THE NEW MOTHER

ALSO BY NORA MURPHY

The Favor

THE NEW MOTHER

Nora Murphy

MINOTAUR BOOKS
NEW YORK

First published in the United States by Minotaur Books, an imprint of St. Martin's Publishing Group

THE NEW MOTHER. Copyright © 2023 by Nora Murphy. All rights reserved. Printed in the United States of America. For information, address St. Martin's Publishing Group, 120 Broadway, New York, NY 10271.

www.minotaurbooks.com

Designed by Gabriel Guma

Library of Congress Cataloging-in-Publication Data

Names: Murphy, Nora, 1990– author.
Title: The new mother / Nora Murphy.
Description: First edition. | New York : Minotaur Books, 2023. |
Identifiers: LCCN 2022058803 | ISBN 9781250822444 (hardcover) |
    ISBN 9781250822451 (ebook)
Subjects: LCSH: Mothers—Fiction. | LCGFT: Thrillers (Fiction) | Novels.
Classification: LCC PS3613.U75256 N49 2023 | DDC 813/.6—dc23/
    eng/20221220
LC record available at https://lccn.loc.gov/2022058803

Our books may be purchased in bulk for promotional, educational, or business use. Please contact your local bookseller or the Macmillan Corporate and Premium Sales Department at 800-221-7945, extension 5442, or by email at MacmillanSpecialMarkets@macmillan.com.

First Edition: 2023

10 9 8 7 6 5 4 3 2 1

For all the mothers. You're a wonder.

PROLOGUE

It wasn't the sort of neighborhood for murder.

It was exactly the sort of neighborhood that comprised the majority of Patuxent County. Expansive colonials dotted quiet, tree-lined streets, cul-de-sacs and looping curves sprouted from slightly busier, but still relatively peaceful, roads.

It was November, but lawns remained green and free from fallen leaves. It was the sort of neighborhood where yard-care services were maintained on contract, and cleaning crews swept into the houses clandestinely and regularly. It was the sort of neighborhood where polite nods and smiles were exchanged when the mail was carried in from boxes. Where a sign advertising the existence of a NEIGHBORHOOD WATCH program was sufficient to make the residents feel comfortable that criminal activity wouldn't come knocking, despite the fact that the neighborhood watch didn't actually exist. It was a neighborhood where doorbell cameras and security systems were superciliously eschewed as unnecessary. Where the parents felt safe letting the children ride their bikes in the street, only glancing out the front window occasionally—no need to purchase those signs that read DRIVE LIKE YOUR CHILDREN LIVE HERE to stake in the front yard.

But there were no children riding their bikes in the street now. There was no one out at all as Detective Jill West turned the wheel of her sedan, directing the car down Ashby Drive. She pulled to a stop at the curb.

The detective paused before climbing out of her car to look out the window at the particular house in which she was interested. It was tidy and stately and almost interchangeable with all the others. At least, it looked that way, didn't it? But it wasn't really interchangeable. It was different from all the rest because—all the evidence she had so far was pointing toward this fact—a murderer lived there.

No, it wasn't the sort of neighborhood for murder. Yet that was exactly what had brought her here.

Part I

THE DOWNFALL & THE LETDOWN

ONE

He had never seen me before, but he knew me inside and out. He'd lived, grown, wriggled inside me for nine months. Here he was. A stranger.

Yet, love was brimming up. Threatening to spill over my edges. It was too much. It felt excessive and counterfeit, almost sickening to my stomach.

They were still pumping Pitocin through my IV—the plasticky contraption was taped to the back of my hand, shooting oxytocin into my veins. It felt foreign and obvious on my skin, even though it had been there for more than fifteen hours. It was the love hormone, was it not? Love and chocolate. They were pumping me with love. Was that the reason for the feeling, or was it natural and real and the strongest force that there was?

Was it all that mattered, the love?

Decidedly not.

I'd asked the nurse if she could remove the IV. She'd told me I needed to finish the bag of fluids and oxytocin. Ideally, they'd leave it in for twenty-four hours after the birth, if I could stand it that long. She was sweet, apologetic. I'd told her it was fine, even though I was afraid I wouldn't be able to sleep with it stuck to my hand, tying me to the wheeling, metal contraption from which the bag of fluids was hanging.

It was an absurd concern. That wasn't the reason I wouldn't be able to sleep.

The nurse had left us alone after that. As panic and an overwhelming urge to cry "Now what?" had gripped me, Tyler had dozed off.

He was still asleep on the plasticky sofa a few feet away from me. I could hear him snoring—softly—but snoring nonetheless, covered in a starchy, white—why were they all so impractically white?—hospital sheet because we'd forgotten to bring a blanket for him from the house. He looked uncomfortable, lying there, but that felt appropriate and fair.

I felt an urge to reach over and shake him, because that he was sleeping was very *unfair*. Besides, it was a reflex. For years, I'd been nudging him whenever I'd heard him snore. But I couldn't reach him now, and I was too scared to try to get up on my own. The effects of the epidural had not worn off completely. My legs felt leaden, tied to cement blocks, like someone was planning to toss me off a bridge and wait for me to sink.

When we had arrived in the room, which was far smaller than the room in which I'd given birth, the nurse had helped me out of the wheelchair while Tyler stood guard over the baby's bassinet with its clear, plastic walls. She'd told me that she needed to make sure I could use the bathroom.

I was still feeling high at that point, from the extra painkillers the anesthesiologist had pumped into my IV before I'd started pushing. I was floating through a haze of airy, rainbow numbness. I couldn't feel a thing.

With impressive strength—although I had rid my body of an eight-pound human, fluids, and placenta, by the looks of my belly, it was all still there, the entire fifty-five pounds I'd put on during the pregnancy—the nurse had supported me, led me over to the toilet, and sat me down. She'd stood over me, making sure I didn't fall off, and we waited until we could hear the trickle of liquid. My cloth hospital gown had drops of blood at the hem.

Tyler's body jolted, then he shifted on the sofa and his breathing evened out, the soft snoring resumed.

Between us was the baby. Oliver. The stranger.

His arms wriggled, his legs fluttered. We watched each other. I knew exactly what he was doing. He'd done just the very same thing every night back when he lived inside of me. Here he was, out in the world, evicted nine days past due with the help of eleven hours of Pitocin drip and one hour and forty-six minutes of pushing. Why should he give up his routine? He showed no signs of sleep. He was free now.

I'd told Tyler to leave the bathroom light on, to crack the door, so that I could see Oliver. The glare reflected off the analog clock hanging on the wall across from me. It was 3:34. I had been awake for twenty-four hours.

Although I still wasn't sure that I was ready, I used my arms to push my legs off the side of the bed, and I sat. The right leg tingled, feeling fighting its way back in. The left one felt heavy and foreign, as if it belonged to someone else. I stood, gripping the cool metal of my IV stand, testing my own stability. I took a step, then another, then gripped the doorframe of the bathroom, and swiveled myself inside. The toilet was just a step too far, but I lunged for it anyway.

I fell. Calves, thighs, palms smacked the floor.

"Nat?" Benign confusion.

I took a breath.

"Nat?" Panic creeping in.

"I'm fine," I called.

A lie. But I couldn't have Tyler coming in here, leaving Oliver unattended. I was relieved he was awake, though. He could take over for a few minutes. Oliver needed to be watched at all times. To make sure he was breathing. To make sure his heart was beating. Besides, it seemed shameful to have collapsed on the bathroom floor. I didn't want Tyler to see me like this, which was perhaps irrational, considering what he had just witnessed—the birth.

I willed my legs to move but they didn't, so I used my arms to pull myself up and onto the toilet. I was stronger than I thought. I was a mother now.

Something poured from me. Perhaps blood. I could hear it more than feel it. I hadn't even felt the need to go to the bathroom. I was only abiding by the nurse's directive—"Try to get up every couple hours to use the bathroom if you can."

If you can. I'd just birthed a child. I could do anything, and following the rules was in my nature. Doing so was a compulsion, as powerful as an addict's need for a fix. I was a deadline meeter, an overachiever, a rule abider.

Or perhaps I *couldn't* do anything. I'd gotten up. But then, I'd fallen.

My supplies were within arm's reach of the toilet—bless the nurse—my squirt bottle, pads, and ice packs. I unwrapped an ice pack and cracked it in half to activate the chemicals and the glorious, cooling sensation.

"You okay?" Tyler called.

I grunted noncommittally. "Just don't come in here," I said.

I steeled myself to stand, but I didn't. Not just yet. I was afraid I might fall again, and I wasn't ready to fall.

I surveyed the room as I sat on the toilet. Blood pooled on the floor. I wouldn't be able to clean it up. I couldn't bend down, balance, wipe the ground. It looked like a crime scene. It looked violent and dramatic. It looked like someone, or something, had died.

And it would take some time for me to understand that something *had* died.

As my son came to life, as he entered the world, something else was in the process of dying.

TWO

"I'm not leaving."

"Nat."

I poked my nipple at Oliver's chin. His mouth, pink and wet like chewed-up bubble gum, turned down at the corners, remained resolutely closed. He was so beautiful. Peach fuzz of golden hair, eyes that were cobalt in the light, black in the dark of night.

"Natalie. Let's go home."

"No," I said. "I'm not leaving." I tried to squeeze out a drop of colostrum, to wave it beneath my baby's nose.

"Home," Tyler said again. He dragged out the word, as if I were a child learning to speak. "Don't you want to sleep in your own bed tonight?" Tyler asked.

Sleep. I almost laughed.

My dad had visited us the previous day, followed by Tyler's parents, then his sister. I'd not managed to change out of my blood-spotted hospital gown before any of them had arrived. I'd not managed to shower until after all of them had gone. Then, once they were, and I might finally be able to sleep, I couldn't. My mind raced, and I watched Oliver.

The night nurse had come in at two in the morning and watched me try to get Oliver to latch. She looked like a ghost, hovering in the doorway in her pale scrubs.

"Have you slept at all?" she asked.

I hadn't. "I'm fine," I said.

"I can take him to the nursery for a couple hours," she said. "Let you get some rest." She eyed Tyler, who was sprawled across the sofa, his right arm grazing the floor, with a measure of skepticism.

The nursery. I knew what that meant. They'd put my son in a plastic bassinet, alongside the other babies. They would all look alike. When time was up, they might bring me the wrong one. Would I even know? When Oliver cried, they'd feed him a bottle—*a bottle*—filled with formula—*formula*.

"That's okay," I said. "I'll be okay."

She had nodded, businesslike, then she took my vitals, dispensed two Midol, and left.

I needed that nurse to come back tonight. To ask me again. I might even let myself say yes. I might not. But, still, I wanted her to ask. I wanted to feel the pride, to hear the little voice in my head telling me I was a *good mom* if I said no. If I was at home, she wouldn't come. At home, no one would come.

"Natalie," Tyler said. "You've been discharged. Oliver has been discharged. Let's go home."

He took Oliver from my arms and began to rock him back and forth, looking down at me, his eyebrows raised in a silent directive. *Come on. Get dressed.*

"You need to get the car seat, right? Pull the car out front."

"Oh," Tyler said. "Right."

I pushed myself out of the hospital bed and began to dig through the duffel bag we had packed together, weeks ago, filled with hope and excitement, getting it ready for when labor spontaneously began. It never had.

"Should I just . . . ?" Tyler looked around the room, as if searching for a third person who could hold the baby. He put Oliver in his bassinet. "Be right back," he said, then he disappeared.

Nothing I had packed fit. I had read that I should bring clothes that had fit when I was six months' pregnant. My optimistically bright and floral maternity T-shirts, which had previously stretched tightly, cutely, over my bulging belly, looked ridiculous hugging my sagging, puckered flesh. I pulled on one of Tyler's T-shirts. It was threadbare and dirty, smelling like sweat and warmth and the body wash he had used the morning before we left for the hospital. There was a smear of deodorant along the hem.

I inspected myself in the mirror. There were swollen, purple circles beneath my eyes, bruise-like, and just as tender. I was a mother now. I'd never looked so hideous.

Tyler burst back into the room, the skin above his upper lip damp with sweat.

"It's so hot," he said. "Ninety degrees already. I pulled the car up out front, left it running to cool it down." He placed the car seat onto the bed from which I'd barely moved for the last two days.

"That's not legal," I said. I was peeking at Oliver every few seconds while packing up my things. "You can't just abandon a running car."

I could tell that Tyler wanted to roll his eyes, but he knew he couldn't. I had just been stitched back together after birthing his child. I was hormonal. He had to tread carefully. He spun away from me and left the room.

"He should know that," I whispered to Oliver, who had dozed off in his bassinet. "He's a lawyer, too."

I struggled to zip the duffel bag. Our belongings seemed to have multiplied, expanded, like belongings tended to do on vacation, like the bellies of the people who had packed them, although our experience couldn't otherwise have been any less like a vacation.

Tyler appeared again, sweatier than before. There were speckles of moisture on his chest. He was out of shape. He'd gained weight during my pregnancy. He'd probably never lose it, and that would be okay. Meanwhile, I was overwhelmed by the repulsiveness of my body, now that our child had departed from it. I was struck by a sense of urgency for it to go back to the way it had been before.

"I found a spot near the front," Tyler said. "We'll go down and you can wait in the lobby while I cool the car down."

He said it as if we were checking out of a five-star hotel.

We both turned to Oliver. He was still sleeping, wrapped in his swaddle. The nurse had wrapped him up for us. Tyler and I still didn't have the hang of the technique. That first night, every time we had changed his diaper, after wiping the sticky, tar-like mess from his bottom, too tired to laugh at how disgusting and difficult it was, we had each tried to swaddle him several times, but one corner of the blanket always popped free. It wasn't tight enough. It wasn't safe. If it was too loose, the fabric could cover his face. It could suffocate him. So, I'd had to watch him, to make sure the fabric stayed in place, to make sure he didn't suffocate.

"I guess we should dress him," Tyler said.

I held up the onesie I had extracted from our bag. It was creamy and silky soft and printed with tiny elephants. Tyler gingerly tugged the blanket loose and Oliver promptly began to fuss in his sleep.

"Maybe we should just wait for him to wake up," I said.

Tyler ignored me, so I stepped forward and pulled the outfit over Oliver's head, a sick feeling brewing in my gut. He seemed so fragile.

We looked down at our child. He was swimming in the outfit, blinking up at us with eyes that were heavy with sleep.

"Do you have shoes?" Tyler asked.

"Shoes?" I was aghast. "He's a newborn baby. He doesn't have to wear shoes."

"Er, socks, then. It seems like he should have something on his feet, doesn't it?"

I lifted Oliver up and approached the car seat. I hadn't brought any baby socks. I didn't even own a pair.

"I don't know," I said. "No one bought me socks for the baby shower. I think that if a baby was supposed to wear socks, people would have bought me some."

"Did you put them on your registry?" Tyler asked.

I hadn't.

I blinked back tears as I pushed the car seat straps to the side, already feeling like I had failed my son. I tucked him in as carefully as I could, then fastened the straps. I'd practiced buckling them and unbuckling them last week, barely able to see what I was doing over my belly.

"Is that tight enough?" Tyler asked.

"Why are you asking me all these questions?" I snapped. "I don't know the answers. Why don't you look them up?"

Dutifully, he turned away from me and began to search for something on his cell phone. I tucked the blanket around Oliver's lap and slipped my feet into the flip-flops I'd worn to the hospital, the only shoes that had fit over my fluid-filled feet at the end of my pregnancy. They still looked grotesque, swollen up to the base of my shins. The nurse had assured me that the swelling would go down in a couple weeks.

She came bustling into the room, then, after a curt knock.

"Are we ready?" she asked. "He looks darling."

"Is this tight enough?" I asked her, fiddling with the car seat straps.

She bent over to look. "It's perfect," she said.

"Yes," said Tyler. "The clip should be beneath the level of his under-arms, no slack in the straps," as if he'd known this all along.

"You'll have to sit in the wheelchair, alright?" the nurse said. "I know you can walk, but it's policy."

"Okay," I agreed. I settled onto it, feeling slightly ridiculous. Tyler slung the straps of our duffel bag over his shoulder and tucked the pillows we'd brought from home under his arms. He had no arms left for the baby.

"Here," said the nurse. "I'll put the car seat on your lap."

She pushed me through the halls, struggling to round corners. She was a petite woman, and her effort felt shameful, a reminder of all the weight I would have to lose. People smiled at me and moved out of the way as we passed. *Congratulations,* they murmured. I smiled back, but I wished they'd stop looking.

Tyler ran ahead of us to start the car and pull it up front.

"Let's go just outside," the nurse suggested. "Better to wait in the shade outside than in here. Too many germs."

I was horrified. I'd not even thought of the germ-infested lobby air as a danger to my baby. I hugged the car seat more tightly to my body, as though I could shield him from illness that way.

The nurse pushed me down to Tyler's car. We bumped over the cracks in the sidewalk and I clenched my teeth, feeling pain echo through my body.

Tyler took the car seat and clicked it into place in the middle seat in the back of the car.

"Do you want to sit in the back with the baby?" the nurse asked. I could tell she'd forgotten his name.

"Yes," I replied, grateful for the suggestion. I hadn't thought of that, hadn't realized that the days of sitting beside Tyler in the car, fiddling with the air-conditioning controls, changing the radio station, feeling his hand reach for mine, were over.

"Bye, sweetie," the nurse whispered as I slid into the backseat. "You'll do great."

I nodded, smiled bravely.

She slammed the car door, and then she was gone.

"Ready?" Tyler asked.

I wasn't. I wasn't the one who wanted to leave.

"Sure," I said.

He pulled away from the curb. Oliver had dozed off. I reached into the car seat and slipped my index finger into the hollow of his curled hand.

Tyler sped past the road that led to our old neighborhood.

"Where are you going?" I almost asked. I'd forgotten. We weren't headed to our little rancher just outside the city limits. We were going to the new house, impractically spacious for just two adults and one small baby. With soaring ceilings and the white kitchen I had thought that I wanted so badly until I had it. With shiny porcelain tile and dove-gray walls. With four bedrooms and glossy, wide-plank wood floors. With a two-car garage that we weren't even using because the previous owners hadn't left the remote openers behind and we were too busy to buy and program new ones.

There was no activity along Ashby Drive. A few weeks of summer vacation remained, but school would be starting soon. Colored markers, scissors, glue sticks, and mechanical pencils had been bought. Back-to-school clothes were hanging in closets and folded in drawers, awaiting their first-day-of-school debuts. The high schoolers were almost looking forward to the day. Would they be *cool* this year? Popular? Would anyone notice their haircuts and tans? As if any of it mattered. They thought it did. I had, too, back then.

It was too hot, too sunny, to set up sprinklers in the front yard or drape Slip 'N Slides along the hill out back. The heat was rising from the pavement in rippling waves. It was the kind of day that conjured thoughts of skin cancer and heatstroke rather than summer fun.

Tyler parked in the driveway and leapt out, rushing over to open the door for me, like we were arriving at my house at the end of a date that had gone extremely well.

"Can you get the baby?" I asked him after pulling myself out of the car with an astonishing lack of grace.

"Of course," he said.

He was so chipper. He'd not been awake for three days and two nights straight.

Meanwhile, I feared that I was dying. The burning pain from the stitches.

The dull ache behind my eyes. It felt like I was being held beneath the surface of a murky body of water. Everything smelled faintly of blood.

I stood in the driveway and watched Tyler unlatch the car seat and remove it from the car. "I'll come back for the stuff," he said.

I nodded and followed him up the porch steps. He fiddled with his keys and I closed my eyes for a second, feeling my body sway, imagining we were standing on the porch of our little rancher.

It had been Tyler's idea to move. We needed more space for the baby things. More bedrooms for the baby and his future sibling, because I was an only child, and I had always assumed I'd have two kids of my own. We wanted a better school district. A garage so we could shuffle the kids and our belongings and ourselves from house to car while protected from the rain and snow.

Sure, those things would be nice. One day. We hadn't needed those things immediately. And we hadn't needed worse commutes. We were already about to experience a massive change that would shatter our lives completely. Wouldn't it be easier to have a smaller house, closer to our respective offices, familiar in its smells and creaks? I could make my way from our bed to the kitchen and back with my eyes closed in that house, without having to climb any stairs.

But Tyler had been insistent. Interest rates were low. It wasn't a good time to move, but it would never be a good time to move. It would only be more difficult once the baby was born. Besides, the perfect house had come on the market. Just over three thousand square feet, not including the basement, move-in ready, with a brick porch and grand portico held steady by white columns. Schools ranked nines and tens. All of those things that should matter in a house but in which I wasn't interested because it wasn't our house. It wasn't home.

Tyler had booked a tour the morning the listing went live, and we made a full-price offer that night. The house was ours before I was able to fully digest how little I wanted it.

Then came the matter of getting our rancher ready to list. New paint. Power washing. Replacing light fixtures. Having carpets cleaned and hardwoods waxed. Fortunately, it sold in a week. It was a darling house, with turquoise shutters and bay windows that looked like eyes flanking the front door, which was as yellow as the daffodils that bloomed out front every April. I had painted the door myself the weekend we had moved in, five years ago.

Suddenly, the move was complete. The rancher was no longer home, while the house on Ashby Drive had not yet taken its place in my heart or mind.

Unpacking took days, and we had tripled our square footage. We bought and assembled complete rooms' worth of furniture. We painted the nursery a soothing green. We hung pictures and measured for area rugs. All of it was at Tyler's insistence. He seemed to believe that filling the house would make me feel more settled. It had only made me feel like I was a guest in someone else's home, sitting on stiff couches, resting my head on strange-smelling throw pillows, gazing at canvas prints that meant nothing to me.

Finally, Tyler located the correct key and pushed the front door open. He placed the car seat on the floor in the foyer. Frosty air, unfamiliar, the smell of a stranger's house, swirled around us.

"You're home," he told Oliver. He turned and went back outside, presumably to retrieve our bag and pillows from the car.

I unbuckled the straps and extracted Oliver. He was still sleeping, but I had read that you should never let your baby sleep in its car seat if it wasn't actually riding in the car. Automatically, I limped up the stairs and entered the nursery.

I laid Oliver down in his crib. He looked so tiny in the middle of his mattress. His eyes opened and he turned his head to the side, staring out between the crib bars. It was like he was in jail. His eyes drifted closed again.

I wanted to unpack my things from the duffel bag. To take a shower beneath the rain-shower head in the master bathroom. To pop a Midol. To lie down. But how could I do any of those things, now that Oliver was here? I longed, ached, to put him back inside me. Then I could go about my business, while knowing he was safe and comfortable and part of me.

There had been so much anticipation leading up to Oliver's birth. It had been the center of our lives ever since we had sat cross-legged on our bed and stared down at the tiny word on the plastic, pee-soaked test last November, while we laughed giddily, nervously—PREGNANT. Everything we had done since was with Oliver in mind, was in preparation for his arrival. Now, here he was, and I hadn't a clue what came next.

I moved toward the door, then paused. I couldn't leave him.

I leaned over the top of the crib, reached for his body, then froze. I couldn't wake him, either.

I sank to the floor, pressing my face into the unusual fleshiness of my arm, trying as best as I could to muffle my cries. It had been a foolish thing to do, crouching down, letting myself collapse. Pain engulfed me. I needed that Midol. I needed something much, much stronger.

Downstairs, the front door slammed. Behind me, Oliver began to whimper. I wiped my face with the hem of Tyler's T-shirt, then pushed myself up from the ground. I couldn't break down. There was this human now, this human we had created.

I rolled up Tyler's T-shirt and settled down in the rocking chair. One of the breastfeeding pillows I had received at my baby shower was on the floor beside me, where I'd stationed it, ready and waiting for action. I congratulated myself for the forethought. I had done quite a bit of planning. Planning, preparation, was what gave me confidence. It was what I did before making presentations to partners at work. Before stepping into a client meeting. Before dialing opposing counsel to negotiate a term in a contract. Preparation and research made me feel competent and intelligent. It wasn't working when it came to mothering. I had planned and researched every tiny thing. Why did I still feel lost?

I arranged the pillow on my lap and settled Oliver on top of it. I poked my nipple into his mouth, which was opening and closing as he fussed. On the third try, he accepted it and began to suck. My breast felt oddly firm, which meant, I suspected, that my milk was finally coming in.

I could hear Tyler climbing the stairs. He appeared in the doorway, leaning against the frame. "Look at you," he said. He was smiling. He didn't look like he was dying. "Settling right in."

I didn't move, didn't speak. I didn't want Oliver to lose his grip.

"My mom dropped off some groceries," Tyler said. "Our fridge is packed. Want me to make something to eat?"

He didn't wait for me to respond, just turned and left. I could hear his footsteps, light and quick on the steps. I hated how free he was. I didn't think I would ever be that way again. The weight of what we'd done, the responsibility of what we would need to do next, for almost two decades, was squeezing the air from my lungs.

Oliver was falling asleep at my breast, so I tickled his head with the tips of my fingers the way the lactation consultant had shown me in the hospital. She'd said I needed to keep him awake so that he could eat, to wake him every two hours for a feeding, until he'd regained the weight he'd lost after birth. I knew this already, of course. I'd read this in all the baby care books I had downloaded onto my Kindle and devoured during the sleepless, restless nights during my pregnancy.

Oliver drifted to sleep anyway, so I sat there, cradling him against me, rocking in the chair.

I heard Tyler clattering dishes and slamming cabinets downstairs. I thought of his mother carrying brimming paper bags into our house and unloading them carefully, putting everything in the wrong place, smiling faintly at the thought of her first grandchild. She hadn't worked a single day since she was twenty-eight years old. She'd left her job when she was eight months' pregnant with Tyler and had never returned. She liked to tell me stories of the exhaustion she'd felt, how difficult breastfeeding was. How her body hadn't made enough milk, so she'd switched to formula after a few days.

She'd never pumped milk into little plastic bottles and lined them up in the communal fridge. She'd never dragged herself out of bed after two hours of sleep and driven downtown to meet with clients and write memos to partners and account for every minute of her time in the software that tracked billable hours.

She had no idea what lay ahead of me. Neither did I.

"I made you some food," Tyler called from downstairs, a hint of pride in his voice.

"Congratulations," I murmured.

I carried Oliver downstairs with me and settled into a chair at the kitchen table, cradling him in both my arms.

"Do you want to, um, put him down or something?" Tyler asked. He'd made sandwiches, little piles of strawberries on each of our plates.

I shook my head, rested Oliver on my lap, my right arm still cradling him, and lifted my sandwich with my left hand. Slimy, deli-style chicken I never would have purchased or eaten fell out the bottom, along with several leaves of butter lettuce smeared with mustard that looked like wet sand.

I started to cry.

"Nat," said Tyler. He sounded alarmed. "What's wrong?"

I shook my head. I couldn't explain it. I couldn't say what I was feeling. It was too shameful, too wrong.

And that was the thing. It felt wrong. Everything did. Everything felt too different. Too overwhelming and impossible. What had I been expecting? What had we done?

I felt broken. Heavy with exhaustion. Hunger was twisting my insides into knots. Pain was ricocheting through me as I sat on the unforgiving wooden chair. I felt like a nuisance to myself. A burden. That my needs and my feelings still existed wasn't fair. How could I possibly care for us both?

A tear rolled down my face and fell onto Oliver's forehead. He didn't stir.

"Nat," Tyler said again. I could tell he was scared.

I wiped at my eyes with the back of my hand. "I just feel a little overwhelmed, being home," I said. "But it's fine. I'm fine."

It wasn't the truth, but it would have to be. What choice did I have?

THREE

From its resting place on the dining room table, his laptop screen went dark, as quickly as the blink of an eye, as lasting as a sudden death. It felt like an accusation. An admonishment. He should have been keeping it awake, his fingers flying across the keyboard. Each key was dotted with a shiny circle, right around the letter, worn by the oil of his hands. He wouldn't have minded a new laptop, but a new laptop would make Erin's eyebrows rise.

Do you really need that?

She wouldn't say anything about it. That wasn't her style. Her antipathy was of the silent and simmering variety. It had seeped between them a long time ago—years ago, he thought—and had been bubbling there ever since.

Seven hundred and fifty words. That was his daily writing goal, as he chipped away at the ninety thousand or so he'd need for the document that would become his novel.

It was a respectable goal, he thought, but perhaps not a particularly ambitious one for a stay-at-home father whose child attended an expensive (*We really can't afford it anymore.*) private school at which she spent six and a half hours, five days a week. Somehow, he still managed not to meet it.

"You should aim higher, Paul," Erin would tell him. "Why aren't you writing more? *What is it that you do all day?*"

He cleans her house. He makes her dinner. He pulls her weeds and rakes her leaves. Oh, and he raises her child. The one she treats with coldness and indifference, as if Petra were a mosquito that flew into the house and took up residence on the ceiling. An irritant, but not enough that it

would be worth it for Erin to dust off the ladder, drag it out of the basement storage room, and *take care of it.*

That was his job.

He paced through the dining room, back and forth between the two
windows, the heavy mahogany drapes rippling slightly in the breeze from
the blasting air-conditioning, waiting for words to flood into his head so
that he could rush over, wake up his computer, and spill them onto the
screen.

Was it still considered writer's block if it had lasted for more than a decade? Or did that just mean he wasn't a writer at all? Was it just . . . *block*?

He moved into the hallway and smushed his finger into the rubbery
button on the thermostat, turning the temperature up, the air-conditioning
down.

"You keep the house too cold during the day," Erin would say, when
the gas and electric bill arrived in her email inbox, the creases between
her brows deepening, her mouth a sharp slash of bleeding red lipstick, the
color she always wore.

The bill wasn't too high. It was only a jab. One of so many that he en-
dured every day.

Her subtext: *go spend the day in an office, use someone else's AC, like
the rest of us.*

He paused before the left window, looking out at the tree-lined street
and stately colonials. There was no one out. Not a soul.

It was ninety-five degrees, the sun beating down on the asphalt like a
fluorescent bulb in an interrogation room. The only movement outside
was the rise of heat waves, rippling up from the ground. There weren't
even any children out playing, savoring the last few weeks of summer
vacation.

They were all in their houses, he supposed, watching their screens, their
tablets. They made tablets especially for children these days, he thought
disdainfully, with parental controls and thick, silicone cases. Petra had
never owned a tablet. She was far too bright for that. He never stuck her
in front of a screen. They spent their days reading and conversing, having
adventures inside the house and out, their imaginations streaking wildly,
erratically, but together. Did Erin thank him for that? Did she appreciate
all those screen-free days he spent with their daughter?

Of course not. She only saw him as a leech. A liability. A burden. Much the same way she seemed to view Petra herself.

"You need to forgive her," he used to tell Erin. "You need to let it go. It's irrational."

That was his theory. That Erin held on to resentment toward Petra since her difficult pregnancy, since Petra's impossible first few months of life.

"Don't be ridiculous," Erin would tell him coldly. "I don't resent her. It's all in your head."

He'd given up on such comments, on trying to help.

Or perhaps the neighborhood kids were at camp, like Petra, not going cross-eyed before their screens. She was at her expensive (*We can't afford that!*) horse-riding camp this week. He hadn't wanted her to go to the camp, but it was only half-day and it only lasted a few weeks out of a long summer, and Petra wanted to go, and what Petra wanted, he wanted.

A car rolled slowly down the hill, past his house, toward the end of the cul-de-sac, the sun sending its charcoal paint aglitter. He recognized the car. It belonged to the new couple, returning home from somewhere. He hadn't yet met them.

The sale had closed, and the moving trucks came and went, first carrying the Tuckers' belongings away, then bringing the new family's in. He'd felt an ache for Lara Tucker, as her absence settled in and became all too real. He would miss her. But he had smiled at his wife and daughter.

"We should walk down to meet the new neighbors, bring them a plate of brownies or maybe a potted plant."

"No one does that anymore," Erin had said sullenly, as though she were the hormonal preteen, while Petra had only shrugged at him.

He had seen them on occasion, in passing. The man in his suits, climbing into and out of his gray sedan. The woman, her honey-blond hair brushing her shoulders as she heaved her heavily pregnant body out of her own car, rubbing her obviously sore lower back, late in the evening, after, he presumed, a long day at the office. She was attractive, at least from a distance—soft and fair. She looked nothing like his wife.

He watched the car slow further as it bumped over the low curb at the end of their driveway. He watched as they climbed out. The man sprang from the driver's seat, while the woman seemed to drag herself from the backseat, still heavy, but no longer pregnant. The man stooped and awkwardly extracted a car seat.

The baby was here. All milky skin, soft like the back of a dog's ear. Inexplicable lavender smell, even before its first bath. He thought of the moment he'd first held Petra in his arms. Everything had felt so solid and simple and sure. *How could they be anything but happy, ever, as long as they had her?* he'd thought. How had it all gone so wrong?

The man struggled at the front door for a while, then they disappeared inside. They were home, a place of comfort and familiarity, yet everything had changed.

He and Erin had moved into this house while Erin was still pregnant, just like this family. Erin had been no help at all during the move. She'd been violently sick every day of her pregnancy, beginning two weeks after the positive test. She had lain on the couch, the first piece of furniture the movers had brought inside, clutching a waxy barf bag, directing the movers as to what went where, while he raced around, unpacking their smaller possessions, the boxes they had brought in their own cars, sweat pouring into his eyes.

He'd been so hopeful that day when they had arrived home with their brand-new baby. The pregnancy was over. The sickness was gone. Erin would return to the way she'd been before, and they had the love of their lives, their existence holding new meaning and importance, as they forever would orbit their tiny daughter, their minuscule and glowing sun. He'd been brimming with happiness. He had his child, and he'd get his wife back. Everything had felt so perfect.

Was this family feeling like he had, he wondered? Happy and hopeful and simply just *full*? Or was one of them feeling like Erin had felt? When the baby was born, when it left the woman's body, had something else snuck in? Something poisonous? Something pervasive?

Only time would tell.

He very much wanted to find out. He wanted to meet this woman who had moved into Lara Tucker's old house. He wanted to see her up close, to discover who she was, and who she might become for him.

But not now. Now, they'd need space. Time to settle in.

He turned away from the window, but he closed the curtains first, pulling them tightly together. To keep the sunlight out, he told himself. To keep the house cool. So that he wouldn't displease his wife.

He laughed, then, because everything he did displeased his wife. His very existence. The rise and fall of his chest as he breathed. The steady beat of his heart.

He returned to his seat at the dining room table, and he woke up his laptop. The empty document blinked accusingly back at him.

You're worthless, it seemed to say. It sounded like Erin.

He slammed the lid closed.

FOUR

My dad held Oliver stiffly, just the same way he had when he'd visited us in the hospital. He looked like he'd not held a baby for thirty-two years.

I felt a pang in my chest, and a tiny bubble of resentment, so unfair, popped to life. Because he wasn't my mom. And did a woman ever need her mother more than when she became a mother herself?

To his credit, my dad seemed to understand this.

"I wish your mom could have met him," he'd murmured when I'd first placed Oliver into his arms.

His eyes were wet, and mine had flooded, too. I'd only nodded, not able to say anything more, because I simply couldn't. I couldn't think about it, couldn't talk about it. That was the only way I could cope with the fact that my mom had become sick with breast cancer five years earlier, that she'd died only eighteen months after her diagnosis, that she'd never been able to meet her grandson, that she wasn't here to hold my hand and tell me what to do and assure me that I was competent and I was strong and I could do this.

"Tyler, how much time do you have left before you head back to work?" my dad asked, still stiffly holding Oliver, watching him closely as though the baby might suddenly spring from his arms.

I shifted uncomfortably on the sofa, and not just because I was physically uncomfortable, although I was. Tyler's return to work was another subject I didn't want to discuss or consider.

"I go back a week from Monday," Tyler replied, sounding very blasé. He didn't sound scared, or full of dread, like I was.

What would happen when it was just the two of us? What mistakes would I make? It was like a swarm of bees, the fear, lingering behind me, buzzing, distracting, occasionally knocking me in the head.

I had called my dad our first night home from the hospital and asked for his advice. Do I have to hold the baby all the time? Can I leave him alone?

Yes, you can put him down in his crib and go do something else, he'd said. *If he's sleeping or he's not crying, you can leave him alone and do what you have to do.*

But he'd sounded uncertain. I suspected he couldn't really remember, or else my mom, who, in her role as school librarian, had worked far fewer hours than my lawyer dad, had handled much more of the child-care responsibilities.

Was his advice wrong? Old-fashioned and outdated? Acceptable during the same time when it was acceptable to let a baby suck liquor off your finger and go to sleep on its stomach? But not acceptable now. Not when we knew more. Did we know too much?

Still, I needed the advice. I needed the rules. They guided me. They gave me purpose.

"What about you, Nat?" my dad asked. "Seven more weeks of leave?"

"Eight weeks," I corrected. But then I considered that my leave had started the day we'd headed into the hospital for the induction. Oliver had been born the next day. Suddenly, it was closer to seven weeks than eight.

I swallowed an urge to cry, while thoughts swirled in my head. They terrified me, these thoughts. Of all the thoughts that knocked on the door of my mind, these were unstoppable. They didn't bother to knock. These leapt out of nowhere, screaming, "Boo." These were the most terrifying of all.

What if I couldn't go back?

Work had been my identity for so long. I was an attorney. It was what I did. I prepared license agreements and negotiated complex commercial contracts. I attended networking events and helped partners draft research papers to be presented at conferences. Now those things seemed alien. And how could I leave Oliver? I wanted to work, but the thought of being apart from my baby made me feel like I had just raced up a flight of stairs and couldn't catch my breath.

"I don't want to talk about going back to work," I snapped. I looked down at my lap, fiddled with the hem of Tyler's T-shirt, still the only thing I could wear comfortably.

"Nat is tired," Tyler told my dad confidingly, as though apologizing for my behavior, and my rage burned. "We had a rough night."

"Oh?" My dad was unruffled, unoffended by my tone.

I could feel Tyler looking at me, silently directing me to explain what had happened, but I didn't want to. I glanced around the room, noticed clean diapers littering the coffee table. A stained onesie was draped over the back of an armchair. A pack of wipes had been left open on a blanket on the floor, where Tyler had taken to changing Oliver. The entire house was like this. There were clothes spilling from drawers. Cat hair was collecting in the corners of rooms. Dust had settled onto nightstands and dressers and shelves. Black rings were already forming in the toilets. A thin layer of grime covered the floors, everything, me.

I'd put a hold on our cleaning service. I didn't want anyone else coming into the house, bringing their germs. After all, I'd be home. Not working. I'd have time to clean the house, I'd thought. How had I been so foolish?

"Oliver wouldn't sleep at all last night," Tyler continued. "I mean, not at all. He never fell asleep."

Even though I'd not wanted to be the one to tell the story, hearing Tyler say it only made my rage burn higher. Because Tyler didn't really get it, did he? He had slept.

Although Tyler did look like he'd been up all night, too. He was standing in the arched doorway between the dining and living rooms, leaning against the wall. I knew the exact shape of him, the way he moved. I'd recognize him anywhere. From behind, from the side, from a distance, from so close up that my eyes crossed. I'd loved him for a decade, ever since a few weeks after we had met, back in college, so hopeful and burdened and stressed we were, or so we thought, in our LSAT prep course. I'd always loved him, but I hated him now. For the slump of his shoulders. For the droop to his eyes. For how *tired* he looked.

It wasn't a competition. *May the most exhausted parent of all be the winner.* There was no winner. Or were we both winners? That's how a good mother would feel—like she'd won, even while she felt like she'd died.

"He just wouldn't stop crying, Dad," I said. "Every time I got him quiet and put him into his bassinet, he'd scream like he was being tortured. He did it the whole night. I just kept nursing him, but it didn't help."

At four in the morning, Tyler had staggered into the nursery, finding Oliver and me still sitting there.

"Here," Tyler had said, arms outstretched, reaching toward us. "Let me take him. Get some rest."

"But he's eating," I'd whispered, even though he wasn't. Just an hour earlier, I had squeezed my breasts, tender and spent, trying to force out a drop of milk. There was none left.

"He's not eating." Tyler had peered down into my arms. "He's sleeping."

I'd let Tyler remove him from my arms. He began to cry as soon as my nipple slipped from his mouth. Tyler sank into the rocking chair while I hesitated in the doorway.

"You just fed him. He doesn't need to eat again for two hours. You can get some sleep," Tyler urged.

I wanted nothing more, yet I felt simultaneously empty and lost without Oliver pressing against my chest. I'd climbed into bed, but I couldn't fall asleep. Not while Oliver was crying. So, I'd returned to the nursery, found Tyler standing in the middle of the room, swaying robotically from side to side. "I don't know what's wrong," he said, a hint of panic creeping in. "He's not stopping. Maybe he's still hungry," Tyler had suggested hopefully. Could it be so simple?

I'd felt tears stinging the corners of my eyes. "I've been nursing him all night long," I said. "I don't think I have any milk left."

"Let me just give him some formula," Tyler suggested.

"It's too early for him to drink from a bottle," I snapped. That was another rule. The words *nipple confusion* automatically, obediently, floated into my mind, even though the concept seemed artificial and absurd.

I didn't admit that there was another obstacle to Tyler's suggestion. We didn't have any formula. My mother-in-law, skeptical of my plan to exclusively breastfeed my son for the first six months of his life, had suggested that I buy some formula for the house, "just in case." But it was exactly for that reason that I had not. If it was there, here, it would be tempting. In a fit of sleep-deprived hysteria, I might shove an unsterilized bottle and a box of formula toward Tyler and order him to take over for the night. If we didn't have any formula, I couldn't do that.

There was a CVS, open twenty-four hours, only five minutes away from Ashby Drive.

But, no, no. I was only following the recommendations promulgated by the American Academy of Pediatrics. They wouldn't recommend something that was impossible. And if it was possible, that meant I needed to do it.

Tyler had sighed, then given Oliver back to me. He had stopped crying immediately, and it sent a shiver of pride down my spine.

"You can sleep," I'd told Tyler. "At least one of us should be sleeping."

Tyler had left then, and I breastfed my son. He fell asleep. I tried to put him into his bassinet, to climb into bed myself. Oliver cried. I tried again. And again. And again.

When Tyler awoke, he returned to the nursery, his cheek creased from his pillowcase. The lines in his skin, the rumpled look of his hair, were like slaps to my face.

"Nat," he'd said. "You okay?" There was fear in his eyes.

I broke. "This can't be normal." Sobs shook my shoulders, chopped my breaths. "I have nursed him all night. If I'm not, he's crying. There's something wrong with him." I could barely understand myself.

"Let's call the doctor," Tyler said definitively.

I'd not wanted to. It seemed ridiculous. "My baby won't sleep. He's crying." Was that not what babies did? I was too ashamed to wake the doctor, was thinking of Elaine, my best friend. She was a pediatrician, often complaining to me about the phone calls she received from new parents. I had promised her that I wouldn't be one of them.

So, Tyler had called. The pediatrician on call, Dr. Williams, had been sympathetic, although admittedly groggy. We were scheduled to bring Oliver in to see Dr. Lee the following morning, but Dr. Williams told us that she had an opening at nine, and suggested that we come in then.

"We brought him to the doctor this morning," I told my dad. I didn't admit that we'd called at six-thirty in the morning. "She said Oliver seems fine, that he might have just been hungry."

"He was cluster feeding," Tyler replied knowingly, reciting the term the doctor had mentioned, as if giving it a name made it something that was manageable, rather than something that felt very, very impossible.

"Well," said my dad. "I'm glad he's okay."

I felt a prickle of hurt. Because this was my dad. And what about me? What if I wasn't okay?

Oliver stirred, his mouth stretched open, and he began to cry. My dad looked alarmed and immediately pushed himself up from the couch. "That's my cue," he said, chuckling. "Time to go back to your parents."

Tyler and I both stepped forward, reached for Oliver. My dad handed him to me. "He's probably hungry again," I said, edging away from Tyler. My dad had been holding Oliver for almost an hour, and I was aching to press my baby against me, to smell his skin, to stroke the top of his head.

"I'm working tomorrow," my dad said as we walked him to the door. "But call if you need help."

"I will," I said, even knowing that I wouldn't. Aged sixty-six, widowed, and living an hour away from his only child, my dad was still working as a public defender. He'd been doing it for forty years now. Sometimes, I worried that he didn't have more in his life. But mostly, I was grateful that he had his work. The relationships, the stimulation, the socialization that it afforded, relieved some of my daughterly duties and concerns. If I needed help, I wouldn't pull my dad away from his job.

Same with my best friend, Elaine. Although she might be an ideal option, in that she was a pediatrician, she, too, was working a busy schedule. And she was expecting a baby soon herself. She and her husband had stopped by briefly the previous evening. Elaine had held Oliver and gushed over his cuteness, but I could tell that she was exhausted from spending the long workday on her feet, moving from appointment to appointment. Her ankles were swollen, her lower back aching. She didn't have the energy to assuage my new mother fears, to teach me how to take care of my son.

My dad clapped Tyler on the back, then wrapped an arm around my shoulders, squeezed once, and then he was gone.

"I'll be upstairs," I told Tyler. I could sit anywhere to nurse Oliver, but I was most comfortable in the nursery, my breastfeeding pillow wrapped around my waist, my elbows propped on the armrests of the glider, which already smelled of sour milk and spit-up.

"Okay," Tyler said. "I'll make us something to eat."

He trailed into the kitchen, and I heard him opening and closing the fridge and cabinets, surveying the items that his mother had dropped off.

She'd stopped by earlier with another bag of groceries. Her helpfulness was a pretext—she just wanted to hold her grandson. Perhaps I should have been more grateful than I was.

But I didn't really want visitors. I didn't want anyone to come. I felt ashamed. Like something dirty, something to be kept hidden. Something incompetent and failing. Like I should shut myself away until I figured things out, until all of it got easier.

FIVE

The next week passed in a sleepless blur. The days dragged, yet they were gone in a blink. They were wet with spit-up and still white with pain. There was, at all times, a panicky feeling fluttering in my chest, like a bird in a too-small cage. At any moment, it might break free, take over, make me scream.

I'd begun to believe that it wasn't going to matter when Tyler returned to work. Ever since the night Oliver had stayed up all night, I'd been tending to him almost on my own, with a sense of desperation, like I had something to prove. *I could do this.*

I spent my days and nights nursing Oliver and holding him while he slept, only asking Tyler to take him here and there for a few minutes so that I could use the bathroom or take a shower. I'd gotten quite good at balancing Oliver on the nursing pillow, holding him in place with my left hand, so that I could shovel some food into my mouth.

I'd begun to think that Tyler might as well not be here. I could handle it. I had everything under control. Except, when he tucked his button-down shirt into his dress slacks and bent down to kiss me, then Oliver, on the tops of our heads, the panicky, caged bird feeling had intensified.

If nothing else, Tyler had been backup. Now what? How would I go to the bathroom and perform my ritualistic postpartum care? How would I eat? Breastfeeding made me ravenous. I was eating as much as I could, as much as I wanted, but still, the weight was falling off me. I was wasting away. Oliver was sucking the literal life from my body. I still had a long way to go before I was back to my pre-pregnancy size, and it was shocking how little I cared anymore.

There was something else, besides the panic. I was struck by a desire to put on my own dress slacks—not that they'd fit—and my colorful Ann Taylor blouses and my suede kitten heels. I wanted to fill my travel mug and head to the office. I wanted a break. That I now viewed a day at Gallagher, Markham & Rice as a break was shocking, even comical.

"It's just you and me, kid," I told Oliver once Tyler was gone, testing it out. "Kiddo." My son blinked at me with his opaque eyes, navy in the dimly lit room. "I think you need a nickname. What are your thoughts? Kiddo?"

I placed him down in the middle of our bed, plenty of room all around him should he somehow, miraculously, make a move toward an edge. I paused—what was the point in dressing? I did it anyway, removing my nursing pajamas and changing into athletic shorts, two sizes bigger than I used to wear, and another of Tyler's T-shirts, keeping an eye on Oliver the entire time. Although I had no plans to go anywhere, I slipped my feet into my sneakers and tied the laces, if only because I might not have an opportunity to do so later.

Oliver was staring upward, so I followed his line of sight. I flicked the switch on the wall and laid down on the bed beside him. We watched the ceiling fan whir, slowly, until it gained speed and the blades blurred into a white circle. It was quite boring, but Oliver seemed pleased.

You'll never get this time back. This is the best time of your life. Reminders, a mantra of sorts. Were they true? I wished. I hoped. Only time would tell. By then, it'd be too late.

"Looks like I found something you like, kiddo," I told Oliver. Of course he didn't reply.

I heaved myself upward, turned off the fan, and lifted him up. "We've got the whole day ahead of us," I said. "What would you like to do?"

I carried him down to the kitchen, stepping carefully on the sleek wood of the stairs—potential danger seemed to lurk everywhere. I poked around in the cabinets and fridge with one hand, wishing I could put Oliver down somewhere, feeling like a guest in someone else's house.

"I'm starving," I told him. I snacked on a handful of blueberries and several spoonsful of peanut butter. Tyler's mother had purchased a massive jar of it, creamy and dry, not like the grainy, oily, so-called natural variety to which Tyler was partial. Perhaps this was the kind he'd eaten during his childhood. Perhaps his peanut butter preferences had evolved over the years.

I'd no idea what to do with my baby, but a thought was tickling the back of my mind. I carried him back upstairs and into the bedroom next door to the nursery. It was an extra bedroom, empty, aside from boxes and gift bags full of baby items I'd received at my shower but which I'd deemed superfluous or inappropriate for a newborn. It was difficult to root through the boxes and bags while holding Oliver against my chest, but that was exactly why I needed what I was looking for.

I found it in a gift bag still overflowing with tissue paper. It had come from a law school friend, Mary Claire. She had two children already. *I swear by it,* she'd told me. *You just tuck the baby inside, and you can do whatever you want to do, have your hands free. They love it because they're close to you. They can hear your heartbeat.*

It looked, to me, like a too-long, rather ugly scarf. I carried it, with the little book of directions, into my bedroom and got Oliver set up on the bed with the spinning fan. I stood in front of our full-length mirror and attempted to fasten the wrap around myself, becoming twisted and tangled and frustrated. "My God," I told Oliver. "I'd never put you in this."

But I'd graduated summa cum laude from college and then law school. I'd passed the bar exam. I'd been promoted to senior associate at my firm and had negotiated hundreds of commercial contracts over the course of seven years of practice. I could fasten a baby wrap.

With the help of several YouTube videos, I figured it out. Again, I stood in front of the mirror as I carefully slipped Oliver inside, pulling the fabric across his back. His head rested against my breasts, the crown of it close enough that I could easily bow my own head to sniff or plant a kiss.

"There we go," I exclaimed. "Isn't this wonderful, kiddo? I can use both my hands now. Bless that Mary Claire." The panicky feeling was pushed away. All my problems were solved.

My sense of accomplishment lasted only a few seconds. Before I could even leave the room, Oliver began to scream.

I rushed back to the mirror and extracted Oliver carefully, then placed him onto the bed while I pulled at the baby wrap wildly, finally whipping it off. I hurriedly sat on the edge of the bed and nursed Oliver. Without the benefit of my nursing pillow or support for my arms, my muscles burned. I stared at nothing until he was finished.

Why didn't my baby love the wrap like Mary Claire's babies? Didn't he want to be close to my chest, to hear my heartbeat?

I needed to get out of the house. I needed fresh air. Even if that air was ninety degrees and humid as steam rising from a bowl of soup.

I contemplated Oliver's car seat. Did he need to be strapped in for a leisurely stroll through the neighborhood? Probably, but I folded a blanket over the pointed clips and fasteners and laid him on top, then draped a second blanket loosely over his legs. The car seat clicked into the stroller, which was waiting for us in the cool and dark garage.

Sweat immediately beaded on my forehead as I pushed the stroller over the bump at the end of the driveway, but Oliver was already asleep. Perhaps this would be our thing. We'd spend hours walking the neighborhood, building muscle, breathing in air scented with chlorine from the neighbors' pools and honeysuckle lining the backs of yards, fragrant, pretty, invasive.

Or perhaps not. I'd not even made it up the hill, to the end of my street, before my groin muscles began to burn, whether from lack of use or overuse, I wasn't sure. But I continued to push. I knew of a loop through the neighborhood that was just under a mile. I'd walked it before, during my pregnancy, hearing and hoping that walking might cause labor to start. It hadn't.

Oliver was staring quietly above at the soaring oak trees that lined the street, rustling in the faint breeze. We were nearing the halfway point on our route when, without warning, he began to scream again.

Curtains were pulled to the side, blinds were parted, as neighbors looked out. *What is that noise?* Dogs winced and whined and strained toward the sound.

Probably not. Probably no one was looking, but it felt like they were.

I looked around wildly, feeling mortified. I reached into the stroller to rub his chest. "Shh," I told him. "It's okay. What's wrong?"

I jiggled the stroller from side to side. He could be hungry, I supposed. He could need a diaper change. He could be crying for no reason at all. It would be approximately the same distance to turn around as it would be to continue our loop. It was the worst possible place for him to have a meltdown.

I clenched my teeth, gripped the handlebars of the stroller, and spun, walking back toward the house as quickly as I could, which wasn't very quickly at all, while waves of pain crashed against me and set tears burning in the corners of my own eyes.

My head was bowed as I pushed, looking at the ground, not where I was going, not at my son. We were hurrying down Ashby Drive, propelled by momentum, when I sensed a presence. Someone doing yard work in his front yard to my right. Out of my peripheral vision, I could see that he was neither tall nor short. He was thin and wiry, dark-haired, maybe a decade older than me. He was raking mulch into flower beds. The earthy, wooden odor slapped me in the face. He'd not been there on our way up our street.

He stood, holding his rake to the side of his body like a cane. He lifted a hand and waved; he was smiling. I'd not met him before, didn't know his name. We were still new to the neighborhood, still running into neighbors for the first time, exchanging names and pleasantries. Thus far, I'd only met a handful of people. And now wasn't the time for introductions.

I nodded toward him, once, curtly. There was a knowing look on his face. Had I seen him out before? With kids, older than Oliver? Kids with odorous armpits and pulsing zits and almost visible angst, but independent (relatively)? He must have kids. His look was one of sympathy, not judgment. A look that said he'd been exactly where I was, on more than one occasion. He'd been through worse. And, here he was, laying mulch on a Monday afternoon.

He'd survived.

Would I?

Downhill was worse than up, fighting the momentum from my extra weight, the pull of the stroller, dragging me toward our house, faster than I was comfortable going. Oliver was enjoying it. His mouth went slack, his eyes drooped heavily.

I parked the stroller in the garage, removed the car seat, staggered into the house, knifelike pain slicing through me.

I broke a rule. Oliver was asleep in the car seat now, and I left him there on the kitchen floor. I was out of ice packs, the magical, cracking ones I'd received from the hospital. I should have hoarded them, secreted them in our duffel bag before we were discharged. I should have figured out where to buy them in bulk. But I'd not known I would need them. No one had told me it would be this bad, that, even two weeks after the birth, it would hurt this much.

I opened the freezer, letting the frigid air dry the sweat from my face. The ice pack was resting in the door, flexible, bright blue, and frostbitten, a match to the stylish lunch box I used to bring to work. The lunch box had been packed away in a kitchen cabinet since the start of my maternity leave.

I folded the ice pack in half and shoved it into my shorts, wriggled and bent it into the V-shaped space between the tops of my thighs. The relief was instant and sweet.

I'd never contemplated such a use for it. It was only one of so many things I had never imagined, had never seen coming. I was so scared to consider what more there might be.

SIX

"It's too early to lay mulch," he'd told her. "We don't lay mulch until September."

This was true, not merely an excuse, not born of laziness. None of the neighbors had done the annual end-of-summer yard cleanup. No one else had pulled weeds or raked dark and fragrant wood chips over their flower beds. (Not that many, or any, of them did this sort of work themselves.) But it wasn't the only reason. It was also far, far too hot for such physical labor.

He used the back of his arm to wipe the sweat from his forehead, but that did not help, only served to moisten his face further, so he dropped his rake and used the hem of his T-shirt.

Of course, Erin got what she wanted. She wanted him to do the yard work, and he told her it was too early. Of course, here he was, doing the yard work.

Paul lifted his rake from the ground and resumed digging it into the mounds of mulch he'd dumped on the gardens lining the house. He'd thought that carrying the bags from the trunk of his car and emptying them into piles would be the most difficult aspect of the chore, but the raking was far worse. A pinching pain was beginning to throb between his shoulder blades, and there was a hint of nausea building in his gut. Probably the beginning of heatstroke.

God, how he hated her.

The thought startled him so much that he froze, the rake hovering just above the ground. It was as if it was a burglar that had broken into his mind, shattered a window, made itself at home. Did it belong? He paused to consider this.

He decided that it did. He wasn't sure when exactly it had happened, or how, but he hated his wife.

He let the thought, the realization, get comfortable, to recline onto a sofa, drape its feet over an armrest, while he continued his work. It was an unwelcome distraction from the dizzying heat.

It wasn't his fault, though. It was Erin's. She'd brought the hatred upon herself. She had probably hated him ever since she got pregnant with Petra, a decade ago. Ever since he had resigned from his job, and they'd made the decision that he would stay at home with Petra for a while, that he would focus on his writing. Even though Erin had been the one to suggest that in the first place. True, it wasn't as though he'd had much of a choice but to resign. The school had made that clear. Resign from his position, or there'd be a formal investigation into the girl's allegations.

Just quit, Erin had said. *We'll be fine.* She was earning so much more than him already, back then. His meager salary as a professor at the local university felt superfluous compared to her soaring earnings, her thriving financial advisory business.

And she'd been so sick, already having grown tired of the idea of being a mother, even before their baby was born. She'd already been looking forward to going back to work.

Erin behaved as though it was his fault she'd been so aggressively ill with morning sickness twenty-four hours a day, for months and months, throughout the pregnancy. As though it was his fault that baby Petra had screeched for hours, and slept for only minutes. None of it was his fault, but he had always taken care of everything as if it had been. He was the one who stayed home with Petra and soothed her cries. He was the one who paced the house with her in the middle of the night. Meanwhile, Erin's life had returned to much the way it had been before she ever had a baby. She returned to her previous path and continued down it, the birth of their child a mere deviation. He and Petra took a new path, together, without her.

Now, Petra was ten, and he was still a stay-at-home father, and his wife seemed to hate him for that, as though it hadn't been her idea in the first place.

He could only imagine how much more Erin would hate him, if she ever found out about Lara Tucker.

Paul glanced toward the end of the street, at the house that sat at twelve o'clock on the cul-de-sac, the house in which the young couple now lived with their brand-new baby.

It used to be the Tucker house, home to Mark and Lara, and their sons, Hudson and Cole.

He was certain that Erin didn't know about Lara. Mark had never found out about them, either. It was so easy, almost too easy. They were just two stay-at-home parents with the unique luxury of leisure time and empty houses, while their children were at school and their spouses were at work, toiling away, earning the money that allowed them to live in such a nice neighborhood. He and Lara had spent quite a bit of that leisure time together, in the Tucker house. Lara was pretty, enthusiastic, eager to have her ego stroked, to be told she was beautiful while he pressed into her, his hands in her hair.

His marriage, his situation, had been far more bearable when Lara was around.

But then came the separation. Mark moved out, which made things even easier for them at first, until the house was listed and sold, and Lara and the boys were gone, too. And in swept the new family with their careers and sedans, and now, their tiny baby.

That was when he heard it, and thoughts of Lara were chased from his mind.

Years ago, during those first few days of Petra's life, the sound had flooded him with stress, choked him with panic. With trial and error, with sheer persistence, he had learned exactly how to calm his crying baby daughter. Soothing her cries was the most rewarding thing he'd ever done. He'd carried her down to the basement, so that she wouldn't wake Erin. He'd fed her bottles and paced the floor with her, until she shuddered and grew heavy and still against his chest.

He tracked the sound, scanning the otherwise peaceful street, searching for its source.

It was the new neighbor, pushing her stroller awkwardly down the street, quickly, yet somehow gingerly, as if she were in a great deal of pain. He could immediately tell that she was anxious and embarrassed by the noise. She shouldn't be. Babies cried. There was no rhyme or reason to it, and the sooner she came to accept that, the better off she'd be. She couldn't possibly soothe her child when she herself was so coiled and prone to sparking, like a tangled and fraying extension cord.

He took a step forward, holding his rake to his side, preparing to drop it to the ground, to make his way into the street, to finally meet the new neighbor.

Immediately, he could tell that the woman was too ashamed, too overwhelmed. She only wanted to get home, out of the heat. It wasn't the right time. Not now. Not when he was drenched in sweat. He couldn't hold a baby. He couldn't meet its mother like this. He would disgust her.

Instead, he smiled at her, and lifted his arm to wave, friendly, but considerate, keeping his distance.

She smiled tightly and gave him a brief nod back, keeping her hands firmly on the handlebars of the stroller. There was no hesitation, no pull toward him, no pause. She continued to scurry back to the safety of her house, within which her insecurity could be concealed.

No, it wasn't the right time, but already, it had become quite clear that she did need him. Unequivocally, she could use his help.

And he could help her. He had been there. He had survived. Petra had flourished. He missed those days, tear-streaked, spit-up-coated, ear-shattering-scream-filled days. Days that had been marred, like almost every day since, like today, by Erin.

And perhaps, she could help him, too. It was the closest he'd come to her since she'd moved into the house at the end of the street, and he could see that she was objectively attractive, if not a bit disheveled. She had moved into the Tucker house, and she seemed to be spending her days there alone. Could she do for him what Lara had done?

He wouldn't mind getting even closer. What color were her eyes? How soft was her skin? Of what did it smell? He wouldn't mind finding out.

But not now. The time was not right.

He turned back to the garden beds. He dug the rake fiercely, bitterly, into the mounds of mulch, finishing the job. For now, it was the only choice he had.

SEVEN

"Look," said Elaine proudly, staring down at her belly. Something bulged against it, ran along its front, most likely a tiny foot.

I watched and smiled. Oliver was balancing on the top of her bump. "Quite handy," she'd said, laughing, when I had first passed her my baby and she'd settled down on the sofa.

"Did you feel that?" she asked Oliver. "That was your future best friend. Girlfriend? Perhaps, wife? You better treat her well."

I stared at Oliver. Somehow, it hadn't yet occurred to me that he was not going to be a baby forever. He would grow up. Go to school. His underarms would smell. He'd mask it with noxious spray. He'd jerk off into towels behind his closed bedroom door. He'd drink beer in friends' basements and lie to me about it. He'd go off to college, maybe several states away. He'd forget to call. He'd get married, to a woman, to a man, to someone. He'd have children of his own. I'd hold them and think of him. I'd miss these days. Wouldn't I?

"Nat?"

"Sorry," I said. "What did you say?"

"I'm sorry it's been so long since I've visited," Elaine said. "Work has just been so busy."

"That's okay," I told her. And, really, it was. I had grown used to being alone with just my baby. "I understand how busy work can be when you're getting ready to go out on leave."

Elaine nodded. "How are you feeling?" She was gently tracing Oliver's hairline with the tip of her finger.

"Um." I rubbed my eyes.

Elaine had been my best friend since the eighth grade. We'd stood side by side in front of a mirror, our upper arms brushing, while we did our hair and makeup for homecoming dances. We'd commiserated about our periods. In college, we'd linked arms for warmth as we stumbled back to our dorm or on-campus apartments, returning from parties or bars. We'd gotten pregnant months apart. She knew everything about me. But the horrors of my labor, of my recovery, seemed too sordid to share even with her. And she was a doctor, well-versed in medical things and blood and stitches, but she'd not yet gone through childbirth herself. I didn't want to scare her. But did I wish that someone had scared me? Was that the problem? That no one had told me about the witch hazel pads I'd need for my hemorrhoids; the magical ice packs; the diaper-like sanitary napkins; the billowing, hospital-issue underwear; the sitz bath and squirt bottle?

"I'm feeling okay, I guess," I said. "It's been more difficult than I thought it would be. I mean, it's been five weeks. The pain is still pretty bad. I thought I'd be able to go for longer walks by now, but I can't."

"Well, you had, what? A third-degree tear?" Said with the cavalier attitude of a doctor, necessary, not unreasonable. She needed to distance herself. "That's pretty severe."

"Right," I said.

"Just be glad it wasn't fourth degree." We both shuddered. "Or a C-section. That's still my biggest fear, I guess. I just want it all to happen naturally," Elaine continued.

"It definitely wasn't natural for me," I said.

"I have the whole day off, so I could sit here for a few hours," Elaine suggested after a pause. "If you want to go have a nap. Do you have any milk for him?"

I shook my head. "I haven't tried the pump yet. I'll try it this week, start freezing some milk for when I go back to work."

"Good idea," said Elaine. She was gazing lovingly into Oliver's face, peaceful and sleeping because he was being held by competent, practiced arms. Was that the way I looked when I looked at my baby? Or was there resentment in my eyes? Did he see it?

"His doctor thinks he might have reflux?" I said hesitantly. "We had an appointment yesterday, and Oliver wouldn't stop crying. The doctor thinks it might be caused by food sensitivities to something that I'm eating."

"Huh." Elaine's brows were wrinkled. Oliver looked so perfect in this moment. "Why does she think that?"

"Well, sometimes it's difficult to nurse him. He's fussy. He doesn't sleep."

A bark of laughter. "He's a baby. That all sounds normal."

I shook my head vigorously. Why did I feel so desperate to convince her that there was something wrong with my child?

"The doctor watched him trying to nurse. And because he will only sleep for such short periods at a time, it could be that he's uncomfortable."

"So what are you supposed to do?" Elaine asked, her thumb softly grazing the plushness of Oliver's upper arm.

"Eliminate nuts, dairy, and soy from my diet, and see if he seems more comfortable," I replied. I felt more overwhelmed by the suggestion now than I had when Dr. Williams had first made it. What did that leave for me to eat? I'd quickly discovered that soy and dairy were hidden in most things.

Oliver began to fuss faintly in Elaine's arms, as though displeased that we were discussing him. Elaine stood and began to bounce-rock him expertly from side to side. She had several years of practice, by this point, from her work as a pediatrician. She had tried to soothe many tiny, crying newborns during appointments. Her daughter would be in capable hands.

"He's so beautiful, Nat," Elaine whispered, looking down into Oliver's face, again peaceful, his eyes now open. "And I see a lot of babies. I think he likes my earrings." She shook her head gently from side to side, sending her dangling earrings swaying, as she smiled down at my son. "So, are you going to try it?" she asked. "Change your diet? It doesn't leave you with much to eat."

"I could try eliminating one thing at a time, but I'm so desperate to sleep. I'd rather starve and sleep than eat peanut butter."

"You're scaring me," Elaine remarked. "Is it really that bad?"

She was my best friend. I couldn't lie to her. "It is. He still won't sleep more than two hours at a time. Usually, it's less. And I have to hold him all day. He won't nap unless I'm holding him."

"All babies have different temperaments," Elaine said. "Some are more difficult than others. It's just the way it is, nothing you can do about it."

She was reassuring herself, thinking about her perfect daughter, that she would have an easy temperament, that she would sleep.

I'd always imagined myself with a daughter, too.

I'd cried during the ultrasound, the warm gel coating my belly, Tyler peering at the screen eagerly over my shoulder as gray and black images swirled, and the technician called out that I was having a boy. She thought they were tears of joy.

"There's his penis," she'd said. "See? There's his nose, his right foot, his left foot. Oh, he's moving. There's his penis again. There's his right hand. There's his penis again. He keeps on showing us his penis."

"Stop it!" I'd wanted to scream. *"Stop saying* penis*!"*

Tyler and I had headed in to work after the ultrasound appointment, to our respective soaring parking garages downtown, then into our respective soaring office buildings. I'd gone straight into the bathroom, dropped my purse onto the floor, and started to cry again. Because I had never pictured myself raising a son. I had only ever imagined myself raising a daughter. Two daughters. How could I reconcile that long-held image with the reality that there was a boy living inside my uterus? I would never have two daughters. I would have a son. I might even have two sons. It was a terrifying thought, and I'd begun to work on conjuring up a new image. One of myself as a mother to an only child.

It was ridiculous to resent one's son for not being a daughter. I knew this. It was cruel. So I tried not to do it. I really did try.

"I guess I'd better go," Elaine said, passing Oliver back to me. "If you don't want to nap. That okay? I have a few errands to run."

I nodded. "It's time for him to nurse anyway." I was so envious, in that moment. Errands. A day off. A day to myself. Perusing the shelves of Target leisurely, the white, fluorescent lights beating down on me, so unpleasantly bright and wonderful. Picking up dry cleaning, wrapped in staticky plastic, which I'd not done for so many months. I missed my smooth pantsuits and silk, melon-colored blouses. I missed extra-large coffees in to-go cups, sipped while I wound through the aisles in the grocery store.

"Hang in there," Elaine said in the foyer, smiling, biting her bottom lip. I pushed away an urge to ask her to take Oliver with her.

I returned to the family room to feed him, dropping onto the sofa, glad that Elaine was gone, relieved that I was alone now, yet also wishing that she would return. I simply couldn't be satisfied.

Suddenly, there was quite a bit of noise as someone pushed his way into the house. There was bumping, something scraping at the wall, a faint groan. I stood quickly, wrapping my arms around Oliver as if to protect him, my heart fluttering in the back of my throat. But it was only Tyler. He staggered into the family room, his arms wrapped around a large cardboard box; he was pushing a second with his foot.

DELUXE CRADLE SWING was printed across the side of each carton in curling teal font.

"What are you doing here?" I asked him.

He dropped the box onto the floor.

Several silent blinks passed between us. "I live here."

I rolled my eyes, returned to the sofa. "Yes, but what are you doing home so early?" He never seemed to be home before six, and Elaine had only just left.

"What are you talking about?" Tyler asked. "It's six-thirty. I thought you'd be annoyed with me for being later than usual. I stopped for the swings."

He wasn't looking at me anymore, but was crouching down before the cardboard boxes, surveying the images printed on the sides.

I held on to Oliver while I pawed at the cushions for my cell phone. It had slipped between two of them, and when I tugged it out, the time—6:37—blinked back at me, layered over my favorite photo of Oliver. Except Elaine had visited me at two in the afternoon, hadn't she? I opened our text message thread to confirm it. She hadn't stayed that long, not *hours*. She had only just left. Where had the rest of that time gone? Had I fallen asleep, without even noticing it? But I didn't feel rested. If anything, I felt worse than I had earlier in the day, but there simply wasn't any other explanation for those missing hours.

I inspected Oliver. For once, he was quiet, looking up at me with curious, cobalt eyes. He seemed intact, which was further evidence that I hadn't slept. It wasn't as if he could have taken care of himself. It wasn't as if he could have gone hours without crying.

"What do you think?" Tyler asked.

I dropped my phone, grateful for the distraction, and looked up to find him pointing at the boxes.

"I don't want them," I said quickly, even though I had never wanted anything more. "Take them back. Return them."

"Nat," he said calmly. "Why?"

"Sleep in motion is not as restful as stationary sleep. It's not as good for them. It doesn't count."

"Natalie, everyone uses these."

"That doesn't mean it's okay," I replied, as Tyler stepped toward us, smiling, arms outstretched, to take Oliver. "Years ago, everyone put their babies to sleep on their tummies. Everyone gave their babies formula and put rice cereal in their bottles. People put whiskey on their nipples, Tyler!"

"And we all turned out fine." He was kissing the top of Oliver's head.

"No, we didn't. Some of us died."

His head snapped up. He cradled Oliver protectively. "If these swings were dangerous, they wouldn't sell them. I went to Target. There were loads to choose from." As if affronted that I'd suggested that Target could be anything less than perfect.

"I'm not saying they're dangerous. I'm just saying that babies are supposed to sleep where it's still. That's how they get their best sleep."

"Well, he's not sleeping that way, though. You said yourself that he's only sleeping when you hold him. You can't hold him all day, every day. All night, every night. You have to take care of yourself. Isn't sleep in motion better than no sleep at all? You won't leave him in the swing all day. Just when you need a break." His arguments came quick and fast, like bullets. I felt like opposing counsel, standing across from him in the well of the courtroom.

Could I hold him all day, though, I wondered? Should I? Should I want to? Was that what a good mother would do? I wasn't feeling great about my counterargument. It could have been stronger, but I was too exhausted to fill its holes.

Just when you need a break. What if I needed a break the entire day? Already, I was imagining putting Oliver in the swing, strapping him in, tucking a blanket around his lap, spinning the dial, turning it on. Back and forth it would rock, creaking. Oliver would fall asleep. I would lie down in front of him. On the sofa. On the floor. I'd go to sleep myself, bathed in the unusual silence, comforted by the absence of my baby in my arms. I'd sleep for hours.

It was wrong, this fantasy. It was delicious.

"I don't want them," I said again. I turned up my nose and looked away. I wandered into the kitchen, began to prepare dinner. This was our routine when Tyler arrived home. He would hold Oliver, to give me a break from him, while I made dinner, as if cooking was a break.

"Alright," said Tyler. He looked dejected. He'd thought I'd be happy to see the swings. He'd thought that I wanted them.

The truth was, I did want them. I wanted them too much. And that was why I couldn't have them. It didn't matter what I wanted. Not anymore. I was a mother now. Oliver was all that mattered. All that mattered was what was best for him.

EIGHT

The seminal advice, as old as time, handed down and regurgitated like curdled milk spit from a baby's mouth, surviving decades of scientific studies and evolving knowledge of best practices.

Sleep while your baby is sleeping.

Unless you have to go back to work in two weeks. Then, pump breast milk when your baby is sleeping and put it in the freezer. This was what the advice should have been.

My goal was to pump twice a day during my last three weeks of leave, and I had been mostly successful at meeting that goal. I was only able to pump at all because of the swings. I loved the swings. I loved them too much.

I'd put one in the family room, in view from the kitchen, and one upstairs, in our bedroom. Tyler had assembled them, set them up, said nothing when he returned home the following day to see that I had moved one to the second floor and that both were plugged in.

Oliver was strapped into the swing in the family room, and I sat on the sofa in front of him, watching, waiting for him to fall asleep. He was fussing, wiggling his legs. He was tired but fighting sleep. It was the most perplexing of all of his exceedingly perplexing behaviors. Sleep was wonderful. It was all I wanted. Why did my son resist it with everything he had?

"It's okay, kiddo," I told him. "Trust me, you're not going to miss anything. Look, kiddo," I said. "Mommy is going to sleep, too." I closed my eyes. For several minutes, the fussing continued. Then, there was silence. I cracked an eye open to see that Oliver's were closed. I exhaled, though the feeling of victory was short-lived as I unzipped my pump bag, pushed the parts together, and pressed the plastic shields against my breasts. I spun the dial on the pump, then listened to the mechanical chugging, felt the pull-twist of my flesh. I leaned forward, as if that would help the milk to flow. It didn't. I waited for fifteen minutes to pass before giving up.

I ran scalding-hot water into a bowl and swirled the used pump parts inside with a drizzle of soap, leaving them there, to soak, or out of laziness because I didn't feel like washing them.

Oliver was still asleep, so I ate lunch as quickly as I could. I was starving all the time, but almost everything I could eat was unappealing. The jar of peanut butter, now forbidden, seemed to blink at me sadly every time I opened the pantry.

I had just finished tying my sneakers when Oliver awakened and began to cry. Overall, I felt satisfied, accomplished. I allowed only two naps in the swing each day. The first was used for pumping and eating lunch. If there was spare time, I would tackle a small chore around the house. After lunch, we'd go out for a walk, ambling, succinct, but we were working up to longer distances. In the afternoon, we'd practice tummy time for a few seconds here and there, for as long as he and I could stomach it. Then, I'd sit in the glider, my feet resting on the ottoman, and rest Oliver against my thighs so that we could look into each other's faces while I read to him—typically something from my Kindle, whatever I wanted to read—and talked to him, about going back to work, about daycare, about the way I'd once filled my days, with writing and research and negotiations. There would be another afternoon nap in the swing, during which I'd pump again. Dotted throughout the day were diaper changes and nursing sessions and attempted naps in his crib or bassinet, which still only lasted a few minutes at a time. Once Tyler arrived home, I'd finally be able to take a shower, washing sour milk from my hair and sticky, dried sweat from my skin, then prepare dinner, all while Tyler held Oliver, bouncing him and rocking him. Usually, Oliver would cry, and there was no amount of rocking or being pressed against his dad's chest that would help him. He wanted only his mother and her milk. I wasn't sure if this should make me feel happy or irritable.

None of it was perfect, and it wasn't exact, but we had a routine, and that was something to which I could cling.

A routine meant a schedule, and a schedule meant predictability. It meant accountability. It meant that no further hours would be lost. If we had a routine, time wouldn't—couldn't—simply disappear into thin air.

I loaded Oliver into his stroller, draped a light blanket over his lap, and pushed into the driveway.

It was September now. School was back in session. The air was still warm, but bearable. Vacation was over. Driveways, garages, were empty, aside from the few belonging to retirees or stay-at-home parents or those lucky people who worked from home. At least, I'd always thought of them as lucky as I braved rush hour downtown, gridlock, long lines to escape parking garages, and blaring horns. It felt like ages ago that I'd sat in my own car, idling at a red light, cursing as I sat through yet another cycle while trying to make a left onto Howard Street, trying to get to the highway, to escape the city. I'd felt trapped then. I'd not known what it meant to feel trapped.

The sun was beating down on my face, and I was thinking only of its warmth and comfort, not of the wrinkles deepening in my forehead, deeper since I'd turned thirty, deeper still since I'd become a mother.

Oliver was snoozing peacefully again, at least. No one was out, and I began to hum softly to myself, a favorite song, as we swung a U-turn and returned home. A Third Eye Blind song, rife with inappropriate language, but without the lyrics, it was fine. Look at me. I was a joyous stay-at-home mother, humming lovingly to her son.

"Good morning!"

I startled, turned my head, simultaneously leaning over the stroller, protecting my child, impressed, relieved, by my instinct to do so.

"Sorry," said the man behind me, laughing gently. He was jogging slowly, almost in place. I'd not heard him approaching. "I didn't mean to scare you."

"It's fine," I said. I straightened, tried to smile, willing him to move along, to continue his run, as was customary, polite, when neighbors spotted each other while out on the streets.

"You're new to the neighborhood, yes?" He slowed to a walk, drifted toward the middle of the street, giving me space. Sweat glistened on his forehead. He was thin and only a few inches taller than I was, with the lean limbs of a person who ran often, covered long distances. His hair was dark and parted, oddly neat and styled for a person out exercising, and the sun was reflecting off his eyes, turning them a glowing amber. I looked away, trying to recall if I'd ever seen him around before, feeling a hint of anxiety, because, while this was my neighborhood, in safe and quiet suburbia, I was a woman, and he was an unknown male.

"Sort of," I said. "We moved here in July." Had it been nearly three months already?

"Thought so," he replied. He reached up to wipe sweat from his forehead with the back of his forearm. "You bought the house at the end of the cul-de-sac? On Ashby Drive?"

"Right," I said.

"I'm just a few houses up from you. You were lucky to get it. We saw a steady stream of people touring it the first day it went up."

"Yes," I said. "We made an offer that day." I reached into the stroller and tucked Oliver's blanket around him busily, unnecessarily, wishing this man would move on. Was he going to walk me all the way down to our street?

"I'm Paul," he said, making a show of wiping his hands on his clothes, then laughing. "I'd shake your hand, but . . ."

But you're disgusting, and please leave me alone.

"Paul Riley," he continued. "My wife is Erin, and our daughter is Petra. She's ten."

"Natalie," I said, because I had to. "My husband is Tyler, and this is Oliver."

As though he'd been directed to, had received a cue, Oliver's eyes opened, then scrunched closed like a Slinky. His mouth stretched wide, and he started to scream.

"Oh dear," said Paul. He stepped toward the stroller and peered beneath the sunshade, then glanced over his shoulder at me. "May I?" he asked. "My daughter was like this. Oh, how she screamed when we went on walks. I know it puts some babies right to sleep. Not my daughter." He laughed softly, as though the memories of his daughter crying in the neighborhood were fond ones.

I shrugged. "Sure," I said, even though I had no idea what he was asking to do.

"There, there," Paul whispered. He reached in, placing a hand on Oliver's chest, patting gently, murmuring with the sort of calm confidence I'd never possessed.

Only two blinks later, Oliver took a gasping breath, then closed his mouth. He blinked up at Paul with interest.

I stared at the man. Paul. Quite suddenly, I noticed that his features were rather handsome. His sweat had stopped pouring, had dried on his now-matte skin. He was trim and fit, not as short as I'd initially thought. He seemed friendly, rather than creepy. Neighborly, not intrusive.

"How did you do that?" I asked as Paul retracted his hand.

It was his turn to shrug. "I have a way with babies," he said, though he didn't sound arrogant. "I love them." Though he didn't sound effeminate, nor pathetic, the way a woman might have, a mother who lived only for her kids, whose only hobby was arranging their photos into scrapbooks alongside stickers and bubble lettering, who devoted more than a decade of her life to each child, only to realize by the time they were teens that she had been relegated to nothing more than a chauffeur, that she'd be valued more if she made money and bought them *things,* because it was things and rides and then cars that made teenagers happy, not hugs or homemade cookies.

"Huh" was my only reply. I was standing quite close to the man, and I suddenly wanted him to place his calming hand on my chest, to coo into my face, to make me feel safe.

"Like I said, my daughter cried a lot. She was a colicky baby. I've had a lot of practice." He laughed again, and I stared at him. I'd had a lot of practice, too, by this point. Why wasn't I so competent?

"Well." Paul stepped away from me, grinning broadly again. "It was great to meet you, Natalie," he said, my name sounding so intimate rolling off his tongue. "And you, Oliver," he added to my son, who was still gazing up at Paul, mesmerized as he would have been by a spinning ceiling fan.

"You, too," I said. I didn't want him to go.

"Back to my run." Paul gave me a wry smile, as if a run midmorning on a glorious, early fall day were a chore.

With a half wave over his shoulder, he jogged ahead of us toward Ashby Drive. I watched the muscles in his tan calves tightening, and I remembered him as the man I'd seen working in the yard the very first time Oliver had screeched on our walk, a few weeks earlier. He'd not approached us that day, not laid his magical palm onto Oliver's chest.

What did he do? I wondered. Why was he home during the day? Perhaps he worked from home, or was a doctor, who worked night shifts. I suddenly felt quite certain of this. I could picture him wearing a long white lab coat, hurrying down hospital hallways. He probably had a lovely bedside manner.

The road curved, and Paul, his pace at least twice ours, disappeared from view. Oliver must have sensed this, as he began to cry again. I moved more quickly.

We slowed as we passed Paul's house. It was pristine, its red door bright, with evergreen-colored shutters, the mulch he'd been laying down a few weeks earlier held in place with stones lining the gardens. I assumed he had disappeared inside, and I wondered if he could hear Oliver's screams as we went by. How could he not?

I tried to mimic Paul's reassuring coos. "It's okay," I murmured, like a good mother would. "We'll be home soon, and you can nurse."

Oliver ignored me.

I didn't realize that I was hoping Paul would come out of his house until we'd passed it completely, and he didn't.

A door slammed and I turned around optimistically. But it was only Mrs. Jensen, across the street from Paul's house. She was a retired preschool teacher, another one who loved babies. She'd raised four of her own, she had told me proudly when she'd stopped by with a glass dish full of blondies, a few days after we had moved in. She'd told me again when I returned the dish, the dessert having been demolished shamefully fast. I didn't even know her first name. She had introduced herself as though I was one of her students.

She waved at me emphatically, her expansive, floral dress fluttering from the movement. A seemingly friendly overture, but there was disapproval on her face. *What is wrong with you?* She retrieved her newspaper from the end of her driveway without stopping to chat, averting her eyes, turning her back quickly after she straightened her arthritic knees. She pretended to be staring at the paper through the transparent blue bag, as though riveted by a headline.

You take him, I wanted to shout to her. *If it's so easy, you take him.*

Every baby is different. That's what the pediatrician told me. Elaine said it, too. Some babies have an easy temperament. Some babies sleep.

Perhaps that's how Mrs. Jensen's four had been. Mine was temperamental. He didn't sleep. She had no idea what it was like to be me.

I hated it. I hated the blaming looks, the accusatory stares. That Oliver was such a miserable little human seemed to be all my fault. No one blamed him, or Tyler. No one felt bad for me. What had I done to make him that way, they wondered? Surely it was something.

But there'd been Paul's face. There had been sympathy in his glowing, golden eyes, catlike in their color, but not in the emotion that they held. Devoid of apathy, brimming with understanding. I wanted to see them again. I wanted to feel seen.

NINE

He'd left the door unlocked when he went out for his run. That was what people on Ashby Drive, in this neighborhood, did. He was terribly thirsty, but he slipped into the powder room on the way to the kitchen, to check his reflection in the mirror above the vanity. His skin was obviously dotted with sweat, but it could be worse. His hair remained in place, his exercise attire was flattering, especially for a man his age.

He splashed cold water on his face, then dried it with the hand towel, knowing that he was also drying his sweat, knowing that it was permeating the towel, knowing that Erin would be disgusted by him if she saw him do it. He slipped the towel back onto the brass ring, imagining with admittedly childish satisfaction her drying her freshly washed hands with it, then moved into the kitchen where he filled a glass with water.

He'd not been expecting that today, this morning, would be the day he finally introduced himself to the new neighbor, but the opportunity had presented itself, and he'd decided to take it, rather than turning and taking his run elsewhere, when he saw her—*Natalie*—ahead of him. She'd seemed a bit standoffish at first, displeased with being approached, but she warmed to him once he had helped her soothe her baby. He could tell she was impressed, even jealous. He could tell she was overwhelmed. She was all alone, her husband clearly having returned to work. It had been the perfect time for him to swoop in and rescue her.

He'd known, from the first time he'd seen her, that she would need his help. Today had been proof of that. What more could he do for her, he wondered?

What might she be able to do for him?

She was pretty, despite her lack of makeup and grooming. Fair-haired, and soft, with a dimple in her left cheek, her eyes a clear blue, a few shades lighter than her baby's.

Suddenly, he heard it again, the rising pitch. He carried his glass of water into the foyer and peered through the narrow windows lining the front door. It was the baby, of course, crying again. Natalie was pushing the stroller down the hill hurriedly, her mortification evident from the speed with which she was moving and the anxious looks she was throwing toward the other houses as she passed. She was about a decade younger than him, he guessed, just about the same age he had been when Petra was born. She, like him, was home alone with her baby. But she wasn't handling it well. He wondered whether she was still on maternity leave, or whether she'd given up her career entirely. It was a shame he hadn't been able to ask, that he hadn't been able to spend more time with her.

But it was early days. Only the first meeting. There'd be time for more.

Natalie glanced at his house as she passed, just a bit longer than she was looking at any others. She wanted him to come back out, to quiet her baby, to ameliorate her shame. He wanted that, too, and he smiled, feeling a pull toward her as he reached for the doorknob. Perhaps now was the right time after all?

His hand was on the knob when he felt a buzzing against his thigh. His cell phone, in the pocket of his athletic shorts, not a particularly comfortable place for it when he went for a run, but he tried to keep his cell phone on him at all times. Petra was back in school now, and it could be an administrator, letting him know that she'd fallen ill, that she needed him. He couldn't risk missing such a call. If he did, and they tried Erin next, she would be irritated. That was his job, as far as she was concerned, his only job: meeting Petra's needs.

Another interaction with Natalie would have to wait for another day, even though it wasn't Petra or her school calling, he realized once he slipped the phone from his pocket, but Erin herself. He answered grudgingly.

"Hello," Erin replied, sharpness and coldness even in those two syllables. "What are you up to?"

He wouldn't tell her he'd just gotten back from a run. He wouldn't tell her he'd just, finally, met the new neighbor woman, if she could still be considered new after a few months. Just like he had never told her about Lara Tucker, his relationship, his closeness, with her.

"Just working," he lied. "You?"

"Working, of course, but I need you to run out to the store for me," she said. "I thought I might go on my lunch break, or my way home, but it's clear that I'm not getting a lunch break and I might be late."

She was always late. "Oh," he replied. "Business picking up?"

She bristled. He could tell, even though he could not see her, and she hadn't made a sound. He knew his wife.

"I'm working on it," she said. "Anyway, I need tampons. I need vitamins. I took my last one this morning. Can you run out for me?"

He turned from the window, rubbed his hand over his face. Did she really need tampons, he wondered, or did she just like to remind him of the hold she had? He was forty-three years old, long past the stage of his life when purchasing women's sanitary products would make him feel embarrassed. That wasn't the problem. If they had a loving relationship, he'd be happy to do her a favor. If their relationship were one of mutual support, he'd do anything she needed, would have no issue running out to the store for whatever she desired. He *did* have the time. But their relationship wasn't like that. She treated him like an employee, delegating some menial tasks for him to handle. She did things, just like this, not because she needed him to, but to remind him of her power. He only wished there was some way he could remind her of his own power. To show her that she was wrong. That he didn't need her.

Lara Tucker had given him that feeling of power. Their sex, pressed against the counter in her kitchen or on top of the bed she shared with her husband. Lara, and the secret he'd shared with her, had made him feel powerful. But Lara had moved to Pennsylvania with her sons, to be closer to her parents, and she'd taken that feeling with her. He missed it.

"Sure," he said. "I'll run out before I get Petra from school."

"Great. Thanks," she replied, and then the phone went silent, without a *goodbye* or a *love you*.

Erin Riley didn't have time for such pleasantries. Not for him. Not for their own daughter. Not that she loved him. He was certain that she didn't. Still, a *goodbye* or *see you later* wouldn't kill her. She seemed to reserve any niceties for her clients. And look where that had gotten her.

Paul glanced out the window one more time. Natalie and her stroller had disappeared, returned to their house. He could no longer hear the baby's cries, muffled now by distance and additional walls. Quite suddenly, he ached to feel the delicate body of the baby, to feel its warmth soaking into his own skin. He wanted to be reminded of how his own daughter had felt in his arms. Sometimes, he felt like he'd give up everything, except for Petra herself, if he could be transported back in time to her infancy. There'd been difficult days. Impossible days. But never had his life held so much meaning, so much importance, as it had when there'd been the life of another quite literally in his hands.

He missed the feeling of Lara, too. The way her hands had gripped his hair, the way she'd breathed into his ear.

Now, he felt completely alone.

He turned from the window again and climbed the stairs to shower. He still needed to spend some time trying to write before he could head to the store and then retrieve Petra from school. Would today be the day that the words flowed? Would they spill onto the page, or would it remain as clear and white as ever?

At some point, Erin wouldn't continue to accept his excuses, his claims that he didn't want her to see any of the book until it was completely finished. She'd demand that he show her something, or, worse, she'd find a way past the password on his computer and she'd look for it herself. She'd discover that, despite almost ten years of work, there was no novel, only erratic thoughts, random scenes. There was no family saga, no story of fatherhood, which was the way he had described the book to his wife, as vaguely as he could.

"What the fuck have you been doing all these years?" she'd say. She only cursed when she was truly enraged.

He'd point to their child. Their bright and beautiful sun. Well-spoken, polite, considerate. "This," he'd say. "This is what I've *been doing.*" Creating her. Making her into the person she was.

It should have been more than enough.

TEN

"I don't think I can do it," I said.

The day that had been long awaited, dreaded, worried over, was here. Oliver was eight weeks old.

I'd folded over the waistband of my black maternity dress pants, which were too big, but I'd not been able to pull my regular dress pants over my thighs. I'd dropped thirty pounds in eight weeks, but I was in pants purgatory. Too small for maternity pants. Too large for my old pants. A voluminous blouse covered my still faintly bulging middle, and a matching cardigan was draped over my arms, reinforcement to combat the powerful office air-conditioning. I'd brushed my hair, which had begun to come out in clumps every time I showered, into a low, loose bun, in an effort to conceal its sparseness.

"I know it's difficult, but you can do it," Tyler whispered somewhat superciliously. He'd been leaving Oliver for weeks now. He was used to it. Or maybe not, but he did it anyway. Meanwhile I'd not been separated from Oliver at all, except for my two postpartum doctor's appointments and a trip to the grocery store the previous weekend, alone, upon which I'd insisted, so that I could "practice" for my return to work. It had done nothing to help me prepare for this. I'd been rushed and panicked in the store and had forgotten so many items that Tyler had to go out later that day to purchase the remaining things we would need for the week.

"What if I don't want to do it?" I hissed. "What if I don't want to work?"

We were whispering. Oliver was snoozing in his bassinet nearby. I didn't want to wake him. Not yet. I still wanted to eat breakfast and prepare my lunch before I had to get him up and ready for daycare—nursed and diaper changed, possibly multiple times, and dressed in a onesie and tiny pants, before we could get out the door. I'd already spent time the previous night, precious time when Oliver was asleep and I should have been sleeping, too, filling baby bottles with milk, laying out the cooler bag that would be used to transport them, packing up my breast pump supplies, preparing the coffeepot, setting the timer.

"Nat, what are you talking about? You have been saying for days that you missed work. You wanted to go back."

He was right. I had been saying that during my last week of leave. I was bored, I'd told him. But his words, repeating my own, stung. Did they make me a bad mother?

Yet, the day was here, and I no longer wanted to go. I was a good mother after all. I wanted to be with my baby. This realization brought no comfort. It didn't matter. I had to go. I'd already been worried that having a baby would kill my career. Calling the partners for whom I worked the morning I was set to return and requesting extension of maternity leave was certain to do so.

"It's just hard," I said, feeling a thickness at the back of my throat. I blinked very quickly, tilting my head upward, trying to stave off tears, to save my mascara, before remembering I'd forgotten to put any on.

Tyler, who had been busily buttoning his dress shirt, looked up quickly, then stepped toward me, his arms open. He pulled me against his chest, and I wondered abruptly when we'd last done this.

Oliver stirred, then fussed, then cried. I pulled away. "He's awake." I stated the obvious, sounding accusatory, as though Tyler had woken him.

"I'll hold him," Tyler offered quickly, eyeing me as though I were a bomb threatening to detonate. "You can finish getting ready."

I stepped around him and snatched the baby. "He needs to eat," I said. I'd thought I had finished getting ready. Did I not look ready?

In the nursery, I fed Oliver, then changed him, slipping him into the outfit I'd specially selected for his first day of daycare—little navy pants, a matching dinosaur-printed top, and minuscule socks.

I found Tyler in the kitchen, drinking coffee and leaning against the island, staring at his phone—reading the news or possibly an email, getting started on the day's billable hours quota. My stomach was already churning, thinking about the impossible feat of meeting my own when I'd be spending at least an hour pumping breast milk.

"I need to make my lunch and eat," I said, holding Oliver out to him. "Then I want to nurse him one more time before we leave."

Tyler glanced skeptically at the clock on the microwave.

"Fine," I said, pulling Oliver back to my body, turning toward the family room. "I just won't eat today." Although Tyler had not spoken, I could tell he was anxious to leave, to get to work. He was typically already at work by this time, but we'd decided we'd drop Oliver off at daycare together for his first day.

"Nat, you can eat," he said. He followed me into the family room, a worried expression on his face.

It was too early to nurse Oliver again, but I wanted to minimize the amount of milk he'd need to drink while he was away from me. The daycare provider required that I supply two extra bottles of milk each day. Breast milk that was not consumed within an hour of being warmed would be discarded, per the daycare's policy. It seemed like it would be impossible to keep up.

After I'd finished nursing Oliver and shoved several protein bars into my purse, we loaded our respective cars. By unspoken agreement, Tyler clicked Oliver's car seat into my car. I glanced at my rearview mirror every few seconds while I drove, checking on my baby in the shatterproof mirror secured to the headrest above him. There was a heavy and sick feeling in my stomach.

It was a short drive. Too short. The parking lot was bustling. Smiling parents, practiced at unloading their infants. Toddlers bounding toward the building, dragging miniature backpacks along the ground behind them. I parked in the spot beside Tyler and carefully extracted Oliver's car seat. He'd fallen asleep. Tyler collected Oliver's insulated bag of bottles and the bag that held Oliver's crib sheet. Oliver would be taking naps in a crib, within a dark, closet-like room in the back of his classroom. This was difficult for me to imagine. He was accustomed to napping in his swings or my arms. Crib naps usually lasted for only a few minutes at best, a few seconds at worst. How would he manage?

Tyler held out his hand to take the car seat from me, but I shook my head, carrying it into the building with some difficulty. I just wanted to keep him close to me for as long as possible.

Oliver's teachers greeted us enthusiastically. Their excitement irritating, rather than comforting.

"There he is!" exclaimed Michelle ("Miss Michelle").

Sonya ("Miss Sonya") was wearing loose-fitting plastic gloves while she changed the diaper of another baby. They were practical and sanitary, these gloves, yet, inexplicably, they bothered me.

Michelle was seated on the floor, legs crossed, holding a picture book aloft over two babies, resting on their circular, flat owl pillows. There were six children and two teachers in each of the infant classrooms at the center. It was a common ratio, and no worse than any other daycare that we'd toured, but it didn't seem like enough. What if all the babies cried at once, or even just three of them? How would they decide who to hold?

The jostling movements and high-pitched voices had awakened Oliver. Tyler removed him from the car seat while I loaded his bottles into the fridge, slipped his sheet over his mattress in his designated crib, and completed the day's paperwork, indicating when he'd last slept, ate, and been changed.

"Would you like to join your friends for story time?" Sonya asked. She was placing the freshly changed baby onto her owl pillow.

I reached for Oliver quickly, somewhat protectively. *Don't cry,* I scolded myself.

Tyler patted me on the back while I held Oliver, my cheek pressed against his head, as though I wasn't ever going to see him again.

"We should go," Tyler whispered. "It'll be fine."

Sonya held out her arms. "I can take him," she said. She was smiling reassuringly, accustomed to managing infants and clingy mothers.

Oliver began to cry immediately, but Sonya quickly started to bounce and rock him expertly, shushing softly into his ear. "He's going to do fine," she said.

"Have a great day," Michelle called as we turned and left the room.

As we walked down the hall, toward the exit, past the other rooms with babies lying on mats and toddlers squealing over toys, I heard crying.

"That's Oliver," I said, stopping in my tracks.

"It could be any baby," Tyler said. He placed a hand on my back, guided me forward.

I let him, even though he was wrong. I knew it was Oliver. I felt it inside of me.

We hugged in the parking lot, our second of the day. I climbed into my car and backed out of my spot before Tyler turned on his engine. I wanted to get ahead of him so he couldn't see me crying all the way downtown.

By the time I pulled into the parking garage, I had pulled myself together. The tears were no longer falling. I took a deep breath, then made my way into the office.

This was good, I told myself. *Work.* I liked work. I was good at work.

But, my footsteps light on the commercial-grade carpet, the motion-activated lights coming to life, following me down the long hall to my small office, my heart felt pierced, incomplete, ripped open.

"Welcome back," came a voice.

Gina Demetriou, a partner in the mergers and acquisitions practice group, had emerged from the communal kitchen, dunking a tea bag into a steaming mug. I'd done only a little work for her, and not for several months prior to taking my leave, but she must have noticed my absence, and now my shrunken, sagging belly, my tearstained face, my broken heart.

"You look great," she said. "How's the little one?"

I opened my mouth to speak, but no words came. I could feel my bottom lip quivering, then the tears resumed. I lifted my palms to my eyes, as though trying to push them back in.

Gina looked startled for a second—this wasn't the sort of thing senior associates did in the halls of Gallagher, Markham & Rice—before she regained her composure.

"It gets easier," she said, smiling at me kindly. But only for a second. It passed quickly, with some modicum of apparent embarrassment on her part, as if her sympathy had escaped unwittingly as a belch, out of place, inappropriate in a place like this. She patted me dismissively on the back, twice. Then she disappeared.

ELEVEN

I pushed the lock into place with a click. A locksmith had come to install it on my office door while I was out on leave, and someone had affixed a tension rod to the internal window beside my door, hanging a heavy, mahogany drape on it.

Gallagher, Markham & Rice occupied the fourteenth floor of a Baltimore skyscraper. One complete side and one partial side of the building had water views of the Inner Harbor. These were the partners' offices. Associates and senior associates had city views, and support staff had no views. Their offices were across the hall from those of the attorneys. This arrangement—when you had time to think about something other than billable hours and how much work you had to do and whether you'd forgotten your paralegal's birthday—felt distasteful, and unfair. The attorneys' offices had internal windows as well, to allow some daylight to filter into the hallways and the offices of the support staff. The internal windows also served, on occasion, to make me feel like an overworked zoo animal, on display for the partners when they were roaming the halls, trying to decide who was to be assigned to the next new case or project. If you were caught tapping at your phone or peeling your split ends, you were sure to be selected.

The windows also presented an impediment to my pumping breast milk during my workday, hence the installation of the lock and curtain, to afford me my statutorily-guaranteed privacy, and then some. The firm had a "wellness room" next to the communal kitchen. It offered a door that locked, a single dimmable, recessed light, a chaise lounge, and a neck pillow. It was a place you could go to cry or have a nervous breakdown during your workday. It could also accommodate a nursing mother, but the firm had elected to pay for the modifications that would make it possible for me to pump in my office. They didn't want me reclining on a chaise lounge in the wellness room, gushing money away, like milk from my nipples. They wanted me sitting at my desk, billing clients, conducting negotiations over conference calls while the other participants mused over the faint, mechanical chugging audible in the background—*What is that sound?*

I pulled the curtain closed and checked the lock again before crawling beneath my desk to plug in my pump and turn on my space heater— disrobing in the aggressive air-conditioning was highly unpleasant. I carefully undid the buttons of my blouse and pulled down the front of my nursing bra, slipping my strapless pumping bra over top, tucking the breast shields inside it. It zipped securely, holding them in place, so that I could have my arms free to work while I was pumping. But I didn't work. I looked out the window. I could see people bustling down the sidewalks. Had any of them gotten more than two hours of sleep the night before? I could see a homeless man in a threadbare, green cargo-style coat. He was rattling a soda cup. Things could be worse.

I looked at my screen, opened an email that had arrived while I'd been setting up my pump. *Shit.* I'd left my timer running, billing some poor client while I'd been unbuttoning my blouse and fitting my pump parts together. I laughed quietly to myself as I imagined entering the details of the time entry. *Removed breasts from shirt and affixed breast pump. Switched motor on. Pumped breast milk and poured into labeled storage bags and placed them in the firm fridge.* At $310 an hour, that would cost Data Lynx, LLC close to $160.

I opened the timer log and modified the time entry, knocking off a few minutes. It was the ethical thing to do, even though Data Lynx would hardly miss the money.

My phone vibrated, knocking against my stainless-steel water bottle, buzzing metallically. I snatched it up, in case it was Oliver's daycare. It was his third day there.

Gina Demetriou was right. It had gotten easier. It was easier, yet still impossible.

In between my pumping breaks, my racing thoughts, and compulsively checking the app the daycare used to provide the timing of diaper changes, feedings, naps, photos, and notes, I'd barely billed five hours my first two days. On Monday afternoon, I'd raced from the office to retrieve Oliver from daycare. His teachers had admitted that he'd had a difficult day, eschewing bottles, refusing naps in his crib.

The second day had been much like the first. I was always poised to receive a call from his teachers, informing me that they couldn't get him to stop crying, that I'd have to come pick him up.

But my ringing phone was not alight with a call from daycare. It was just spam. I swiped across the screen to reject it, then navigated to the app, checking on Oliver's progress. He'd taken several fifteen-minute naps. It wasn't enough sleep for a baby his age. Not nearly enough. He was too little to be away from me. Eight weeks of maternity leave had felt like an eternity until I'd had a baby. I should have requested more, even if it had been unpaid. We could afford it. But I'd been so worried about what the partners would think of me. Harriet Katz, a senior associate in my practice group, two years older than me, had a baby last year. She'd taken her eight weeks of leave and returned with dry eyes and a smile on her face, thanking God for her wonderful nanny, saying she was so relieved to be back at work. She'd billed nineteen hundred hours over the following twelve months and made partner by the time her daughter was taking her first steps.

A nanny. Was that the secret? Was that the route I should have taken? A top-rated, highly recommended childcare center had felt so much safer. I didn't want a stranger in my home, alone with my child. Daycare centers had cameras and accountability. There were other babies for socialization. But Oliver was far too young for socialization. Those other babies were nothing more than competition for the arms of the teachers, foul odors, and loud noises disturbing his already stilted sleep.

The nanny option seemed so obvious to me now, but the thought of finding a good one was more overwhelming than the thought of keeping Oliver at the daycare. I rubbed my hands over my face, then returned my attention to the contract I'd spent the morning drafting. My focus was short-lived, my attention drawn to the bottles dangling from my body. Milk was no longer dripping through the valves, so I unhooked everything and replaced my bra and shirt.

I labeled the bottles and tucked them into a soft-sided cooler bag in the communal fridge. Breast milk seemed like a private substance, not to be left on display for my coworkers.

I returned to my office, closing the door behind me, reaching for my curtain. I paused, let my hand hang in the air. Then, I left it closed. I clicked the lock.

Just for a few minutes, I told myself. I couldn't abuse the curtain. People would check my billable hours in our case management software and grow suspicious. But the urge to lie down was overpowering. So I did, on the floor behind my L-shaped desk, resting my head on the pillow I'd brought in toward the end of my pregnancy, to support my aching back or prop up my swollen feet.

The floor was hard, rife with crumbs and hairs. It was disgusting. The firm didn't have it vacuumed nearly often enough. I closed my eyes. There was quiet. Had I left my timer running again? I didn't care.

I needed to work. I needed to bill. But my head hurt. My eyes felt heavy. There was a fogginess, gray and stifling, smothering me, like a swaddle blanket, pulled over my face. I should reach up, pull it off, break free, take a breath. I couldn't. I lay there. Someone might call me, or knock, or come in. Had I locked the door? I had, hadn't I? I couldn't remember. I wouldn't fall asleep. I wasn't capable of napping.

My desk phone chirped twice. An internal call. I blinked. My vision swirled, my head thrummed with pain. My back felt twisted, my neck crippled. The fog felt thicker. I checked the time. Two hours had passed.

I checked the time again. That couldn't be right. If I couldn't sleep in my own bed, if I couldn't sleep while reclining on the sofa with my baby wrapped in my arms, then I couldn't sleep on the unforgiving floor of my office amidst the dust mites and crumbs and fallen hairs.

But, if I hadn't fallen asleep, where had the time gone?

I ignored my phone. I ignored my thoughts. It was time to pump again.

TWELVE

"Remember, you have tennis this afternoon," he said, glancing at his daughter in the rearview mirror, then quickly back to the road.

"I know," Petra replied, her gaze trained on the window, watching houses—mansions, really—set on one-to-three-acre lots streak past them.

Petra's friends lived in these sorts of homes. His own home was spacious and comfortable, set on a respectable lot in a well-established, even enviable, neighborhood. But they didn't have an in-ground pool or a movie theater. They didn't have a tennis court or horse barn.

Petra was still little. She was still perfectly content to reap the benefits of her friends' pools and theaters and horses. But would that always be the case? He dreaded the day that she realized that, while she had quite a bit, she didn't have as much as her friends. He dreaded the moment she felt inferior, wrongly so, for such superficial reasons.

It was one of the downsides to the school, he supposed. Erin had certainly become a proponent of pulling her out, of placing her into the highly rated public school to which their house was districted. With Erin's business struggling, things had become tight, and the tuition, more than thirty thousand dollars a year, did seem exceedingly exorbitant, considering the alternative option was excellent and free. Except, Petra loved her school. She loved her friends. She wanted to stay. That meant Paul would do whatever he had to do to keep her there, notwithstanding Erin's protestations, which had been, of late, relentless.

He checked on his daughter again in the mirror when he paused at a stop sign, before making the right onto the long circular drop-off lane outside Glenwood Academy. She'd requested French braids this morning, and he'd managed them quickly, his fingers working through her silken, iced tea–colored waves, then secured the ends with yellow elastics that matched the school symbol embroidered on her polo shirt.

The first time Petra had requested French braids, a couple years earlier, he'd apologized and told her that he didn't know how.

"Ask your mother," he'd said absentmindedly as he flipped blueberry pancakes out of a skillet and onto her plate.

"I have to get to work," Erin had interjected. "I don't have time to braid your hair." She'd kissed Petra on the top of the head so quickly it almost hadn't happened at all, then disappeared into the garage.

Petra had settled for a ponytail that morning, her disappointment popping silently.

Paul had taken Petra to school, then spent the day watching video tutorials about French braids and practicing on several of Petra's dolls. The following morning, he'd brushed her hair out gently.

"Ponytail is fine," she'd said, answering his unasked question. She was accustomed to providing her requested hairstyle, as if she were barking out a drink order in a bar.

"Not French braids?" he'd asked.

"You don't know how to do French braids, Daddy," she'd told him sullenly.

"Let's see about that."

When he was finished, he'd walked her into the bathroom, then passed her Erin's handheld mirror, the heavy one with mother-of-pearl on the handle, so that he could show her the back of her head.

He'd never forget the look on her face that morning as she'd examined her hair, her golden eyes wide.

"Not too busy today," he remarked as he coasted to a stop in front of the school, behind a navy Tesla from which a tiny, dark-haired child was tugging a massive musical instrument case. "Are we earlier than usual?"

Petra considered this as she unbuckled her seat belt and opened the door. "Maybe a few minutes." She removed her backpack from the car, then walked carefully to the driver's side window, which he rolled down.

"Have a great day," he told her. "Love you."

"Love you, too." She leaned in, as he leaned out, and they pressed their cheeks together for the briefest moment, kissing the air, then switched cheeks. Petra delighted in this form of salutation. "Very European," she'd remarked knowingly when he had first introduced her to it.

He watched her walk past the teachers stationed on the steps outside the stately brick building, then file into the school amongst the other children. There was a hollow feeling in his gut as he pulled away from the curb and made his way back to Ashby Drive.

As his car broke the crest of the hill, he noticed movement below, at the end of the cul-de-sac. He slowed, then turned the car carefully into his driveway. Natalie was in her own driveway, loading things into her car. He sat and watched her until she was finished, waited until she'd slammed the doors and her taillights lit up.

Typically, he would have directed his garage door to open and pulled the car inside. He never parked in the driveway, but this time he did. He climbed out and turned to face the street, just as Natalie's car was heading past. He smiled, lifted his arm to wave at her cheerfully, hoping she might pull over and pause to chat. He hadn't seen her lately, though he'd wanted to. He'd been contemplating stopping by to see her, to bring her something, a belated welcome gift, or something for the baby, but he'd been afraid he would seem transparent, strange, for waiting so long. Now, he wished he'd done it anyway.

Her car turned left at the stop sign, then disappeared from his view.

She'd waved back at him as if he were anyone, or no one. She'd been wearing a cardigan and dress pants, ballet flats so slim she might as well have been barefoot. She was off to work. Back to work. She was taking her baby to daycare. She had no need for his practiced coos or expert rocking. She had no need, no time, for him anymore. She'd moved on with her life, and he was disappointed. He'd thought there would be more time to get to know her. Her leave had been far too short.

He supposed he should move on, too. He'd missed his chance.

But he wasn't ready to move on. He'd been so sure that he could be of use to her, and she to him. He was thinking of her honey-colored hair, her softness and prettiness, and the droop of her shoulders. The desperation in her eyes while her baby had screamed down Ashby Drive. The hopeful way she had looked toward his house.

It was not too late. He was not ready to let this go.

He opened his garage, and he pulled inside.

He would find a way to get what he needed. He always did.

THIRTEEN

My face was inches from the mirror. I tilted my head from the left to the right, frowning. It was the kind of pimple you considered covering with a bandage, telling people you'd had an altercation with your cat, or perhaps the fingernail of your infant son. Like getting up after two total hours of sleep, it was a less than ideal way to start a Monday. It was a gift from my still-coursing hormones.

I dabbed concealer onto it, which only seemed to make things worse. I tried to ignore it while I drew eyeliner along my lash line, smudging it with my finger, then wiggled mascara onto my lashes. My tube of mascara was powdery, nearly dried out. Each blink sent specks of black falling onto my cheeks.

I grimaced at my reflection, then tried to pat on a little more concealer, realizing too late that I'd used the same fingertip I'd just used to smear my eyeliner. The zit was now black and shiny, bruised-looking. As though he knew what I'd done, Oliver began to cry from his bassinet.

"Perfect timing," I said. It sent a tiny jolt of pleasure through me when I made such biting little remarks.

I scrubbed the black from my cheek, leaving the zit redder and angrier than before, then padded into the bedroom to get Oliver from his bassinet. Tyler was just beginning to stir as well. I was up earlier than usual. I had a mediation to attend at eight and needed to be out the door by seven, so Tyler was taking over the morning shift. I would be responsible for retrieving Oliver from daycare on my way home.

I would only have time to nurse Oliver once before I'd have to leave. It was a day that called for multitasking. I carried Oliver downstairs so that I could grab a cup of coffee.

In the kitchen, my foot slipped into a puddle of brown liquid, fragrant and warm, pooling in the cracks of the hardwood floors. I followed the trail, across the floor, up the face of the cabinets beside the sink, to the swirling gray countertops, to the coffee machine, in which there was no pot. I'd set the timer but left the carafe perched upside down in the drying rack. I groaned, a startlingly animalistic sound, and hurriedly tucked Oliver into his swing so I could clean up the mess. I had not factored in time to remedy such a snafu, and I needed coffee. Oliver began to cry, wanting to nurse.

Tyler wandered downstairs, already dressed for work, his hair neatly combed into place, his teeth brushed. It took him all of three minutes to get ready in the morning. He took in the scene silently—my error was clear—then stepped around me, reaching for the roll of paper towels.

"You can feed him," he said. "I'll do it."

I stormed back to Oliver and carried him up to the nursery, to the glider chair where I kept my special pillow, where it was easiest for me to nurse. Tyler found us there a few minutes later, only a single mug of coffee in his hand. For himself.

I passed Oliver off to him, gripping my pajama top closed. I'd noticed that any glimpse of my engorged breasts, larger than they'd ever been, invited erotic thoughts from my husband, which couldn't have been any more inconvenient or abhorrent. "I need to go," I said.

I thundered down the stairs, filled a travel mug from the fresh pot Tyler had brewed. My flats stuck to the floorboards. Tyler had done a poor job of cleaning up the coffee, but remedying his failings would have to wait.

"Bye," I yelled on my way to the garage.

"Good luck," Tyler replied. "Love you."

"Love you, kiddo." I whispered it. Although I didn't cry when I left him, not anymore, my heart ached. It was like departing the house without my left arm.

The sun was shining as brightly as though it was the middle of the day, and it made me feel disoriented and tardy. It wasn't until I was merging onto the highway that I was struck with the sickening certainty that I'd forgotten something.

The throbbing sensation from my right cheek provided a reminder. I'd forgotten to make another attempt at covering the pimple. I pawed through my purse, keeping my eyes trained on the road ahead, feeling around for a spare tube of concealer that I knew was not there. I didn't have time to stop at a pharmacy to buy some. It was better to show up with a raging zit than to show up late. Besides, I needed to pump before the mediation started. The leading partner for the case we were mediating was Les Wilson. I knew there would be no natural opportunities for me to pump, aside from the lunch break. Even that wasn't guaranteed. It might be a working lunch, contained within the conference room we were sharing. With some partners, I'd feel comfortable asking for the breaks I needed to relieve my aching breasts and express the milk necessary to feed my child. Les Wilson was not such a partner.

I swung into a spot on the third floor of the garage and arrived at my desk with fifteen minutes to spare. I quickly locked the door and tugged my curtain closed, then began to whip out my pump supplies and breasts. I logged in to my computer and shuffled my notes and legal pads into order as my pump got to work.

There was a tap at my office door. I rolled my eyes, considered ignoring it. Milk was still dripping from the valves. Another tap. I turned off the pump and leaned forward, shaking the remaining milk down, removing the plastic shields from my skin with a squelching groan. I left the pumping bra on, but buttoned my blouse, pulled my blazer closed. When I unlocked my office door and tugged it open, it was to find Les Wilson was standing there, shifting from foot to foot. His gray hair was unartfully combed over a thinning crown, held in place with something shiny and stiff and feminine smelling. Perhaps a product he'd borrowed from his wife. I knew he had one, despite that his left ring finger was optimistically bare.

"You're here," he said. He was looking at my breasts.

"I'm here." I returned to my desk chair, sat down. The bottles of milk were warm and obvious on the desk in front of me.

"Print out a few copies of our Confidential Mediation Statement, will you?"

I nodded, turned to my screen, navigated to the client's file.

Les remained in my doorway. "You did send it to the mediator at least forty-eight hours before, didn't you? I don't think you copied me."

I blinked, a crash of doubt, of horror, washing over me. The mediator had requested that both sides prepare a statement, for the mediator's eyes only, providing a recitation of pertinent facts, any perceived impediments to settlement, a list of goals for the session, and the desired outcome. Les had asked me to draft it with our client and email it to the mediator once it had been finalized. I had completed it and I had sent it over, but my flushed face belied my instinct to defend my competence.

I knew I'd finished it. I remembered discussing it with the client's representative late last week, after spending much of the day getting caught up on the file. I had proofread it, too. But had I actually emailed it to the mediator?

I must have, because I wasn't the sort of person who forgot such things. I met deadlines. I executed tasks to completion. I followed up. I was partner material.

Was.

I scrolled frantically through my sent mail folder.

Les took in my expression. He knew.

"Well," he said. Now he was staring at my zit. "That's what malpractice insurance is for, I guess."

By which he meant: *that's what malpractice insurance is for: new mothers.*

What could I say? I hadn't committed malpractice. Forgetting to send a Confidential Mediation Statement to a mediator with whom our firm worked all the time wasn't malpractice. Les could give it to him now. There was time to look it over before the mediation session started. It was sloppy, yes, and it was out of character. It was a mistake.

I still cared about my career. I was still here, wasn't I? I was here. I was awake. I was dressed. I was just so fucking tired.

Les took a step backward, into the hallway, but I could still see him. I could still hear him. Others could, too. "I'll explain what happened," he said.

I didn't know what he meant by that. I didn't ask.

"No need for you to participate in the mediation." As if it were a favor. He left, not closing the door behind him.

I left my baby for this, I thought, as I screwed the lids on my bottles of milk, my hands shaking. Instead of taking them to the fridge, I pulled my door closed, leaned against it, sank to the ground. This was bad. I should be upset. But the overwhelming feeling rushing over me, as if it were a blast of cool air from the HVAC vent above my desk, was relief. I could pump twice more today. Maybe three times. I could leave my curtain closed and lie down on my office floor with the dust mites and dead skin cells from the associate attorneys who had come before me. Seconds, minutes, hours would pass. I would leave. I would get my baby. He was what mattered. He was all that mattered.

These were the thoughts of a good mother, I believed.

These were the thoughts that would take from me everything else I'd once had.

FOURTEEN

"Do you want me to get him?" Tyler whispered into the darkness.

Him. Our son. He was only a foot away from me. I could reach out and touch him, if I chose to, without getting out of bed. I could pat him on the tummy. I could cover his mouth with my palm.

"I want him to stop crying."

There was a pause. Not a silence—Oliver was still shrieking as if he'd had a nightmare, as if he'd been electrocuted—but, a pause.

"So, do you want me to get him?" Tyler asked again.

I sighed, loudly, then threw the covers off myself. Why did he even ask? Why did he give me the choice? When he asked, my competitive nature, my desire to be a good mom, the best mom, swept in and forced me out of bed so that I could shove my inflamed nipples, burning hot with pain, into my baby's mouth.

I reached into the bassinet and picked Oliver up. In a startling moment of clarity, I considered how easy it would be to make him stop. I was powerless, but I had so much power, at the same time. I started to cry, too, because I was a monster. Nothing made sense. Nothing was clear. Except that. That felt more and more obvious to me every single day. I was a monster. I was a mess.

Hearing my shuddering breaths, Tyler pushed the covers aside as well and struggled out of bed, his foot catching on the loose sheet. He stumbled into the wall. "I got him," he said.

I ignored him, carried Oliver into the nursery, and settled into the glider chair. I was beginning to hate the chair. I was beginning to have violent fantasies about the chair. I'd spent countless hours there since Oliver's birth. I might as well be stuck tied up in the chair, my ankles bound together, my wrists strapped to the armrests, my mouth taped shut.

Tyler appeared in the doorway. He looked like a ghost. I was sure I did, too.

"Natalie," he said, so quietly I wondered if it had been in my head. He rarely called me Natalie. For so long, since college, since we had applied to the same law schools and shared a tiny studio apartment downtown, I had been Nat.

Soon, he would call me Mom. Or Mama. In the presence of Oliver, that's who I'd be. Sooner than we could imagine, Oliver would become uncomfortable if he heard his father referring to me as Nat. I'd become so used to it that at Christmas one year, I'd hear him saying "Mom," and I'd look up. But he would be speaking to his own mother, offering her a fresh fork for dessert.

Mom. It was the greatest honor. It was homogenizing. It was all-consuming, devouring, crushing.

"I'm worried about you."

What could I say? I was worried about me, too.

"I'm fine." I leaned my head back, tilted it to the side.

Tyler stepped into the room, hesitantly. He sat down on the cream area rug, already becoming discolored from shoes not removed at the front door, cat paws, and sunlight. He sat down, his knees bent, his arms stretched backward, his palms flat, propping himself up.

"What are you doing?" I asked.

He didn't answer for a long time, and if there wasn't a reflection on the whites of his eyes, I might've thought he had fallen asleep. "I don't know," he said at last. "Solidarity?"

I snorted. "That's stupid." I gingerly switched Oliver to the other breast. "You should go to bed."

He didn't leave, just sat there, watching me. I closed my eyes.

I felt Oliver's sucking slow, then stop. There was a pause, then it resumed. Three small pulls. Pause. Nursing in his sleep. I inserted the tip of my pinky into his mouth to break the seal, then lifted him up, cupping his head in the hollow beneath my collarbone.

"Want me to hold him up?" Tyler asked.

I shook my head, tipped it, resting my cheek on the top of Oliver's head.

"I'm worried about you, Natalie."

I rubbed Oliver's back gently, to encourage a burp, to help the milk settle, the way the pediatrician had shown me.

"Natalie," Tyler said again.

I opened my eyes. "Please," I said. "Just leave."

"What?" Tyler recoiled as if I'd slapped him. He pushed himself to his feet.

"Just leave me alone."

He took a step backward, then another. There was fear in his eyes before he averted them, turned, and left the room. Fear of me.

I couldn't blame him, and I couldn't explain it. I just wanted to be alone.

After some number of minutes, more than ten, but less than the thirty I was supposed to wait before laying him down, I carried Oliver back to our bedroom. He was asleep, breathing softly and steadily, so I lay him down in his bassinet. My hand caught under his upper back, but I carefully wiggled it out, biting my lip, holding my breath, hoping I wouldn't wake him.

Tyler was silent but stiff in bed beside me. The air was thick with alarm. But I did nothing to try to reassure him that everything was fine, that I was not, in fact, losing my mind. I simply lay on the edge of the mattress, watching my baby sleep. I didn't have the capacity to manage Tyler's stressors, his concerns about me or my stability.

Eventually, I sensed his body relaxing. He began to snore faintly, as he often did in the early fall, when his seasonal allergies acted up. Oliver was peaceful, too. I had an inexplicable feeling that this was going to be his best stretch of sleep for the night. Perhaps two solid hours.

I closed my eyes, wished there were a switch I could flip, a button to press, to turn myself off. To switch myself to sleep mode. Instead, my thoughts raced by like a cheetah in pursuit.

The same scene was running on a loop in my head. A scene from earlier in the day. Me, sitting at my desk, my breast pump whirring, milk dripping into bottles. I was staring at my computer screen, reading a blog about baby sleep.

I'd heard footsteps, then a grunt. I'd looked up, closing my browser. It was Les Wilson, of course, standing in the hallway, a brimming red accordion file tucked under his arm. My first thought was that I had been caught browsing something not work-related, when it should have been the fact that I could see Les Wilson at all.

I'd locked the door but forgotten to close the curtain.

I was too tired to remember everything, to remember anything. Seconds, minutes, hours seemed to go missing from my life. I didn't do things that I was supposed to do. I did things, then couldn't remember why. I felt like the last one to arrive at a party. Everyone else was laughing. I'd missed the joke.

I hadn't told Tyler what had happened, nor had I told him about forgetting to email the Confidential Mediation Statement prior to last week's session, nor that I'd been uninvited from attending. Tyler wouldn't understand. He didn't know what it was like to so displease a partner.

Neither had I. Until it had happened. Twice, within a week, I had disappointed the same partner. And if any of the firm's partners cared to check out my billable hours since my return from maternity leave, they'd all be disappointed. I wasn't pulling my weight, let alone theirs. And the partners liked associates who more than pulled their weight. Who billed enough hours to cover their salaries and expenses and then some, so the partners could gobble up the extra profit and transform it into second homes, boats, bathroom remodels, and custom art for the living room.

My mind was stuck on that mortifying moment, Les Wilson looking into my office, at my exposed breasts, at the chugging pump, his expression both lascivious and appalled.

As I worried and dwelled, time passed, then Oliver awakened and began to cry. I had missed my chance for sleep. I checked the time on my cell phone, ignoring the little icon at the top of the screen telling me that several new work emails had come in since I had last looked. It was 3:12. I'd have to get up in three hours, to get ready for work. That meant I was most likely not going to get any sleep tonight.

I screamed. Rather, it was more like a groan, in frustration, or like the sound that might come out of a warrior charging into battle. But I wasn't charging forward. I was waving the white flag. I was giving up. I couldn't do this anymore.

Tyler threw the covers off himself and scrambled out of bed. He picked up Oliver and backed away from me, like I was dangerous, and maybe I was.

"What is wrong with you?" he asked.

I ignored him, thinking only that I'd never seen him leap up to tend to our crying child so quickly, and that was a point that would, I was certain, be unfairly lost in what was about to come next. Because I was in the wrong. I was the crazy one.

My throat clicked when I tried to swallow so I sat up and reached for my water bottle, seeking to quench my insatiable thirst. My body felt sucked dry.

But the bottle was empty. I'd drained it at some point during the night, and I hadn't felt like going downstairs to get a refill, winding my way along long hallways and slick, wooden steps. I tossed the empty bottle into Oliver's bassinet like I was spiking a football into the ground.

Tyler was staring at me.

"What?" I demanded. But it wasn't a question. *"What."*

Tyler's eyes were wide as he rocked a crying Oliver, to no avail.

"It's almost four in the morning," I said. "I've not yet gone to sleep. Not fallen asleep a single time. Soon, I have to get ready to drive thirty minutes to work, then sit in my office for at least eight hours. I won't be getting any sleep at all. Do you realize that? Do you know what that feels like?"

Tyler softened. His shoulders slumped, as if in relief. *That's all?* his body language seemed to say. *That's the only issue?* As if it was nothing.

"Then let's take shifts," he suggested. "I know you don't want to give him formula, but this isn't working. It's too hard on you."

"Seriously?" I asked. "Listen to yourself." I pointed to Oliver. "He's still crying. He will continue crying until I nurse him. There is no 'taking shifts.' He hates bottles." *He hates you.* I almost said it, even though it wasn't true. I felt cruelty and poison pulsing at my temples. "He's not going to drink bottles or formula while I'm in the house. He knows I'm here. He smells me. You can't even soothe him." Had I gone too far? How was it fair that I should have to care?

Tyler stared down at our baby, cradled in his arms, as if noticing him for the first time. Oliver continued to wail. I threw my legs over the side of the bed and stepped toward them. Tyler didn't turn away from me or cower over our son. He let me take him from his arms.

The rage that had shaken me only seconds before, that had caused my outburst, drained away as I wrapped my arms around my baby. He began to nuzzle at my breasts, nosing for the one thing he wanted the most, the thing that only I could give him. But I didn't feel pride or love this time. I just felt numb.

I carried him into the nursery and pulled my top open. Tyler followed us.

"Have you looked into a nanny?" he asked. "Maybe we could find someone who could live here for a bit. A night nurse, or something?"

I shook my head. He didn't understand. A night nurse wasn't going to help unless she smelled like me and felt like me and made milk like I did.

Tyler cleared his throat. "What about—" He paused, nervous about suggesting whatever it was he was about to suggest. That's what I'd become. Someone my husband feared. Someone with whom he could not communicate freely. "What about a sabbatical?"

The word punctured the fog in my brain. *Sabbatical.* I knew what it meant, of course, but I hadn't a clue about logistics. Did you get paid? Did you lose your insurance? Were you entitled to one? Was requesting one grounds for termination?

"I'm not suggesting you become a stay-at-home mother," Tyler continued hurriedly. "Just, a break. Maybe you could get some more rest during the day. Have a bit less stress. Eight weeks wasn't enough time off. Once he starts sleeping better at night, you could return."

"I don't know," I whispered. How could I explain what I was thinking? What if what I wanted wasn't for work to go away? What if what I wanted was for my baby to go away? Just for a little while? "I don't think my firm would really go for that."

"Well, I guess you could at least ask. At least think about it," he added as he was turning away. He left the room. I could hear his footsteps slapping against the wood floors, returning to bed for a couple more hours of sleep.

I looked down at Oliver, and I nodded. I'd think about it. What choice did I have? What else did I do, but think?

I had thought many times, in the throes of unimaginable exhaustion, as I pushed myself to do what was best for Oliver, that I would die for him. It was, I believed, simply an expression. Hyperbolic and magnanimous. The epitome of a mother's love for her child. A willingness to make the ultimate sacrifice, even though she desperately hoped she would not actually have to make it.

But it was becoming clearer and clearer that, actually, I might die. I might die taking care of him.

Maybe I was dying. Maybe I was already dead.

Part II

THE BREAK & THE STIRRING

FIFTEEN

There was a bounce in his step after he sprang from the bed, its weight lessening, my side shifting downward. Despite that our gross monthly income had been cut in half, Tyler was happier now. He was happy to have our two-month-old baby spending his days with his mom, rather than two strange women and five other infants.

Tyler disappeared into our closet, the entrance to which was closer to my side of the bed, his footsteps becoming slower and more creeping. He thought I was asleep.

He emerged, still buttoning his shirt, the pale blue one with the faint navy stripes. It had been a Christmas gift from me last year. He wore it every single week. He tucked it into his pants, then sucked in his stomach and buttoned them with almost comical effort.

Tyler froze, leaned toward me. "You up?" he whispered, like he was reading a text message from a drunk twentysomething looking to get laid.

I nodded against my pillow.

He sighed, sat down on the edge of the bed, on top of my right shin. I tugged it out from under him.

"Why can't you sleep, Nat? He's sleeping." He tipped his head toward Oliver, who was encased in his latest sleep contraption, a sort of dress with the bottom closed up and weighted beans that rested on his chest. It had worked last night. It had helped him sleep. But like with every other sleep aid we had purchased with such optimism after reading dozens of five-star reviews, sure that *this* would be the solution we needed, I knew it wouldn't last.

I didn't know what to say. I didn't know the answer. *Sleep when your baby is sleeping.* There was no advice for what to do when you couldn't.

Tyler sighed again, patted my thigh, *There, there. It'll be okay.* He stood, kissed me gently on the side of the head, glanced at Oliver, then disappeared.

He'd not told me that he loved me. I knew he was still upset about last night.

"I feel so distant from you," he had told me, after he'd brushed his teeth and wandered into the nursery, wearing a plain undershirt and blue plaid boxers, his arms crossed tightly, as if he were cold.

The light was dim, and I was nursing Oliver, trying to put him to sleep so that I could brush my own teeth, crawl into bed, pretend that sleep would come for me, too.

"Nat?" he asked when I didn't reply. "Did you hear me?"

"Hmm?" I asked, lifting my eyes to meet his, pretending that I hadn't.

"I said"—Tyler cleared this throat, sank to the nursery rug, leaned against the wall across from me—"that I feel very distant from you. I feel like we're not okay."

"We?" I asked. "What do you mean by 'we'?" His statement was outrageous. Of course I wasn't *okay.*

"Me and you," said Tyler. "Our relationship." He was hugging his arms around his knees.

"We're fine," I said. Oliver had fallen asleep, but I freed my left nipple from his mouth and switched him to the right side, trying to fill his belly as much as possible.

"You never touch me anymore," Tyler said quietly, though his tone was rather petulant.

"I'm not cleared for sex yet, Tyler. You know that." My own tone was scolding, and I had reminded Tyler so many times that my doctor had told me to wait ten weeks for sex, longer than the typical six after a vaginal birth, that I'd forgotten she'd really only said to wait eight.

"I'm not talking about sex, Nat." Tyler rested his chin on his forearms. "I'm talking about connecting. We aren't talking. We aren't showing any affection."

"Well," I said, staring down into Oliver's perfect little face, "things haven't exactly been easy for me. I don't sleep. I don't get any time to myself, let alone time for you. I don't really feel like being nagged about my failings."

"I'm not nagging you," Tyler said. "I'm just sad."

"And I'm sorry about that."

"I miss being close with you. I miss the way things were before."

"Alright," I said. "Let's give him away, then."

"Natalie," Tyler admonished, using my full name as if he were a parent shaking a less-than-stellar report card in my face. "That's an awful thing to say."

"You said it. Not me."

"That wasn't what I meant."

I pulled Oliver's body more tightly to mine and used my toes to set the chair rocking.

"It feels like all you care about is taking care of Oliver." Tyler tried again. "That's all you ever talk about anymore. It's all you do. Nurse him and hold him and catalog his sleep." He was picking at a hangnail absent-mindedly. He tugged it loose and cast it aside. I pinched my eyes closed in revulsion. Everything about him disgusted me in that moment.

"I didn't choose for things to be that way, Tyler. I didn't want to have a baby who is so miserable. Who won't sleep ever. Who just wants to be held all of the time."

"So, let me help you," Tyler said. "Let me take him tonight."

I shook my head. I was so tired of hearing him say it. I was so tired of him trying to *help*. We both knew he couldn't help me. Oliver wouldn't allow it. All Tyler had to do was offer to help, like a good dad, then sleep through the night, then go to work. While I died trying to do it all.

"We can't argue in front of Oliver," I said testily, although it was my voice, my animosity, that had risen.

"He doesn't know what we're saying," Tyler retorted. But, realizing he was getting nowhere, he'd stood, his knees cracking.

"He can hear the tone," I said, rolling my eyes. "He can feel the tension."

"See what I mean?" he muttered on his way out of the room. "He's all you care about."

I rolled my eyes again, but Tyler was right. I did feel the distance, the resentment. It was palpable between us, like a murky fog or a wall that was opaque and soundproof, through which I couldn't see, smell, hear, or touch my husband. He was also right that I didn't care. There simply wasn't room.

Tyler's suggestion had been a reasonable one. My job had evaporated into nothingness, yet there was still no space to worry about, to focus on, my marriage. The void left by the abrupt demise of my career—this was not histrionic, I felt certain my career wasn't sleeping, but dead, likely never to be resuscitated—had immediately been filled in, swallowed up by Oliver.

But he was also wrong. Because this was not a bad thing. Because this was not something about which we should be arguing. Because Oliver should have been all he cared about, too.

Let's just get through this, I wanted to say. As if we were living through a war, or one of us had been diagnosed with cancer.

I heard Tyler's car door slam, heard the bottom of his car scrape as it backed over the bump at the end of the driveway, as it always did. Did he feel relieved when he left us?

I climbed out of bed and peeked at Oliver. He was still sleeping peacefully, but I knew that as soon as I left the room, he would know, even from the deep darkness of his sleep. He would awaken and he would cry. Still, I took advantage of his slumber to dress myself, brush my teeth, and pile my hair into a looping knot on top of my head, getting ready for my day as if I had something to do, someplace to go.

I had looked down on stay-at-home mothers in the past. Right or wrong, I'd felt like they were anti-feminist or old-fashioned. Maybe they were simpleminded, I'd thought, content to spend their days wiping runny noses with tissues balled up in their coat pockets, dispensing animal crackers, changing diapers, washing allegedly washable marker from floors and walls. Maybe their careers hadn't been as fulfilling as mine, their incomes not as high, so there wasn't much to give up when it came time to have children. Maybe they'd always dreamed of becoming mothers. That was all very beautiful and sweet, but where would that leave them when their child started school, and then became a teenager and felt embarrassed by his mother and wanted money and things far more than he wanted her time and affection? What would they do when they realized they had given up their lives when they hadn't needed to? They could have had it all. Or, at least, more. The stay-at-home moms would wait in the school drop-off line, feeling sanctimonious, and the working moms would be there, too, feeling sanctimonious. Who was right? I'd always thought I had known.

They were both right. Rather, they were both wrong.

Still, I wasn't one of them. I wasn't a stay-at-home mother. I was on a *sabbatical*. A sabbatical was supposed to be temporary.

My firm had agreed to me taking time off. They had agreed too quickly, seemingly relieved to be rid of me and my somnolence, the odor of malpractice floating around me like a cloud of gnats, almost putrid, as if clients could sniff it out the instant they walked in the door. It was unpaid leave, of course, but I was still considered an employee of the firm. I was clinging to that fact. That facetious, for-appearances-only remnant from my pre-baby life. Because I couldn't have it all—career and motherhood. I'd tried, and I'd failed.

It had been decided that Oliver would stay home with me. Without my income, we would be able to pay our bills, squirrel away some money for retirement and college. We would be *fine*. But we couldn't justify the daycare expense. Besides, why would we want to? If I wasn't working, I would be caring for my baby. It was only natural. The most natural thing there was—a mother, raising her child, doting on him twenty-four hours a day. And, with a child like Oliver, it was quite literally twenty-four hours a day. Tyler had been appalled when I had suggested we continue Oliver's enrichment at the daycare center, at least for a portion of the day.

I'd pretended to be kidding.

But Tyler had readily agreed that it made sense for Oliver to finish the week at daycare before I started my leave. I'd had two days at home, by myself, and I'd spent them sleeping as much as I could. I'd eaten in bed, dropping English muffin crumbs between the sheets and sloshing coffee onto my nightstand. I'd gotten up only to pump and use the bathroom. I'd read, relishing the fact that I was doing so without my nipple burning in my baby's mouth. They were the best two days I'd had in months. I was a monster.

The feeling of restfulness, of optimism and peace, I'd been left with after two days of sleep had quickly diminished, pried from my grasp by my thirteen-pound child. He still awakened often, sometimes only thirty minutes after I'd put him down. He now slept a single three-hour stretch during the night, but it came in the early morning hours, when I was already too crazed to take advantage of the time.

But why did it matter now? I had no responsibilities anymore. No emails to check or miss. No appointments into which I could rush, spots of milk staining the front of my blouse. No malpractice with which I could flirt. This was exactly why I'd taken the sabbatical. So that it wouldn't matter if I was so exhausted that I almost welcomed death.

Oliver hadn't awakened after all, when I'd left him to get ready, so I stepped into the hall and paused in the doorway, listening for any sign that he was stirring, then hurried barefoot down the stairs and rummaged through our kitchen for something I could eat. On the island was a recipe card Tyler's mother had brought by over the weekend. One of several. She was perplexed by, yet interested in, my restrictive diet and had researched and printed out several recipes I was able to eat. Vegan muffins. Vegetable soup. Dairy-free pancakes. Even macaroni and cheese, the sauce made from pureed sweet potatoes and carrots and nutritional yeast. She'd thought she was being considerate, but I found the cards taunting, almost cruel. When would I have the time, the ability, to make these things? What would have been thoughtful was her making them for me and slipping them into the freezer with instructions for reheating.

Why not? I thought. What else did I have to do? My child was asleep. I could make muffins.

I gathered the ingredients and got to work, feeling more domesticated and optimistic than I had in weeks. Tyler would be so impressed when he got home. I was doing so well, baking homemade muffins while caring for our child. This thought almost made me want to stop. I didn't want to contemplate why that was.

Could he not have an affair? I wondered, as I held the mixer in the bowl, blending up the oil and flour and vanilla extract. *I feel so distant from you.* Connect with someone else, then. I didn't care. Just leave me alone.

We didn't have any liners for the muffin pan, so I sprayed it with cooking oil and poured the batter in, hoping they wouldn't stick too badly. I was just closing the oven door when Oliver began to fuss, so I hurried back upstairs to get him, to nurse him, to change him.

In my bedroom, we laid atop the bed, on our backs, watching the ceiling fan spinning above us. It remained one of his favorite activities. But my thoughts were stuck on Tyler. *I'm just sad,* he'd said. As if I wasn't? How dare he burden me with his feelings? With everything I was going through, that was a weight I couldn't bear.

Unable to take it one more second, desperate to escape the house, I climbed off the bed, laced up my sneakers, and headed down to the garage. I tucked Oliver into the stroller, and my phone into the cupholder. Usually, Tyler texted throughout the day, to check in, to see how I was doing. Not today.

I walked quickly, anger, frustration, pumping my legs and pushing my breath out in sharp huffs. We covered our two-mile loop quickly. Oliver, perhaps sensing my *Don't Fuck with Me* energy, was quiet, gazing at the blueness of the sky and the swaying branches of the trees lining both sides of the streets. By the end of our walk, as I pushed the stroller over the bump and back into our garage, my groin muscles were quivering— childbirth had done something seemingly irreparable to them.

As soon as I stepped inside, I smelled it. Fire. The air felt hazy and thick. I ran into the kitchen, threw open the oven door, was met with licking flames as a billowing cloud of smoke was released.

"Shit!" I shouted. I slammed the door closed and turned off the oven, just as the fire alarm began to blare, outrageously loud, and Oliver screamed in terror.

"Shit. Shit. Shit."

I tossed him against my shoulder as I pushed a chair over to the alarm and climbed on top. I waved one of the recipe cards in front of the fire alarm with my left hand, trying to clear the smoke away, trying to make it stop, while Oliver screeched in my other arm. The combined volume of the screaming smoke detector and my terrified child was enough to churn my stomach with nausea.

What had I done?

Going to work on so little sleep had been impossible. But I should have known that staying home with my baby would been even more impossible.

Had I just forgotten about the muffins? Or had time mysteriously evaporated, darting quickly away from me, taunting and elusive, the way it seemed apt to do of late?

Once Oliver was calm, once I nursed him and put him back to sleep, I'd not be able to take a break. To lie down myself. To take a bubble bath, or even a quick shower. To enjoy a meal—to enjoy a muffin. I'd be tossing out the charred, black pan. I'd be scrubbing burnt scraps from the bottom of the oven. I'd be spraying air freshener and opening windows. So that Tyler wouldn't know that I'd almost burned down our new house. So that he wouldn't think I'd done it on purpose. So that I wouldn't have to wonder—*what if I had?*

SIXTEEN

He mixed the batter by hand, foregoing the red KitchenAid mixer that sat, shining, on the counter across from him. It would have made things easier, the mixer, but he knew that the muffins would be moister, more tender, if he didn't overmix. He tipped the bowl over the prepared muffin pan, filling each cup, then slipped it into the oven. While he waited for them to bake, he tidied up the kitchen, washing the bowl and wiping down the counters with a sponge and a spritz of organic, plant-based cleaning spray.

He was so careful to buy only safe cleaning products. He had been, ever since Petra was born. They were pricier, of course, than their chemical-filled counterparts, but they were worth it. That would probably be the next thing Erin would try to take from him. *Too expensive,* she'd hiss.

She had been on a tear the previous night, after Petra had gone to bed. Two more clients had given her notice that they were terminating her services, moving their money to another financial planner. With the negative review still lingering out there on the web, both he and Erin suspected that they, like the other clients who had already left, would not be easily or quickly replaced. It meant more of a hit to her income. It meant more tightening the purse strings, more economizing.

"We need to pull Petra from that school," Erin had told him as they stood on their deck. She'd been sipping from a glass of red wine, two shades darker than her faded lipstick. "The spring tuition is due in a few weeks. We can't keep paying for that."

"We can cut other things," Paul had replied quickly. "We don't need to cut that."

Erin had slammed her stemless glass down on the railing of the deck.

"That's exactly what we need to cut," she'd said. "She can go to public school like all the other kids in this neighborhood. It's a good school. It's free."

"Petra loves her school," he said carefully, trying to keep his voice even. "It would be so hard on her to change it, even worse to do it in the middle of the school year."

"We don't have a choice, Paul," Erin had said, lifting her glass again. "Unless, of course, you decide to get a job and pay the tuition yourself."

He'd looked at her for a long time, then said quietly, "You know that would be difficult, after what happened back then. And I've been out of the workforce for a decade." It was the truth. He didn't know what options he would have.

"Well, why don't you give it a try?" She tipped her nose up, seemed to look down at him over it, even though he was a good six inches taller. "Or you could finish up your novel. Sell it. It *must* be good. You've been working on it for ten years."

Rage had whistled through him, then, like steam bursting from a kettle. He'd pressed his lips together, as if to hold it inside.

"Public school will be good for her." Erin had drained the rest of her wine, then moved toward the sliding door. "I'm not paying the next tuition bill," she said before she'd disappeared inside.

Paul flipped on the oven light and peered through the door. Just a few more minutes. He'd let them cool for a while, then put them in a container and take them down to Natalie.

He had seen her out walking the last couple days, but he'd also seen her husband going to and getting home from work a few times. She had either taken vacation time, or she'd changed her mind and extended her maternity leave. Or perhaps she'd left her job completely. Perhaps a week away from her baby had proved too difficult for her.

He would bring her the muffins, and he would find out.

He needed a distraction. He needed to turn his mind, his thoughts, to something other than his wife, her threats to pull Petra from school, their increasingly painful marital discord, the fact that there was no novel to show her. Perhaps he'd be able to hold the baby. He'd take in its smell, and that would transport him back to the time when Petra had been that young and small. He'd promised her, then, that he would always do what was best for her. He always had, and he always would.

The question now was: what was best?

He needed that tuition bill to be paid. He needed to keep her in her school. He just didn't yet know how.

Perhaps, too, he'd find comfort in spending time with Natalie. They might grow closer. She'd moved into Lara Tucker's house. It would be rather ideal if she could fill the void that Lara's absence had left in his life.

This time, when he peeked into the oven door, he could see that the tops of the muffins were just beginning to crack. They were golden brown, lemon wafting toward him through the warm air. He slipped the pan from the rack and placed it on the counter.

They were perfect.

SEVENTEEN

While I'd never gotten the hang of the scarf-like baby carrier, with the help of Oliver's improved head control, I'd discovered, early that morning, that I could use the more structured baby carrier I'd been gifted at my shower. It was like a backpack that could be worn on the front, meant to carry a small human instead of bulky textbooks, with adjustable straps and clicking buckles.

Oliver seemed to like it. He could glance around him, take in the sights, while still pressed against my warmth and my heartbeat. His pale legs, bare and velvet-soft, dangled from the bottom of the contraption in the appropriate M-shape, safe for the development of his narrow hips.

The baby carrier had allowed me to style my hair for the first time in more than a week—which was an unnecessary exercise and perhaps a waste of this precious time, except that it made me feel slightly more human—then move downstairs and prepare breakfast, even eat it, standing at the counter, dropping crumbs into the fuzz on the top of his head. I'd been able to go outside, to stroll through our backyard, then into the woods, taking in the gently swaying trees and gulp after gulp of crisp, early fall air.

"You like this, do you, kiddo?" I asked him now, dancing around the family room. There was an unfamiliar sense of levity making my steps light. Despite that there was a baby tethered to my front, I felt freer than I had since the start of my sabbatical.

I heard my phone ding from its resting place on the kitchen counter and I danced over to check it, expecting to see a text from Tyler.

I entered my PIN to unlock it—the device had stopped recognizing my face and fingerprints; annoying, but understandable: I didn't recognize me, either.

How's everything going? Haven't heard from you in a while!

Elaine. She was right, but I couldn't bear to see her. She'd offered to stop by last weekend, with her husband, her round belly, her rosy air. Dan and Tyler could catch up, and so could we. Maybe go for a walk.

I'd told her about the loss of my job, of course. Rather, my *sabbatical*. I'd told her over text. I didn't want to discuss it in person. I didn't want her to ask me if I was okay. I was afraid of what I might say.

Things are fine . . . still not sleeping. How are you feeling?

It was what I was supposed to say. *Not sleeping at all! Feel like absolute death! It's been ten weeks but it still feels like my stitches are going to burst every time I sit on the toilet.*

But I had done my duty of asking her how she was feeling. That was the thing I missed most about being pregnant. Everyone asked you how you were feeling all the time, with such genuine concern.

I placed my phone facedown on the counter and carted Oliver to the hall closet to slip on my sneakers. He was just beginning to whine, and I wasn't ready to give up the carrier yet.

"Want to walk down to the woods again?" I asked him. "Want to see your trees?"

I pushed through the French doors and picked through the grass, to the tree line. Oliver gazed at the trees in rapture. He loved to look at the woods.

I walked along the edge of the woods, back and forth. Oliver hiccupped and quieted, staring at the swaying leaves, just starting to turn. Would he like them better that way, I wondered? Was it the lushness, the green, that he loved, or would he like them more when they were brittle and red, shot through with gold, like trails behind sparklers on a hot summer night?

The location of the house had been a selling feature for us. It sat at twelve o'clock on the cul-de-sac, and it backed to a thick swath of woods, at least a hundred yards deep, with a stream running through the middle. There was a path that sprouted from the cul-de-sac, between our yard and that of our next-door neighbor. It led to the edge of the woods, then abruptly stopped. A path to nowhere. The Realtor had suggested it was to designate a county-owned easement so that environmentalists could get to the stream, to check on its health.

It was preserved land, the woods, because the stream fed into the Chesapeake Bay, miles and miles away. It could never be built upon, never be cleared. You knew, from looking at the map, that there was another neighborhood beyond the woods. I suspected that in the winter, once the branches were bare, the leaves fallen to the ground like soggy piles of clothes, you would be able to see glimpses of the other houses, yellow lights in windows in the dark of night. For now, though, it felt quite private and remote at the back of our yard. The path was public, but because it was a path to nowhere, it didn't seem particularly popular.

I walked a few more yards, into the woods, then a few more, ensuring that there were no deer in the vicinity. We were surrounded by the trees now, on both sides. Oliver stared pleasantly out at them. I walked a little deeper still, to the edge of the stream.

Abruptly, I understood the appeal. The stillness, the silence, the earthy smell. It was restorative, calming, like an afternoon at the spa, which was something I'd probably never do again. Not, at least, until Oliver was older and wanted nothing to do with me.

I felt Oliver's cheek resting against my chest and I peered down into his face. He'd fallen asleep.

I continued to walk, winding along the stream. In the middle of the woods, I couldn't see the houses on either side of it. The woods were too thick and deep, the trees too abundant. There was a makeshift path adjacent to the stream, thin and worn brown into the otherwise ample covering of leaves, vegetation, weeds. I saw another, on the other side of the stream. I didn't know whether they had been created by the frequent steps of deer, or of people like Oliver and me, seeking solace and peace in nature. I followed the path for a few more steps, then turned and went back the way I'd come.

As I entered the house, I caught the tail end of our doorbell. A package, most likely. I couldn't recall ordering anything, but that didn't mean I hadn't. Running errands had become unfathomable. I was ordering everything online, from eye drops to groceries to diapers to sanitary pads for the blood that occasionally still dripped from my body.

But when I peered through the windows flanking the front door, I was surprised to see the man who lived a few houses up, the man who had reached a sweating arm into Oliver's stroller to soothe him like it was the simplest, most natural thing in the world, standing on my porch.

He must have taken my surprise for displeasure because he apologized when I opened the door.

"Sorry—I hope I'm not intruding." He brandished a container. "I brought you some muffins. I noticed you've been home with the baby, and I know how hard it is to find time to eat or make anything nice for yourself when you're caring for an infant."

Did he? I stared at him, still startled by his presence on my porch.

"Paul," he said, as if reading my mind, as if knowing I'd forgotten his name. "Paul Riley."

"Natalie," I replied, and he nodded. He hadn't forgotten mine.

"I don't want to impose," he continued, pushing the container toward me. "I just wanted to drop these off."

"No, no," I said, snapping out of my daze, instinct and manners taking over. "Please come in. This is so nice of you."

I led him to the kitchen, and we stood at the island as sunlight streaming through the back windows cast golden squares across the countertops and floor. I placed the container in the center and couldn't resist popping off the lid.

They were beautiful muffins, plush, creamy tops, soft and round like a baby's bottom. Pale yellow and flecked with poppy seeds. They were probably rife with forbidden butter and milk. I knew I'd eat one anyway.

"These look amazing," I said, thinking of the charred black remains of my muffins that weren't, still smoldering in the bottom of the trash can.

Too much baking soda. That had been my downfall. I'd used a tablespoon, instead of a teaspoon, in the batter. There was also the fact that I'd forgotten about them. I'd left them in the oven four times longer than I should have. The batter had risen too much. It had oozed over the sides of the pan, ballooning and roiling and sparking into licking flames.

Fortunately, the fire had died quickly with the oven door closed, the heat turned off. I'd cleaned the evidence of my transgression, like it had been a fiery and messy affair, washed away in the shower while my spouse was at work, like the one I wouldn't have minded Tyler to have. Oliver had snoozed in his swing while I'd worked. I'd wrapped the muffin tin, unrecognizable and lumpy and repulsive, in two trash bags and tossed the entire thing into the can in the garage.

I knew that the next time Tyler's mom visited, she'd go poking around the kitchen, looking for her recipe cards. "Did you make anything?" she'd ask. "What about the muffins? Did you try the muffins?"

"My mother's recipe," Paul said now, smiling humbly.

"You made them?" I couldn't stop staring at the muffins, felt practically lustful toward them.

"I love to bake," he replied, shrugging. "And cook."

"I'm sorry I almost missed the doorbell," I said, suddenly worried that he'd been waiting long, that he might think I had been contemplating not answering the door at all. "I was walking out back, by the woods. My baby likes to be outside. He loves the trees."

"I can understand that. The woods can be so peaceful. My wife goes walking back there sometimes. She says it calms her. She works a lot, gets quite stressed."

I nodded, smiled politely, as a silence fell over us, as I grasped for something to say next. I was saved from my awkwardness, my abrupt lack of social acumen, seemingly yet another thing I'd lost, when Oliver began to cry and flail from within the baby carrier I was still wearing. Because I'd stopped walking, he had awakened, startled, displeased.

"Oh dear," I said, reaching down for the clasps, trying to free him. I unclicked the wrong one, and the carrier began to release from my body, Oliver still trapped inside. I caught him, holding him close. "Shit," I muttered, my cheeks burning.

Paul stepped closer. "Here," he said, tentatively. "I'm well practiced with these baby carriers. May I?"

"Please," I said, because I really did need help.

His fingertips brushed my arms as he undid the buckles.

"Could I hold him?" he asked, sounding so innocent, so hopeful.

"Sure," I replied, wondering whether I was being foolish. I didn't know this man, and here he was, in my house, his hands on my child. But, in this moment, I longed for nothing more. Besides, he was a father, more experienced at holding babies than I was, and he had managed to soothe Oliver before.

Paul extracted Oliver from the carrier, and held him against his chest, upright, just the way Oliver liked. He whispered into his ear and rock-bounced in my bright white kitchen. Oliver immediately fell silent, craning his head to stare at Paul.

There was something, as I stood there, watching them, the pale-yellow muffins, homemade and fragrant, mere feet away. It was a stirring. A warmth.

It was a freedom. I pulled the baby carrier from my body and dropped it onto the island. I sat down on a stool, which wobbled slightly beneath my weight. Tyler had probably assembled it wrong.

It was a happiness. I propped my feet on the bottom bar of the stool, and I reached for a muffin, which was softer and more delightful than I could have ever imagined.

It was delicious and bright. Comforting, like the companionable silence that had fallen over us in the absence of Oliver's cries.

It was a break. It was everything I needed. I finished my muffin, and I reached for another.

EIGHTEEN

I was standing at the kitchen counter, drinking my coffee like it was medicine, an antidote to a poison I'd ingested, when Tyler came flying into the kitchen, alert and important, wearing a black suit, his dress shoes click-slapping against the hardwoods. He had a trial today, not downtown, but at our local courthouse, nearer to our house than his typical commute, yet he was ready earlier than usual.

I'd risen even before him, so exhausted that I wasn't.

"You're leaving already?" I asked. I knew the trial wasn't scheduled to begin until nine-thirty. The courthouse wasn't even open to the public this early.

"I had a thought in the middle of the night," he said, sloshing coffee into a mug. "I need to look at my outline, check something in my exhibits."

I cringed as he began to bustle around, removing a banker's box from his car, dropping it on the floor in the living room, settling onto the sofa with his laptop. It felt like he was trying to make as much noise as possible.

Might as well add that to the list of things for which I despised him lately. Also, the fact that he could have an important thought in the middle of the night, and simply roll over and go back to sleep, confident that he'd still remember it in the morning. I couldn't remember what I'd eaten an hour after I'd eaten it. I could barely remember what I was, and wasn't, allowed to eat. I lost entire hours from my day. I remembered almost nothing.

And I despised his nonchalance over his pressure-filled day. He'd stand in the courtroom, beside his client, across the well from opposing counsel and the opposing party, with the court clerk, law clerk ahead of him, the black-robed judge looming above. He'd feel confident and competent. He'd slept.

He had deadlines, and days full of conference calls. Negotiations, and thirty-page contracts, drafted and reviewed with the requisite level of detail. Excitement, and stress, but stress that invigorated and pumped adrenaline through your veins.

He still had all of those things. While I had traded them in for days and nights full of sopping diapers and cries from my baby that filled me with a different sort of stress, and nipples that constantly burned, no matter how many times I slathered them with waxy lanolin.

I settled onto the love seat opposite Tyler and watched him work, feeling an anesthetizing numbness falling over me like an ice-cold ocean wave. How different our lives had become. How little we had in common.

"Oliver is sleeping," Tyler finally whispered, as he shoved papers back into an exhibit folder and slipped it into the box. "You should go back to sleep."

Back to sleep, I thought. *Back*. As though it was something to which I could return, rather than a foreign and unfamiliar place about which I could only daydream.

He was right, though. Oliver was sleeping. A marathon session by his standards. Probably, it was only because he knew that I couldn't. He hurt me like that, Oliver. It felt purposeful and cruel. I somehow knew that he would be breaking my heart forever.

"Alright," said Tyler, zipping up his laptop bag. "I guess I'll go. Meet my client in the hall and go over a few things."

I could picture them there, hands tucked into the pockets of their dress pants, voices hushed, because opposing counsel was only a few feet away. *Take me with you*, I almost begged.

He moved into the kitchen to retrieve a travel mug full of coffee, his water bottle, something to eat. "Since you're up, can you help me?" he asked, juggling his things at the front door. "Help me load the car?"

He shoved his coffee cup and water bottle at me, slipped his laptop bag over my shoulder before I could protest, then moved to the living room to retrieve his box of evidence.

I glanced toward the stairs, not wanting to leave Oliver alone inside the house, even for a few seconds, even if I was only going to the driveway. A few seconds felt long enough for anything to happen.

If I told him no, it would be an example demonstrating that I only cared about Oliver, filed away and dispatched during our next argument on the subject, ridiculous as it seemed.

So I went out to the driveway, barefoot and in my pajamas, self-conscious now that it was light out, and placed Tyler's belongings on the passenger seat of his car. He tucked the box in his trunk and slammed it, rattling the entire thing, then met me by the driver's side.

"Good luck," I said, and we kissed spuriously, with coffee breath and distracted thoughts.

"Thanks." He was already in his car before the word had disappeared into the dewy October air.

I waved from the porch as he began to back out of the driveway, thinking that we must have looked like the perfect picture of a young family, in the event any neighbors were watching. Dad was busy and successful. Mom stayed home with the beautiful baby, in this spacious house, in a neighborhood with highly rated schools and virtually no crime.

I turned and reached for the front door, pushing down on the lever, shoving my weight against it—the door always stuck, it was a repair we'd not yet tackled. But it didn't give this time, no matter how hard I shoved.

It didn't give because Tyler had locked me out.

I spun. His car was already swiveling around, turning to head up the hill, toward the end of the street.

"Wait," I yelled, running toward his car, the soft arches of my feet catching stray mulch and pebbles. "Wait," I screamed again, my breasts uncomfortably full with milk, overdue for Oliver's next feeding. Tyler's car sped up the road as though he was very aware that I was chasing him and was trying to escape. "Wait." The third died in my throat. Because Tyler was gone, and it was ridiculous to attempt to catch up to a car traveling upward of twenty-five miles an hour, and the shame, the thought of the neighbors seeing me running up the street in my pajamas, chasing my husband's car, screaming at him to stop, had begun to outweigh my desire to catch him. The perfect picture had shattered. What would they think? That he'd left us? That he'd departed after a fight and I was trying to stop him?

My cheeks burning, my heart thudding, from the exertion of my sprint, from adrenaline and anxiety, I punched the code for the garage into the keypad on the wall, directing the doors to open. But inside, the door to the house was also locked.

It was a cool morning, and goose bumps puckered my flesh as I ran through the damp grass, trying the French doors on the deck and the sliding door leading to the walkout basement. Everything was locked. I heaved at the windows next, each one I could reach, growing less concerned about what the neighbors might think, and more consumed by the fact that my husband had locked me out of the house with no phone and no shoes, with my baby inside.

I tried the sliding door to the basement one final time, then dropped to the ground on the stone patio before it. I had no way to get into the house. My only options were break in or go to a neighbor's house to borrow a phone. I knew Tyler's phone number, but he might not answer. He'd be conferring urgently with his client, reviewing his outline for his opening statement, organizing his code- and rule books and exhibit folders on the trial table. He would ignore an unknown number. My in-laws had a key, but I didn't know their phone number by memory. My dad had a key, but he was an hour away, far too far.

Should I call the police?

I felt it in my bones, in the cortisol that shot through my veins, in the uptick of my heartbeat, before I heard a thing. Oliver was crying. Our room was at the back of the house, two full floors up from where I had fallen to the ground. He was there, in his bassinet, alone and upset.

Without thinking, I grabbed an oversized brick from the perimeter lining the mulch-filled flower beds that wrapped around the house and slammed it into one of the basement windows, with the force of a mother. It cracked into a tangle of veins but didn't break. I tried again, and this time, it did, glass shooting into the house. The strength of the blow pushed my hands and forearms into the hole, and the glass scraped at my skin. Blood dripped down my arms as I reached inside to unlock the window. I pushed it open and climbed in, stepping, unavoidably, onto the broken glass that now littered the floor.

I ran up two flights of stairs—the house had never felt so excessively, superfluously large—to the bedroom, to the bassinet, where Oliver was lying on his back, his arms thrown upward, his face turned to the side, peaceful, unaware of my presence, of my horror and fear, my confusion.

I swore I'd heard him crying.

The blackout curtains were still drawn. He'd been asleep for four straight hours. Those hours should have been mine. I ached for them. Instead, I was riddled with anxiety, pumping with adrenaline, bloodied and cut.

I blinked at him for several minutes, the confusion constricting my chest, then I bundled up my hair and stepped into the shower. The cuts burned as I washed them, inspecting them for pieces of glass. I slapped bandages on those that were still oozing, then dressed and moved through the house with paper towels and a bottle of all-purpose cleaning spray, wiping my blood from the floors.

The sight in the basement sent a jolt of shame through my core. I cleared away the broken glass, but the evidence of what I'd done remained. The window would need to be replaced entirely.

The evidence of what Tyler had done, really. This wasn't my fault. How had he locked me out? Had he done so automatically, out of habit? Had he placed his box on the porch while he locked the front door, because that was what he always did? Had he locked our son in the house alone while his mind was on his trial?

I couldn't help but wonder, as I stared at the shattered window, whether he'd done it on purpose. I felt like I was being set up for failure.

Even though he, really, was responsible, he'd be appalled by the damage to our beautiful new house. He'd grumble over the cost of replacement, even though we could easily afford it. He'd sigh about the inconvenience of scheduling someone to come to the house to fix it, even though I would manage it without any assistance from him.

I would tell him that Oliver had been crying. That I'd needed to get to him immediately. That there wasn't time to borrow a phone, or to wait for someone to arrive. Because he had been crying, hadn't he? I'd heard it. I'd felt it.

I nursed and changed Oliver hurriedly after he finally did awaken, wondering whether I'd ever felt more alone. I bundled him in the stroller and pushed up the street. By now, the kids were at school. The parents were at work or shut away in home offices, trying to focus, resisting itches to start loads of laundry or unload the dishwasher. The retirees were puttering within the depths of their houses, waiting for the late-morning sun to burn away the frosty air.

I was craving something warm and comforting, like the bright softness of Paul's muffins. I'd already moved the rest into my own container, and washed Paul's with care, while Oliver had slept in his swing the previous afternoon. The container was resting in the basket at the bottom of the stroller now. I'd only had it a day and could have excusably kept it far longer. I didn't need to return it. That wasn't why I was going.

I rang the doorbell boldly, without warning, just as he had done with me.

He wore faded jeans, a long-sleeved polo shirt, and a surprised, but not displeased, expression on his face. The sun set his golden eyes alight.

I held out his container. "I'm returning this," I said. "And, I'm wondering," I told him, smiling wryly, "whether you can recommend a good contractor?"

NINETEEN

There was a feeling of pride, blossoming, pulsing, as I moved through the aisles of Target, Oliver weighing heavily within the straps of the baby carrier. People smiled pleasantly as I passed, impressed by my skill, by the cuteness of my child.

He was strapped to my front, my purse was hanging over my right shoulder, and my red basket was dangling from my left hand. There was a twinge in my lower back from the weight of it all, but I could manage.

After changing Oliver earlier that morning, I'd discovered that the bag in the diaper pail was full, the bag roll was empty, and we were out of refills. I thought that I had been gifted a complete year's worth of baby supplies, yet I seemed to be ordering something every day.

We needed refills. We needed them immediately. Overnight shipping wouldn't do. Even same-day shipping was inadequate. I wondered whether I should ask Tyler to stop on his way home. Use a trash bag until he got home from work, and I could run out to the store? I felt ridiculous. I could go out, bring Oliver with me. He was an infant, not an atomic bomb.

The baby carrier made things easier. He was far too small to ride in the basket near the handlebars of a shopping cart, and I was suspicious of the carts atop which a car seat could purportedly be latched. They were absurdly bulky. I'd seen other mothers struggling behind them, as if they were pushing a Mini Cooper through the aisles.

I located the baby supply aisles and diaper pail refills quickly. Feeling rather pleased with myself, perhaps overly confident, I wound around the store. I dropped a bar of vegan chocolate into my basket, and, in a gesture of benevolence, a bar of dark for Tyler. I could use a new pair of tweezers, couldn't I? If I was the type of mother who could take her baby to Target, surely I could recommence grooming my eyebrows. A purple bath bomb and a box of tissues also made it into my basket, and I was feeling quite buoyant as I loaded my items onto the conveyor belt, and they moved toward the pleasant cashier in her red T-shirt and vest. I wouldn't have minded browsing longer, but I didn't want to press my luck. Oliver might awaken and begin to scream at any time, shattering my moment of maternal competence, my brief foray into parental capability.

As it turned out, the cracks into my competence and capability were already there, as with our basement window.

The window was scheduled to be replaced on Monday morning by a company recommended by Paul. He'd known exactly who I should call; he had arranged for his own windows to be replaced the previous year. He'd listened, the sympathy obvious and honest on his face, as I told him what had happened. He'd looked through his phone for the appropriate number and he'd held Oliver for me while I called it.

I had told him everything.

I had told him more than I'd told Tyler. With Tyler, I'd said that Oliver had been screaming. That I'd had to get into the house.

But the shrieks I'd thought I could hear, that had reverberated through my body as I'd slammed the brick through the window and stepped on broken glass, had not been the sort of cries from which my baby could recover. He wasn't capable of such self-soothing. It had never happened before, and he'd been pale and dry-cheeked when I arrived in the bedroom. The calm before a storm, not after it.

There was only one explanation. Oliver hadn't been crying. I'd only imagined it.

Tyler had been extremely apologetic, although his frustration was lurking, monsterlike beneath the surface. He seemed to believe, notwithstanding his accidentally, automatically—he claimed this was the case—locking the front door after he stepped through it, that I should have been able to determine an alternate solution to breaking and entering.

I wasn't competent. I was a sham. A pig in sheep's clothing. A little girl merely dressed like a mom. When I pawed through my purse, my fingertips grazed errant breath mints, tubes of lip balm that I could never find when I needed them, and three pens. What I didn't find was my wallet.

"Your total is $43.76," said the cashier, as I stared at her in horror.

"Um," I said, still pawing through my bag as if my wallet, which was quite large and not actually capable of hiding, might reveal itself. "I'm so sorry. I forgot my wallet."

"Oh," said the cashier in surprise. She was young and new, unsure how to handle this turn of events.

I rolled my eyes theatrically, aware of the closeness of the woman standing directly behind me. "I think I left it in my diaper bag, and then I brought my purse with me."

"You know," said the woman behind me, smiling banally, lackadaisically, "I got rid of my purse entirely. It was actually very liberating. I just use my diaper bag now." There was a rosy-cheeked toddler, stony-faced, propped against her hip, and she was loading her prospective purchases onto the belt with almost pompous ease. She had the smooth, well-rested face of a woman who was getting both dependable sleep and regular facials. She didn't look very liberated to me.

But I was just like her, was I not? I was a more hideous, more hideously exhausted, version of her.

"I'll just have to run home to get it, then come back? Would that be okay?" I asked the cashier.

She was relieved to be offered an out. "Of course," she said. "I'll leave your things right here." She bent to place my plastic bag onto the floor.

I practically fled from the store, and I sped home. The wallet was, indeed, in my diaper bag. Oliver had fallen asleep in the car. Once I'd returned to Target and parked, I stood in front of the open car door and stared at my baby.

Couldn't I just leave him in the car?

How I hated myself for the thought.

I didn't bother with the baby carrier, just raced inside with Oliver cradled against my chest, supported with my right hand, my credit card in my left.

There was a line at my previous register, longer than the ones at others, yet I stood in it anyway with nothing to purchase, only a dozing baby in my arms. The woman in front of me glanced back curiously. *They sell babies here?* As if I'd picked him off a shelf. But who would ever do that? I hated myself for that thought, too.

I smiled brightly at the cashier. "I'm back," I said to her confused expression. She'd forgotten my little snafu entirely. This should have brought me comfort. "I forgot my wallet earlier," I explained.

"Right!" She bent to retrieve my things, and I managed to swipe my credit card and tuck my wrist through the holes of the plastic bag without dropping my child onto the sticky floor.

Shame continued to warm my face the remainder of the day. As I breast-fed and burped my child and held him upright and stared at nothing. As I changed diapers and shoved them into the pail, with its new refill bags, without an iota of victoriousness. As I ate the last of Paul's muffins and re-sisted the urge to visit him again, to tell him what I'd done, to listen to the fact that it was okay, and actually quite funny when you thought about it.

I had searched for his name online, curious about who he was, ex-actly, after leaving his house the previous morning. I'd scoured Facebook and LinkedIn on my phone, while Oliver nursed then slept at my breast. There had been other Paul Rileys, but none that looked like him.

His wife, on the other hand, Erin Riley—there'd been no shortage of results on her. She was Ivy League–educated, and she owned a small fi-nancial consulting company in a suburban office building not far from our neighborhood. It seemed as if she was very successful. Her hair was thick, shiny, and almond-colored, her features were unremarkable, and her lips, unsmiling, playing the part of serious finance-type person, were a bright red. I wasn't sure why I cared about any of this.

Tyler burst through the front door, with no warning. I knew better than to question his presence so early, knew better than to give any indi-cation of the fact that time seemed to slip away from me some days, like the hours were a horde of toddlers who scattered erratically at a theme park. I couldn't keep track of them.

But I checked the time—just after five. It was unusually early for him to be home—my sabbatical had afforded him the prerogative to work as much as he pleased.

He had good news, apparently, was practically overflowing with joy and pride.

I sat on the sofa in the family room, nursing Oliver, while Tyler knelt to the floor before us, like he was going to propose, his eyes crinkling in delight.

"Nat," he said, placing his hands on my upper arms. "I made partner."

My first reaction was confusion. Partner? As though I didn't know what the word meant, didn't understand the significance of the term.

My second was anger, a ball of fire, red and echoing, like a shot from a cannon. Third came the slow burn of envy. I could already tell it would never die.

Partner. *I made partner.* These were, perhaps, the three words every private practice attorney yearned to say, from the moment they started the timer to bill their first tenth of an hour.

"Wow," I said. It was all I could manage.

"They told me today. Promotions and raises aren't supposed to be announced until next week, but Jim told me early." He was beaming at me, but not looking for my approval. He didn't need it. He had what he needed now.

"I had no idea you were going to make partner this year."

"Me, either," he said, with childlike wonder, while sickness was twisting my gut. Because we'd graduated from the same law school—my grades had actually been better. I'd made Law Review, Order of the Coif. Tyler hadn't. We'd both begun careers with large firms downtown. And he'd made partner at age thirty-two, a mere two months after our child was born. His income, his ego, his importance would skyrocket. And here I was. On a sabbatical, with stinging nipples at the ends of drained and sagging breasts, spending my days changing diapers and shoving the dirty ones into a diaper pail for which I forgot to purchase refills, my seven years of higher education useless and inconvenient, like a persistent mosquito buzzing around my face. *Unfair* felt a callously inadequate descriptor for this place where we found ourselves, but it captured the general idea. And *why*? Why were we here? Because I could feed our child with my body, while Tyler could not? Because, as an educated person, capable of understanding the benefits of breastfeeding, that was what I was expected to do?

Tyler prattled on about the way they'd told him. The reasons he'd been promoted. What would come next, while I sat there, holding Oliver, who had fallen asleep, more disinterested than me in his father's success.

"Let's order a nice dinner," he said. "Have something delivered."

"Sure," I said. "You pick." I hadn't the energy to remind him about my restrictive diet.

He chose Italian, which left me with virtually no options, as cheese and butter abounded on the menu. But I ate my shrimp with marinara, on angel hair pasta, with no parmesan on top, and pretended to be happy for my husband.

When it was time for bed, later than I usually attempted it, Oliver settled quickly, seemed to be sleeping soundly, as if in cahoots with Tyler, who wrapped his arms around me after we climbed between the sheets, and pulled me close.

Apparently, the promotion, the prospect of more money and power, had turned him on, and I bit back horror and disgust as he kissed the back of my neck, felt a firmness poking me in the back.

"Is it . . ." Tyler asked, hesitantly, courteously. "Is it okay? It's been ten weeks."

"Okay," I said, even though it wasn't okay. But I had been cleared, weeks ago, actually, and the more I put it off, the more impossible it would seem. "But, not with Oliver right here." It felt wrong, with our child mere feet away.

"Right," said Tyler, as though he'd forgotten about our son entirely. Perhaps he was too busy dreaming of the way his profile would look on the firm's web page. TYLER FANNING, PARTNER.

He climbed out of bed and took my hand, led me to the never-used guest room, which we'd fully furnished anyway. I reclined on the bed, bracing myself, knowing that it would be worse if my body was tense, but unable to relax.

I gasped, cried out. Tyler mistook the exclamation for pleasure. "Oh, Nat," he murmured into my ear, his breath hot and wet and reminiscent of the garlic sauce he'd eaten with dinner, a fact I might have found endearing a year ago, but which, now, just made me sad.

How did he know me so little? I was not in rapture, not consumed with lust. I was thinking of the Wusthof knife tucked into its smooth, wooden caddy resting on our swirling countertops in the kitchen. The largest knife. The one we used to slice whole watermelons on warm summer afternoons. I felt as though it had been plunged inside of me. I'd never look at it the same way again, would wince every time I used it.

And I had never hated my husband more, as he moved above me.

I hated him for his pleasure and his obliviousness or indifference to the pain twisting my face. For his exorbitant salary and bonuses, which would soon become even more exorbitant, and the way they made me feel like a leech. For his liftoff, his ambition, while I was ground into the sidewalk like an ant beneath the high heels I no longer wore. For his freedom, flaunting and buoyant, while I wilted and died. Hopeless. Trapped.

TWENTY

Dark sunglasses, too big for my face, were pushed low on my nose, as I moved gingerly up Ashby Drive. I couldn't remember the last time I'd worn them and had dug them out of a storage bin shoved to the hall closet, filled with random items that had seemed important enough to pack when we were moving from the little ranch house, but apparently not important enough to unpack even three months after moving into our new house that still felt new.

It was inevitable, and I was actually surprised it had taken this long, but I'd been struck by a migraine the previous evening. I'd had worse, ones that had sent me to the floor of the bathroom, gripping the toilet, and ones that had prevented me from leaving bed at all.

I was a mother now, and staying in bed wasn't an option.

I'd staggered to the bassinet each time Oliver had cried the previous night, the pain pounding in my head almost anesthetizing the horror of getting up seven times between eight and six. When I wasn't holding Oliver, I'd simply lain in bed with my forehead pressed into my pillow, the pain too intense to fall asleep.

I was doing just that when Tyler got up to get ready for work, and still when he was preparing to leave the house.

"Nat?" he said doubtfully. "Are you okay?"

"Migraine," I whispered.

"Oh," he replied.

He should have offered to take the day off work. He should have realized that I couldn't care for Oliver in my current state. He should have stayed home to help me. Instead, he said the worst possible thing that he could have said.

"Do you want me to call my mom?" he asked. "I'm sure she could come by and help you."

"Get out," I hissed in reply, pressing my face deeper into the silkiness of my pillowcase.

Tyler left, then Oliver cried, and I'd decided that I simply needed to carry on as though I didn't have a migraine. What other choice did I have? Spend the day with Diane Fanning bustling around my house, reminding me, both implicitly and explicitly, of all the ways in which she was a perfect mother and that she had raised a perfect son, despite the evidence to the contrary, staring us right in the face, his absence the clearest manifestation thereof? *No, thank you.*

I got up then, took two Tylenol, and changed and fed my baby.

A walk, I'd decided. Fresh air would help. The day was cool and gray and inoffensive to the senses.

Besides, there was someone else who could help me, someone far preferable to my mother-in-law. I could stop by his house on my way back, see if he wanted to hold Oliver for a bit. I was certain that he would. He'd been so delighted to see me on his porch the previous day.

Was it me he so enjoyed, or was it my baby? I didn't know, and I didn't care.

I must have looked ridiculous in the sunglasses, on a day that didn't call for them, but even the faint sunlight pushing its way through the overcast sky was too much for me to handle. We moved slowly and carefully, Oliver dozing in his stroller. *Keep sleeping,* I willed silently. *I need you to be an easy baby today.* It would be a first.

It was still early October, and the temperature was fluttering in the low seventies. It was, I believed, the best weather of the year, besides, possibly, late May or early June. It was a lovely time to be home, to be outdoors, rather than trapped between the tiny four walls of my city office.

I felt odd as I pushed through the streets—something was off. The headache, I assumed, the sleepless night. Months of them in succession. It was adding up. It was a dreamlike state in which I found myself as I wound through the streets. Rather, more accurately, it was a nightmare.

I'd intended on the two-mile loop, respectable, but not overly ambitious. Somehow, somewhere, I'd gone wrong. Nothing looked familiar.

The neighborhood was large and tree lined, the streets weaving and looping and connecting, filling the area between Elkhorn Lane, a busier street than the peaceful roads off which the driveways sprouted, and the woods and stream that ran behind the neighborhood. It was a good neighborhood for running, Tyler and I had discussed when we'd bought the house, offering many variations of loops and routes. Neither of us had taken advantage of that since moving in.

I began to walk more quickly, scanning my surroundings for something that looked familiar, a house, a street name. Nothing did. There was no one out.

I turned around, walking as quickly as my damaged muscles would allow, ignoring the pain squeezing my brain. Turn around and retrace my steps, I decided.

But had I already turned around? I couldn't recall, and I didn't recognize anything around me. Without warning, tears burned my eyes and my breath came quickly, far too quickly. My chest constricted. I kept moving until I couldn't. I doubled over, the stroller's handlebar slipping from my grip. It began to roll away from me, and I watched it go as blackness pressed inward from the outskirts of my vision.

Footsteps, approaching rapidly. Someone was chasing me. *Oliver*. I needed to get to Oliver. I pushed through the blackness, stood, but I fell to my knees again. The footsteps were louder and closer. They passed me. A man. Dark-haired and spry, in shorts and a jacket. He ran right by and grabbed the handles of the stroller, pulling it to a stop.

I let myself collapse then. It was over. Oliver was gone. My immediate feeling, through the pain pressing against my chest and head, was relief. I'd be able to sleep now. Now that Oliver was gone.

The man turned and began to push the stroller back toward me. Unlike the surroundings, he was familiar. I knew him.

He crouched beside me and placed a hand on my back. "Natalie," he said. "What happened?"

I cried in earnest then. I let go. Because I knew that I could.

"It's okay," said Paul, his hand still pressing gently against my back. "I'll get you home. Can you walk?"

He helped me stand, and I tried to take a breath. This time, it worked, filling my lungs. Some of the darkness dissipated.

Paul held the stroller with one hand, his other arm wrapped around my waist. We walked home that way, in silence. I was conscious of how this must look, concerned what the other neighbors might think, but not enough to push him away.

When we reached my house, I stood frozen before the garage. The front door was locked. The garage doors were closed. I didn't know the code.

Paul read my mind. "Don't think," he said. "You know it. Just type it in."

I lifted the lid to the keypad and I pressed my fingers into the rubbery buttons. He was right. I did. 0–8–0–4. My due date. We'd picked the code before Oliver was born, assuming it might be his birthday, but he'd not been evicted from the womb for another week.

Paul carried Oliver's car seat inside; mercifully, he was still sound asleep. My baby had no idea I'd almost fainted on the side of the road, that I'd gotten us lost, that he could have rolled away from me and tipped over, fallen out, his head smacking the pavement. I sank onto the family room sofa and my shoulders shook.

Paul hurriedly placed the car seat onto the rug before me so that I could watch my son, then stepped into the kitchen. He returned with a glass of water, which I drank slowly, even though my stomach churned with nausea.

Paul dropped onto the sofa beside me. "Should I take you to the hospital?" he asked.

I shook my head. It was a mistake. The pain roared.

"You're okay now." It wasn't a question, and I appreciated that.

Oliver began to stir. I'd known he would, now that he was no longer moving.

Without missing a beat, Paul slipped my son from the car seat and held him against his chest. "What happened?" he asked.

"I don't know," I admitted. I realized I was still wearing the sunglasses. I slipped them from my face. "I have a migraine. I thought some fresh air might help. I got lost. Nothing looked familiar to me. I panicked. I don't know how that happened. I was trying to walk a route I have walked before. I must have become distracted and made a wrong turn."

He studied my face. "You weren't lost. You were only about a half mile from Ashby Drive."

I shrugged. Was that supposed to make me feel better? I was so confused, so panicked, I might as well have been in California.

"You're just tired, Natalie," Paul continued. "You just need to get some rest. Don't worry about it."

The tears felt like acid behind my eyes. I shook my head.

"What?" he asked. "What is it?"

"It's not just that," I admitted. "I'm not just tired. I'm forgetting things."

"Like the garage code?" he asked, still rocking Oliver. "That's nothing. It happens."

"I'm forgetting a lot of things. I feel like I'm not really living. I feel like I'm watching from the outside."

His brows crinkled with concern.

"I'm losing time," I said.

There it was. I'd thought it would be a relief to say it, but my words felt fluorescent and tacky. They didn't belong out there. I longed to put them away.

"What does that mean?" Paul asked, patting Oliver's back. His face had gone slack with sleep.

"Sometimes, all of a sudden, I realize it's a half hour, or an hour, or more, later than I thought it was. Time slips away from me. I can't remember anything."

Paul watched me, seemingly lost in thought, as he rocked back and forth with my baby in his arms. The muscle memory seemed to kick in when he was holding Oliver. He knew exactly what to do without even thinking about it.

"That doesn't sound like anything to worry about, Natalie," he said, after the silence had stretched so long that it had begun to feel awkward. "That sounds completely normal. I mean, I remember the same thing happening to me when Petra was a baby. I was so sleep-deprived. It gets better. I promise."

I nodded miserably. I didn't know if he was right, but my mind was too weak, limp, like something overcooked or broken, to argue with him.

"Why don't you go upstairs and lie down?" Paul suggested. "I can watch Oliver for a bit. Maybe take him out for another stroll, since I didn't get to finish my run, if that's okay." He grinned.

I hesitated, but I wasn't sure why. Something instinctual, perhaps. Because he had given me no reason not to trust him. I was the one who was untrustworthy. I was the one who had put my baby in danger. It was Paul who had saved us.

"That would be really nice," I said.

I took more Tylenol and carried another glass of water and my phone upstairs to bed. I had left the phone resting on the kitchen island when I'd left for our walk, distracted by the migraine, or something. If I'd brought it with me, maybe I wouldn't have thought I was lost. I could have pulled up a map and found our way home. Maybe I wouldn't have panicked.

I slipped into bed and sipped my water. I could hear Paul's silky, soothing voice as he chatted to Oliver downstairs, footsteps off and on. I lay down, even though I knew I wouldn't be able to sleep.

Yet, somehow, I did. Sleep pulled me under, dark and stifling.

I awakened several hours later, pulled back out by the sense that someone was watching me.

He was. Paul. He smiled sheepishly. "Sorry," he said. "Petra will be getting out of school soon, and I need to run a quick errand first."

I sat up as quickly as I could, brushing away the unfamiliar fog of slumber, embarrassed by my mussed hair and sleep-stale breath. "Of course," I said. "I'm sorry. Thank you so much for your help. I feel better." It should have been the truth, but I wasn't sure if it was.

"Anytime," said Paul. He passed Oliver to me. "Take care of yourself," he added.

He paused, and I thought for a second that he might bend down and kiss me on the top of the head, or perhaps somewhere else. Thinking better of it, he nodded once, turned, and he was gone.

TWENTY-ONE

He hurried down her stairs, into the foyer, then out the front door. He turned the lock before pulling the door closed behind him, even though it was perfectly safe to leave the front door unlocked. He always did when he was home.

Apparently, though, her husband was in the habit of locking the door behind him. Paul thought of the morning she'd shown up on his doorstep, with his empty container, telling him she needed the name of a contractor. Her husband had locked her out of the house, she'd said, she thought her baby was crying, and she'd smashed a window to get to him. Turns out, he hadn't been crying at all—she'd only been imagining it.

Then, there was this. Getting lost in her own neighborhood, crumpling to the ground in the street, letting her stroller, her baby, roll away from her. She was an unbridled disaster, this one, hurtling recklessly through motherhood.

Paul jogged down the steps of her front porch, then made his way down the driveway, wondering if the other neighbors were watching him. Had they seen him walking her home, his arm around her? Had they seen him entering her house beside her, while her husband was at the office, and his wife was at work?

Were they getting the wrong idea? Were they getting the right one?

She was forgetting things. She couldn't remember the code to get into her own garage. She was losing time, too. He'd told her it sounded completely normal for a sleep-deprived, new parent. Nothing to worry about. He'd even told her that the same thing had happened to him.

It hadn't, but he'd said it anyway.

For Paul Riley had worked it out. Just like he'd known that he would.

He'd allowed his mind to wander, away from his miserable wife, away from her failing business, away from her cold demeanor toward him, toward their daughter, away from her failings, all the ways in which she was a blight upon what might otherwise have the potential to be familial perfection, suburban bliss, away from the fact that, despite almost ten years of work, there was no novel, a fact that Erin might discover at any time.

When he had least expected it, his mind had stopped wandering through these problems, these pieces. It had landed upon the solution, upon one particular wildflower, in a meadow lush with weeds.

An exhausted, desperate, new mother. Alone and lost. Lost time, in fact. She was suffering, perhaps, from postpartum depression. Maybe even something more serious than that. Her mind was not well.

Which was, actually, quite perfect.

Perfect for him, at least.

The solution to his problems was *her*.

Now, it was just a matter of waiting for the right moment. For the perfect time to make his move.

TWENTY-TWO

I knocked my knuckles against the window, testing its sturdiness. It held, it hurt, my fingertips were smarting, stinging. Oliver was looking into my face, his expression the baby version of an eye roll. But would it hold against a brick? I hoped I wouldn't have to find out.

The doorbell rang. The contractors, recommended by Paul, were long gone.

It was Paul himself standing on my porch, something charcoal gray and wrapped in plastic in his hands. Smiling, reaching out. The relief, when I took the plastic-wrapped item from him and released Oliver to his arms, was palpable, sweet. But gone in a blink. The sweetness was soon chased away by a sour aftertaste. The pervasive sourness of mom guilt.

"I got you this," he said, after we'd moved deeper into the house, to the family room, into which the late-morning sunlight was streaming. "I thought it might be helpful."

"Oh," I said, startled by his thoughtfulness, pleased that he'd been thinking of me, that he had seen me. That he knew I needed help.

"It's a baby carrier," he explained, rock-bouncing to the right then left, Oliver pressed against his chest. "I know it just looks like a scarf or something, but there's a way to wrap it so that you can hold your baby close to you. I used to have something similar for Petra when she was a baby. Mine was a gift from a friend, though, who'd been to Africa. In many villages there, the women always wear their babies all day. They nurse seamlessly that way."

"Oh," I said again, inspecting the packaging, glancing at the brand, which was familiar. I'd read it on the tag of the gray scarf-like baby wrap I'd shoved into Oliver's dresser after the morning I'd tried it out. I hadn't seen it since. "Thank you so much, but I actually, um, I have one of these. I couldn't get the hang of it, though."

"No?" he asked. "I thought Oliver would be just the sort of baby who'd love it. Always wants to be held. Just like Petra. Let's give it a try." He reached for the package.

"Well, here," I said, handing it back to him. "Let me just go get mine. Since I already have one. You could return this one."

I ignored his protestations that it was nothing, it hadn't been expensive, and hurried upstairs. To accept a gift from him felt overtly inappropriate, far too intimate. After digging my own rejected, charcoal-colored wrap out of the dresser, I returned downstairs, having once again left my baby alone in the arms of a veritable stranger. A veritable stranger, though, who was better with him than I was. Paul was continuing to rock-bounce, as Oliver looked placidly over his shoulder.

"Right," said Paul. He glanced around, then placed Oliver into his swing and buckled the five-point harness faster and more easily than Tyler ever had. I let him take the wrap from my hands. "May I?" he asked, but he was already twisting and looping it around me, his fingers grazing my back, his face so close I could feel his breath.

"I tried this before, but Oliver cried in it, so I shoved it in his dresser and forgot about it until now. I have another baby carrier, too," I said, desperate to make conversation. "One of the backpack sort, that you wear on your front."

"Oh, this is much better than those," he said. "Softer, more womb-like."

He retrieved Oliver from the swing and helped me tuck him inside the outer fold of the wrap.

He stepped back, admired us. "There," he said. "Maybe this will make things easier for you."

I nodded and bounced gently, my hands pressed against Oliver.

"So, um," I said, not sure what to do next, as I continued to sway, "were you home quite a bit when Petra was born?" I was embarrassed to realize that even with all this time we'd spent together, I had never asked what he did for a living, never asked why he seemed to be home so much.

Paul laughed, the skin around his golden eyes crinkling outward, like rays from the sun. "I've been home ever since," he said.

"Really," I remarked, rudely startled by his revelation. "I didn't realize. You're a stay-at-home father?"

"Well, I'm a writer, too. I used to be a college professor. English. But my wife's career was taking off before her pregnancy. We'd been trying for a long time to have children, were beginning to wonder if it would ever happen. She was focusing on growing her business. Suddenly, she was pregnant, and we decided it would be best for the family if she returned to work rather quickly and I stayed home with Petra. That way, I could care for her and devote some time to my writing. It's been my greatest joy, to have that time with her."

I blinked at him, unseeing. *His greatest joy? Best for the family? She returned to work. I stayed home.* Tyler and I had both been senior associates when Oliver was born. We were earning almost the same salary and bonuses, Tyler only slightly more, evidence of our respective firms' implicit biases against me and in favor of him. Why had it been so obvious, so automatic, that it would be me to take the sabbatical? It could have easily been Tyler who stayed home to care for Oliver, to hold him all night, to be slowly, steadily, broken by lack of sleep.

Except, Tyler was a partner now, and, besides, I was the one who fed Oliver, who kept him alive with my body. If only Tyler could lactate. Why was there not some innovation for just that? A sort of faux breast that he could wear, with a bladder of milk inside, warmed to his body temperature? I laughed, amused by silent and secret thoughts, much like a person who had lost touch with reality a long time ago.

"I'm sorry," I told Paul, embarrassed again. "I just can't imagine my husband doing something like that. As you can see," I said, gesturing to our kitchen, gleaming and white, the absolute image of suburban, domestic perfection, "here we are. It's me at home, not at work. Here I am, taking care of our baby."

Paul shrugged modestly. "It made more sense for our family. Petra was a difficult baby. Like Oliver, it seems. She wanted to be held all the time. She was colicky, would scream for hours every afternoon. Erin couldn't stand it. She couldn't come home from work until Petra's afternoon episodes were over. I wore her around the house all the time. It helped."

Oliver suddenly began to squirm against the soft, gray fabric and whine.

I hurriedly extracted him from the wrap. "It's probably time to nurse him," I said apologetically, but Paul didn't appear remotely disturbed by the shrieks. He held out his hands and I passed Oliver to him. Paul held Oliver against his chest and patted his back while I un-looped and removed the baby carrier. I folded it neatly, influenced by Paul's presence to do something tidy and careful, rather than leaving it in a crumpled ball on the kitchen counter. I put it down beside the baby wrap Paul had brought.

"Erin didn't breastfeed Petra very long," he said. "Only a few weeks. She said she wasn't getting any milk. But I don't know."

I was astonished to note that Oliver's screams had already quieted to displeased squeaks. Perhaps he didn't need to eat after all. Perhaps he just smelled, heard Paul, wanted to be held against his chest, instead of mine. It was hurtful, but only for a second. More than anything, it was freeing.

"Yes, Petra was a very difficult baby," Paul continued, as if I'd asked a question. "And Erin had a horrible pregnancy, too. She was violently ill. Sometimes, I wonder if she's never quite forgiven our daughter for that. It wasn't her fault, of course, but rationality doesn't always prevail when it comes to our children, does it?"

My phone began to vibrate on the island nearby, alight with the words, KIDS FIRST PEDIATRICS. Oliver's doctor. I snatched it up in surprise— why would his doctor be calling?—and answered the call after muttering a quiet "Excuse me" to Paul.

"Mrs. Fanning?" asked the voice.

"Yes," I said, although hearing the name still made me think of my mother-in-law.

"This is Melissa from Kids First Pediatrics. Checking whether you were still coming in for Oliver's appointment this morning? If you can get here in the next fifteen minutes, we can still see him. Otherwise, you'll have to reschedule."

I blinked blankly, my eyes meeting Paul's. His brows were drawn low in concern as he continued to pat my son's back.

"I'm so sorry," I said. "I completely forgot. I can be there in fifteen minutes." Could I? I'd have to collect the diaper bag, pack Oliver in the car. It was a ten-minute drive. Was the bag stocked with diapers and wipes? With the swaddle blanket I'd need to wrap him up in the cool exam room after he'd been weighed and measured by the nurse?

I hung up the phone, tossed it back onto the island. "I have to go," I told Paul, a flutter of panic, franticness in my tone. "I forgot about Oliver's doctor's appointment. We're late."

"It's okay," he said, continuing to sway and pat Oliver's back. "Get ready. Get what you need. I'll hold him."

"Thank you." I breathed, relieved for the help, then dashed upstairs to collect the diaper bag, which was, of course, not stocked with the things that I needed. That just wasn't the sort of mother that I was.

Back downstairs, I added my wallet to the bag, then pawed through it, double-checking the contents. I reached out, took Oliver from Paul and began tucking him into his car seat. "I'm so embarrassed," I admitted. "I can't believe I forgot his appointment. I mean, it's not as though I have a busy schedule."

"Yes, you do," Paul said calmly, with the same even and soothing voice he used to murmur in Oliver's ear. "You have the busiest schedule of all. I know exactly how it is. Don't worry about it. You just need more support."

He held the diaper bag out to me, and I swung it over my shoulder, lifted Oliver's car seat.

"Thank you so much," I said again, swallowing quickly, not sure why I felt like I was fighting a wave of tears. Was it shame, or the unusual blush of kindness? He was so forgiving, so lacking in judgment. So unlike Tyler. Tyler would be appalled that I was a stay-at-home mother—sorry, *on a sabbatical*—yet, I'd forgotten to take our son to his appointment. Which is why I wouldn't tell him.

"You'll show yourself out?" I called to Paul, as I rushed toward the door. He was still lingering in my kitchen, his energy so steady and peaceful that I wanted to run back in and press my arm against his, in case a bit of it might rub off on me.

"Of course," he said. "And good luck. Don't worry about it. You're doing great."

I closed the door on his words, but brought them with me, let them idle, unmoving, in my brain as I clicked Oliver's car seat into place, hoping for them to provide absolution from the mom guilt that was back, that had never really gone away at all, that was pumping through my heart, that was squeezing the breath from my lungs. More than anything, I wished they were true.

TWENTY-THREE

I spun the wheel slowly, turning out of the doctor's office parking lot, still not sure how I'd forgotten about Oliver's appointment. I had no memory of scheduling it. No bells had been rung by the call from the receptionist. No *That's right!* I couldn't help wondering if it had been the office's mistake, rather than my own. I comforted myself with this particular anecdote, this fallacy.

But Dr. Williams had bustled into the exam room, unsurprised by our presence, seeming to know exactly the purpose for the appointment: another weight check for Oliver. As it turned out, he was doing remarkably well. It was not unexpected. I felt that I did nothing but nurse him.

"How's he sleeping?" she had asked. "Did you make any changes to your diet?"

"I did. I cut out everything." That was how it felt. "But he's still only sleeping thirty-minute-to-two-hour stretches. Occasionally three hours."

She glanced up at me briefly over the frames of tortoiseshell glasses.

"Does he seem more comfortable? Is he spitting up less?"

Because I'd not known about the appointment, I'd not had time to prepare answers to these questions.

I'd pinched my eyes closed, tried and failed to think. "I believe so," I'd told her. "The spit-up incidents haven't seemed as . . . voluminous. Or frequent."

"Well, great, then."

It was as though she had slammed the lid on something. Case closed. As long as Oliver was more comfortable, was gaining weight properly, everything was *great*.

Had I known about the appointment, I was certain I would have had questions for Dr. Williams. I would have typed a list of them in my phone because my memory was such that I needed to put every import- ant thought into writing before it was lost forever. Just as I had prepared no answers, nor did I have any questions, so the appointment wrapped up quickly, and Oliver and I had been back in the car, with the obliga- tory, age-inappropriate sticker, my arms aching from lugging his car seat around, the shame of my forgetfulness still lingering on my skin like a sunburn.

I slowed to a stop at a light, thought about calling Tyler and telling him about the appointment. But I was afraid I might accidentally admit that I had forgotten it and had almost not made it there in time. I was afraid he'd be disgusted by me. I was afraid I deserved it.

Besides, I wasn't in the mood to speak to my husband, had no interest in hearing his voice or the background noise of his computer keys tap- ping or the voices of other busy professionals on the streets of the city.

As I approached the end of my driveway, I noted the presence of an- other car, one I didn't recognize, parked near the house as though it had every right to be there. It was a burgundy compact SUV. It didn't belong to anyone I knew.

Curious, I parked in the street, instead of behind or beside the car, as though I were the guest. Oliver was still fast asleep, exhausted from all the tears in the doctor's office. He stayed that way even as I awkwardly ex- tracted his car seat from its place in the middle seat. It was the safest place for it to be, but God was it cumbersome to get it in and out. I understood why parents opted for vehicles larger than mine. Like, for example, the one belonging to my visitor.

I walked toward the SUV, peered into its untinted windows. There was no one inside, no one sitting in the driver's seat and waiting for my return.

I moved up the front walkway, just as I had so many times before. On the front porch, I froze, my keys dangling from my right hand, the left still holding onto Oliver's car seat, my body tipping that direction uncomfort- ably from its bulky weight. Something wasn't right. I stared at my front door.

The wreath. It wasn't mine. I blinked at it. It was a fall one, decorated with red, gold, and orange foliage.

The storm door swung open with its usual creak, and a woman appeared. She was in her sixties, with a graying bob and black-framed glasses, over which she was peering at me. She didn't step onto the porch, just hovered in the doorway, not quite inside, and not quite out. There was fear in her face, confusion. Had I not been a woman, especially a woman with a baby, perhaps she wouldn't have even opened the door. I could feel fear of my own.

"Can I help you?" she asked. She glanced down at my hand, still holding my keys. I could have just been hanging on to them, having just locked my car. But I had selected one particular key and was gripping it between my index finger and thumb, preparing to insert it into the dead bolt on the yellow front door.

"I'm sorry," I said, blinking up at her. "I must have the wrong house."

I turned and hurried back down the walkway and climbed into the car.

"That's alright," I could barely hear her call after me. She was relieved. I wasn't.

The storm door clicked closed, then the door behind it. She'd probably locked it. She was right to.

I pressed my foot onto the gas and peeled away from the curb, away from the little white rancher with the window eyes and the daffodil-yellow door. Away from the house that always had and still did feel like home.

What would have happened if that woman hadn't come to the door? Would I have tried a key? Would I have broken in, just like I'd broken into my new house, smashing a window with a brick?

I'd never met the people who had bought our rancher, but our Realtor had told us that they were an older couple, retired. They'd wanted to downsize, find a home with no stairs, to be close to their grandchildren. We'd been doing the opposite. We'd needed to upsize. More space for the kids. More space so that we could, once they became older, escape them.

"It could have happened to anyone," I remarked. Oliver was still sleeping. I supposed I was talking to myself. "I was just on autopilot," I continued. "I went to the old house without even thinking. I was distracted. That's all." It sounded so innocent. No big deal.

Sometimes, I lied to myself in that way. I did what I needed to do.

It wasn't what I wanted. What I wanted didn't matter anymore.

In this moment, though, I wanted to get what I wanted, and all I wanted—a tiny ask, really—was to feel better. To feel like everything was okay. To feel like nothing was wrong with me.

My fingers hovered over the buttons on the dashboard of my car for a second, while I debated calling Tyler, telling him everything. He was my husband, after all. Wasn't that the point of him? A supportive shoulder, a kind and listening ear. But I very much doubted that would help matters at all.

There was someone else, though, who very well might help. Someone who wasn't my husband. Someone who was something unknown, undefinable to me. A friend? Or just a neighbor? I wasn't sure. I didn't care. He was a person who could make me feel the way I needed to feel.

I returned my hand to the wheel, and I drove to his house.

TWENTY-FOUR

When the doorbell rang, he was chopping vegetables for a casserole, sliding them into a container, mincing fresh garlic, swiping the leaves from sprigs of rosemary. He'd assemble everything before he went to get Petra from school. Then, he'd be able to focus on her. To sit at the kitchen table beside her while she ate a snack and did her homework. To drive her to her piano lesson and be able to relax while he was there, the back of his head resting against the wall, his eyes closed, as he sat in a folding chair outside the room, listening to her progress, pride welling up in his chest. When they got home, he'd simply have to pop the dish into the oven. Such prep work was crucial to truly enjoying one's children. He wondered, quite often, how working parents did it all. The answer, he suspected, was that they didn't. One simply *couldn't*. Something was lost. Something was done in inferior fashion, be it work or parenting or domestic life. Maybe all three. Working parents were spread too thin.

Not like him. But his task had been interrupted. He wiped his hands on a dish towel and moved toward the front door, was unsurprised to see Natalie standing there on his porch. She couldn't seem to stay away.

He smiled as he swung the door open, and her eyes were shining. With tears, relief, comfort. They were closer than he had even realized—she thought so, at least, and that was what mattered.

"Come here," he said. He took the car seat from her and placed it on the floor, just inside the door. In the event anyone happened to be watching, he reached for her, pulling her toward him. He hugged her there, in the doorway, wondering a second too late if it was too soon for such a gesture.

It wasn't. Her body seemed to melt into his for several seconds before she extracted herself, then moved deeper into his house. "What's wrong?" he asked as she stood in the foyer, staring at the ground.

"It's getting worse," she said. She bit her lip so firmly he half expected it to bead with blood.

He picked up the car seat again and ushered her into the kitchen, setting her up at the breakfast table with a glass of water.

"Can I make you a tea?" he asked. "Chamomile?"

"Um." She blinked at him as though overwhelmed by the offer.

"I'll make you one," he said. "No problem."

He pushed the chopping board aside and tucked the containers into the fridge while he waited for the kettle to boil.

"I'm sorry," Natalie said. "I'm interrupting you."

"Not at all," he replied. "You are welcome here anytime. *Anytime.* Both of you."

It was important that she understand this. It was important that she continue to stop by.

Paul poured them each a mug of tea, noticing his phone screen come to life on the counter as he moved past it. A notification. He'd missed a call from Erin. He hesitated, considered calling her back, then delivered the teas to the kitchen table, carrying his phone with him. Erin would call again. She always did, on the rare occasion that he didn't answer.

"So," he said, as Natalie looked into her cup as though it might tell her future, dunking the tea bag up and down, "what's going on?"

Oliver began to stir, so she reached out a leg and began to rock the car seat to and fro with her foot. "I left the doctor's appointment," she said, "and I drove to the wrong house." She covered her face with her hands. "I mean, how does that happen? I drove to our old house, instead of here. We haven't lived there for three months, Paul."

He slumped, as though relaxing in relief. "That's all?" he asked. "Natalie, that could happen to anyone. You were just distracted. It was only muscle memory."

"But I got out," she protested. "I walked to the front door with Oliver. I had my keys out. The woman who lives there now, she opened the door. She was scared. She was scared of me." Natalie rubbed her hands over her face. Oliver began to cry in earnest.

"Let me," Paul said. He stood and extracted the baby from the seat.

"I forgot my son's appointment. I forgot where I live. I forgot to do something for work, did you know that? My firm was disappointed in me. I was a liability. I was a more serious mistake waiting to happen. Before I left, I forgot to close my privacy curtain while I was pumping. My boss saw my breasts, Paul. I forget everything. I forget my wallet. I forget what I've done and where I've gone. I broke into my own house." She began to laugh, then. It was rather unsettling.

"You're too hard on yourself," he said. He stepped closer to her and placed a hand on her shoulder, solid and reassuring. He wanted her to become accustomed to his touch. He wanted her to think nothing of touching him back. "You should be kinder to yourself, Natalie. What you're doing is so hard. It's the hardest job there is."

"Other people do this," she said. "You did this. People do this all the time. Other people are able to do other things while they take care of their babies. They keep working."

"But every baby is different. Oliver is very difficult. But he will grow out of it. I bet that when he's a toddler, he'll sleep like a champ. He'll potty train easily. It won't be like this forever."

His phone rang again, vibrating on the table in front of them. Erin.

"Sorry," he said. "This is my wife." He rolled his eyes. "Let me just make sure everything is okay."

She looked embarrassed, then, for crying at his kitchen table while his wife was at work.

"Hey, can you pick up my prescription?" Erin said when he answered.

"Sure," he replied. "I'll get it before I pick up Petra."

Of course. Her antidepressants. She'd been taking them for years, though not as long as she should have been. She'd probably needed them after Petra's birth. She'd been suffering from something, too, he suspected, like Natalie. Her indifference toward baby Petra, her temper, her general apathy. He'd not considered that it might be postpartum depression until much, much later. Even then, he still maintained the belief that his wife simply wasn't a good mother.

"Great." He could tell she was about to hang up. Message delivered. She could have just texted such a short message, but she always preferred to call. Perhaps it was ingrained in her, from the way she had been trained to treat her clients. Phone calls made for better client service than written communications, which could be easily misinterpreted.

"How's it going?" he asked.

There was a pause. "Fine," she said. He didn't usually ask her that. She didn't return the question.

"Our neighbor just stopped by again," he told her anyway, his eyes on Natalie. "With her baby. I know you've been looking forward to meeting her."

Erin was silent. *No, I haven't.* He could tell that's what she wanted to say. But she was too polite.

"Alright," he continued, "I'll let you go."

He hung up the phone, hoping it had been enough for questions to begin forming in Erin's mind. A young woman, alone with her husband. *Again.*

She never knew about Lara, but she knew about Kristie Larsen. About Kristie's allegations. Erin would not like this. Not at all.

Paul returned his phone to the table.

"I should go," Natalie said. "I need to feed Oliver."

"I'll walk you out," he said quickly.

"You don't have to do that," she replied. She held her tea mug uncertainly.

"Leave that," he told her, as he tucked Oliver back into the car seat. "I'll get that later. And I know I don't have to. I want to." He looked up, met her eyes, watched the blush creep along her cheeks.

He carried the car seat to the car for her and clicked it into the base in the backseat. He remembered how to do it, still felt like it was just yesterday that he'd been slipping Petra into her own car seat.

Natalie stood nervously beside her car. "Thank you," she said.

He wasn't sure what she was thanking him for—carrying the car seat, the tea, or his words. He stepped toward her and pulled her against him again. She wasn't that much shorter than he was, but he rested his cheek on the top of her head for a second. Her breasts were pressed against his body. She was much taller, much softer, than Erin, than his usual type. He had always preferred petite women, but he could feel a stirring of attraction while he held her. He tried to tamp it down. It would only get in the way of what he needed to do, and he had to remain focused on that. He turned his thoughts to the baby wraps he'd swiped from her kitchen counter after she'd left him alone in her house. He'd found a gallon-sized Ziploc bag in her pantry and had tucked the wrap she had used inside.

He'd concealed the closed bag, along with the other wrap, beneath his windbreaker before leaving the house. After returning home, he'd hidden the wraps in a duffel bag on the top shelf of his closet before returning to the first floor to begin washing and chopping vegetables for that night's dinner. It had been too easy. He hoped that continued.

They broke apart, and he gripped her upper arms. "You're doing *great*," he told her.

She nodded once, smiled wryly. *You're kind, but you're a liar,* it seemed to say.

She slid into her car, and he waved her off.

He'd not been lying. She was doing great. She was doing exactly what he needed her to do.

TWENTY-FIVE

It was automatic, a foregone conclusion, that we'd spend the day together. The weekend had been excruciatingly slow, needlessly long, without him. Finally, Monday had arrived, and there he'd been, on my porch.

"I wanted to see how you're doing," he told me, the worry clear on his face. He cared about me.

I'd invited him inside, into the family room at the back of the house.

"I'm okay," I'd told him. I supposed that was the truth.

"Petra is on a school trip until Wednesday," Paul had said as we moved down the hall. "She's in New York. I'm lost without her."

So, I'd let him borrow my child for much of the day. How kind of me. How generous. He had held Oliver for hours, passing him back to me only when it was time for him to nurse, which I had done in Paul's presence without a second thought, as though he were my husband. He had even changed Oliver twice, which perhaps should have given me pause. But what could I say? I trusted him immensely. I trusted him with my baby. I trusted him more than I trusted myself.

Tuesday, it was, by unspoken rule, my turn to appear on his porch. I held off until the afternoon, hopeful, despite the unspoken rule, that he would be unable to stay away, from me, from Oliver. That I'd find him on my front steps in the morning. But it was past one, and he hadn't shown up, and it turned out I was the one who couldn't stay away. I packed Oliver into his stroller and pushed up Ashby Drive. Petra was still in New York with her classmates until Wednesday evening. Erin was at work. I rang the doorbell then stepped back and waited, jiggling Oliver's stroller.

Paul opened the door within seconds, like he'd been standing just inside, waiting for us. Instead of stepping to the side to let me into the house, he hurried out and extracted Oliver from his stroller.

"There he is," he exclaimed, as though he'd not seen Oliver for weeks, when it had been less than twenty-four hours. I might have been offended that he didn't seem nearly as excited to see me, but I wasn't.

I followed him into the living room, tidy as ever, with artfully draped throw blankets, carefully placed candles, their wax-covered wicks still cream-colored and intact, and abundant coasters resting on corners of end tables that were shiny and free from water marks or coffee rings.

The Rileys' house was certainly pristine, though I didn't know whose doing this was, Erin or Paul. It was hard to imagine keeping my own house so neat. Maybe it would be easy with a ten-year-old like Petra. I'd not yet met her. When I visited the house, she was always at the expensive private school to which Paul and Erin sent her, despite that the local public schools were some of the best in the state, even the country. But there were pictures of her all over the house. Photographs in frames on the mantel, bookshelves, and tables. Petra at her piano recital, in her soccer uniform. Baby Petra asleep in Erin's arms. Toddler Petra with red, patent leather shoes. There was a canvas print hanging on the wall in the living room—a seemingly recent portrait, Petra standing in front of one of the local lakes.

Paul's laptop was open, resting on the dining room table, its screen dark.

I froze, suddenly self-conscious about my uninvited presence.

"I'm sorry, am I keeping you from your writing?" I asked.

"No, no." Paul brushed me off quickly. "Not at all." He didn't elaborate, and I didn't ask him to.

I moved to his sofa, sank onto it. Immediately, I felt a rush of something warm. My period, returning already? I shifted uncomfortably. The last thing I needed was to bleed on his sofa.

"Could I use your bathroom?" I asked.

"Sure," said Paul. He pointed to the hall, then snapped his fingers. "Actually, I forgot. There's something wrong with the toilet down here. I need to call a plumber." He removed his hand from Oliver's back to rake it through his hair.

"I'm sorry," I said, hesitating in the doorway.

"You can go upstairs. There's a hall bath up there."

"Thanks," I said, turning toward the foyer, then climbing the stairs to the second floor of the house.

It was uncharted territory for me. I had never been upstairs.

The hall bath clearly belonged to Petra. Fluffy pink mats dotted the floor. The walls were lavender, and the shower curtain was printed with neon butterflies.

I kept walking. Past Petra's bedroom, which was similarly outfitted in stereotypically girly fashion. I don't know why, but I'd expected more sophisticated taste out of Petra. I stepped past a generic guest bedroom. Past an office with cherrywood and an L-shaped desk and cream-colored executive chair. At the end of the hall were double doors standing open. They led to the master suite.

It was filled with a large sleigh bed, two dressers, matching nightstands. The bed was neatly made with a white-and-cobalt-striped comforter. Complementary area rugs rested on the hardwood floors on each side of the bed. Something soft in which to dig her toes after a peaceful night of sleep. A rose-gold eye mask was resting on one of the nightstands. Erin's nightstand. Beside it was a squat glass, only a few fingers of water remaining, lipstick staining its rim. Did she sleep in it, too, I wondered, reapplying before she slipped into bed?

I moved into the bathroom. It was nice enough, but not as updated as my own. The tile wasn't as modern, the vanity and color scheme dark instead of the whites and grays currently favored. I stood in front of Erin's sink. There were expensive-looking glass bottles and jars lined up along the edge of the vanity, where the granite met the wall. Anti-wrinkle cream, serums, perfumes.

I paused, closed my eyes, shutting down one sense in an effort to strengthen another. I heard nothing. Oliver wasn't crying. I felt peace—no cortisol coursing through my veins. I wasn't straining for any indication that Oliver was awake, that he needed me. He was in capable hands. He was safe and calm. And that meant I was free. When was the last time I'd bothered with my own anti-wrinkle cream? My pregnancy- and nursing-safe skin serums? When had I last plucked my eyebrows? No wonder Erin had these things. She had the time, the ability, to use them. And while she was working full-time, providing for her family, too. I had no idea what that must feel like, but I ached for it. I longed for it like it was something I had lost, instead of something I'd never had.

I leaned toward the mirror, grimaced. I located a pair of tweezers in the top drawer and got to work. Although I recalled purchasing a new pair for myself during the debacle that was my last trip to Target, I'd never bothered to use them. I lifted each of Erin's face creams and inspected the ingredients.

I used Erin's toilet, examining my underwear, which were slightly wet, but not filled with blood. It hadn't been my period, after all, likely just a gush of urine, set free by the weakened muscles of my pelvic floor. They sometimes failed me that way. When I sneezed. When I laughed too hard, as though wetting myself were punishment for enjoying a moment of mirth.

I washed my hands with Erin's organic Mrs. Meyer's soap, and dried them on her plush burgundy towel, odors of lemon and olive oil wafting from my skin. Without thinking, I unscrewed the lid of a jar of face cream and smoothed some onto my neck and jawline.

Immediately, I was horrified. I was supposed to be using the hall bath, and here I was, helping myself to Erin's things. When I returned, Paul might notice that I smelled like Erin.

I dampened a tissue and wiped at my skin vigorously until redness bloomed.

Downstairs, Paul was still walking the living room floor with Oliver in his arms. He said nothing about my extended absence, nor my freshly groomed eyebrows. He didn't tell me that I smelled like his wife. He said nothing at all.

We settled into what had become our usual routine. He rocked and spun his way around the room, Oliver in his arms, occasionally mentioning how comfortable, natural, it felt to be holding a baby again, while I sat on the sofa nearby, melting into it, allowing myself to experience the crushing exhaustion I always seemed to be fighting. We chatted, idly, companionably, our words ebbing and flowing, about our lives before our children, and how they changed.

Our eyes met, our bodies stiffened, when we heard the garage door creaking upward, a car door slamming, then the squeak of a door being pushed open. Someone was home. Erin, of course. This was not part of the routine. Not at all.

She emerged from the hall, strode into the living room. Her living room. She wasn't surprised to see me. Perhaps she'd noticed my stroller parked out front.

It was the first time I'd seen her in person, despite that I'd spent hours in her home. Her hair was thick and golden brown, brushing her clavicle, left exposed by her emerald-colored, boatneck sweater. Her lips were a slash of crimson.

"You must be Natalie, our new neighbor," she said after we'd all stared at each other in awkward surprise. She stood in between the living and dining rooms, her thin arms crossed in front of her flat chest. "I've heard so much about you. And baby Oliver." She peeked at him, at his little face resting against her husband's shoulder. Was she remembering when her own child had been that young and small and fragile? Was she marveling at her husband's almost uncanny way with infants? "He's precious," she said.

"Nat," said Paul, stepping in. "This is my wife, Erin."

Her mouth formed a thin line, as did mine, only for a second, while I wondered why he had called me Nat. Usually, always, I was *Natalie*.

"It's so nice to meet you," I said. "Your home is beautiful."

I felt anxious, socially inept. What to say next? Would she ask me what I was doing here in her house, with her husband, in the middle of the afternoon? It would be a reasonable question, but I wasn't sure of the answer.

But Erin said nothing more. She took a handful of steps, to a credenza pressed against the back wall of the dining room. She popped the stopper from the mouth of a half-empty bottle of red wine and poured a serving into one of two glasses perched on a tray nearby.

"Can I offer you a glass, Natalie?" she asked after she took a sip. Red wine stained the side of the glass. Her lipstick left behind a half-moon of color.

"Oh, no," I said. "I can't. Thank you, though."

She nodded, moved across the room to stand beside her husband.

In her presence, I felt bovine-esque, milky, and soft, as compared to her birdlike petiteness, her delicate wrists, her narrow hips and child-sized hands, the way she moved, sharply, with efficient elegance.

"I remember those days," she said. She took another sip and her breath fogged the inside of her glass for a second. "Tell me," she said, taking another step closer to Paul, "how are you settling into the neighborhood?"

"It's been very nice," I said. "It's a lovely place to raise a family." A canned response. Would I ever mean it?

"Have you spent time with many of the neighbors, or is my husband the only one fortunate enough to benefit from your visits?"

With the right tone, it might have been a charming comment. But hers was tinged with sarcasm, like a paper with blackened edges, burning from the outside in.

"Um, I've met a few people," I said, not sure if it was technically the truth. I had met a few people, in passing. Mrs. Jensen. The retired couple who lived two houses away. The family across from the Rileys whose grown children and grandchildren always seemed to be visiting. I knew there was a family with two teenaged boys, perhaps twins, who lived next door to me. They had four cars, and I could always tell when it was the teenagers or their friends coming to or leaving the house. Their engines roared, their speed was always a little too fast. On the other side was a middle-aged woman, who lived alone. She seemed to work long hours. I'd seen her checking the mail, dressed professionally, moving stiffly like a person who'd spent a long and sedentary day behind a desk. We always waved to each other, but had never said more than hello. Paul was the only person with whom I'd become friendly. He was the only person I'd cared to get to know more, with whom I wanted to exchange more than just distracted waves in passing.

"Well, you've not yet been to the annual block party," Erin continued. "You'll get to know people better there."

"That's right," said Paul, snapping. "Have you heard about that, Nat?"

Nat. I shook my head.

"It's the Saturday before Halloween every year, in the afternoon," he continued. "The kids can dress up. The adults, too, if they want. People take turns hosting it. This year, it's our turn. We'll have it out back."

"Sounds nice," I replied. It didn't.

"And motherhood?" Erin asked. "How's that been for you, Natalie?"

My heart began to pound. It shouldn't be a terribly personal question, but for me it was. Admittedly, though, it was my answer that made it so personal. If my response was "It's amazing, perfect, beautiful," well, that could be shared with anyone. And coming from her, with her icicle-sharp demeanor, it felt like an accusation.

"It's been difficult," I admitted. "He's not much of a sleeper." I nodded toward my son, still cradled against Paul's chest, asleep and angelic, as if proving me a liar.

"I understand," Erin said. She smiled, revealing teeth stained burgundy with her afternoon wine. "Fortunately, I had Paul. He took more of the overnight shifts than I did."

I smiled back and nodded, and an uncomfortable silence fell over us. Paul didn't step in to remedy it, so I pushed myself up from the sofa. "Well," I said, "I'd better get home. Time to nurse him, put him down," I added.

"Right," Erin said, already moving to the door to show me out. "Nice of you to stop by." The sarcasm wasn't veiled this time, wasn't hinted at. She might as well have slapped me across the face with it.

"And so nice to finally meet you," I murmured as I held out my arms to accept my baby from Paul. Our eyes locked and our fingers touched. Why was she here? What did she want? It was her house, yet it felt like she was the intruder.

Erin held the front door open for me, waiting for me to move through it. Her over-plucked brows were drawn low. She didn't say goodbye. She didn't smile or wave.

I glanced back at her. She hadn't closed the door yet. Our eyes met.

"Bye, Natalie," she said, her tone pleasant. But then, she slammed the door. The dead bolt flipped into place.

It felt like a clear admonishment. *You're not welcome here.*

I slipped Oliver into the stroller a little too roughly. He started to cry. Gripping the handlebars tightly, I pushed it hurriedly down the hill, back to my house.

Yes, I am, I thought wildly. *I am welcome.* I needed Paul's comforting words. The competent hands with which he held my son. She wouldn't take that from me.

TWENTY-SIX

My house was safer than his, after his wife had surprised us the previous afternoon.

What if I'd been nursing Oliver, when she'd come in, I'd wondered later? What would she have thought if I'd been sitting on her sofa, in her house, with her husband, my breast on display?

I was relieved, then, to find him on my porch. There was a thick, black picture frame dangling from his right hand.

"Oh," I'd remarked in surprise and pleasure as he held the frame aloft, smiling.

"Any interest?" he asked, tilting the frame so that I could see the picture inside, while I held Oliver over my shoulder and swayed back and forth. "This was hanging in Petra's nursery," he continued. "I figured it should be put to use, rather than just collect dust in my basement."

It was nothing like the pastel cartoon jungle animals, the swirling, kitschy word art, that currently adorned Oliver's walls. This was an oil painting, realistic and raw, still wet-looking, but almost photographic in its accuracy.

"It's beautiful," I said. "I love it." But as with the charcoal baby wrap, something felt wrong about accepting a gift from Paul. "You don't want to hang it somewhere else in your house? It wouldn't have to hang in a nursery." It certainly didn't look like typical nursery artwork.

"Oh no," Paul replied. "Erin was never fond of it. She couldn't wait to take it down when Petra moved into her big-girl room. Like I said, it's been relegated to the storage room in our basement for years.

"I'll be happy to hang it for you," he continued cautiously, as I ushered him into the house. "Only if you want to hang it, of course. No pressure."

"That would be wonderful," I said. "Thank you."

We trailed into the family room, a hundred times messier than Paul's own. I didn't mind it. He didn't make me feel self-conscious about such trivial things.

"Should I hold him for a bit first?" he asked hopefully.

"Mind if I do a few things while you do?" I asked.

"Not at all."

I passed Oliver to him, then went into the kitchen. I swallowed a Midol and unloaded the dishwasher before returning to the family room, sinking onto the sofa beside him. For a moment, I felt light, almost happy. My phone vibrated from within my sweatshirt pocket. I slipped it out, entered my PIN, and read the message.

Everything okay?

Tyler.

I locked the screen without responding, tossing the phone onto the cushion beside me.

"You seem happier," Tyler had told me last night, while we sat on the sofa in the darkened family room, Oliver dozing in his swing.

The venom, immediate and strong, that had rushed to my surface, like blood to a cut, was astonishing. Ashamed, I pushed it back, stanched the flow, as if with a paper towel.

"Trust me," I said. "I'm not happy."

In that moment, I'd been seething, still, over being made to feel so unwelcome in Paul's house, by Erin. Tyler had been home late. Oliver had screamed virtually nonstop the rest of the afternoon, until exhausting himself and finally going to sleep in his swing. How could Tyler have thought that I seemed happy?

My husband's face, so plump with rest and collagen and extra weight, fell only slightly, only for a second, until the recollection that he'd been made partner, that he had everything he wanted, returned the sparkle to his eyes, the uptick to his lips.

"Why?" he asked. He reached toward me, grasped my hands. "What can I do?"

"There's nothing you can do," I said. "He only wants me all night." That was the truth, and it didn't need saying, but I said it anyway because it hurt Tyler, much like the way he'd hurt me by making partner in the face of the abrupt demise of my own career.

"He's too dependent on nursing," Tyler said. He extracted his hands from mine, pulled them back to his lap.

"No shit," I said.

"We need to teach him to be soothed in other ways," Tyler continued, ignoring my blatant animosity. "If he could be soothed in other ways, I could help you at night."

It was a conversation we'd had many times before, never to any avail, and I was exhausted of it. "We can't teach him, Tyler. We can't teach him anything. He's a baby. He's too little to be trained."

I said it, but I still didn't know if it was true. Clearly, Oliver had learned that if he cried and cried, he would, eventually, be offered my breasts. Could he unlearn that lesson, too? But, at what cost? Would he feel abandoned? Unloved? Would I ruin him? Break him? These were my greatest fears. They were ridiculous and extreme, but what if they weren't? It was that little hint, that tiny *what if* that pushed me harder than I could stand to be pushed.

"We can try," Tyler was saying. "We can try to teach him."

I'd ignored him, stared at the television screen. My eyes began to cross, the images blurred and doubled.

"Maybe," Tyler continued, "it's time to stop nursing him. You've been doing so well. But if it's killing you to stay up breastfeeding him every night, is that really what's best for him?"

"Tyler," I said, appalled. I continued to stare at the bright and flickering screen. I couldn't bear to look at him.

"I know," he said quietly. "I know." Soothing, sympathetic. But he didn't know. Not really.

"Why does it matter if I'm so tired?" I asked. "This is why I stopped working. There's nothing to sleep for."

"For your health," Tyler said. "You need to sleep for your health."

I tilted my head toward Oliver. "Well, I have to stay up for his."

"Everything okay?" Paul asked, eyeing my discarded device.

I laughed, though it made me sound crazy, not amused. "Not really."

"Want to talk about it?" he asked.

I looked at him. We were so close that we could have kissed. But I didn't want to. I longed for him to hold me, but it wasn't a sexual longing. I couldn't have had a sexual thought if I tried, at that point, and I certainly didn't want to try—it would conjure only thoughts of that sharp and reflective Wusthof, of slicing pain and parched skin, sucked dry of all moisture by the breastfeeding. This was a different sort of longing entirely. In this moment, I hated Tyler for being nothing like Paul. For being partner. For sleeping. For burdening me with more than my fair share of responsibility for keeping our child alive and making him happy. For burdening me with his feelings. For failing to take notice of how disquieting my own had become.

Meanwhile, Paul was comfort. He took nothing from me, only gave. He was relief and hope.

There was so much I could have told him. That I was so tired, I was scaring myself. That my memory still refused to hold on to much of anything. That I loved my baby with a fierceness that almost felt deadly. But, despite the love, there was despondency wavering just below my surface.

I didn't want to talk about any of it. For once, I wanted to forget.

"I just want to rest," I told him. "To relax. To feel like I'm going to be okay."

He watched me in silence for a few seconds, then he stood. He cradled Oliver with one arm, then held his other hand toward me.

"So, rest," he said. "Right now. Show me where you want me to hang this picture, then lie down. I'll take care of him."

"No," I protested immediately. "I couldn't."

"You can. You need to." He stretched his hand even closer.

I reached up, and I took it. I let him lead me upstairs, to the nursery, where we surveyed the open wall space.

"You know what?" I said. "Let's replace that picture with the one you brought." I pointed to the cartoon giraffe, pastel, almost patronizing.

"You got it. Now, go lie down."

I hesitated in the doorway. "But how will you watch him while you hang it?"

"I'll put him to sleep, lay him down for a nap."

"Oh, no." I laughed. "Oliver doesn't nap in his crib. He only naps in his swing, or while he's being held."

But Paul only smiled at me, patiently. "I'll see what I can do."

"Do you have somewhere you need to be?" I asked. "What if I fall asleep?"

"Natalie, that's the whole point. Don't worry about it. I've got nothing but time."

I hesitated a second longer, but then I did as he said. I left.

Maybe his firmness, his demands that I take care of myself, should have bothered me. They were so direct, so much more than the vague suggestions offered by my husband. Who was he to tell me what to do? Except, it was exactly what I needed. It was what Tyler should have done. It was what Tyler never did.

TWENTY-SEVEN

Once Oliver was deeply asleep, Paul laid him down gently atop the crib mattress. The baby stirred slightly, surprised by the abrupt lack of warmth and movement, but Paul leaned over the side of the crib and patted Oliver gently on the tummy until he slipped back into slumber. It truly wasn't that difficult—he couldn't see what Natalie found so impossible about putting her baby to sleep. He suspected the issue was that she was so insecure, so anxious all the time. She feared nothing more than being a bad mother, being incompetent. Babies were so intuitive. They drank that anxiety up. They needed a calm and confident presence. He'd always been that.

He moved quietly out of the room. The door to the master bedroom was closed over, but not all the way. He knew she wasn't really resting. She was lying there, her body tense, straining for the sound of her baby crying out for her.

He descended the stairs silently. The picture was still propped against the wall in the foyer. He moved past it, into the family room. He felt lucky to find that her phone was still resting on the sofa, partially concealed within the crack between two cushions. He slipped it out and entered her PIN.

He had watched her type the numbers in, slowly, stolidly, the way she did everything. Had she been faster, had she used biometrics to get into the phone, he wouldn't be able to do this. But she hadn't.

He added himself as a contact, only his first name—*Paul*. They had never exchanged numbers, had only been walking to each other's houses. He fired off a string of messages, from her phone, to his.

I need to see you.
Please.

Please don't ignore me.
I need you.
I'm coming up there.

His own phone was in his pocket, but he figured that was okay. His location data was turned off—it always was; he didn't need Erin knowing his whereabouts all the time. If the police reviewed phone location records, if it got to that point, they wouldn't be able to determine that his phone was in her house, not his own. Either way, their signals would be bouncing off the same tower. When he got home, he'd open the messages on his own phone, then block her number. That would explain why they were the only ones.

He deleted from her phone the texts he had just sent, then returned it to the sofa. He retrieved the painting from the foyer and carried it up the stairs. Oliver was still asleep in his crib, his features slack and relaxed, his left arm thrown upward in bliss. As quietly as he could, Paul stretched to remove the giraffe picture from the wall and replace it with the one he'd brought.

When he'd told Natalie that Erin had always hated the painting—it was too lurid, she'd said, too graphic—he'd been telling the truth. It had been collecting dust in the basement ever since Petra had moved into her big-girl bedroom, not that he'd cared. Bringing the picture had only been an excuse to see Natalie. To make it seem as though he was doing her a favor.

He knew that he shouldn't be seen walking to her house anymore. He knew that from now on, it was better that she be seen coming to him. He no longer wanted the neighbors to think they were having an affair, that their relationship was mutual. That wouldn't help him. His attraction toward her had been pushed aside, hidden away, by his purpose, his plan.

Now, he needed people to believe that Natalie was obsessed with him. That she was getting too close. That her affection was unwelcome, that he'd enjoyed her, and her baby, at first, but her attention had begun to make him uncomfortable. She wouldn't leave him alone.

When the body was found, all eyes would be on him. That was inevitable.

But, with his careful planning, with the evidence he was creating, it wouldn't stay that way for long. Suspicion would shift.

Paul stepped back, admired the way the painting looked hanging against the cool, green wall, admired the way Oliver was still asleep in the crib, despite the noise he'd made hanging the artwork.

For a second, he felt bad for Oliver. He'd lose his mother. It didn't seem fair. But his mother was a mess, and he would still have his father, just the way Petra had, in a way, only ever had Paul. Oliver would be fine.

He only needed one more piece to click into place. It was almost time.

Part III

THE VICTIM & THE MURDERER

TWENTY-EIGHT

"Is everyone coming this year?" Erin asked as she shook a bag of chips into a basket and placed it onto one of the card tables lined up on their deck. She stepped back and surveyed the area, as though admiring her work, as if emptying a single bag of chips into a basket hadn't been her only contribution.

Paul had bought Halloween tablecloths and napkins, faux spiderwebs, orange twinkle lights. He had purchased all of the food—snacks, and finger foods only. This was the tradition of the party. It was meant to be informal and relaxed, to take place outdoors, weather permitting. It wasn't a full dinner party, even though, every year, someone brought something that required plates and utensils, something that the host was ill-equipped to serve.

There were coolers brimming with ice, cans of sparkling cider, beer, and bottles of wine. Traditionally, neighbors brought their beverage of choice to the party, but Erin had told Paul to buy some options, not complaining once about the cost. In fact, she hadn't complained at all about the expense associated with hosting the party, although she'd continued to complain about every other purchase he made, including the groceries he bought to feed the family every week (*Must you get everything organic?* she had asked on Thursday, while inspecting the crumpled receipt that he'd neglected to toss into the recycling bin.)

This was because while Erin wouldn't allow Paul to forget their financial struggles for a single second, she'd do whatever she could to hide them from the neighbors. Of course, some of them used her for their financial planning needs. It was possible they had seen the negative reviews that disgruntled client had posted over the past year.

Erin had made a poor investment choice for the man. It happened. But he'd felt that she didn't listen to him. He'd been close to retirement age, and she'd been aggressive when he'd asked for caution. He had lost quite a bit of money, retirement had been postponed, so he'd fired her and left a slew of extremely unflattering reviews all over the web.

Erin had contacted the websites, asked them to take the reviews down, but with no success. He was a bona fide client. The reviews were cruel, but they weren't technically untrue.

Other clients had left since. New clients had been more difficult to find. The result had been a steady decline in her income—their family's income—over the past year. The result had been Erin, whose career was everything to her, who had sacrificed so much more than she should have for said career, who was already prone to being rather serious and prickly, becoming fairly unbearable to be around. The result had been Erin threatening to pull Petra from her private school, trying to force Paul to get a *real job,* demanding information about the progress of his novel—a novel that still didn't exist.

"I think so," said Paul, in response to her question. "Not the Wilsons. Their sons have soccer games. But most everyone else should be here."

Petra darted into the backyard then, as though shot from a cannon. Her costume, a unicorn outfit, had apparently given her new energy and vigor. A swirling rainbow horn was held to her forehead with an elastic band.

"People should be here soon," she said excitedly. "Are we ready, Daddy?"

That she'd directed the question to him alone filled him with a jolt of pleasure. He looked around with animation. Petra had helped him arrange the games for the children that morning—hanging a jack-o'-lantern piñata, setting up the pin-the-tail-on-the-black-cat poster board, hiding Halloween-themed favors around the yard for the kids to find.

"I think so," he told her. He held out his arms and she launched into them. "You look wonderful."

He snapped his fingers after he'd released his daughter. "You know what," he said. "I think Mommy needs something, doesn't she?"

They both looked at Erin. She wore a black sweater and ankle pants, leopard-printed flats on her feet. She looked like she had just returned from the office. In fact, she had gone into the office that morning, even though it was Saturday. To her credit, she was trying to work her way out of their financial downturn.

"Yes, Mommy," Petra said. "You need a costume."

Paul had gamely donned his khaki vest and wide-brimmed safari hat. He wore the same half-hearted costume every year.

"I'm a leopard," Erin said, lifting her left foot and wiggling it to show off her printed shoes.

"More like a panther with leopard paws." Petra was laughing.

"I got Mommy something," Paul said. "It's in our bedroom, on the dresser. Go and grab it for us, will you, darling?"

Petra blinked at him for a second, then sprinted back inside.

Erin turned her displeased expression upon him. She hadn't noticed that her red lipstick—she might as well have it tattooed on, he sometimes thought—was bleeding into the skin around her lips. He hated when that happened. It almost made him feel bad for her.

"You know," he said. "I think the new neighbors are coming. Natalie and her husband, with the baby."

"You think?" She crossed her arms around herself, even though it was an unseasonably warm afternoon.

"She told me they were stopping by."

Erin watched him. "She still been inviting herself over?" she asked. "Inviting herself in when I'm not home?"

He rubbed a hand over his face. "Yes, she has." He sighed, gazed toward the tree line at the back of their yard.

"What?" Erin asked. She pulled her arms tighter.

"There's just something about her that makes me uncomfortable," he said, as though grudgingly. "She seems a little—I don't know—obsessed with me."

Erin's mouth tightened.

"It wouldn't be the first time that's happened," he reminded her. "That's why it makes me so nervous. That's why it makes me nervous to tell her to go away, to leave me alone. I'm afraid what she might do if I embarrass her like that. That's what got me into trouble before."

Erin didn't agree, but she tilted her head, seeming to indicate acknowledgment.

He was referring, of course, to the reason he'd resigned from his job ten years ago. He could barely see her face clearly anymore, the student, but he would never forget her name. Kristie Larsen had been a freshman in his American Literature course. She was a young freshman, though.

She'd skipped a few grades, and everyone knew this. Being a young college student didn't make her a prodigy or enviable in the eyes of the other students, who were fairly cruel. She wouldn't be able to get into a bar, or purchase alcohol. She was of little use to them.

Kristie had taken a liking to Paul. Every day during office hours, there she was. She'd invite herself in and sit in the guest chair closest to his desk. She was well read and intelligent. He'd enjoyed her company, had thought nothing of her frequent presence. He'd believed that she only needed a friend, someone to talk to, because she was too bright, too young, for her classmates.

He didn't find her attractive. She was a big-boned young woman—she was still a girl, really—with hair that frizzed around her face. He wondered what might have been different if she'd been delicate and pretty and more his type.

But, she wasn't, and so the day she'd practically launched herself at him, planting a kiss that had landed somewhere near, but not on, his mouth, he'd grabbed her arms firmly and pushed her away. "No," he'd said, as if she were a jumping dog.

She had left his office in tears.

She had run directly to the dean. She had reported him.

As it turned out, there'd been rumors swirling around the campus. Rumors he had not heard. Other students had noticed all the time Kristie had been spending in Paul's office. They didn't like Kristie, and it was so salacious, so fun, to talk about the fact that she was having an affair with Professor Riley. Never mind that she wasn't. Never mind what those rumors did to him, to his family.

Kristie's report to the dean had been like gasoline on the rumors. They had exploded through the campus.

Paul had pleaded his innocence. He'd told the dean that she had been the one to make an advance. But with the young woman's report, and those rumors, the damage was done.

"Alright, Paul," the dean had said, sounding exhausted. "Just resign, and we'll put this to bed."

He had told Erin everything, the entire truth. Things were still okay between them, back then. She'd been pregnant, but not quite so bitter as she became once Petra was born. They had decided that the best option, the only option, was for him to resign.

They'd moved out to the suburbs and decided that Erin, whose career was taking off, would take a short maternity leave, that Paul would be the one to stay home with the baby. He'd finally write that novel he had always wanted to write. If it didn't work out, he would go back to work eventually.

It didn't work out, but he never had wanted to go back to work. His life became so full once Petra was born. So fulfilling and happy. Erin was, she always had been, a cancer to that.

Natalie wasn't like Kristie. Not really. But if he could make it seem like she was—

"Just, keep an eye on her for me, would you?" he asked his wife. "I'll try to keep my distance but, well, I tried back then, too. And look where that left me."

Erin met his eyes, nodded once. There wasn't much she would do for him anymore, but she would do this. What had happened with Kristie had hurt her, too.

"I have to say," she said knowingly, in that superior way she often spoke, her nose tipped upward, "this was my fear, when I came home and found her in our house, making herself at home. Making herself too comfortable. I swear to God, she smelled like my face cream. She'd been in my bedroom, in my bathroom, I could tell." She squinted at him. "There's something off about her."

He scratched at his cheek. "Really," he said, but he already knew this. He'd smelled it, too.

At that moment, Petra flew into the yard, carrying a pair of cat ears attached to a headband. Paul had purchased it from the party supply store when he'd bought everything else, somehow knowing it would work with whatever his wife chose to wear.

"Here you go, Mommy," she said.

Erin stared at the headband with disdain for several beats. She looked like she might swat it out of her daughter's hand.

But then, to his surprise, she took it. She tucked her hair behind her ears, then slipped the band over her head. "Let's get this party started."

TWENTY-NINE

Oliver was dressed like a lion. I'd put the costume on him at the last possible minute, knowing he would hate it. I had been correct. He was flailing and screeching in my arms.

Tyler stood in the living room, peering out the window. He'd been watching the other neighbors spill from their houses and make their way to the Rileys'.

"We should go," he said. "I know you wanted to go late, to just stop by, but it started over an hour ago. We'll miss the whole thing."

Tyler was happy to go to the party. I knew exactly why.

"So nice to meet you. And what do you do?" the neighbors would ask him politely.

"Oh, I'm a partner at a law firm," he'd reply with cavalier modesty.

I didn't want to go to the party. (*And, what do you do, Natalie? Oh, I'm a stay-at-home mother.*) I could get away with saying I was a lawyer, too. That I was taking a little time off. That I was taking a sabbatical to spend more time with my baby. I knew such a response would make me feel like a wolf in sheep's clothing.

And I didn't want strangers peering into Oliver's face, breathing their germ-infested breath into his perfect little nose, his underdeveloped immune system. Besides, I'd forgotten how to socialize. I didn't know what I could say and what I couldn't. Which remarks about raising a newborn might garner hilarity, nostalgia? Which would bring about shame, nervous chuckles, knowing glances exchanged above the rims of cups?

But I'd have one friend, one ally, at the party. I didn't want to offend him by not showing up—he knew I didn't have alternate plans. I imagined him collecting Oliver from my arms, literally taking him off my hands, carrying him around for the duration of the party as if Oliver was his own child, while I slumped in a lawn chair then melted into the grass in an invisible puddle of fatigue.

"Alright," I said, irritably, "let's get this over with."

Tyler eyed Oliver, still screaming in my arms. "Should we take the costume off? He doesn't seem to like it."

"He's fine," I said. No matter what we put him in, he'd cry. How did Tyler still not understand that? "Let's go."

I slipped Oliver into his stroller, then stepped aside for Tyler to take hold of the handlebars. He looked embarrassed as he pushed the stroller up the hill, as Oliver's cries echoed up and down the street.

The stroller bumped awkwardly over the grass as we entered the Rileys' backyard. People milled about, their voices too loud, their artificial laughter as unsettling as the cries of my baby.

The first person who met my eyes was Erin. She wore a black sweater and pants, her lips painted red, cat ears perched on her head. Instead of rushing forward to welcome me, to remark over how darling my baby looked in his costume, to offer me something to eat or drink, she watched me the length of two blinks, something resembling contempt flickering in her eyes, then sipped her red wine and continued chatting with another neighbor, whose name and address I did not know.

"This was a bad idea," I muttered to Tyler, who ignored me. He had his networking face on—the one he'd worn in our pre-baby days when we had attended bar association events together, events brimming with judges and lawyers, young and old, naïve and experienced.

Why did Erin hate me? She certainly seemed to. She seemed to hate me from the moment she found me sitting in her house with her husband. Perhaps she was mistrusting, nervous. Perhaps I should assure her that there was nothing to worry about. That Paul and I were only friends.

But that might only draw attention to our relationship, to our closeness. How many men befriended women a decade younger than them? Spent time together while their spouses were at work?

We had the truth on our side. We *were* only friends, strictly platonic, though I could see how it might appear otherwise from an outsider's perspective. That was not my problem, I reminded myself. That was hers.

I scanned the yard for Paul, spotted him on the deck with a child wearing a unicorn costume, whose hair had the same almond-colored silkiness as Erin's. The inimitable Petra, I presumed. I veered toward them, relief inflating my chest as I drew closer to him. Tyler followed me with the stroller.

I climbed the deck steps and met them in front of a card table loaded with snacks, abandoning Tyler below as he worked to extract Oliver from the stroller.

"This must be Petra," I said. "I've heard so much about you."

She smiled shyly, but politely, up at me.

Paul visibly stiffened. "Yes," he said woodenly. "This is Petra."

He placed his hands on her shoulders—almost protectively—then began to steer her away from me. He didn't tell her who I was.

"Petra, help me refill this basket," he said, reaching for a nearly full basket of chips resting on the table. "Excuse me," he muttered belatedly, as he disappeared into the house with his daughter.

Tyler arrived at my side, Oliver in his arms. "That Paul?" he asked as the sliding door closed behind them. Tyler, unlike Erin, didn't seem to harbor any suspicion. This was possibly, likely, because he was not aware of just how close Paul and I were, just how much time we'd spent together over the past month.

"Yes," I said, feeling slighted and stung. "That's Paul."

An older couple sidled up to us and introduced themselves. Martha and Bill. Their children were grown, long gone, and they were retired from the federal government. We exchanged pleasantries, and they moved on. A younger couple, perhaps our age, appeared as well. They lived at the corner of Ashby Drive, were childless, and worked in the tech industry, from home. They'd chosen the neighborhood for its peacefulness, for its spacious houses with abundant room to work from home. Their names were lost to me the moment they shared them. I was staring at the sliding door.

Paul reappeared. My eyes never left him, so I could tell that his were avoiding mine.

I glowered as the young couple wandered away, was replaced by another older couple, the one that lived across the street from the Rileys. They introduced themselves as Tom and Penny. The woman reminded me of smaller and friendlier Mrs. Jensen, who was also present, lurking nearby wearing a billowing muumuu.

Oliver began to cry again, and I reached for him automatically, began to sway and bounce, rubbing his back. He rooted at my breasts, even though I'd fed him just before we left. I looked for Paul again, noticed him standing in the grass below.

"Excuse me," I said, then descended the stairs. There was a shattered piñata hanging from the eaves of the deck, its guts littering the ground. I stepped over them.

My gaze found Paul's, but immediately he was in motion, brushing past me. I stood there alone, watching him stop at his wife's side. She'd been standing with the woman I recognized as my next-door neighbor, Linda, the woman with whom I'd only ever exchanged waves and hellos. Paul bent to whisper something to his wife, and she turned away from Linda, and toward me, the contempt still present in her eyes, now more boil than simmer.

I looked up, saw that Tyler was making his way down the stairs, too.

"Vijay Antin is a lawyer as well. Did you know that? They're a few houses up from us. IP law."

"No," I said. "I didn't." I didn't care, either. Tyler was beaming. He'd probably uttered the revered phrase—*I'm a partner at a law firm—Katz, Harris & Jones—have you heard of it?*—several times by now.

Oliver began to whine again as the Antins approached us.

"Your husband tells me you've done some intellectual property law as well," Vijay said, his eyes crinkling.

"Yes." My voice sounded far away. "Mostly licensing agreements."

He continued to prattle on, his words like some gibberish language spoken rapidly by a babbling toddler. My eyes seemed to cross. There were two of him standing before me. Oliver cried louder.

"Sorry," I interrupted him. "I need to walk him around a bit, try to get him to sleep."

I stepped around the Antins, leaving Tyler there to discuss riveting things like contract terms and commercial disputes—things I had, at one time, actually found riveting.

Again, I scanned the yard as I paced along its perimeter, looking for Paul. I located him on the opposite side, standing alone.

Perhaps I'd been imagining his coolness. Perhaps he was only acting like a host, ensuring that he was spreading his attention fairly, that his guests were taken care of. Still, I didn't understand. How could he treat me with such apathy?

I hurried across the yard toward him. He saw me approach, his face grim.

"Paul," I pleaded once I'd reached him. "Is something wrong?"

His mouth became a thin line. He didn't reply, only turned away, trying to brush past me.

I adjusted Oliver, pressing him against my chest with my right arm. My left shot out, grabbing onto Paul's. "Wait," I whispered.

"Don't touch him!"

The shrillness of the words, their high-pitched quality, caused them to rise above all the other sounds filling the yard, above the chatter and laughter and crunching of chips and click-swish as cans of soda and water and beer were opened.

Erin was hurtling toward me like a bowling ball, her red lips bared, her tiny fists clenched like the curling paws of an animal dead on the side of the road.

She stopped right before she reached me, but close enough that I could feel the heat of her breath, smell the sickening, wet-leathery scent of the red wine she'd drunk.

"Don't touch my husband," she whispered.

"I wasn't," I said faintly. "I didn't."

But my hand was still wrapped around Paul's arm. I dropped it to my side, wiped it on my pants, as though I could clean him from my skin.

Another hand landed on my shoulder. I looked up. Tyler.

"Let's go," he said.

I could feel all eyes on us as Tyler collected the stroller from the base of the deck stairs and pushed it over the grass. I clutched Oliver against my chest like a shield. As we left the yard, I noticed Mrs. Jensen standing beside an overweight and balding man who I assumed was her husband. She backed away from us like we were wasps.

Tyler was silent as we pushed onto the street, the only sound the creaking of the stroller wheels. Oliver had exhausted himself, finally put to sleep by the movement. My left hand was cupped over the back of his lion's mane.

Tyler didn't speak until we reached the garage doors of our house.

Something was burning, tingling on the back of my head. The stares of the neighbors, as they had watched us go. What must they have been thinking?

"What," Tyler hissed, "the *fuck* was that?"

He *never* cursed. He was livid. Not with Erin. With me. He expected the worst of me. He thought that this was my fault, that I'd done something.

"Why did she say that, Nat? Why did she tell you not to touch him? Why did you grab his arm like that?"

I stared at my husband. I could have lied. I didn't need to.

"I have no idea."

THIRTY

Don't touch him!

The party had wrapped up quickly after Erin's words had sliced through the air. Only a whisper, but it had quieted the crowd, drawn their eyes, more so even than a scream. Tension had rested brittlely over the group. Laughter had dissipated. Small talk had fizzled. The fun was very much over. It was time to go home.

What was that about? the neighbors had whispered to themselves as they trailed away from the Riley house.

Good. They were meant to wonder. This time, he wanted rumors to abound. He needed gossip to trickle amongst them like the rainwater running down to the gutters at the bottom of Ashby Drive.

He was just glad Petra hadn't noticed. The children had been oblivious to Erin's fury, busy with pin-the-tail-on-the-cat, organized and led by Petra, up on the deck. He'd known that's what they were doing, he'd known that Petra was otherwise occupied. That was the only reason he'd hissed into Erin's ear, let Natalie get as close as she did.

Of course, he hadn't known that Natalie would grab him. He hadn't known that Erin would storm toward her. Things had gone better than he'd ever imagined they would. He was shocked that Erin had lost control in the presence of the neighbors, that she had allowed her perfect veneer to slip. It showed him that the challenges with her business were taking more of a toll on her, mentally, than he had even realized.

"Thank you," Paul said as he slipped a tablecloth from a card table and folded it into a neat square. "Thank you for standing up for me."

Erin was leaning against the deck railing, finishing off her bottle of wine and watching him clean. She wasn't helping. She felt that not cleaning was her prerogative, as financial provider. "You need to be firmer with her, like I was," she said, as though her words to Natalie had been calculated, rather than an uncontrolled explosion.

"I know," he said. He collected a few empty cans from another table and tossed them into the recycling bin, which he'd rolled out back. "She just seems so vulnerable. I think she's having some postpartum issues. You know me." He smiled sheepishly. "I'm a softie."

Erin drained her glass of wine. Darkness was falling quickly, and her hazel eyes looked almost black. "Well," she said, "I'm not."

She lifted a beer bottle from the floor of the deck, then returned to the railing. Without warning, she spiked the bottle downward. It crashed into the recycling bin below and shattered, the sound of glass breaking as startling as her words—*Don't touch him!*

She turned to face him. "I'm not going to let her do this."

He wasn't sure what *this* was. He was sure, though, that Erin cared little about him. But she cared about status. She was a successful businesswoman. She was in control. Her disgruntled client had taken control away from her. So had baby Petra, all those years ago. Her pregnancy had taken the reins, driven her into illness. Then Petra had been uncontrollable, inconsolable. Kristie Larsen had taken her husband's career. She wasn't going to let it happen again. He'd been counting on that, on this.

"Next time she comes here uninvited, next time she comes to see you, tell me." Erin retrieved her wineglass, glared into it, as if someone else had finished her drink while she was in the bathroom.

"Next time she tries anything, let me know. I will handle it."

THIRTY-ONE

COUPLE ON TRIAL FOR KILLING THEIR BABY, read the ticker running along the bottom of the screen.

I'd discovered the trial, broadcasted live on Court TV, early in the morning. Tyler would be appalled if he knew I was watching it. But I couldn't turn away.

My fascination did not mean that I would ever do something to my own baby. I would never hurt him. I loved him so much that it felt crushing and wrong. But I could understand how a mother might. This might seem dichotomous. But motherhood was dichotomous, if nothing else.

Oliver was lying on the floor, on his colorful play mat, with arches stretching over his head, from which toys and bells were hanging. Every few seconds, I leaned forward and sent the mobile, with its purple and turquoise butterflies, spinning. Oliver gazed up at it in rapture.

I'd thought he was too young for the play mat, but he seemed pleased with the setup, with the music. It was an activity he could do that did not involve my arms or nipples and, therefore, I was pleased with it, too, annoying music notwithstanding.

I punched one of the pillows on the sofa—they were awful, crunching and seemingly filled with plastic—and rested my head on top of it, lying on my side so that I could see both the television and Oliver.

The mother, Jessica Graham, was on the witness stand. I'd missed something and had no idea why she was testifying. Criminal defendants generally didn't. She was being cross-examined now. It wasn't going well. The prosecutor was asking her about the way she and her husband had disposed of their infant son's body. Wrapped in plastic bags and secured with duct tape. Tossed into a well on their rural property.

I had missed the part I'd most wanted to see. The part where she explained *why* they'd done it. Had it been an accident? Or had they shaken him in a moment of blind frustration and rage because he simply would not stop crying, not realizing how fragile he was? How easy it was to do him harm?

I became aware of a faint vibrating, and I thought it was coming from the television, someone's cell phone, inside a bag on the floor, resting against the leg of a trial table. *Oh no,* I thought, because there were few things worse for a lawyer than having a cell phone make a sound in the courtroom. But the proceedings didn't stop, the judge didn't admonish anyone, and I realized it was coming from my own, which had fallen onto the ground.

It was Tyler, calling to check in, or else, calling to demand, again, that I explain what had happened at the Halloween party on Saturday. He'd asked me Saturday night. He'd asked me all day Sunday.

Why? Why, why, why?

"You don't even know him," Tyler had told me.

"Well . . ."

I'd told him the truth then, feeling as though I had no other choice. Rather, I'd told him part of the truth. He'd known about the muffins, of course. He'd eaten several of them, but he had seemed to forget about Paul's existence since then. I'd told him that Paul and I had continued to chat when we passed on the street, when Oliver and I went out walking. I'd told him that Paul was a stay-at-home father, that he was wonderful with babies. I'd said that I'd even let him hold Oliver. That was it.

I had not told him that Paul had brought me a baby wrap or a piece of artwork. Tyler thought I had ordered that myself. He had never noticed or questioned the lack of corresponding charges to our credit cards. I had not told him that Paul had been in our house, in our bedroom, even. I hadn't told him that I'd been in Paul's. That I'd seen his bed, that I'd rubbed Erin's lotion onto my neck. That I'd nursed Oliver on her sofa. That I'd confided in Paul more than I'd confided in my own husband. That he'd wrapped his arms around me.

My mind was too lumbering, too slow, to keep my false facts straight, and everything I said seemed to lead to more questions, then more and more. It had been a relief when Tyler rolled out of bed this morning and left for work.

Besides, I didn't know the answer to the most resounding question of all: *why had Erin said that?* Why had Paul been so cold? I truly didn't understand. It was unbearable. Had I done something wrong? I could only assume that Erin suspected that we were having an affair. She'd certainly given every indication that was how she felt. She assumed the worst. She blamed me. I was a threat to their marriage.

But this was all speculation. I needed to know. I needed to feel Paul's forgiveness, to be washed with the comfort and relief he provided, and on which I'd become so dependent.

It was lunchtime, I realized, and Tyler was probably taking a break. He had the luxury of breaks during his workday, since he didn't squander away billable hours producing milk for our child. He could run out, braving the streets busy with suits and dress shoes, to wait in line for a fourteen-dollar sandwich. He could let his mind wander while he peed, instead of forcing himself to think about a case so that he could bill those two minutes to a client. Two minutes seemed like nothing, but it rounded up to 0.1 hours, and it added up.

"Hi," I answered.

"Hey," he replied uncertainly.

"What's up?" I leaned down to spin Oliver's butterflies.

Tyler didn't respond.

"What?" I asked, exasperated. "What's wrong?"

"I can't stop thinking about what happened on Saturday," he said. There was something new in his voice now. Something that hadn't been there Saturday night, or even Sunday.

"Well, stop," I told him. "I think you're thinking about it too much. You're making something out of nothing."

"It's not nothing."

"What is it then?"

"His wife told you not to touch him. She was suspicious. I mean, it's like she thinks you're having an affair with this guy."

And there it was. I'd been wondering when he might come out and say it. A pinched silence traveled down the line, bounding back and forth between us.

"Natalie." Tyler's voice was small. It sounded like he was going to cry. "Are you having an affair with him?"

"*No*," I gasped. "Don't be ridiculous."

"She clearly thinks so. Why does she think that? And all this time, you've been spending time with him. I had no idea. I have no idea what you're doing while I'm at work. All this time, you've had this *friend*, and I had no idea."

"I'm by myself, Tyler. I'm by myself all the time, and he's just my friend. He's just a neighbor. It's not like you ever asked me. I wasn't hiding anything from you. It just never came up."

I was tired of talking about this. We'd been over all of it before.

"You don't even know him, Nat," Tyler said quietly.

"Yes, I do," I said. "I told you. We've talked. We're friendly."

"No, you don't. He's a stranger." His voice was thin and crisp, like he might shatter at any second.

"What are you talking about?" I asked, resigned. "He's not a stranger."

"What did he tell you about the reason he's a stay-at-home dad?" He was gaining strength now, gaining steam.

"Just that Petra was a challenging baby and his wife's career was taking off. Why?"

"He's lying," Tyler replied.

"And you know this, how?" I asked.

"Look him up," Tyler said. "Search for his name, and the name of the college where he used to teach. He resigned from his position. He was asked to leave because he had an inappropriate relationship with a student."

I shook my head, but there was a feeling of dread bubbling to life deep within me.

"She was sixteen years old, Nat."

"Who?" I asked numbly.

"The student. She skipped several grades and was attending college. He was twice her age," Tyler continued. "There were rumors of an inappropriate relationship, and he was forced to leave his position."

"No," I said. "That's not true."

Oliver's head snapped toward me. He started to cry. I lifted him off the floor and tugged my shirt up to nurse him, cradling the phone between my shoulder and ear.

"Listen to yourself." Tyler's voice was rising. "You're defending him," he said. "You let him hold our child. You don't even know him."

There it was again. *You don't even know him.* But I did. It couldn't be true. It didn't fit. It made no sense.

"His wife was right to tell you not to touch him. Don't see him again," Tyler said. Stern, again. Scolding. He'd said it before. "He's a predator. Now you know. Don't go anywhere near him."

I blinked angrily, tears blurring the television screen. Jessica Graham was still on the stand. Tyler thought Paul was the monster. That Paul was the one who we didn't know at all. He had no idea.

"Fine," I said. It was better, easier, to just agree with him. He wasn't my keeper. He wasn't my boss. He could not tell me what to do. My career had been pulled out from under me. My entire life, as I'd known it. I now held my life in my arms, fifteen pounds and fluttering eyelids and solid but fragile warmth and petal-soft skin I could touch and smell forever. I loved him so much it felt impossible and stifling and heavy in my chest. I'd brought him into this world. He existed only because I'd decided for him to exist. And yet, being with him day after day, minute after minute, second after second, had driven me insane. How could I explain it?

"I have to go," I said.

"Okay, love—"

I tossed my phone aside, and turned up the volume on the television, forcing my attention to the trial of the *State of Ohio v. Jessica Graham.*

A mother on trial. And I almost laughed, at the irony of it. Because she was on trial for killing her baby. But we were always on trial anyway. We were on trial all of the time. Because we lost our tempers on occasion, when we were expected to exhibit Herculean patience at all times. Because we fed our toddlers processed, rocket ship–shaped cheesy crackers. Because we packed juice boxes rife with high-fructose corn syrup in lunch boxes. Because we sometimes let pee diapers sit for a while, but only pee, we promise. Because we accidentally fed our babies purees laced with arsenic, even though no one told us it was there, and wasn't it the manufacturers' faults? But no, it was our fault, because we should have somehow known it was there and because we should have been making homemade baby food in the same Ninja blender we had purchased to make our weight-loss smoothies. Because we occasionally let our baby cry in his crib for five minutes when he awoke from his nap because we were so exhausted that we couldn't even fathom lifting him from the crib.

Because we ordered our own ice cream cone and let it drip sloppily onto our sagging stomachs while we ate instead of stealing just one lick from Dad's, who was, of course, entitled to a judgment-free cone of his own.

Because we were mothers.

THIRTY-TWO

I wasn't just on trial. I'd been convicted already. I was rotting in jail. Whatever happened to due process? To innocence until guilt was proven?

I hadn't done anything wrong. The neighbors had stared at me like I was a low-class prostitute. My husband thought I was a cheater. Erin Riley had shrieked like I was a raccoon stealing the food for the party, rabies pulsing through my veins.

And—this was what hurt the most—Paul was treating me like I was nothing to him. My friend had slipped away. And had he ever really been my friend? Had I even known him at all?

It wasn't fair, and I was so tired. I was so tired of everything not being fair, of waiting, of wondering. I was, very simply, tired. And I needed answers.

Tyler was at work. Erin, in all likelihood, was, too. As far as I could tell, the way Paul discussed her, work was all she did.

I stepped into the garage, slipped Oliver into his stroller, and bundled a blanket around him. He began to fuss as I pushed onto the driveway.

"Not now," I said irritably. "I have something I need to do."

Miraculously, he listened.

She was there, on his porch. He must have sensed her before she even rang the doorbell. She did so, and it chimed through the house. He closed the lid of his laptop and tugged his phone from his pocket.

She's here, he typed. He sent the text. Her office was only a few minutes away, in a suburban low-rise office park with views of Elkhorn Lake. Assuming she saw the message, assuming she wasn't in a meeting, she would be here soon. He took his time moving to the door, waited there, out of sight, until she rang the bell again.

God, she was desperate.

He could sense, could feel in his gut, that it was time.

"Hello," said Paul. The sun had dipped behind clouds that had rolled in at some point without my noticing. His golden eyes were darker than usual, as if they were absorbing some of the color from his burgundy, long-sleeved polo. I recognized the logo on his chest—a woven alligator. It was an expensive brand, an expensive shirt. Probably a gift from his wife.

He leaned against the doorframe.

"Can we talk?" I asked. I tugged my sleeves over my hands, even though I wasn't cold. The newly November air was balmy, thick with humidity, in the most unsettling way.

Paul moved aside somewhat reluctantly, waited as I extracted Oliver from his stroller and stepped into his house.

He led me into the living room. "Can I get you something to drink?" His body language was closed off, his mannerisms stilted.

"I don't want a drink," I said. Why did I feel like I was about to cry?

Paul didn't sit, so neither did I.

"Could we talk about what happened on Saturday?" I asked. "I don't understand."

He sighed, rubbed his hand across his chin.

"I'm afraid," he said, "that my wife doesn't want me to see you anymore."

Erin wasn't the only one who felt that way. I thought of Tyler. *Don't go anywhere near him.* He'd be livid if he knew where I was.

I sank to the sofa. Oliver protested. Almost without thinking, I lifted my shirt and nursed him. I needed him to be quiet. I needed to focus, and when my baby was crying, I could think of nothing else.

"But, why?" I asked.

"Natalie," he said. "You can see how it might look. You're young and beautiful. Here, in our house, while she's at work."

"No, I'm not," I said. I wasn't sure what I meant, which part I was denying.

"She's jealous, I think. She's afraid that something has happened between us, or that something might happen. She doesn't want me to spend any more time with you. I tried to keep my distance at the party, but she saw you try to approach me, and she lost it. If she knew you were here . . ." He shook his head.

"But it's not like that," I said. "Nothing has happened. We don't have that sort of relationship."

Paul rubbed his face again. "I know. That's what I told her. But you have to admit that it's a little bit hard to believe."

I didn't want to admit it. But he was right.

I stared at the wall across from me. At the portrait of Petra hanging above the wood-burning fireplace and the antique tool set on the hearth before it. Neither of us spoke for a long time.

"There's something else that's bothering me," I began hesitantly. "I read something about you."

Paul shrugged. "What did you read?" His face was impassive, his tone flat.

"About the reason you left your teaching position," I said. "There was an article about it."

He snorted. He didn't look away from my eyes. "There was more than one article about it."

I peeked down to check Oliver. He was falling asleep.

"None of it's true," Paul continued. "I hope you know that."

I waited.

"It was nothing but rumors. That girl"—for some reason, the term made me bristle, even though at sixteen she was still a girl, which was the *point*—"was having a difficult time. All the other students knew she was younger. At that age, being younger wasn't a good thing. She didn't have friends. She came to my office hours often. She was a gifted writer, and I told her that her challenges felt like the end of the world, but they'd pass. All of a sudden, there were rumors. The kids spread them. All of it was just more cruelty toward her. They could be so selfish. They never stopped to think about what it would do to me. The student made an allegation that wasn't true, and the rumors somehow got back to the dean, and I resigned. To be honest, I'd been thinking about it anyway at that point. Erin was pregnant and becoming increasingly stressed about taking an extended period of leave." He shrugged. "It was shameful, a blight to my reputation. The local media even picked it up, even though there was never any proof. But ultimately, it was for the best. From then, I devoted my life to Petra. I hope she never finds out about those rumors."

I chewed my lip. I could see it. He must have been one of the youngest professors, and certainly the best-looking. I could understand the other female students feeling jealous when they saw the youngest of them all receiving attention from Professor Riley.

"I hope you believe me," he said, quietly, seriously.

A slow burn crept across my cheeks.

"Why?" I asked. "Why does it matter? Our friendship is over." I said it because I wanted him to correct me, to tell me that wasn't true.

He didn't have time to respond.

This time, I had no warning that she was here. The garage door hadn't rumbled upward loudly. I'd not heard the slam of her car door. She'd not had to fumble with her keys to get inside.

The slow burn on my face burst into flames.

She looked sloppier than I'd ever seen her. Her lipstick was smeared above her top lip, like she'd reapplied it in a moving car. Her eyes flicked from my face to my breast. Oliver had dozed off, still sucking in his sleep. He woke with a jolt when I pulled him free, tugged my shirt down without bothering to rehook the flap of my nursing bra.

"I think it's time you went home, Natalie," Erin said. Her words were melting, dripping ice.

"Why?" I asked. "Why are you being so mean to me?"

I sounded pathetic. Like a child on the playground, the butt of the popular clique's jokes. "There's nothing going on," I continued. "I swear. Nothing has happened with your husband. I mean, nothing will happen, either. It's not like that."

She pointed to the door. She didn't care, didn't want to hear it.

"Please, just go," she said. "This is our house, and I'm asking you to please go, and don't come back."

I wanted to drop to my knees and plead with them. But she seemed relatively calm, and I had Oliver in my arms. Besides, she was right. This was her house. This was her husband. Perhaps I should just go.

I looked at Paul, hoping he would take my side, hoping he would tell her she was acting insane. He wouldn't look at me.

Erin opened the front door. Her eyes were cast down as I stepped onto the porch.

My hands shook as I tucked Oliver into his stroller. I could feel her flashing eyes boring into me.

I glanced back at her. She stepped outside and closed the door. Our eyes met.

Before I could turn. Before I could wrap my fingers around the handlebars. Before I could walk away, embarrassed, but unscathed, she stormed forward.

Her tiny, birdlike hands wrapped around my arms. She was half a foot shorter than I was, but she gripped me tightly.

"I am *dead fucking serious* when I tell you, *stay away from my husband*." She released me as quickly as she'd grabbed me, then spun away, and she was gone, into the house, the door firmly closed, the locks in place.

I couldn't help but cry as I rushed home. Not delicate, seeping tears. Angry, staggering sobs shook me as I pushed down the hill.

Of course, Mrs. Jensen was outside, ambling toward her mailbox. She always seemed to be out when I didn't want her to be, nosy, witnessing my shame, my motherly failings. How long had she been there? What had she seen?

She froze as I hurried past, as though fearful that I might launch myself toward her like Erin had done to me. I ignored her.

The sky was darkening like a day-old bruise. It was too late in the year for a thunderstorm, but it felt like one was coming. The wind whipped at my hair.

Once inside my house, I slipped off my T-shirt and settled onto the family room sofa to finish nursing Oliver. I held him in place with my arms, my muscles tense and tight. My phone vibrated in the pocket of my jogger pants, and I shifted to my left to jiggle it out. I was hoping it would be a message from Paul, telling me to come back, it was all a mistake, he'd chosen me after all, even though we never communicated that way. I didn't even have his number, and he didn't have mine.

It was from Tyler.

Stuck in last-minute settlement talks. Will be very late. Sorry.

The apology was an afterthought, and it didn't matter. He didn't have to be sorry. Not when we were so dependent on his money, his self-importance, his billable hours, the exorbitant rate he charged. Not when he'd spoken his piece. He wasn't rushed to get home, to make sure I was being a good little girl, staying away from Paul. He simply trusted that I was, or else he didn't care as much as he claimed to.

I tossed my phone to the side. It bounced off the sofa cushion and fell to the floor. I stared into space while Oliver ate. On the blank wall ahead of me, I saw Paul and Erin standing side by side, a perfect-looking, trim, and tidy couple. Erin's wine-soaked teeth and thin, red smile. Her designer home, magazine ready in its neatness. Rage bubbled beneath my surface. It wasn't valid. I had no right. Still, there it was.

Or was it she who had no right?

Stay away from my husband, she'd whispered. It had been so shocking, so snakelike, the words almost as startling as her grip on my arms.

How dare she say that? We hadn't done anything wrong.

Oliver rested sleepily in his swing while I replaced my shirt. I stormed through the house, cleaning up, shuffling through the fridge and pantry, contemplating dinner options. I assumed Tyler wouldn't be joining me. All the while, my rage simmered. I felt removed from myself, blinded, deaf, numb.

Stay away from my husband.

Darkness fell much earlier than usual. Lightning flashed; thunder shook the house. Oliver dozed in his swing. He seemed to like the background noise of crashing lightning and thunder. I paced and let my rage bubble and pop. I was tired of struggling to hold it together. To be quiet and perfect. To be a mom.

Before, when I was with Paul, hope had stirred to life. There'd been companionship and relief and comfort. When I was with Paul, and Oliver was in his arms, having a life outside of motherhood, my own life, with work and hobbies and self-care, felt possible. Erin had snatched that away.

Stay away from my husband.

There was a tiny human with me all the time. I could never escape him. But now, in this moment, I had never felt more alone.

THIRTY-THREE

"Erin," he said. He stepped toward her, reached for her arms, just the same way she had grabbed Natalie only minutes before. He'd watched her through the living room windows. But he didn't shake her. He didn't make a threat. He held her steady. "Calm down."

She pulled herself from his grip.

"I don't relish acting that way, you know?" she said. She was seething, practically rabid. He'd never seen her so angry. "I did it to protect you. To protect our family."

"I know," he said calmly. "I know."

He watched as she paced through the house, like a crazed animal in a too-small cage.

Natalie must be safely inside her own house by now. Mrs. Jensen—bless her—had been outside, getting her mail. She'd seen the whole thing. Petra would be at school late, rehearsal for the school play. He wasn't due to get her until half past six. They'd stop for pizza on the way home, and milkshakes, slurped through neon curly straws. Just the two of them. After today, it would always be just the two of them.

But it couldn't happen here. He needed to get Erin out of the house.

"Look," he said, "maybe you should go out for a walk. Cool down."

She shot him a look, continued her pacing.

"Get some fresh air in the woods," he suggested. "That usually calms you down." He moved into the kitchen and retrieved a stainless-steel tumbler, one with a lid. Typically, he used it for coffee, brought it with him in the car when he dropped Petra at school. He popped the cork of a half-full bottle of red wine and poured some in. "Take this," he said. "Calm down. I'll go get Petra after her rehearsal. We'll bring a pizza home. Okay?"

She didn't agree with anything he'd said, but she took the tumbler, then a long, slow pull from it.

He moved into the kitchen. If he was hovering, if he was too insistent, she wouldn't go, out of sheer contrariness.

The front door swung open, then closed again.

He moved to the front windows and peered out. She'd slipped on a windbreaker—one of his—and was walking quickly down the hill, the flaps of the unzipped jacket billowing behind her like a cape.

This had always been his plan. He knew that he couldn't kill her in the house. He had always wanted to kill her in the woods, particularly once he'd learned that Natalie also liked walking there. Doing it outdoors seemed safer. That was his only option. To follow her there when she went out for a walk. To do so without being seen.

And there she went.

Paul sprinted up the stairs. He pulled a sweatshirt over his head, then stepped into his old sneakers, the pair he wore for yard work, knowing that when it was over, he'd have to get rid of everything he was wearing.

It had been a balmy day, and a storm was coming, but the weather was due to turn cooler, more seasonable, over the next few days. Perhaps Petra might want to sit by the fireplace, to roast marshmallows, to take her mind off the fact that her mother had gone missing. He'd keep the fire burning after Petra went to bed. He'd add a few items in with the extra logs. He'd sweep up the ashes that remained and toss them out with the trash before the body was even found.

The baby wraps were still in his duffel bag on the top shelf of his closet. He slipped the one concealed in the plastic bag into the waistband of his pants.

He stopped by the pantry to slide a pair of black latex gloves onto his hands. He wore them to preserve his skin when he scrubbed the kitchen sink, disinfected the counters. His *serial-killer gloves,* Erin used to call them.

He was smiling as he slipped through sliding door at the back of the house and moved to the back of his yard, to the tree line. There were two yards he needed to get through before he reached the woods. Trees dotted the backs of the yards, separating them from the yards of the houses on the street behind his. They'd offer some cover, and so would the hood of his sweatshirt, but not enough. The storm was getting closer. The wind was picking up, the sky was dark and swirling, clouds racing across it.

Don't think too much, he decided. *Just go.*

He ran.

As he slipped into the thick cover of the trees, the first raindrop, thick and fat, smacked against his forehead. Thunder rumbled in the distance.

He moved quickly, but as quietly as he could, as he tried to catch up to his wife.

For a second, he feared that Erin hadn't gone into the woods after all. Had she not walked past Natalie's house, but right up to it? Had she rung the doorbell? Had she confronted her again?

Then, he feared that Erin had already turned around, chased home by the weather. That he might run straight into her, face-to-face.

But then, he saw her up ahead, the windbreaker still floating ethereally behind her, the tumbler still clutched in her right hand. She was moving away from him, toward the storm, instead of back home. The wrong direction.

The right one, for him.

He followed.

THIRTY-FOUR

The feeling of despair, of loneliness, had only strengthened since I had been chased from Paul's house. I refused to accept that as the end to our friendship. But I couldn't go back there.

Stay away from my husband. I needed to let him come to me.

When he did, would I tell him what Erin had said to me? What she'd done? I still hadn't decided.

The more troubling thought rushed in next: what if he never came?

I was in the glider, its cushions thin and sunken from the many hours of use, when the doorbell rang. My heart leapt, something stirred. I held Oliver upright and hurried down the stairs.

But it was not Paul standing on my front porch. It was the person I least wanted to see in this moment, besides, I supposed, Erin Riley herself. It was master's degree–possessing but not using, homemade cupcake–baking, pot roast–cooking Diane Fanning, stay-at-home mother extraordinaire and my mother-in-law.

I contemplated, for just a second, closing the door in her face. It simply wasn't fair. She'd given me no warning, and neither had Tyler.

"Hi," she said brightly, her gaze focused on Oliver, practically salivating at his proximity. When had she last seen him? It had been a few weeks, at least. Every time Tyler had suggested that his parents come by, I'd told him, vehemently, *no.* He was too scared of me to veto my voice, to say too bad, they were coming anyway, they wanted to see their grandson.

Why? he'd ask me. *Why can't they come?*

The truth was I couldn't bear to be around Diane. She had happily abandoned her career to stay home with her kids. She'd been home ever since, doing nothing, doing everything. She felt like my nemesis. Her presence ravaged me with guilt, and I was already guilty enough.

"She's too perfect," I had told Tyler once. "I can't stand to sit with her and listen to her stories about how easy and wonderful and amazing motherhood is."

"Trust me. She isn't *perfect*," he had replied, sternly, his eyes not meeting mine, stuck on some memory from his past. He didn't share it.

I wished he had, but I didn't ask. I needed to hear it, and the fact that he didn't get that without my asking was simply more evidence of his failures, his ineptitude. Add it to the jar, to the chart, like a sort of reverse poster for gold stars.

It wasn't just that. It wasn't just that she made me feel inadequate and broken. She bored me, the way she discussed the most banal things with such interest. Was she born that way, or had her mind atrophied from lack of stimulation? Had the mundanity of motherhood liquefied her brain? Had it seeped from her ear when she was distracted with slapping a Band-Aid on a skinned knee? Either way, I found her sad. Yet, she seemed so happy. She was perplexing. She was everything I didn't want to be. And here I was, being catapulted down her same path despite my best efforts and years of higher education.

"I don't want to impose," Diane said.

I stepped to the side, and she entered the house. I was conscious of the dirt and the clutter. Diane's house was always pristine, never mind that she didn't clean it herself.

She ignored the mess and parked herself on the living room sofa.

"We haven't seen you in a while, Nat," she said hesitantly. "I thought I'd come by and see how I could help. I can watch him for a few hours if you'd like. You can take a nap, run an errand."

It was tempting, though I knew I wouldn't be able to, with her sitting downstairs. It would take me hours to fall asleep, and by the time I did, it would be time for Oliver to eat again. I'd awaken to his cries, feeling even more exhausted than before. But I could do something else. Take advantage of the time to accomplish something. That way, I could also avoid sitting with Diane and chatting about the recipe cards she had left for me and the beauty of motherhood.

But the realization struck me like a dodgeball to the chest, knocked the air straight out of me. There wasn't anything I needed to do. Not anymore. This was my only thing.

It would be rather satisfying, though, to take her up on her offer, to let her try to soothe my child to no avail, to show her how he only wanted me, to make her understand how difficult that was. She thought she understood, but she didn't. She hadn't fed her children with her body. She hadn't had babies like Oliver.

I passed Oliver to Diane and sat in an armchair across from her. "It's okay," I said. "I can't nap." I didn't tell her that, actually, I had managed to nap a couple of times, while my neighbor expertly cared for my impossible baby.

She smiled sympathetically, but she was looking down at Oliver, cradling him, gazing into his face. "Could you lie in bed with him?" she asked. "Maybe you could get some sleep if he laid in the bed beside you."

"He can't lie in the bed with me," I said, horrified. "It's not safe."

She shrugged nonchalantly. "I did it all the time."

There was simply no point arguing. "Well, I would worry that it's not safe," I said. "I wouldn't be able to sleep."

Oliver began to cry, and she startled, shifted in her seat. "What's wrong?" she asked.

"He doesn't like to be held that way," I told her, even though she'd been asking Oliver, not me. "He likes to be held upright and to walk around."

"Oh dear," she replied. She obeyed, lifting Oliver up and pressing him against her shoulder. She began to pace along the perimeter of the area rug.

"No wonder you're so exhausted," she said after several minutes of silence.

I bit my lip, nodded, suddenly feeling on the verge of a meltdown myself. But I knew that I couldn't. Not in front of Diane. She'd worry about my competence. She'd worry about Oliver. Then, she'd come back. She probably would anyway. She'd broken the seal, like a first drunken trip to a bar bathroom in college. She'd be back again and again.

"Anyway, how are you doing, Nat?" she asked, still walking along the rug, her icy-blond bob cupping her cheeks, her head tilted downward, checking on her grandson and her footing.

"I'm okay," I lied.

"Do you miss your job?"

The question surprised me, and I surprised myself by answering honestly. "I miss the mental stimulation. I miss feeling busy. I miss my office and my work. But I miss the way it used to be. With Oliver, staying up all night, every night, I couldn't manage it."

She nodded, as though she understood.

Eventually, Oliver dozed off in her arms, and she settled back onto the sofa, leaning against the cushions. She looked tired, but utterly content. It was clear on her face. What, I wondered, was clear on mine?

Unable to bear the awkward silence, she launched into her typical small talk. *Whole Foods was out of that salad dressing Tyler loves so much. I was going to bring you a few bottles. I was thinking of going out walking later, but I think I already got my exercise today, don't you? Ha-ha. Chilly today, isn't it? The leaves are falling quickly. Seems like it happened earlier than usual this year. That storm did a number on them. Strange, that was, wasn't it? Such is Maryland weather, I guess.*

Finally, Oliver stirred then began to punch and fuss in her arms.

"It's probably time for him to eat," I said.

"Oh." She brightened. "I could give him a bottle?"

"I don't have any bottles." There were a few bags of milk in the freezer, solid and speckled with frost. It would take ages to warm them up. I couldn't wait ages for her to leave. "Sorry."

"Right," she replied. "No problem." She grabbed her jacket and moved toward the front door.

"Remember," she said, placing a hand on my upper arm. "I'm here. Anything you need."

What I needed was for her to *not* be here, but I nodded and smiled as she bent down to kiss the soft spot on Oliver's head.

I closed and locked the door behind her and trailed into the family room. I'd just settled onto the sofa when the doorbell rang again.

Back already. Had she forgotten something? Did she need to sniff her grandson one last time? To plant one final kiss into his sparse hair?

But this time, it *was* Paul standing on my porch. He wore a bulky sweater, jeans, and chestnut boat shoes. His dark hair was slightly rumpled, as though he'd just awakened from a nap.

Relief and affection came rushing into my house behind him, but only for a second, as everything that had happened over the last few days came rushing back to me. *Don't touch him. Stay away from my husband.*

He didn't reach for Oliver. He began to pace from the front door to the foot of the staircase, then back. There were lines of concern contorting his face. "I was wondering," he said, "have you seen Erin lately?"

"No," I said with surprise. "I haven't seen her since yesterday."

He froze, his eyes searching mine. "You saw her yesterday. And?"

When she had surprised us in his house. When she grabbed me. How could he forget?

"Yes, with you. At your house." I stared at him unblinking. Was I losing it? Was he?

He shook his head vigorously, impatiently. "Then, she came here. What happened?"

I squinted at him. "Oh," I replied. "Um, no, she didn't," I continued. "I saw her at your house. I went home. I haven't seen her since. Why? Is something wrong?" I crossed my arms. I was irritated. I felt I deserved an apology for the way they both had treated me, not a grilling.

"She's missing," he said, his eyes now closed, as if the words were unthinkable, and I supposed they were. "My wife is missing."

"Missing," I repeated, like I'd never heard the word before. "Missing."

He pressed the heels of his hands into his eyes. "Missing. I've told the police, but they're not doing anything. Not yet. I'm going door-to-door."

He dropped his hands and turned away from me. He still didn't tell me he was sorry for all that had happened. He didn't ask me how I was. He hadn't even looked at Oliver.

His shoulders shook, his iciness seemed to melt.

"Sorry," he said, lifting his head. "I've only been to half the street. I have a lot more to do. But, could I trouble you for some water, maybe a cup of coffee, borrow your bathroom? I could use a break for just a couple minutes. I didn't sleep at all last night."

I hesitated, then nodded. How could I refuse? "Sure," I said. I pointed to the powder room, even though he knew where it was. "I'll meet you in the kitchen."

I rushed into the family room and slipped Oliver into his swing. He protested, punching his arms out, his brows low.

"Just give me a few minutes, please," I whispered.

Oliver blinked at me, then began to cry. I groaned, almost a growl, then held him against my shoulder as I moved into the kitchen. I filled a glass with water from the spout on the front of the fridge and placed it on the island, then started a pot of coffee. I bounce-walked Oliver around the room while it brewed, trying to shush his cries.

I didn't hear Paul approaching over the sounds of Oliver's wails, but then he was there. His face looked red and matte, as if he'd just splashed it with water, patted it dry with my hand towel.

I pointed to the glass of water, and he took it, swallowed half quickly while I filled a mug with coffee with one hand, still holding Oliver in my other arm.

"So," I said, unsure where to begin, "you haven't seen Erin since yesterday afternoon? You haven't heard from her? Have you called her?"

He tilted his head toward me, an almost pitying expression on his face. I nodded. Of course he'd called her.

"She left her phone at home. She stormed from the house, not long after you left, and she left her phone behind. I haven't seen her since."

"And you've reached out to her friends and family? She isn't with them? Did she take her car?"

He shook his head while he took a long sip of coffee.

"I've done everything I can think of, Natalie. Now I'm asking all the neighbors. No one's seen her. No one's said they've seen her."

"Right," I replied. I felt stuck, slow, my thoughts stolid and plodding, while he stood there, studying me, his own thoughts seeming to flash through his eyes.

"What?" I asked.

He shook his head, slid the water glass a few inches away from him, toward me. "I have to keep going," he said. He brushed past me, walked to the door.

Oliver fussed against my neck. I patted his back as I followed.

Paul didn't thank me for the coffee, and he didn't say goodbye, just stepped silently onto my porch.

Abruptly, he spun to face me. "If you know anything more, tell me," he pleaded. "Tell me right now." His sudden fierceness reminded me so much of his wife, while I'd stood on their front porch just the day before.

I took a step back, retreating into the foyer, my knuckles pale as I gripped the door. "I don't know what you're talking about," I said. "I have no idea where your wife is."

What about me? I wanted to say. *Remember when you cared about me?*

He didn't seem to. He didn't seem to care at all.

Just like Erin had done to me, I slammed the door in his face.

THIRTY-FIVE

He buried his face in his hands as he jogged down the steps of her porch, but it was to conceal a smile, not tears.

He felt lighter now, the baby wrap no longer concealed within the waistband of his jeans, pressed against his stomach. Now, the plastic bag that had held it was folded into a neat square, tucked into his back pocket. The baby wrap was safely tucked into a shoebox on the floor of Natalie's closet. The box had been covered with dust, and it held a pair of high heels she had clearly never worn. Perhaps she'd forgotten to return them until it was too late. He was certain she wouldn't bother opening the box, looking inside. Natalie hadn't asked him why he'd used the upstairs bathroom. He suspected she hadn't noticed. She hadn't heard a thing.

He'd need to ensure that the wrap was found, that the police searched for it. He needed to point them to Natalie.

If they were able to test the wrap for DNA, it would have Erin's, of course, probably his, too, but it would also have Natalie's. He'd looped it around her. He'd helped her slip her baby inside of it. Then, she'd used it to kill his wife.

At least, that's what the police would think, if things continued to go his way.

And thus far, things had gone so well, so smoothly, that he felt as though it had been his destiny to kill Erin in the woods the previous afternoon. Everything had been clicking into place so easily. Too easily? He was almost suspicious of the ease. Almost.

Once he was sure that Erin was gone, once she was still and gray, her neck a bright, tattooed red, he had tucked the baby wrap back into the plastic bag, concealed it in the waistband of his jeans, then used his shoe to push some fallen leaves onto her body. Her fair skin, her brown hair, seemed to blend in with her surroundings well. If anyone happened to spot her, it would be because of the damn windbreaker, but he didn't feel as though he should take it off her body. She'd dropped the tumbler of wine. Deep red liquid spilled from it, seeped into the ground like bloodshed, even though hers had been a bloodless death.

He'd followed her fairly deep into the woods, knocked her down by the stream. He knew there were no cameras there, no witnesses. If there was any evidence that implicated him, it would be of a physical nature. He could only hope the falling rain, the drops heavy and thick as a toddler's tears, would help with that. She'd not managed to fight back for long, to rake her nails against his skin. She was too small, too surprised by the way he'd leapt on top of her and held her down. She'd reached, for his hands at first, tearing at them, trying to push them away, but then, she'd gripped the baby wrap. She tore at it, trying to pull it away from her skin. He had been too strong.

Although she'd not succeeded in ripping the wrap, he had torn away the tag that bore the brand name and the instructions for washing it, and arranged it beneath Erin's lifeless hand, hoping it would be protected there. He wanted the police to find it, to determine what it came from, to trace it back to Natalie.

There would be circumstantial evidence against him. Evidence of motive, opportunity, but he would be careful to ensure that there was better evidence of motive, of circumstance, that pointed to someone else. He already had been careful of that.

He'd run back home the same way he had come, hoping that he was beyond the view of any neighbors, or any security cameras stationed above back doors, then removed his shoes in the grass, walking barefoot into the house. He stripped and shoved his clothes—his sweatshirt, long-sleeved polo, jeans, and shoes—into a paper bag, which he hid on the firewood shelf in the garage. He stacked a few pieces of wood on top of it, as if to remind himself to burn it the next time he set a fire, which would have to be soon. He'd add the other baby wrap, too. The one still hiding on the top of his closet. The one that hadn't been wrapped around Erin's neck. This way, there would only be one to be found. The one that mattered. The one that had, that would, set him free.

He'd showered then, changed into clean clothes, and gone to retrieve his daughter.

Rehearsal had gone well. Petra was beaming when he picked her up from the auditorium. He drove her straight to their favorite pizza place.

"Let's get another one to go," he'd told her, before he asked for the check, while the waiter stood at their table to bear witness. "Take it home for Mommy."

Of course, the house was silent and dark when they arrived home.

"Where *is* Mommy?" Petra had asked.

"I saw her this afternoon, but she must have gone back to the office," he said. "I bet she's working late."

"But her car was in the garage. Wasn't it?"

His daughter was too smart.

"Right," he said. "Maybe she walked."

She certainly *could* have walked to work, her office was close enough to their house, though, to his knowledge, she never had. But Petra seemed satisfied with this explanation, so they'd gone inside, rinsed off the crazy straws they had brought home from the restaurant, and gotten ready for bed.

The following morning, Erin still wasn't back. He'd become visibly anxious about her absence. Although he hated to deceive his daughter in that way, she would become a witness in the inevitable investigation. He had to remind himself that this was all for her, for them. She would be better off in the end.

"I'm sure everything's fine," he'd told Petra in the school drop-off line. "I'll find Mommy when you're at school." He had kissed her on each cheek, then waved her off.

He made a stop on the way home, at Erin's office. Her assistant was sitting at her desk, her silver hair tucked neatly behind her ears, tortoise-shell glasses low on her nose.

"Oh," she said in surprise. "Hello, Paul." She peered more closely at him over her frames. "Is everything okay?"

"Donna," he said, "tell me, is Erin here?"

Donna would have to find a new job, he supposed. She'd been with Erin for a long time. At least since Petra was born. Donna had given Petra birthday and Christmas gifts every year, even though she had, Paul knew, four grandkids of her own.

"No," Donna said, her surprise evident. "She usually would be, by this time, but, well, I don't need to tell you that, do I?"

They blinked at each other for several long seconds.

"Everything okay?" Donna asked again.

"No. I'm afraid not. I don't know where Erin is."

Donna had more questions, of course. *When did you last see her? Where do you think she could be?*

He ignored them. "I'm sorry. I have to go."

From the car, then while pacing through his house, he had made some phone calls. Erin's sister, who lived at the beach in Delaware. Her parents, at their condo in Lake Tahoe. Erin's best friend, Stacy—her only friend, as far as he knew. None of them had heard from her the previous day. He didn't like igniting their panic, but he didn't see how he had any other choice. He called the local hospital, provided a description of Erin, but there were no unidentified female patients at the time.

His final call had been to the Patuxent County Police Department.

"My wife is missing," he told the desk sergeant, his voice wavering.

He knew everything he said was being recorded. From now on, every step, every word, every breath, would be observed with microscopic attention, with intense judgment. He was the husband. He knew the way this was likely to go. It was his job to make sure that didn't happen.

He answered the sergeant's questions, rattling off Erin's full name, date of birth, phone number, and home and work addresses.

"Her phone is here, though," he said. "In the house. No point calling it. I tried anyway," he admitted.

He was surprised Erin hadn't taken the phone with her into the woods. She was usually so tied to her phone, wanting to be accessible to her clients all the time. But the clients had been calling less than they used to, there were fewer of them, and that she hadn't taken it was only further evidence that what he'd done was fate. It was what he was supposed to do.

"It's not been twenty-four hours yet," the policeman said. "But I'll send someone to the house."

"When?" Paul asked, his growing hysteria apparent. "My wife is gone. Our daughter—Erin wouldn't do this without telling us. She wouldn't just disappear."

"That's what everyone says, sir. Then, their wife or daughter or husband or whoever it may be turns up safe and sound. A miscommunication is all. Happens all the time."

"Not Erin," Paul insisted. But he'd said his piece, and he could have kissed this man for his blasé attitude. He hung up the phone and waited for the police to arrive, until he decided that he should have been doing more. He should be looking for his wife. In the neighborhood. In the woods. He should be speaking with his neighbors. What had they seen? What did they know?

Paul bounded up the steps of the Wilsons' house, next door to Natalie's. His smile had fallen. He was every bit the worried husband.

Terry Wilson opened the door, still wearing her scrubs. She had probably just returned from a shift at the hospital. She looked tired, like an overworked working parent. He would never be like her.

Paul raked a hand through his hair. "I'm sorry to bother you, Terry," he said. "But I need to know—have you seen my wife?"

She hadn't. None of them had.

Paul descended the steps of the Wilsons' porch, glanced around him. Linda Molloy's house remained still and quiet. She lived on the other side of Natalie's house, and hadn't been home to answer the door. He wasn't surprised. Linda and Erin had always been friendly, although Linda was more than a decade older, divorced, her children grown. She still lived alone in her big family home, and she owned her own CPA business. She and Erin had referred clients to each other. He'd have to return later in the evening if he wanted to catch Linda. He was anxious to see if she'd heard or seen anything—after all, he'd run near the back of her yard on his way into the woods.

He was headed to the Jensens' house when he noticed a navy sedan pull to a stop in front of his own home. A woman climbed out, a cop.

He met her in his driveway, and she showed him a badge. "Detective Jill West," she said.

Paul led her inside, and he told her what had happened.

Well, he told her the pieces he needed her to know.

His wife had arrived home from work early the previous day, in the afternoon. His neighbor, Natalie, unknown last name, had stopped by. Erin wasn't happy that she was there. She walked Natalie out. He stayed inside, but he thought that they'd argued. When Erin returned to the house, she seemed upset. She'd gone to speak to Natalie again, privately, or so he thought. And she'd gone out for a walk, he said, to calm herself down. She had never come back.

"What was the nature of their conflict?" Detective West inquired.

"Well, Natalie had been visiting me while Erin was at work, and Erin didn't like that. For a while, I felt bad for the woman. She seemed so isolated, taking care of her baby alone all day. I'm a stay-at-home father, I know how lonely it can be. I was kind to her, but to be honest with you, it became a bit much, her coming by all the time."

Detective West wasn't taking notes. She only watched him, ginger eyebrows raised.

"And have you spoken to this woman since your wife left? Did your wife actually go there?"

"I did. I was going door-to-door," he said. "Natalie told me Erin never stopped by. She told me she hasn't seen her since she left our house." He shook his head. "But I don't know."

"Alright."

Her affect was cool, flat, and emotionless. He didn't know whether that was how she forced herself to be, out of self-preservation, or whether that was how her job had turned her.

"My wife works a lot. I thought she might have returned to her office. She could walk there, in theory. But without her phone? Without telling me?" He shook his head.

That which was concealed inside the brown paper bag in the garage seemed to pulse with secrecy as they spoke. Detective West didn't notice.

She glanced down at her vibrating cell phone and excused herself, moving into the hallway.

"I've got to go chase something down," she said when she returned. "I'll check in tonight, and tomorrow morning. If nothing has changed, we will open an investigation."

He protested, to deaf ears. She deflected his objections with rote and meaningless expressions: *lack of resources, budget cuts, busy caseload, wife an adult, not missing long.* He was pleased when she left rather irritably.

It was actually quite perfect. He'd stop at the store for graham crackers, blocks of chocolate, and marshmallows before he picked up Petra from school. He'd build a fire in the living room fireplace. They would roast the marshmallows over the licking flames and Petra would soon understand that Erin being gone wasn't really all that different from the way it had been before. In fact, it was better.

She would go up to bed, and Paul would then do what he needed to do. He'd keep the fire going long into the night, as long as he needed to, until everything was gone.

He glared at the detective as she slid ungracefully into her car. By the time she returned, by the time she *opened an investigation,* he would be ready.

Back to his rounds, he decided. Back to the Jensens'. He couldn't wait to hear what Carol Jensen would have to say.

THIRTY-SIX

The woman on my front porch wore a gray herringbone suit and plain white blouse. Her black shoes were chunky, rubbery, sensible. Her short red hair was pulled back into a tiny ponytail. She reached into her pocket and removed a badge.

"Mrs. Fanning?" she asked.

I studied the badge distractedly, knowing that it, her, her presence at my house, uninvited and unexpected, had something to do with Erin Riley. PATUXENT COUNTY POLICE DEPARTMENT, it said.

"I'm Detective Jill West," she continued. "Could I come in?"

Wordlessly, I stepped to the side, allowing her to enter.

We moved into the living room, and I was conscious of the mess, just as I'd been conscious of it when Diane had stopped by the previous day. But not, apparently, conscious enough to do something about it after she'd left.

"What's going on?" I asked nervously, anxious to fill the silence.

"I'm interviewing all the neighbors," Detective West said, "about the disappearance of Erin Riley."

"It's awful," I said automatically.

"When did you last see Mrs. Riley?" the detective asked. She had a notepad in her lap, but she was looking at my face, straight into my eyes, like she was a human lie detector test.

"Um," I said, thinking, forcing the ungreased and underused wheels of my mind to turn, "I saw her Monday afternoon. I'm friends with her husband." I paused, swallowed. That sounded *bad*. "He helps me with my baby sometimes. I was at his house in the afternoon, and Erin got home. We chatted for a bit, then I left."

Stay away from my husband.

I pressed my lips together, lest the words explode out. Something very insistent was telling me not to let them.

I realized abruptly that Oliver was still sleeping in his swing in the family room, resting gently on top of a blanket—not strapped in—and panic began to inflate my chest. Should I ask her if we could move into the family room? Should I ask for a break, so that I could go retrieve him?

I would do nothing, I decided. He'd cry when he awakened. He always did. I'd rush in to get him, pretend that I hadn't forgotten about my child, pretend that he'd been sleeping somewhere safe, a place the rules permitted him to sleep unattended.

"What time was that?" Detective West continued.

"I think it was about two," I replied. "I'm just guessing," I added. "I can't remember."

I couldn't remember anything. What day of the week it was. Doctor's appointments for my son. Emailing Confidential Mediation Statements. How I'd spent seconds, minutes, hours of my days. Where I lived. Who I was.

"And you didn't see her again after you left her home?"

I wished she'd look away, blink, something.

"No," I said. "I don't think so."

Silence fell upon us. I could hear the mechanical creaking of Oliver's swing.

"Where do you think she went?" I asked.

"I can't say yet," the detective replied, which wasn't the same as *I don't know.* "If you're friendly with her husband, haven't you spoken with him about it?"

"He stopped by to ask me if I'd seen her. Yesterday." I shook my head. "He said she was missing. That's all. He seemed very anxious."

"Naturally," Detective West said. "His wife has vanished."

"Right." I plucked a cat hair from the sofa, tossed it to the floor, as though that were a better place for it.

"Are you certain that Mrs. Riley didn't come here?" she asked abruptly.

"Here?" I asked. My voice cracked. "No," I said. "I mean, I am sure." And I was. So why did I sound like I was lying?

"She didn't leave her house, and walk here? To continue the conversation with you?"

I shook my head wildly. "She didn't come here."

Did she?

My silent question went unanswered.

"You may have noticed police and others searching the area." Detective West closed her notebook with a slap. *You're useless,* it seemed to say.

"No," I replied, startled. "I haven't."

"Her husband has organized a search party. You haven't helped?"

"He didn't ask me to help," I said, feeling a sting. "But I don't think I could help anyway. I have to look after my baby," I continued.

The detective glanced around, then nodded knowingly. Because I wasn't looking after my baby, was I?

She stood and moved toward the door.

"Thanks for speaking with me," she said. "If you think of any information that might be helpful, please do call the police."

"Of course." I tried a smile, but it felt wrong. She looked at me strangely before stepping outside, onto my porch.

I closed and locked the front door behind her and hurried into the family room. Oliver was still sleeping. I paced the room. It was a strange dichotomy, one of so many. I longed for him to sleep, yet when he did, I found myself bored, half wanting him to wake up.

When Tyler waltzed in the door at half past six, I had dinner ready. He seemed impressed.

"Don't get used to it," I said. Oliver had been oddly peaceful and quiet the remainder of the afternoon. I'd laid him on his activity mat on the kitchen floor while I cooked. He'd not whined to be held a single time.

Tyler prattled on about a new case he was working on while we ate. Finally, once his plate was clear, he asked about my day.

"A detective came by," I said robotically.

He swiveled in his seat. "What? Why?"

"About Paul's wife. Erin."

"Right," he said. I'd told Tyler that Erin was missing. He seemed rather callously disinterested in Erin's well-being. Perhaps it was loyalty, after the spectacle Erin had caused at the block party. Perhaps he didn't blame me for that, for any of it, after all.

"She had nothing new to share, really," I told him. "Just wanted to know if I had any information."

"Hasn't *Paul* told you anything?" Tyler asked.

"No. I haven't seen him since the party. Since you told me not to," I lied. I *couldn't* tell him about what had happened on Monday afternoon— *Stay away from my husband.* He would be livid with me. It would only prove the points he'd made. "He was going door-to-door, asking if people had seen Erin, and he asked me, too," I continued. "But that's it."

"Probably for the best," said Tyler. He stood up to clear our plates.

"What do you mean?" I didn't get up to help him.

"Well, his wife just vanished from their house while he was home?" he asked. "Come on. It seems suspicious."

"Maybe someone picked her up," I said. "Maybe she was out walking, and someone abducted her."

Tyler didn't reply over the clanging of the dishes as he tucked them into the dishwasher.

While he finished cleaning up, I placed Oliver into his swing. I chewed at a nail, thinking about what Tyler had said. What, exactly, was he suggesting?

"You seem shaken," Tyler said. He was half looking at his cell phone, probably skimming over an email.

"Well, yeah," I said. "Our neighbor is missing. She just disappeared. It's a little alarming."

It wasn't the truth, but it sounded right. The truth was, it was disturbing just how unshaken I was. It was something else that had me shaken. *Don't touch him. Stay away from my husband.* She'd grabbed me. Neighbors might have seen her. What would they think?

"Right," Tyler said, still looking at his phone. "Why don't you take a little break? Go for a run or something?"

There was that rage again, so familiar, it almost came as a comfort.

"Go for a run?" I repeated. "Listen to yourself. I can't run, Tyler. Have you seen me run at all since I pushed an eight-pound human being out of my vagina?"

"I'm sorry," he said, appropriately chastened. "I forgot."

"Jesus Christ. Must be nice." I focused my gaze on Oliver, on the rise and fall of his chest, making sure that it was still rising and falling.

"Take some time for yourself," Tyler continued. "That's all I meant."

I shook my head, continued to stare at Oliver.

"What about a bath? Can you take a bath?"

A bath. The standalone Jacuzzi tub had been quite appealing when we had first toured the house. I'd pictured myself in there with a glass of Pinot Grigio and a flickering candle. Except, I'd been pregnant when we moved in. I couldn't drink wine and I couldn't recline in a hot bath—too scared I'd overheat the baby. But now I could. In theory.

"You tell me," I said to Tyler. "Can I take a bath?"

"Of course," he said, leaping up from the sofa, placing his phone onto the armrest, as though Oliver had awakened already and was starting to scream. "I will watch him."

I turned away to conceal my rolling eyes. He made it sound like he was babysitting, not parenting. He looked at me, as though awaiting his instructions—*I'll be home by nine, help yourself to anything in the pantry.*

Upstairs, I wiped the tub clean with a wad of toilet paper. It had collected dust from lack of use. I filled it, adding a drizzle of bubble bath, then undressed, letting my clothes fall to the floor, averting my eyes from the mirrors hanging on the wall across from me.

I had just sunk into the water, rested my head against the back of the tub, and closed my eyes, when Oliver began to cry. Tyler's murmuring traveled up the stairs. He would need me, and soon.

I cracked an eye. The bubbles were dissipating already. I could see my angry, red nipple, grotesque in its raw meat–like appearance, rimmed and puckered from Oliver's persistent gums. I used my fingertips to pull a mound of bubbles across the surface of the water, to cover it up. Oliver continued to cry.

I sank deeper and deeper, beneath the surface of the water, letting it swallow me up. Oliver's wails traveled through the ceiling and floor, or perhaps a vent, dulled, but still audible. The pressure from the water swirled around me, my lungs began to ache.

"Nat?" So quiet, I could barely hear it. The crying, I could hear. I could feel it in my gut, my chest, my blood, more powerful and piercing than the lack of air.

Don't touch him. Stay away from my husband.

And now Erin was gone. Paul seemed to hate me for it, as if it were my fault.

I pushed myself up to the surface, opened my mouth, let the oxygen rush in.

The stirring was gone. The hope. Everything that my time with Paul had given me was gone now.

I wiped the water from my eyes. Tyler was standing in the doorway, Oliver in his arms, a look of horror, of fear, on his face, as if he'd found me drowning. And maybe he had. Maybe I was.

I heaved myself out of the tub.

THIRTY-SEVEN

It was an ugly bush. It had been ugly ever since we had bought the house. Ugly and close to death. At a certain point, we'd known, we would have to put it out of its misery. But why now? With his own hands?

Tyler had unearthed a reciprocating saw from somewhere in the basement, while I looked on disapprovingly, Oliver in my arms.

"Where did that even come from?" I asked.

Tyler glanced at the box, shrugged. "I can't remember. I bought it for some project at the old house."

It was true. He had a spurt of activity, playing handyman, when we had first moved into the old house, trying to fix various items that had come up on the home inspection report but that the seller had refused to repair. He'd not done the same thing when we had moved into this house. There'd been fewer things to do. The house was newer, in better shape.

But there was that bush on the side, scratchy and sharp, green and yellow but also tangled with dried and dead branches, brown, disintegrating. We had agreed that we would eventually tear it out, put in something more attractive and less dead-looking.

The lawn service had stopped coming for the year. Fall cleanup, leaf raking, and weed pulling weren't included, and weeds abounded in the garden beds lining our house.

In the morning, Tyler had emerged from our closet in a hideously old pair of jeans and a threadbare sweatshirt. "I'm going to work in the yard," he'd said.

My head snapped up. "What? Why?"

"There are weeds everywhere. That bush is almost dead. It's embarrassing."

"Okay," I'd said, adjusting Oliver in my arms. "Then call our service for an estimate. Why would you do it yourself?"

Tyler shook his head. "I'm perfectly capable of doing it myself."

He disappeared downstairs, and irritation bubbled, because that wasn't the point—his capability. Because he should have been holding Oliver. Spending time with him. That's what he should have *wanted*. What kind of a person chose non-urgent yard work, work we could have easily afforded to have someone else, a professional, perform, when he could instead spend time with his son?

The bush was on the same side of the house as the path that led to nowhere. I sat in a chair at the dining room table and watched Tyler work. Oliver was on his play mat on the floor in front of me. The excruciatingly upbeat song, so at odds with my mood, was blaring repeatedly.

He'd begun enthusiastically, the saw whirring as he hacked at branches, tossing them into a tangled pile. He had taken a break to come inside to dig out his thick, fleece snow gloves. I assumed the dried branches were pricking his skin. He looked ridiculous. I would have laughed if I weren't so angry.

He had slowed, then, his energy waning, but he persisted. Once the bush had been fully dismembered and nothing remained but a knobby stump, he began to drag branches across the yard, into the woods. He disappeared there, out of my view. I turned from the window and carried Oliver to the family room to nurse him, sitting on the sofa, facing the double levels of windows.

The leaves had gone from amber, gold, and red to pale brown and were dropping rapidly. Our yard was covered. It would need to be raked. I wondered whether Tyler would elect to tackle that chore himself as well.

Tyler emerged from the tree line and made his way inside, his forehead and chest damp with sweat.

"All done?" I asked coldly.

He removed his gloves, bits of branch falling to the floor. "I'll dig out the stump and pull the weeds tomorrow," he said. "Should we have some lunch?"

I laughed, a sharp bark of a sound, so bitter and crackling that it seemed broken.

"What?" Tyler asked innocently, folding the backs of the gloves over so that they would stay together.

"You're going to spend all day tomorrow doing yard work, too?"

"It needs to get done, Nat," he said, shrugging.

"Then hire someone. You haven't done any yard work since we moved in here. Why now?"

"We only have one income now," he replied with almost aggressive patience. He was plucking tiny yellowed and browned needles from his shirt and tossing them onto the floor. "We don't have as much money to spend on things like that."

"Are you kidding me?" I asked. "You have got to be kidding me."

He just looked at me, defiance in his eyes. Not fear. Not yet.

"You just made partner, Tyler. Your income has skyrocketed. We have plenty of money. That's an excuse."

He looked rather smug, and I hated that I'd said it. "An excuse for what?" he asked.

"Because you don't want to hold your son. You don't want to spend time with him. You'd rather be working in the yard than spending time with him."

"That's not true," Tyler said. He shook his head sadly, as if he pitied me. "He doesn't want me to hold him. He only wants you. If I was holding him, he would only cry for you."

"Oh, so that's a reason not to do it?" I asked. *"Oh well, he doesn't like me. Too bad. I'll just give up and not have a relationship with my own child?"*

Oliver was beginning to wriggle in my arms. Our voices had risen. I stood up and draped him over my shoulder.

"No," said Tyler. "He's a baby. I will be able to have a relationship with him when he's older. When he's not breastfeeding. Now he only wants you."

"That's the stupidest thing I've ever heard," I said.

"Is it wrong?" he demanded. "Am I wrong?" His eyes were wide. I couldn't remember the last time he'd been this angry with me.

"Yes," I said. "You're wrong."

He threw up his hands, then crossed his arms. I thought he was going to storm off, but he didn't. He had something else to say.

"You could try," I continued. "Maybe if you tried, if you spent more time with him, he would get used to you and he would find you comforting. Maybe you'd be able to get him to stop crying."

"You don't let me try," he exploded. "You don't let me try." Quieter that time. He was looking at Oliver. "Every time I have him, and he doesn't stop crying immediately, you take him away and you breastfeed him. I don't get a chance."

I stared at him, feeling the tension between my eyebrows, feeling my shoulders rising toward my ears. *No.* That couldn't be right. He gave up. He brought me Oliver. He admitted defeat. Didn't he?

"The other night when I was taking a bath, you brought him to me. You told me you would watch him, then you brought him to me when I was in the bath."

"That is so unfair," Tyler said. "He hadn't eaten for a while. He was hungry. You just picked one example. That's probably the only time I brought him to you. Every other time you just take him away from me."

"Because I can't stand to hear him cry," I shrieked. The rage had bubbled too high. It was spilling over now. "You can't soothe him, and I just want him to stop. Because the sound of him crying makes me want to die. Do you understand that? I want to die when he's crying."

Tyler fell silent. He looked away from me. He didn't understand. He couldn't. It wasn't mental. It wasn't in my head, imagined, the feeling when Oliver cried. It wasn't something that could be cured by deep breathing or therapy. It was a physical reaction. The stress hormone crashing over me in waves. The need for my child to not cry was the most powerful thing I had ever felt, aside from the love that I had for him. The love that was still there, always there, driving everything, no matter how shattered I felt.

"I need a break," I said. "When you are home, I should get a break. I have him all the time. Twenty-four hours a day. You should want to spend time with him." I was repeating myself, I knew, but my thoughts were blurring and my mind was fogging. I'd had three hours of sleep the previous night—total, not consecutive.

"I don't get a break, either, Nat," Tyler said. "I work a ton of hours. I get home and do stuff around the house. I hold him whenever he lets me."

"*Work is a break.* Work is so much easier than what I do every day. And you get a break every single night," I cried. The rage had simmered down now. Not gone, but dormant. I felt desperately sad. "You sleep every single night. I don't. I stay up almost all night. I have for three months now. Do you understand what that is like?"

Tyler shook his head. "That's been your choice. You're such a martyr," he said, his voice icy, his words clipped. "Why do you have to be such a martyr?"

The word caught in my mind, like a speck of gold in a sieve. It hung there, glistening. I couldn't process it, was too tired to recall what exactly it meant. But I liked the sound of it. It felt right, like a pair of worn sneakers, molded to the high arches of my feet. It didn't sound like a bad thing.

"Whatever," I said. I could no longer remember how or why the fight had started, and I was too exhausted for it to continue. It didn't feel like either of us had won.

Tyler stepped around me without another word. I heard him climbing the stairs, then, a minute later, the shower turned on.

He'd shower leisurely, enjoying the sound of only the water pounding on his back and the tiled floor. Oliver always seemed to be screaming when I showered. He'd dress, then come downstairs. He'd probably fire up his laptop and bill a few hours as the day wore on. He'd drink a couple beers, watch something on television. He'd do what he wanted to do, his life resembling its pre-baby state so closely.

I put Oliver in his swing and sank onto the family room sofa. I absolutely refused to make lunch. I already knew that Tyler would come downstairs and glance around, expecting it to be done. The unfairness of it all was crushing. And why? Why was it like this? I didn't understand. I'd done everything I could not to fall into this role. Yet here I was. I felt like a mindless milk machine. I might as well be a cow. You could put me out in the barn, walk me out when needed. In the meantime, I'd stand there, banal, mundane, quiet. Using and needing very few brain cells.

I thought about crying. It might provide a small measure of relief, of release. It might elicit some measure of sympathy from my husband. But then, I thought of Paul. Was he the real reason I was falling apart? Was it just that I'd been relying on him to give me what I needed, and he wasn't available right now? Perhaps I was only missing his help and his comfort.

Things were so fresh, so confusing, with Erin having just gone missing, I told myself. He just needed time. In time, he would be available again. I just needed to hold on.

THIRTY-EIGHT

My knees were aching as I sat folded on the floor in Oliver's bedroom, removing tiny onesies, pants, and footie pajamas, and even tinier socks from his dresser and piling them into a storage bin. Oliver always seemed to be outgrowing clothes, and pulling too-small things from his dresser, replacing them with new ones, felt like an incessant, never-ending chore.

It seemed, although he'd not told me I was right or apologized, that Tyler felt badly about our fight. He'd not headed back out to the yard this morning to finish his work. He'd muttered only that he'd be calling our lawn service to handle it, would ask them rake up the leaves, too. He'd been doting on Oliver much of the day. Playing peekaboo, offering to give him bottles, reading him picture books while peering down at him. Oliver gazed at the images in wonder.

Tyler had suggested he watch Oliver while he napped in his swing so that I could *take a break*. I could have gone out for a walk or lain in bed, tried to fall asleep myself. But I could walk with Oliver, and I knew I wouldn't be able to fall asleep. Perhaps in an effort to demonstrate to Tyler just how hard I worked all the time, I'd decided to tackle Oliver's dresser, even though the chore wasn't urgent. I typically chipped away at it, pulling out a few items of clothing when I was preparing to change him, or packing some away after I did his laundry.

Even though there was a great deal of pressure and discomfort emanating from my groin as I sat on the hard floor, at least it was quiet. Being away from Oliver when he wasn't crying, having him out of my sight, gave me time to miss him, and I needed that. We both did.

I could hear murmurs from the television traveling up the stairs from the family room. Tyler must have grown bored and turned it on. I could only hope he didn't wake Oliver. I needed more time.

I tucked a few too-small onesies into the storage bin and snapped on the lid, then pushed it into the spare bedroom, which was still used exclusively for baby items. When we'd bought the house, we had talked about how it would become Oliver's childhood bedroom. We'd move him in there after we had our second child, and the baby would take over the nursery. Now, these thoughts sent a spike of horror through my gut.

"Nat," Tyler shouted from downstairs, his tone desperate, shocked.

Panic flooded into my mind. *Oliver.* I ran faster than I'd run in months, maybe even a year, down the stairs, into the family room.

But Oliver was still sleeping peacefully, swaying back and forth in his swing, the tinkling music playing from the mobile on top. Tyler was not looking at him, but at the television screen in front of him.

It was a picture of Erin. Her blown-straight hair, bright and smiling eyes, her lips, red, as always.

The picture disappeared, was replaced by a reporter, standing outdoors.

I looked at the text emblazoned across the bottom of the screen in bold, white font.

Body of Missing Patuxent County Woman Found in Woods.
Erin Riley.

Husband has identified her body, the reporter was saying.

"That's our woods," Tyler said, pointing to the television.

He was right. It was our woods. I'd recognize it anywhere. Thick with trees and vegetation that had become obscured by the fallen leaves, surrounding the stream, neighborhoods on either side of it. The reporter was on-site, in its midst, surrounded by yellow caution tape. Uniformed bodies moved in the background.

"We haven't seen any news vans or police. You'd think they would park here if they walked into the woods," Tyler said.

I didn't reply.

"Maybe they parked in the neighborhoods on the other side of it, or farther down," he continued in my silence.

There's been no formal ruling as to cause of death at this time. We will await results of the autopsy, but a police spokesperson has indicated that the death is being treated as suspicious.

Tyler was looking at me. "Holy shit," he said. "She was murdered."

"You don't know that," I snapped, still watching the screen, although the images had blurred before my eyes and dizziness was sweeping over me.

"That's what they just said," Tyler retorted.

"They just said they don't know yet," I told him. "I heard it."

"Did her husband say anything to you about what might have happened?" Tyler asked.

I shook my head numbly. "I told you," I said. "I haven't talked to him since he was going door-to-door, asking all the neighbors if they'd seen her."

"Good," Tyler said suddenly, fiercely. "You should not be hanging around that guy ever again."

"What guy?" I asked, even though I knew.

"Her husband."

"*Paul.*" I couldn't help myself.

"*Paul,*" he said, imitating my tone, "could have killed his wife."

My defense of him was automatic and assured. "Don't be ridiculous," I said. "He didn't kill his wife. She went for a walk. She left alive, alone. She never returned."

Tyler shook his head, exasperated. "So he told you. You don't know that."

"You don't know him," I said. I pictured Paul, his gentle, capable hands, cradling Oliver, rubbing his back as he walked him around his living room. He couldn't have hurt his wife.

"You don't know him, either." Tyler was almost shouting now. "Listen to yourself. You sound insane."

And I was. I'd been insane for a long time now.

"He could be dangerous," Tyler continued. He was *activated* now, excited to prove his point. Excited to paint me as the monster that I was. "And you go to his house. You invite him into ours. You let him hold our baby."

We both looked down at Oliver, still sleeping in his swing, despite the rising tension and voices. His *Goddamn Swing* was how I'd come to think of it. Goddamn Swing. We both loved it so much, Oliver and me. Too much. Why couldn't we just put it in our bedroom, let him sleep there all night? What, exactly, was so unsafe about it? He was strapped in, facing upward, with no blankets or other suffocation risks. It was just a rule. Yet another rule. Sometimes, they felt random, these rules. They felt personal and promulgated for the sole purpose of making new motherhood as difficult as possible.

"Stay away from him," Tyler demanded, drawing my attention back to him, away from the Goddamn Swing. *Stay away from my husband.* "I don't want you spending time with him anymore."

I stood there with my arms crossed, looking at him. I didn't know Paul, he'd said. Well, in this moment, I didn't know my husband. Anger and frustration flashing in his bulging eyes, while he once again told me what to do. Directed me to stop doing my one thing, the one thing that I had. The one thing that had provided me with relief and comfort and hope. After I'd lost so much else. How dare he?

"You already told me that," I said, my voice eerily calm. So calm, too calm. "I already told you I wouldn't."

Paul didn't want to see me, either, that much was clear. But I felt desperate for that to change. That I hadn't agreed with Tyler's theory, his suspicions, had not gone unnoticed.

It was like a switch flipped. Tyler slumped onto the sofa. The anger drained away. He rubbed his hands over his face. "Nat," he said. There was a long pause. "Please be careful. I can't lose you. Why do I feel like I'm losing you?"

I gazed down at him, blinked. Once. Twice. I said nothing. I turned and left the room, back upstairs. Oliver was asleep. It was still my time, still my break, and I was going to use it.

He was wrong again.

I can't lose you.

He'd already lost me. I'd lost myself.

THIRTY-NINE

"Bed rest," she said, echoing her text message, the one that had sent me hurtling into the car, with Oliver, of course, on Monday morning, for a spontaneous visit to my best friend.

I sat on the edge of her bed, Oliver in my arms. Downstairs, her husband, Dan, was clattering around. He'd greeted me with a look of panic on his face. He'd taken a few days off, he'd told me, but that was all the time he could afford to take until the baby was born. Elaine would be on her own, on bed rest.

The pleasant perfection of Elaine's pregnancy had come to an end the previous night. She had started to bleed and had rushed to the hospital for an ultrasound, where it was discovered that while the baby was fine, Elaine's placenta was covering the opening of her cervix. The baby's source of food and life was blocking its way out. Elaine was placed on bed rest for the remainder of her pregnancy, was directed to wait, like a vegetable, to see if the placenta would shift. Wait for any signs of another bleed. If there was any more blood, she might need an emergency C-section.

"I can't believe this is happening," she said. "I was feeling so great. I had no idea that I had this issue."

"I guess you wouldn't," I said, patting her leg. I'd trade places with her in an instant. *Put Oliver back in my uterus, please. Hook him up to everything he needs. Confine me to a bed.* God, it seemed like nirvana.

"I was scheduled to have an ultrasound in a couple days. My doctor said it would have been discovered at that time. The placenta wasn't covering the cervix at my last appointment."

She was repeating herself. She had been ever since I'd arrived.

"And I can't work," she continued. "It's not like I can work from home.

My practice will assign me to all the telehealth patients, people who want to see someone via video. But that won't be very many. They might have to cut my pay. They can't afford to pay me all these weeks of leave, plus twelve weeks of maternity leave."

"I'm sure they can," I told her. "It's just a matter of whether they want to, or the partners would rather take advantage and gobble up as much profit as they can."

"You're so cynical," she said, looking at me sharply.

I shrugged. She'd get there soon.

"Anyway," she said, holding out her arms, "should I take him?"

I thought she'd never ask. I passed her my son, and she lifted him up, his head wobbling only slightly as he stared into her face while she murmured and cooed. He looked on with interest.

"I won't be able to rock him or walk him around," she said. "But we'll see how he does." She pressed Oliver against her shoulder and began to rub his back. "What's been going on with you?" she asked. "I haven't seen you in a while."

"Oh, um, the same, I guess. Just staying home with Oliver. Not sleeping much."

"Still?" Elaine asked. She looked worried. She should be.

"Still. He's been getting one stretch of sleep that's three or four hours long. Other than that, he wakes up every hour or so. Sometimes less."

"God, I thought it would have gotten easier for you by now." She was still rubbing tiny circles onto Oliver's back. His head was drooping sleepily toward her neck.

"Me, too."

There was a companionable silence, then, "What about that woman who was murdered?" Elaine asked. "Have you seen that on the news? She lived on your street, didn't she?"

"Yes," I replied, as discomfort crept in. "She lived just a few houses up from me. It's awful."

"What do you think happened?" she asked. "I mean, they don't think it was random, do they? It was probably her husband. It's always the husband."

"I don't know what *they* think," I said, bristling. "But I know her husband, actually," I added, sniffing, crossing my arms. "It couldn't have been him."

"Do you?"

"We had become sort of friendly," I explained. "He's a writer and stay-at-home dad. He loves kids. We met when we were both out in the neighborhood one day, and he's spent some time holding Oliver, giving me a break. He's a very nice person." I thought of all the things he'd brought me. The butter-soft muffins. The artwork now hanging above Oliver's crib. The baby wrap. I thought of my panic attack in the neighborhood, how he'd rescued me. Elaine only wanted to place blame on him to make herself feel better. Everyone would feel safer if it had been a targeted attack.

"Oh," Elaine replied, her surprise evident. "Well, I'm not sure who it could have been, then. I just hope no one else goes missing or gets killed. I hope it's not a serial killer or something."

"I highly doubt it," I said, shifting on her bed. It was like we were sitting together, squeezed onto one of our tiny dorm room beds in college, chatting long into the night. Except, it was nothing like that.

"You've never mentioned this man to me before," Elaine said quietly, hesitantly. "Is there something going on with him?"

I looked at her. "What do you mean?"

"I mean"—she lowered her voice further—"do you *like* him?"

Now she sounded like a twelve-year-old girl, not a college student, and certainly not an adult. Was I supposed to squeal "Yes!" and leap up to jump on her bed excitedly, embarrassed?

"It's not like that," I said, not sure if I was telling the truth. My feelings had become so complicated, so confusing in Erin's and Paul's absences. "It's just nice to have someone close by who loves babies. Someone who understands what it's like to put your career on hold to care for your child. It's nice to have someone who can take him and give me a break."

"Okay," Elaine said uncertainly. "I get it." But it didn't sound like she did. And I wouldn't have, either, back when I was in my third trimester, when my greatest fears, my greatly naïve fears, had been about childbirth and childbirth alone. But she'd probably understand soon.

I pushed myself off the edge of her bed. "I'd better go," I said. "Time to nurse Oliver."

Panic flashed in Elaine's eyes. She didn't want me to leave.

"I'll come back and visit you after Dan goes back to work," I said. "I can keep you company sometimes."

"Okay," she said, pacified. "That would be nice."

I collected a dozing Oliver, gave her hand a quick squeeze, and departed.

FORTY

When I slowed down on the hill of Ashby Drive, on my way home from Elaine's, I noticed a navy sedan parked in front of my mailbox. Detective West was back. I'd known that she would be, but I'd hoped that it wouldn't be so soon.

She met me in the driveway as I was extracting Oliver's car seat. He'd fallen asleep in the car, of course. I'd been planning on waking him to nurse, then trying to put him down for a nap so I could take a little time for myself. Now, I'd have to leave him in the seat so that I could be interviewed by the police.

"Good morning," Detective West said brightly, as though she were a friendly neighbor who'd spotted me while she was out front watering her azaleas.

"Oh, hello," I said, as if I'd just noticed her, too. "Can I help you with something?"

She nodded toward my sleeping baby. "Asleep in the car, I see. They do that, don't they? It never failed with my son, too. I used to drive around for hours, sometimes in the middle of the night."

I stared at her. Was she telling me the truth? Or was she lying, trying to draw herself closer to me? Trying to trick me into opening up to her?

"Could I come in and chat for a few minutes?" she continued, then began walking toward my house, not waiting for me to reply.

I heaved the car seat off the driveway. "Alright," I said.

She followed me up the porch steps and into the living room, where we took our seats after I had positioned the car seat so that I could watch Oliver sleep.

"I want to speak with you again," Detective West said, "about the day Erin Riley went missing."

"Okay," I said, shifting uncertainly on the sofa. "I think I told you everything." Instantly, I regretted my use of the word *think*.

The detective tucked a loose crimson hair behind her ear. "You said you left the Riley house, and you never saw her again."

"Right," I replied, nodding, waiting.

"She didn't come to your house that afternoon?" The detective was staring into my face.

"Erin? I already told you she didn't." Why was she asking me again?

"Are you sure?"

I looked up. Suddenly, I saw her. Erin. On my porch. In my house. No. Just in my yard. Us, walking together in the woods. Arguing. Sharp voices, leaves crunching beneath our feet. Snippets of memories knocked at my mind. But they weren't memories. They weren't real.

"I'm sure," I said.

"Because apparently she had mentioned she was going to speak with you. Apparently, a neighbor"—she looked down at her notes—"told us that Erin Riley was seen approaching your house late Monday afternoon."

I blinked dumbly, meeting her eyes, then shook my head. "No," I said. "Maybe she was approaching the woods, the path that leads there, beside my house."

Detective West waited for me to continue. I couldn't help but do just that.

"Did the neighbor actually see her at my house, or just walking toward it?" I asked. "Because if she was just walking toward it, then she was also walking toward the woods. And that's where she was found."

"I'm afraid I don't need to answer your questions, Mrs. Fanning."

I nodded, as if her words hadn't bothered me at all.

"That isn't all that a neighbor saw," she said. "Can you tell me about the argument you had with Erin, on her front porch?"

"Oh," I said, as if I'd forgotten, when in fact it remained one of the few things I couldn't forget. "Like I told you, Erin seemed a bit jealous—for no reason, of course—of my friendship with her husband. She wasn't thrilled that I'd been in her house. It wasn't that big of an issue. There was nothing for her to worry about, but I would have respected her wishes." *If she hadn't been killed.*

"I heard that it got quite heated. I was told that Erin actually grabbed you."

Stay away from my husband. Venomous, snakelike, lashing toward me.

"I suppose she did," I said. "She was angry, but I did nothing to escalate the situation. I left. And I never saw her after that."

Mrs. Jensen. Who else could it have been? I'd seen her when I was rushing home, after leaving the Rileys' house, hadn't I? She was out to get me. She saw me for what I was. She heard my baby screaming while I walked him around the neighborhood, screaming in a way that I'd never heard any other baby scream. She judged me for my ineptitude in the face of her own soft and natural motherliness.

"Well," said Detective West, pushing herself up from her seat, "if you change your mind, if you remember something, please let me know."

Which was a kindlier way of telling me to stop lying.

But I wasn't lying.

I walked her to the front door, then stood there, looking out the front window for a long time. I watched her climb into her car and drive away. I stared at Mrs. Jensen's house. There was no movement visible, but she was probably standing at her front window, too, looking on with satisfaction. I watched the Riley house, peaceful and pristine as ever.

How was he doing, I wondered? When would I see him again? He'd been so cold when I'd last seen him, almost accusatory. I didn't understand, but I needed to.

It was all I could do to not burst from my house and ring his doorbell. But I couldn't. It was far too early. I turned away from the window and moved back into the living room to watch Oliver sleep in his car seat, as if it were any other Monday afternoon. As if everything hadn't changed.

FORTY-ONE

I waited until long after the detective's generic navy sedan had disappeared. I stood before Oliver's car seat and watched until his eyelids fluttered then pinched, his mouth turned down then opened, until a low wail began. I shushed him, nursed him, patted his back, changed him, then pushed into the garage and tucked him into his stroller.

The detective had probably visited Paul's house before she had visited mine. She wouldn't be back so soon. It was too early to go, with suspicion swirling around me, but perhaps it was also the best time to go and see him.

On his front porch, though, I paused, thinking of Petra. Was she inside the house? Would I be intruding?

I should have brought something with me, like the lemon muffins he had brought for me. That's what you did when someone died. That was the neighborly thing to do. Yet, here I was, nothing in my arms but my baby, nothing to offer them.

November was making its presence known. It was colder every day. The trees were becoming more and more bare. I held Oliver tightly against my chest, tugging the lapels of my jacket around his little body. His chin was resting against my shoulder, taking in the sights of the outdoors, his still quite thin hair lifting in the faint breeze. I'd forgotten a hat for him. Did I even own a hat that might fit? The obligatory pink-and-blue-striped hospital hats he'd worn as a newborn would be far too small by now, not that I knew where they were. I knew I'd saved them, but they could be anywhere. I should have tucked them carefully into a memento box, along with his inked footprints and a lock of his hair, to take out as he grew, to finger and smell. I'd probably lost them.

I lifted an arm to knock, then dropped it again.

I shouldn't be here.

I turned and bent over Oliver's stroller, preparing to place him back inside, to return home, but there was a squeak and a brief rush of air, and when I looked over my shoulder it was to see Paul standing in his open doorway, the corners of his eyes crinkling in a smile that didn't reach his lips.

I straightened, acting as though I'd been lifting Oliver from his stroller, not putting him back inside it.

"I thought I heard something," he said.

"I'm sorry," I told him, tucking Oliver beneath my jacket once again. "I know I shouldn't be here."

His brows lowered, creases formed between them. "Why?"

Did he really not get it? *Stay away from my husband.*

"Well, it doesn't look great, does it? Erin is gone, and I'm here at your house." I didn't know how else to explain it. What was I to him? What was he to me? The stirring was there, becoming a fluttering at the top of my chest.

He said nothing, just watched me with his golden eyes.

"I just wanted to see how you were doing," I said, disappointed. "How's Petra?"

He sighed, crossed his arms. He seemed warmer today, but he didn't invite me inside. He really didn't get it. We shouldn't be out here, talking, for all the neighborhood to see.

"She's not doing well," he said. He rubbed his hands over his cheeks, against the dark stubble, flecked with gray. "She's in her room, won't come out. I'm surprised, really. She was never very close with Erin. It's always been the two of us that were close. But, I suppose, she's older now. She'll be a teenager soon enough. Teenage girls need their mothers."

"I'm sorry," I replied, shifting nervously on my feet. I didn't know what else to say. I hoped that Petra was the only reason he wasn't inviting me inside.

Paul's head lifted, his brows wrinkled again. "I thought I saw," he told me, "the detective driving past a bit ago. Was she at your house? Looked like she was coming from the end of the cul-de-sac."

"Oh," I replied, startled by his question. "She was. She wanted to ask me if Erin came to my house. She said a neighbor saw her walking toward it." I shook my head and shrugged, as best as I could with Oliver in my arms, as though bewildered.

Paul was blinking at me. "Right," he said. "She was walking to your house."

There was a coldness wrapping itself around me. Solid and icy and not at all caused by the crisp and fresh November air.

"She didn't walk to my house," I said.

"That's what you told me. But when she left, she'd said she was going down to speak with you. She must have had something more to say to you that afternoon. She never returned."

Despite how it would look, I sat down, perched on the edge of the steps leading to the Rileys' front porch, beneath Paul.

What was he talking about? Why hadn't he told me this when he'd first stopped by, the day he was going door-to-door? Or had he? I couldn't remember.

"Why do you think she wanted to talk to me?" I asked. *Stay away from my husband.* What more might she have wanted to say? Oliver began to squirm against my collarbone. He didn't like it when I sat.

"I'm sure you know, Nat." There was an air of frustration, exasperation, a whiff of *We've been over this.* "You know she wasn't thrilled to find you in the house, in the middle of the day. You know she was angry. I thought she might want to confront you again, to ask you whether there was something going on between the two of us. I let her go. I knew you'd tell her there wasn't, put her mind at ease."

My cheeks burned. He was right. Erin was right. I shouldn't have been in her home that day. She'd been right to say what she said. And I shouldn't have returned, after she disappeared, nor after she was killed, after her body was found. I shouldn't be here now.

I stood up, turned, and tucked Oliver into his stroller.

"Natalie," Paul said.

I didn't look at him.

"Where are you going?"

I gripped the handlebars of the stroller. "I shouldn't keep coming here," I said. "I'm sorry about everything."

"It's not your fault," Paul said. His words were kind, but he was backing away from me. "I like spending time with you and Oliver."

"Well, it looks wrong," I said. I pushed farther away. It was the last thing we needed, to have the neighbors, Mrs. Jensen, see us together.

"I don't care how it looks. Why does that matter?"

"It matters because you told the police your wife was coming down to talk to me right before she disappeared. Someone told her that we'd argued. She grabbed me. Did you know that? She was so angry that she grabbed my arms. She told me to stay away from you. Then she was killed. They might think I was the last person to see her. But I wasn't."

Paul was still blinking at me, innocent and surprised. "Jesus," he said. "I didn't think of it in that way, Nat. I was just telling the police the truth. That was what she said. But if you say she didn't come down to speak with you, then I'm sure you're right. She probably went straight into the woods to walk and clear her head. Maybe it was a random crime. She was attacked in the woods. Or maybe it was suicide."

"Still," I said. "I'd better go. If I can help in any way, let me know."

Paul nodded slightly. He was still watching me quietly. I wondered if my words sounded as hollow to him as they did to me. There wasn't anything I could do for him. His wife was gone. His daughter was devastated and motherless. I couldn't bring her back.

There was a burning behind my eyes, as there always was. It worsened in the afternoons. I pushed the stroller down the hill, toward my house, zombielike, feeling staggering and awkward, feeling the eyes of my neighbors on me.

There she goes, back home. She was at the Riley house. She stood out front with Paul. Can't help herself. I've seen them together quite a bit this past month, and now, his wife is dead. I don't know, I couldn't speculate about something so awful—yes, yes you could. You could and you will. You already had.

It was a dryness making my eyes burn, I thought. Human beings' eyes weren't meant to be open for as many hours a day as mine were. For three months, I'd been getting only a handful of hours of sleep a day. It had become automatic, but that didn't mean it was easy. Oliver cried. I got up. I nursed him. I put him down. Tyler slept beside me. Over and over again, in a blurred loop like a wheel racing down a hill. Racing toward what, I didn't yet know, but surely it wouldn't be good for me.

I eyed the path that led to the woods, to nowhere, by the side of my house as I pushed into the driveway. That must have been how Erin got in there. I closed my eyes for a second, swaying, unsteady on my feet. Did I see her that day? Had she come back? Images flooded in, like they had before, when I was sitting in my living room with the detective. Memories of a swirling sky and sharp voices and flaring, fear-filled eyes. Erin's. Of a wavering, pulsing rage. My own. Of sudden, knifelike movements.

But no. That hadn't happened. She had never come to my house. So, why had she told Paul that she was going to? Why had someone seen her walking here?

I opened my eyes and hurried the stroller into the garage. Oliver began to cry as I lifted him from the stroller. He wriggled in my arms. *You're a mess. You're a monster,* he seemed to say.

I held him tightly and rushed to the sofa, arranged the pillows beneath my elbows, and settled down to feed him. "I'm doing the best I can," I said defensively. He lunged for my nipple and began to nurse. He was heavy and solid in my arms. He wasn't upset with me. He wasn't ashamed. He loved me with every piece of him, even though he was too young to know that he did. I was his everything, and he was mine. He didn't think I was a monster or a mess. That was all in my head. That was just my mind, letting me down again.

FORTY-TWO

He stood on his porch, arms crossed, and watched her go. He was pleased that she'd stopped by to see him, and he'd wanted her to understand that, but it was equally important that the neighbors, the police, believed the opposite.

She had been the last person to see his wife alive. Mrs. Jensen was witness to that. She had seen Erin confront Natalie on the porch last Monday afternoon. She had seen Erin grip Natalie's arms. This particular piece of evidence had not been his doing but was yet another stroke of good luck.

Mrs. Jensen had even seen Erin striding toward Natalie's house in that billowing windbreaker, before turning away from her windows. The storm had been rolling in, and it had been time to prepare an early dinner. She'd stepped away from her window. She'd seen nothing more. She'd not known that Erin hadn't in fact gone to Natalie's. That she had, instead, proceeded straight into the woods.

There was this—the confrontation at the party, then on his porch; Erin being seen walking toward Natalie's house; that being the last time she was seen; Natalie continuing to stop by, uninvited, in the face of his wife's murder. There was also what he was going to do next.

Paul moved into the kitchen and slipped his cell phone from the pocket of his jeans. There was music pulsing softly from upstairs. Petra. He would go up to check on her when he was finished. Her mother's sudden disappearance, then death, seemed to transform her into a teenager in the blink of an eye. His bright little sun was blazing, licking with flames. She was ridden with angst, prone to abrupt mood swings. But they would get through it. It was nothing he couldn't weather.

Now, he would be able to continue staying home with her, without having Erin constantly in his ear, at his throat. Petra would remain at her school. He'd be free from Erin—no need for alimony or child support, for a messy divorce, for a custody battle.

Once Natalie was arrested for her murder, the life insurance proceeds would come through. Several million dollars. He'd invest it wisely, live comfortably off the interest income and their savings. Perhaps with Erin's impatient and stifling presence gone—the antithesis to a muse— his writer's block would lift, and that novel would finally flow.

He searched for Detective West's number, her mobile line. She answered almost immediately.

"I thought you should know," he told her, "Natalie stopped by here again."

"Did she?" The detective, so formidably straight-faced, so incessantly cool, finally revealed the slightest uptick of interest.

"I'm afraid so. She came right to my house, uninvited. I couldn't be-lieve it. I'll be honest with you, Detective. She's making me quite uncom-fortable." He paused to chew on his lip, although she couldn't see him. "Now that we know that Erin is gone, I'm thinking about everything in a new light. What I'd thought was her friendship feels more and more like an obsession. Erin didn't like it. She wasn't going to let it go. I'm scared of what Natalie might have done." He choked on a welling sob. "What did she do to my wife?"

There was a long pause during which he feared he'd gone a bit too far.

"I'd like to hear more about this," the detective said at last. "I'd like you to write everything down for me. I can come by now. Does that work for you?"

"Of course," he said. "Please come."

He hung up the phone, then navigated to the string of text messages he'd sent to himself from Natalie's phone, that day in her house when he'd hung the painting in Oliver's nursery while she'd been resting obliviously in her bed. He took a screenshot, emailed it to himself, then moved into the first-floor study. It was used for Petra's homework room, but she didn't need it now. She wouldn't, for a while. He wasn't sure when she would be ready to return to school, though he trusted that the school would do what was needed to help her catch up. That was the level of attention that he paid for.

He awakened the family computer, opened his email, then the image of the messages.

I need to see you.
Please.
Please don't ignore me.
I need you.
I'm coming up there.

They seemed a bit too obvious to him, looking at them now. Would he be doubted for taking this long to show them to her? He hoped that he could explain his delay by saying that until Erin's body was found, he'd been clinging to hope that she was hiding somewhere, taking some time for herself. Now that she was gone, his neighbor's obsession with him seemed important. He'd been blind to the severity of the danger before. Natalie continuing to stop by to see him had opened his eyes, as had the discovery of Erin's body, in the woods, the woods in front of which Natalie lived, the woods in which she, like Erin, had liked to walk.

In fact, he remembered mentioning to Natalie that Erin had enjoyed walking in the woods. Natalie would have seen her heading there. She would have known where to find her. He would tell the detective that.

He'd been ready for the call about the body. He knew that the police were finally combing the woods with dogs who'd been trained to detect Erin's scent. He'd handed over pieces from her laundry hamper to the police, for the dogs to smell, to become acquainted with his wife's odor. While the search parties of friends and family, arranged and led by him, had managed to miss her corpse, the dogs had not.

By then, though, all physical evidence of his presence in the woods had been destroyed. At least, that was his hope. He'd had to identify her body, of course, a formality, as he'd known better than anyone that it was her. But it had given him an opportunity to collapse in shock and grief. After that, the police had come to search his house, looking for any indication as to what might have happened to his wife. He'd been happy to have them search. It would only help to clear him. He had nothing to hide. The baby wrap was safely in Natalie's closet, out of his own.

Paul printed several copies of the messages, then closed his email, shut down the computer.

They were fine, these messages. They painted a picture of a woman obsessed. Of one-sided affection. Of a woman who was frustrated. Who was not willing to accept rejection. Who wouldn't let Erin tell her no. *Don't touch him!* How dare she?

Natalie was desperate. She was desperate for Paul to do for her what he'd done for Erin and Petra. She was desperate to be with him. Erin had stood in her way, and so she had killed her.

Paul had thought it so often, it was almost beginning to feel like the truth.

The doorbell rang. The detective was here.

FORTY-THREE

We danced around each other in the kitchen like roommates who were civil but didn't quite get along—one had drunk the other's wine or eaten the other's granola one too many times. Tyler's eyes were cast down as he filled his travel mug to the brim. He replaced the pot in the machine, and I reached for it immediately, poured two inches of liquid into my mug. Neither of us uttered a word.

I could think of things to say to Tyler. *What do you have going on today? How did you sleep?* I could recount the previous night for him, like I used to do, describing in detail every time Oliver awakened, tell him that he'd spit up all down my back at one-thirty when I'd been holding him upright and pacing the upstairs hall, explain how he'd peed in my face at two-thirty when I'd been too slow with the clean diaper. I could think of things I could say. I just didn't have the energy to actually say them. I didn't have the desire to crack the ice between us, to chip away at the bitterness.

Tyler snapped the lid on his travel mug and glanced up, meeting my eyes only briefly. He bent to drop a kiss on the top of my head as though he were a distracted grandfather.

"See you later," he said quietly. "Love you."

It was automatic for him. He still said it without thinking. For how long it would remain that way, I wasn't sure.

The front door closed with a squeak, shaking the house slightly. I could hear him locking it behind him. Was he thinking of Erin Riley when he did so, I wondered? Was he trying to keep us safe? Or was this just automatic, too, like it was the morning he had locked me out of the house?

I threw back my coffee like a college student downing a shot of liquor, and perhaps I might as well drink it from a shot glass. My days of leisurely nursing cup upon cup of coffee were long gone, and they wouldn't return until I stopped nursing my baby. I'd made it three months. I had nine more to go. It was a horrifying thought, but I accepted it resignedly. Oliver deserved it. And the relief of stopping would be easily crushed, outweighed by guilt over giving up.

I tucked my empty mug into the dishwasher, realizing only after several drips of coffee had fallen onto the plates in the rack below that the dishes were clean. Tyler's breakfast dishes were resting in the sink. He'd not bothered to unload the clean dishes, to load in the dirty ones. Not when I, his unemployed wife, could do so for him. I slammed the dishwasher closed.

I lay down on the family room sofa, pulling a throw blanket over myself, the baby monitor resting on my chest. I'd forgotten my Kindle, my phone. I didn't want to turn the television on, lest I wake Oliver. The minutes ticked by, and I stared at nothing. My breasts filled and hardened, preparing for the next feeding with no effort or thought required. This was my life. This was my purpose.

At seven-thirty, there came a faint tap at the front door. I startled, peered at the tiny screen of the monitor. Oliver hadn't stirred once. As usual, he'd saved his longest stretch of sleep until after I felt too crazed to fall asleep myself.

I padded into the living room and looked cautiously out the front window. My heart sank. The navy sedan was parked in my driveway again. She was here so early, standing on my porch. It must be important, urgent. Had there been a break in the case?

I opened the front door and crossed my arms self-consciously over my braless chest.

"Good morning," said Detective West. She didn't smile. "Can I speak with you?"

As if I had a choice. "Sure." I stepped aside, let her enter.

I did have a choice, though. I knew that—I was—*was*—a lawyer. I didn't have to talk to her. I didn't have to let her in. I could demand to have an attorney present with me. But that was what a guilty person would do, I thought. She'd done nothing, said nothing, to indicate that I was a suspect in Erin's death, had she? She was merely interviewing me as a neighbor. As a possible witness to something important.

She sat down on my living room sofa like she'd been here a thousand times before. "I know it's early," she said quietly. "I'm sorry. But I figured you would be up." She smiled wryly.

There it was again. An attempt to commiserate, to draw me close. To make me comfortable. To trap me.

"It's fine," I whispered. "But my baby is sleeping upstairs." I looked meaningfully at the monitor in my hands.

She nodded. "I wanted to speak with you," she said, her voice so respectfully low that I had to lean toward her to hear, "about your relationship with Paul Riley."

She watched me, scarcely blinking, waiting, as though her question was perfectly expected and clear, that it required no further elaboration.

"My relationship," I said. "What do you mean? We already discussed that. Paul Riley is my neighbor. We are friendly. His wife was killed. It's very tragic."

"You're friendly," she repeated. "He's your neighbor. That's it."

"Yes," I replied, bewildered. "That's it." We'd been over this before.

She waited.

"He loves children. Neither of us is working right now," I continued. "Sometimes we spend time together during the day. He holds my baby." What more did she want from me?

"In fact, you were in his home the afternoon before Mrs. Riley disappeared."

"Well, yes. I told you that. I left the house when Erin got home from work. I didn't see her again."

"There was nothing romantic about your relationship, then." Detective West watched me, her face placid.

"Romantic," I repeated, as though it was a foreign word. And it was. "No. I'm married. He's married. He was married." I swallowed. "We were only friends."

"Were." She pounced on the word. "Not anymore?"

"I'm not sure," I replied. "He is grieving, with his daughter. It's very sad."

"Did you want more from him?" she asked. Her tone was so innocent, cloaked with benign curiosity, like we were teenagers gossiping about the boy who sat next to me in biology class.

"No," I said quickly, relieved that the single word was draped in horror, at least to my own ears. "I am married. I'm a mother. It's not like that at all. It's just nice to have company. Taking care of a baby all day can be very isolating."

"I know," Detective West replied.

I remembered what she had told me about her son sleeping in the car. How she'd driven around in the middle of the night. Maybe that's what I should do. Drive through the streets. It was something to pass the time.

"Weren't you a bit too close to Mr. Riley, though? Obsessed, one could say?"

My hand flew to my chest. *"No,"* I said, defensive. "We were only friends. It was mutual. Erin might have thought there was something going on. She might have been jealous and suspicious, but there was no reason to be."

A brittle silence stretched between us. I watched Oliver on the baby monitor, wishing he would stir, cry, give me an excuse to get up.

"Why are you asking these questions?" I asked, suddenly desperate to understand what was prompting her to bring this up again. Mrs. Jensen, I suspected, watching us walk to each other's houses, seeing his arm around me, seeing us embrace. *Don't touch him! Stay away from my husband.* Erin's hands gripping my arms. I'd been back just yesterday, had sat on his porch.

"I'm afraid I can't tell you that," the detective said. I wasn't surprised.

"Well," I said, shifting nervously on the sofa, chilly and exposed in my baggy sleep shorts and milk-stained shirt, "I don't know what more I can say. I wish I could help you."

She nodded, her little crimson ponytail bobbing.

"We hope to get a break soon," she said. "We have collected all evidence possible from her body and the place where it was found. An autopsy has been performed. We will figure out who did this. I won't stop until we do."

It was my turn to nod. "Good," I said. It suddenly felt like the wrong thing to say, but there it was.

"We recovered a piece of the murder weapon from the scene," the detective continued, her eyes still boring into mine. I could feel them, even when I looked away. "It's been tested for DNA. Results pending."

Was she going to ask me for a sample? Should I tell her no?

"A piece of the murder weapon," I repeated. "How was she killed?" I asked. Something was telling me I shouldn't give up my DNA. But she'd been in my house. Perhaps she already had it. She could very well have collected something of mine without me ever noticing. That wouldn't be legal, I reminded myself. Not without a warrant.

But did she have one?

"I was wondering when you might ask," she said.

A chill trailed down my spine.

She slid a plastic bag from her pocket, held it toward me, close enough that I could see it, but not close enough that I could rip it from her hands.

"Erin Riley was strangled with a piece of fabric. There were fibers on her neck, and there was a piece of it left at the scene. There must have been a struggle. The tag ripped off. This tag, which has the brand name. We were able to identify the weapon, based on this tag."

She tilted the plastic bag gently from side to side. The tag inside was familiar. I'd studied it before. The brand name was printed neatly at the top. I knew exactly what it was from.

I dug my fingernails into my thigh as cold dread pressed against my neck, goose bumps prickled up and down my arms.

"Do you recognize this?" she asked.

My thoughts spun. Deny it? Was there a point?

I said nothing.

In the next moment, a piercing scream filled the room. For a second, I thought it was my own.

But it was Oliver, rescuing me. I stood on shaking legs. The detective did, too, but sturdy and in no rush.

"Sorry," I said, barely a whisper, "I better get him."

"I'll show myself out," Detective West replied.

I nodded and left her there, hurried up the stairs to get my baby. I lifted him from his bassinet, pressed my cheek against his, as I heard my front door close, then the detective's car rumbled to life.

"Thank you," I whispered into Oliver's neck, even though he didn't, couldn't understand that he'd saved me.

He had. But only for now. I knew she'd be back.

FORTY-FOUR

Erin Riley was strangled with a baby wrap.

My baby wrap.

I'd been frozen ever since I'd seen the tag, zipped into the evidence bag. In a daze, a trance, even more so than my ever-present state of fogginess, bewilderment, incomprehension.

Should I have admitted that I knew what the tag was from?

No. Something, something piercing through the fog like the nose of a plane, had told me to keep quiet.

I fed Oliver, changed him, laid him on his mat, changed him, fed him, laid him in his swing, changed him, fed him, laid him in his crib, picked him up promptly when he awakened and screamed, fed him, held him, unmoving, in the glider in the nursery room, for what felt like hours. It was mind-numbing. For once, that was exactly what I wanted. To numb, to freeze, to silence my thoughts.

I didn't go out for a walk, didn't want to be seen walking toward or passing the Riley house. Paul didn't come to me. I didn't eat, either. I should have. My milk supply would dwindle without sufficient calories, but every time I entered the kitchen, the urge to vomit twisted through me.

Oliver was on his activity mat again, the grating music rattling my brain, the fabric butterflies spinning above his face.

Abruptly, I sprang into motion. I could fix this. I could put my mind at ease. If only I could find my baby wrap, folded neatly somewhere, fully intact, the tag attached to one end. That would mean no one had used it to kill Erin Riley.

I moved Oliver to his swing, barely pausing to strap him in, then turned the motor and music on.

The spare bedroom. It had to be there, with all the other baby things, either discarded or packed away for later use. I thundered up the stairs, down the hall, into the bedroom. I rifled through gift bags I'd still not managed to unpack, tossing tissue paper aside, letting it flutter to the floor like dandelion seeds caught in the wind, only remembering too late that I'd used the baby wrap at least once. I had tried it out. Where had I put it?

I moved on to the storage bins, packed with clothes Oliver had already outgrown. I grabbed handfuls of onesies and footie pajamas, dropping them onto the floor. I dug through to the bottom of the bins. If the wrap was there, it would stand out, much larger than everything else. It wasn't.

I moved into the nursery and pawed through his dresser, leaving it no messier than it had been before. I wasn't the sort of mother who lovingly folded his clean laundry or rolled it into stackable cylinders. Instead, I shoved handfuls of things into the drawers. He was a baby, had no need to worry about wrinkles.

It wasn't there. Nor was it in his closet.

I knew that if it was in the house, it would be in the nursery or spare bedroom. I looked in the guest bedroom anyway, then moved on to my own bedroom, my heart sinking. I knew it wouldn't be there, and it wasn't. Not in my closet. Not in my dresser.

I pushed the last drawer closed, rose, turned toward the door.

Tyler was there. He'd materialized, returned home, at some point. In his arms was a red and wet-faced Oliver, whose mouth was wide, a scream rising like a siren.

I stepped toward them, my arms outstretched.

Tyler jerked Oliver backward. "He was screaming," he said accusingly.

"Yes, he tends to do that."

Tyler took another step back. "You were letting him scream downstairs alone."

"No, I wasn't, Tyler." There was that rage again. "He spit up all over me," I lied. "I was just changing my clothes. He was sleeping in his swing. He must have just woken up."

Tyler's shoulders sagged. He passed Oliver to me. We both just wanted the screaming to stop. Maybe it was the last thing we had in common.

"Why are you home so early?" I asked, even though I had no idea what time it was. I could only tell, by the daylight still streaming through the windows, that it was far earlier than Tyler usually arrived home from work. I climbed into our bed and arranged the pillows so that I could nurse Oliver.

"I'm home," Tyler said, his voice still pinched with irritation, "because the police came to my office to speak with me."

"The police," I echoed, my tender breast in my hand, inches from Oliver's face, but just out of reach. He punched and wailed until I shoved it downward.

"A detective." Tyler slid a small card from his pocket and read from it. "Detective Jill West."

I could feel dread brewing in my gut, steeping, growing stronger with every second that ticked by, every tiny suck and release of Oliver's mouth.

"She's the one investigating," I said, working with every fiber of myself to keep my voice even and calm. "She's the one I spoke with. What did she want to know?"

"If I saw anything or heard anything, the day Erin went missing. I told her I wasn't home. I checked my calendar. I worked late that day."

"I know," I said. I remembered. The thunderstorm. Pacing the house alone.

"But why did she come to my work, Nat? She could have come by our house in the evening or on a weekend. She spoke with the receptionist. She identified herself as a cop. It's mortifying. I'm a *partner* now. It looks bad."

As if we needed to be reminded of that.

"Did she tell you she wanted to speak with me? Did you tell her she could find me at work?"

"No," I replied, quickly. She'd not said any such thing. It was clear, she'd not wanted me, or Tyler, to know she would be paying him a visit, nor had she wanted to interview him in my presence. She'd wanted to know what he would divulge when I wasn't around. So did I.

"That's not all," Tyler continued.

He was eyeing me with disapproval, as though I were an empty soda cup on the side of the highway. I looked down at Oliver, stroked his forehead.

"She asked me about your relationship with Paul. *Relationship,*" Tyler spat. "As if you're having an affair with the man." He was blinking at me quickly. We had discussed this so many times, yet it seemed he was still afraid that I was.

"That's ridiculous," I said. I shifted on the bed beneath Oliver's weight. "We've been over this, Tyler. It's ridiculous."

"I mean, Natalie," Tyler said. Full name, stern. I was in trouble, like a five-year-old who'd snuck a cookie before dinner. Like a five-year-old who'd done far, far worse. "A police officer shows up at my office and questions me about my and my wife's whereabouts on the day a neighbor was killed. Then, she questions me about my wife's relationship with the woman's husband. Like my wife was cheating on me. Like she had a motive to want this woman dead."

"I know. It's insane," I said. "What more do you want me to say?"

"It's insane," Tyler echoed. "I know it is. I know that Erin was jealous of you. She seemed crazy, that outburst at the party. But it still looks very bad."

Right. Because that was what mattered. Appearances. How it looked. It was this neighborhood, with its dark mulch and pristine colonials and luxury cars. Everything looked so perfect. Tyler wanted us to fit in. If we were back in our little rancher, with its character and quirks, maybe he wouldn't care so much. Maybe he'd care about what actually mattered.

"Why?" he asked.

My head snapped up. "Why, what?"

"Why did you have to spend so much time with this man? Paul?"

I switched Oliver to the other side, adjusted my pillows. "I don't think that's a fair assessment," I said. "He was very neighborly and kind. He was good company during the day. He liked to hold Oliver. You have no idea what it's like, Tyler, being home with him all day every day. It's exhausting. It wears on you."

"So, ask my mom for help. She's around. She could hold him and help you every single day."

I snorted.

"Ask a friend, then. Anyone. Why him?"

It was a reasonable question. I didn't know the answer. Because I didn't want to ask Diane? Because the people I might've wanted to help me, Tyler, Elaine, my dad, were always at work? Because Paul was not? He was close, he was here? He was convenient? Because Oliver liked to be held by him? Because his arms seemed magical? Because he got it? He'd been there? He'd survived, he'd thrived? Because he showed me another way, another world? A world where the baby was cared for and happy and I had a career on top of it all? A world where I could *have it all,* whatever that meant.

"None of this would be happening if you hadn't spent so much time with him. His wife wouldn't have thought you were having an affair," Tyler said quietly. "The police wouldn't think so, either."

"You are acting like this is all my fault," I hissed. "You're acting like you think I killed her."

"Of course I don't think that," Tyler said. "I think her husband killed her. I think he's dangerous."

I blinked at him. "Paul."

"*Yes,*" said Tyler. "Who else could it have been?"

I shook my head. Just as before, I couldn't see Paul hurting his wife. I couldn't see him hurting anyone.

But if not him, then what had happened? Why did suspicion seem to be falling on me?

I removed my nipple from Oliver's mouth and tugged my shirt down. He'd fallen asleep, and I was likely stuck here until he awakened. Climbing out of bed with him would be too precarious. I'd wake him up.

I stared at the wall, behind my husband. I couldn't meet his eyes. I was afraid of what he'd see in mine. Would he know that I'd seen Paul since he demanded that I stop? That Erin had confronted me the day she was killed (*Stay away from my husband*)? That she'd held on to me? That she'd been seen walking down to our house? Would he think that it was me who was the dangerous one, like the detective seemed to think?

"Let me take him," Tyler said, arms outstretched.

I looked down at Oliver, his features slack with sleep. If I said no, Tyler would be angry. If I passed him off, Oliver would awaken and scream for my smell and my milk. I couldn't win. I never did.

I loosened my arms. "Okay."

Tyler extracted Oliver from my arms and held him against his chest.

Oliver stirred immediately, then wriggled. His eyes flew open, met those of his father. He screamed.

Tyler sighed, a groaning sound, thick with frustration. He passed Oliver back to me. Even though he'd only just eaten, I nursed him to sleep again, because I knew that would soothe him the fastest.

I'd known it would happen when I handed him off. I'd known, yet I'd done it anyway. I did it to hurt Tyler. Because he had hurt me.

He was blaming me for everything, and it wasn't fair. It wasn't my fault.

If only I knew, if only I could figure out, exactly whose fault it was.

FORTY-FIVE

She returned to the scene of the crime.

That's what someone might say, if they saw me. That's what the detective seemed to believe.

Maybe it would jog a memory. Maybe it would help me understand.

It was still gray and still cold. The fallen leaves were damp and silent beneath my feet as I moved into the depths of the woods, close to the stream, near but not on the path worn by deer or some other animal or people, people like Erin, who had enjoyed the peace and earthy smells of the woods, before she was murdered there. Oliver had enjoyed them, too. No one would enjoy these woods ever again. I walked until I reached the trees with remnants of yellow caution tape tied to their trunks, the stray ends fluttering in the faint breeze.

I closed my eyes, felt my dizzy body tilting from side to side. This was where it had happened. The back of Erin's head, her shiny, almond hair, her slim neck. Someone had looped the baby wrap around it.

My knees buckled and I fell to the ground, like that first night in the hospital bathroom, hours after Oliver was born. My legs and hands smacked the ground, cool but still soft, not yet frozen solid. There was no blood this time. Not now. But there was still shame. There was fear and confusion. So much had changed since that night.

Oliver.

I opened my eyes. I looked down, but Oliver wasn't in my arms.

I pushed myself up with shaking arms. He was at home. I'd been compelled into the woods. I had left him behind. *He'll be fine*, I'd thought. Now, it felt ridiculous. I ran.

Burning lungs and thundering heart, my breath led the way, puffs of white moisture suspended in the air. My foot caught on a fallen tree limb, concealed beneath the covering of leaves. My ankle bent and I fell. I was up and running again before the pain registered. My breasts were throbbing with milk. I could feel it dripping into the pads of my nursing bra.

I burst from the tree line and into my yard. As I climbed the deck stairs two at a time, I could hear Oliver screaming from inside the house. I stripped off my jacket as I entered.

This time, I'd not been imagining it. Oliver was really, truly screeching. For how long, I had no idea. But he was safe, strapped into his swing, his face red and shiny, like an overripe tomato left to rot on the plant. I hurriedly unbuckled the straps and pulled him from the swing.

He'd worked himself into such a state that it took him a few seconds to latch onto my right breast. The left one leaked steadily into my bra. The letdown came quickly and furiously, signaled by his cries, by my need to comfort him.

My ankle was aching, my heart still pounding, my groin stung, protesting the speed at which I'd run through the woods.

A car door slammed. I stood precariously, still holding Oliver to my breast.

I peered through the cracks between the living room curtains, watched a navy sedan back out of my driveway, a red-haired head turned to the side. Didn't those cars have backup cameras? Or was she just so accustomed to looking over her shoulder when she was driving backward that she continued to do it that way?

It was such an irrelevant thought, given the circumstances. It seemed only further evidence of how far I'd fallen.

She was not arriving, but leaving. Did she ring the doorbell while I was in the woods? Had that woken Oliver? Had she waited and waited, listening to him cry? Had she peeked in the windows? Had she known I was here, avoiding her? Or worse, had she known that I wasn't?

There wasn't anything I could do besides continue to feed my baby, so that was what I did. When I was finished, I held him upright and paced the house, rubbing his back while he burped wetly, sending spit-up down my back.

I carried Oliver upstairs and placed him on the bed beneath the spinning ceiling fan. I stripped off my shirt and bra, tossing them into the hamper, then pawed through my dresser for fresh ones.

But I couldn't find a bra. I needed to do laundry. I could always go bra-less, often did. Except I could have sworn the pink one—the one that had a broken and itching hook in the back, the one I usually avoided—had still been in the drawer that morning when I'd donned the black one then dug around for a pair of socks that didn't have holes in the toes.

I reached my hand through the crack over the back of the drawer, the hidden, unfinished wood scraping roughly against my skin. My finger-tips grazed the familiar fabric of the bra and I tugged it out. The pink one. I was right. I'd known it was there.

I froze with the bra in my hand. Oliver cooed on the bed behind me.

I tugged it on, then a long-sleeved tunic, as I ran down the hall, to Oliver's bedroom. I opened his drawers, one by one, reaching my hand over the back of each.

I'd missed it. Had I missed the baby wrap, too?

But there was nothing behind Oliver's drawers besides more tiny clothes, those that I had shoved in deeply, messily. I hadn't folded anything since before Oliver was born and I'd so optimistically filled his dresser with soft and Dreft-smelling things, using my cutely bulging belly as a shelf while I worked.

No, the baby wrap wasn't there, but it had to be here, somewhere.

I tore through the house, starting with places where it might make sense for the wrap to be. Places I'd already looked. Oliver's closet. The spare bedroom. Amidst the clutter dotting the living room and family room. Then, I looked everywhere else, places it would make no sense for the wrap to be. The basement, the storage area in the unfinished portion, rushing upstairs every few minutes to check on Oliver, who had, miraculously, dozed off on my bed.

I searched my closet, pushing aside clothes I hadn't worn in months. I rifled through bins of scarves and bags I never used. Shiny and brand-emblazoned purses and cross-body bags I used to drape across my shoulder when I attended events at which I smiled until my cheeks hurt and held chilled glasses of wine that sweat down my fingers, events from a time that felt like a lifetime ago. Finally, I found it. Tears pricked the backs of my eyes when I saw the soft, gray fabric, folded into a tight rectangle, resting inside a shoebox with a pair of heels I'd intended to return but never had.

But the relief shriveled and died as quickly as it had come. Because the tag was missing. The tag was not attached to the edge of the wrap. It was zipped into a plastic evidence bag in the possession of Detective West.

I froze, my hands hovering over the frayed threads where the tag had been torn from the wrap, my mind trapped.

I'd been searching for proof that I couldn't have killed Erin. In fact, here it was. Slapping me in the face.

I had not put this baby wrap here. I knew that.

And I had looked everywhere, yet I'd only found one. But there had been two baby wraps. Mine, and the one Paul had brought me. A gift. He'd looped it around me, helped me use it.

My mind broke free. No longer trapped. The wheels turned. Someone else had returned this wrap to my house, had hid it in this box. I knew that now. And I knew why.

The doorbell rang, and I crashed. Into reality, into pragmatism, into truth.

But was it too late?

The detective was back.

Part IV

THE CAT & THE MOUSE

FORTY-SIX

It had only been a couple hours since I'd seen Detective West's car backing out of my driveway, yet so much had changed.

"Hello," I said, after opening the front door for her. "Come in."

She followed me into the kitchen and made herself comfortable. I stood nearby, swaying, Oliver pressed against my chest and peering over my shoulder.

The digital recorder was slim and silver. She placed it on the table in front of her, her hand hovered above it.

"Mind if I record our conversation?" she asked.

Yes, screamed everything inside me, everything I knew, everything I had learned during my three years of law school and ever since.

"That's fine," I told her, even though I understood that if I told her no, she couldn't legally do it. Maryland law required the consent of both parties to record a conversation.

She slid a piece of paper toward me.

"Do you recognize these?" she asked.

Although I didn't want to, I stepped closer, looked down at the page. It was filled with a printed image, a screenshot of a text message thread. I read the words in the colored bubbles.

I need to see you.
Please.
Please don't ignore me.
I need you.
I'm coming up there.

"Um—no," I told her. "I don't."

"That your phone number?"

I squinted at the page, at the phone number at the top of the message thread. Fear burned like acid in my stomach. What had he done?

"Yes," I admitted. I had to. "But I didn't send those messages."

"Apparently, you did," she said. "You sent these messages on Thursday, October twenty-ninth."

"To whom?" I asked, even though I knew.

"To Paul Riley. He blocked your number after he received them."

I closed my eyes. Thursday, October 29. He'd been in my phone. There was no other explanation. But how could I say that? It felt ridiculous, it would sound even more so to Detective West.

"I don't even have Paul's phone number," I told her. "We never exchanged numbers. We didn't communicate by phone." I shifted Oliver as I located my own device. "I'll show you," I said. I navigated to my contact list, organized by first name. I scrolled to the *P*'s, and I froze, because there it was. *Paul.* Saved in my phone. Of course it was. He was ten steps ahead of me.

"It's there, isn't it?"

The phone slipped from my fingers, clattered onto the table. I took a step back, made no move to retrieve it.

"It was a friendship at first, wasn't it?" she asked. Her voice was kind. I could have slapped the kindness out of her. It was so convincing, and I was so aching for a little kindness, especially since Paul had snatched his away from me. He'd done so much worse.

"It was mutual. You enjoyed each other's company. But it wasn't enough. You wanted more, and Paul knew that. Erin knew that, too. She wasn't happy. She told you to stay away from him, multiple times. He tried, but you wouldn't let that happen. Stopping by uninvited. Following him around at the neighborhood party."

I shook my head, but she wasn't wrong. The things she said were facts. But they were so twisted, so taken out of context, that I could hardly recognize them.

She slid the paper back toward herself, then reached out again, something else in her hand. The plastic bag, the tag from the baby-wrap-turned-weapon was inside.

"I know what this is," she said.

My eyes flicked to the tag, away again.

"The brand name is printed here, and Paul Riley identified this as the tag from a baby wrap that he purchased for you. It was a gift to you."

"No," I told her.

"He bought you a baby wrap. He left it here. Then, it was used to kill his wife. To get her out of the picture. To get her out of the way."

I looked at the tag. I looked at the recorder, resting there on the table, glittering beneath the recessed lighting, as though wide-eyed and open-eared, waiting for me to admit that she was right.

I had nothing to admit.

Facts, each a piece to a puzzle—pieces that had been muddled by gray fog, pieces that had been missing completely, pieces that had looked like something else entirely—had come into focus. They'd shifted into place.

All this time, I thought I had been awake. I thought I'd been too sleep-deprived to function, too lost to comprehend what was going on. I thought I had lost myself. I had been free-falling.

As it turned out, I hadn't been awake at all. All that time, I had been asleep. Asleep at the wheel—Paul had taken hold of it. He was driving me straight toward a crash. The moment was here. The collision was coming. Was there any time left to stop it?

I wanted to tell her. I wanted to tell her everything I now knew. But I couldn't. Not yet. I might only have one chance to prove what had happened, and I needed to better understand before I took that chance. I needed more.

I clutched my baby, my life, against my heart. I looked at the detective. I found her knowing eyes. She didn't know anything.

"It would be helpful, Ms. Fanning," she continued, "if you'd let us take a look around your house. It might help to clear you from this mess."

My pulse thrummed. Would she reach into her jacket, remove a warrant? Was her request merely a formality, an opportunity for me to cooperate?

I thought of the baby wrap. I'd hidden it before I'd answered the door, but had I hidden it well enough? I couldn't take the risk of finding out.

"No," I said. "I don't think so."

"So you're not providing your consent?"

"I'm not."

She simply shrugged. She stood, lifted the recorder, clicked it off. My breath exhaled, escaped in a low whistle—relieved, for now.

"That's fine," she said, nonchalance visible in her face. Her subtext was clear. She didn't have a warrant, but she wanted me to believe she could get one soon.

I didn't believe her. If she could get one, she would have. She didn't have enough. She needed more.

I walked her to the front door. She smiled before she stepped outside. "We'll be in touch," she said.

I knew she would. She would be back.

FORTY-SEVEN

I flipped the dead bolt behind her, as if that might keep her out. How much time did I have before she returned? How close was she to getting a warrant?

I had to act as if it was imminent.

I retrieved a Ziploc storage bag from the pantry and carried Oliver upstairs. He was unusually silent, perhaps intuitive to and counteracting the adrenaline and fear that was making my heart pound, blood roar in my ears. We stood in front of the thick, canvas print that hung in the nursery, above his changing table. *You Are So Loved,* it read, in white, cursive lettering, against a black background. A gift from someone—I couldn't recall who—at my baby shower.

Hanging on the wall across the room was the painting Paul had brought. I was struck by a sudden urge to pull it down, to tear through the canvas, to smash the frame.

Instead, I laid Oliver carefully down in his crib. "Just for a second," I whispered. I handed him a toy, colorful, linked rings, which he gripped and lifted in front of his face, squinting with interest. I removed the print from the wall and placed it facedown on the floor, revealing the baby wrap, which I'd flattened and hidden behind the canvas, before rehanging the print and letting Detective West into the house. I placed the wrap carefully into the plastic storage bag, squeezed the air out, and pressed my fingers along the zipper to seal it.

It rested snugly in the print's frame, behind the canvas, and I hooked it carefully back onto the wall. It was not a foolproof hiding place. I was virtually certain that, if the police returned with a warrant, they would find the wrap. They would test it. I'd touched it. I presumed that this was the wrap that I had used to hold Oliver, that it was the same one that Paul had later used with me, helping to loop it across my body and tuck my baby inside. I remembered now. I'd rushed out of the house that day, to get to Oliver's forgotten doctor's appointment. I'd left the baby wrap behind. Both of them—the one I had used, gifted by Mary Claire at my shower, and the one Paul had brought for me, still in its packaging, which I'd suggested he return. I'd never noticed their absence. Never given them another thought.

Paul had taken the wraps with him when he'd left. He must have. Had his plan been forming, even then? His plan to kill Erin, his plan to implicate me in her death.

I lifted Oliver from his crib and returned downstairs, moved into the living room, looked out the windows. I could see Detective West's car parked outside the Riley house, and anger flared. What was he telling her? What more did he have? I'd not known about the text messages, nor that he'd managed to hide the baby wrap in my house. Apparently, that wasn't enough for a warrant, but he might have other evidence up his sleeve, which could push her back here, which could override my lack of consent for her to search the house.

I watched, motionless. Oliver had dozed off, his head tucked into the hollow above my collarbone. After several minutes, Paul's front door swung open, and Detective West strode down the porch steps. She was moving quickly, busily. She slid into her car, and the brake lights flashed red.

My pulse thrummed, but instead of turning the car and returning to my house, she peeled away from the curb. She was leaving. For now.

I felt more awake, more alert, than I had in months. Perhaps I was still confused, but I wasn't a fool. I knew it with everything in my bones. I was running out of time.

FORTY-EIGHT

He watched her back her unmarked sedan out of Natalie's driveway. She'd not been there long, not nearly long enough to search the house, which meant that she hadn't found the baby wrap. Which meant that she had no warrants. Not for a search, and not for an arrest.

He didn't understand.

The police had the tag from baby wrap, which he had identified. They had the text messages. They had the statement, from Mrs. Jensen, that Erin had gripped Natalie's arms, that there'd been an altercation, and that she'd soon after seen Erin tearing toward Natalie's house. They had his own statement—albeit a false one—that Erin had gone to confront Natalie again, and that she'd headed into the woods for a walk. There, she'd been killed. What more did they need?

The car pulled to a stop at the curb outside his house, and he was opening the door to her before she'd even knocked or rung the bell.

"Do you have news?" he asked hopefully. This was genuine, the hope.

Her lips were turned down. "Could I come in for a minute?"

"Of course." He ushered her inside, and they settled down in the living room, she on an armchair, he on the sofa across from her. He leaned forward, elbows on his knees, hands clasped together, as if in prayer.

"I spoke with her." Detective West crossed her legs. "I showed her the tag from the baby wrap again, advised her that you'd identified it. I showed her the messages."

"And?"

"She didn't admit anything. She acted like she didn't even know she had your number."

She'd not been acting, but it was a good sign that the detective thought she was. It was a good sign, too, that Natalie had not previously noticed his name as a contact in her phone. She'd not caught on. Not yet.

"What else?" he asked. "There must be more."

"Well, I asked her if I could search the house. She declined."

He knew already that the house had not been searched, but it did surprise him to learn that Natalie had been asked, that she'd refused. Did this mean she was not, in fact, still clueless? Or was it just her background, her training as a lawyer, that was guiding her? She knew her rights, and that was not a factor in his favor.

"And you can't search anyway?" he asked. He unclasped his hands, leaned toward her.

The detective smiled. It was patronizing, and he didn't like it.

"Not without a warrant." She stood, smoothed her dress pants, which had bunched unflatteringly around her thighs. "But rest assured, Mr. Riley, we are watching her movements. We will see what she does next. Getting a warrant, finding that baby wrap, is our top priority."

He nodded and tried to smile back at her, but it felt more like a grimace.

"She's not been bothering you anymore, has she?" the detective continued. "Has she been back here?"

"No," he admitted. He wished she would come. That might help things along. But perhaps he'd been too cold during their last interaction. She might not know what was happening, but she seemed to understand that she should stay away.

He followed the detective to the front door and held it open while she stepped through it. He closed the door behind her and let the silence, in her absence, fall over the house. The silence seemed to roar around him. Petra was upstairs, her bedroom door firmly closed. He missed her chatter, her upbeat music, the way she sang along to it in her high-pitched voice, oblivious to its lack of tune, to the lyrics she was getting wrong.

He glanced at his watch. Erin's sister, Brenna, would be here soon to retrieve his daughter. She had asked if Petra could come stay with her for a few nights. He would have declined—he didn't want to be apart from his daughter—but Brenna had already spoken to Petra directly, and Petra wanted to go.

Fine, he'd decided. But just a couple of nights. Perhaps a change of scenery might be good for Petra. He was expecting Brenna any minute. She'd texted him when she'd left her beach house in Delaware, nearly three hours earlier. He assumed she'd run into some traffic.

He wished Petra would agree to return to school. She was too sad, she claimed, but he thought that if only she would go, if only she would resume some semblance of her former routine, she would begin to feel better. She would see that life went on, in Erin's absence. That it wasn't truly all that different without her.

That it was, actually, much better.

Better, yet still unsettled. Things would not feel settled until Natalie was arrested for the murder. It was taking longer than he'd thought.

He knew exactly where the baby wrap was, but he couldn't very well point it out. The police needed something more to get there. He needed something more to help them.

FORTY-NINE

Detective West drummed her fingers along her steering wheel. Just as she was about to pull away from the curb, her phone rang. She jammed her thumb into the button on her dashboard to answer the call through her car's Bluetooth system.

"Price," she said, "please tell me you have good news."

"No," said Officer Price. "She wouldn't sign it."

"Damn it." West lifted a hand, as if to slam it into the steering wheel, but didn't. She lowered it slowly, returned it to the wheel. She'd not been expecting good news. She'd not been expecting anything.

That was why she hadn't told Natalie Fanning, or Paul Riley, that she'd sent Officers Price and Hernandez to present the judge on duty with an application for a warrant to search the Fanning house. The duty judge, for the previous twelve and following forty-eight hours, was the Honorable Marlene Porter. She was a notoriously defense-friendly judge. West knew that the application was weak. Perhaps Judge Hart would have signed it, but even that wasn't a sure thing. Most others wouldn't. And Judge Porter? Decidedly not. It had been a shot in the dark, and she'd missed.

She needed more, so that she could revise the warrant and present it again. She hoped that by the time Judge Porter's duty ended, she'd have a stronger application, and a friendlier judge to review it.

"Sorry," said Officer Price. He sounded ashamed.

"Not your fault, Price," she replied. "Thanks for trying."

There was a pause. She'd been about to end the call, but sensed that there was something more that Cameron Price wanted to say. He was young and ambitious, eager to please. He'd been overtly thrilled to be assigned to support West on the case. These were factors that could make him either very helpful, or exceedingly annoying, to work with.

"What is it?" she asked.

"Just wondering," Price said, "what you were thinking. Are you still focused on Mrs. Fanning?"

West eased to a stop and flicked on her turn signal, preparing to make a left turn out of the neighborhood. She considered Price's question. It wasn't a bad one. She'd been working so furiously, almost frantically, since Erin Riley's body had been found. She'd not taken much time to put together a theory of the case.

"The husband certainly seems to think that Natalie Fanning killed his wife," she replied, aware that she'd not actually answered the question.

There was another pause. "And do you agree? Or do you think it was the husband? It usually is, isn't it?"

West frowned, jammed her foot onto the accelerator, swinging the car onto the street that ran perpendicular to the Rileys' and Fannings' neighborhood. It wasn't a busy road, and a sidewalk ran along either side of it. More neighborhoods were dotted along it, along with a low-rise office complex, about a mile to the north of the Rileys' house. That was the office complex from which Erin Riley had run her financial planning business.

"I've interviewed her assistant at work, her best friend, her sister, and her parents. I've spoken to all the neighbors. It's interesting. No one has told me anything that leads me to suspect that Mr. Riley was involved. Erin was very private, it seems, even to those closest to her. Everyone described her as extremely focused on her career, while Paul has been devoted to their daughter. This seemed to work for them, as far as we can tell. Mr. Riley let us search the house. There's been no evidence of infidelity between them." She shrugged, although Price could not see her. "I've no physical evidence to go off. Not yet."

"Right," Price said. She could hear a faint tapping in the background, as if he were taking notes. He was so eager.

"Meanwhile," she continued, "there does seem to be a one-sided interest in Paul from Natalie Fanning. There are those text messages. Erin was displeased with their relationship, which was apparently strictly platonic, per Paul's insistence. But it seems Natalie wouldn't stay away. She didn't admit to sending the texts. She didn't admit to recognizing the tag from the baby wrap. She didn't let us search the house." West tapped her fingers along her steering wheel. "She's hiding something. And there's something off about her. Something odd."

"Do you think," Price asked, "she and Paul are in on it together? Maybe he's only pretending her interest was not returned. Maybe they plotted to kill her together."

"It's possible," she admitted. She had considered this. "But remember Natalie's married, too. She's not really free now, to be with him. And besides, there's something rash and irrational about this one. Something angry. The baby wrap as the weapon. I think that means something, to take something like that, to use it to kill someone." It screamed, to West, something unwell. Of a person who was not well. From what she'd seen thus far, that was Natalie. Not Paul.

"So, what's next?" Price asked.

"We're waiting on physical evidence results to come back from the scene. We'll see if that gets us anywhere. In the meantime, I think we've got to find that baby wrap. We've got to search the Fanning house. Maybe we'll need to search the area again. It might not be in the house."

"She might've already destroyed it," Price pointed out.

"She might," West agreed. "But either way, we need to know."

"We need a warrant. But we can't get one. We need something more." Price sounded deflated, and she was struck by an urge to reassure him.

"We'll find more," West said. "And we'll get that warrant."

FIFTY

I'd always thought she was against me, but could she, perhaps, be my savior? Who else might know more, might be able to shed light on what was going on, but the neighborhood busybody? My very own nosy neighbor?

I'd decided to wear Oliver, though not, of course, in the gray, scarf-like wrap. That remained concealed behind the canvas print in Oliver's bedroom, until I could figure out a way to get it out of my house.

I'd thought about destroying it. Lighting a fire, burning it there. Taking it into the woods and digging a hole to bury it. But there'd been, off and on, since shortly after Detective West had driven away from Paul's house the previous afternoon, another unmarked police car parked along my street.

Tyler had noticed it when he'd arrived home from work.

"There's someone sitting in the front seat," he'd remarked as he'd stood in the kitchen, holding Oliver, while I poked at a sauté pan of vegetables with a wooden spatula, steam rising from it and heating my face.

"I think it's a cop," I'd said, trying to sound nonchalant. "You know, because of Erin's murder. Watching the neighborhood, I guess."

Watching me.

It had not been there constantly, but every now and then, it was there. There might have been others around, better concealed. I couldn't do anything to raise suspicion further.

The car was there now, as I descended the porch steps, made my way down the driveway.

A uniformed officer sat inside. I glanced at him as I passed, but I didn't wave, and neither did he.

I held Oliver's feet in my hands as I walked down the street. His head was encased in a navy knit hat. I'd finally remembered to order one on-line.

We were just out for a walk, like any other mother and baby. Nothing to see here. Nothing suspicious.

As I passed Mrs. Jensen's house, I paused, as though struck by the idea to approach it suddenly. I turned, walked down her driveway, and rang the bell.

I wanted to know what she'd seen. What, exactly, had she told the po-lice? What had she told Paul?

A curtain twitched, and I spun toward it. I caught a glimpse of Mrs. Jensen in a floral, long-sleeved housedress. I waited for her to move to the door, to pull it open.

She didn't.

I considered ringing the doorbell again, but knew it was ridiculous. She'd made it quite clear that she knew I was here, that she was choosing to not open the door.

Stung, my cheeks burning, I left. I didn't feel like maintaining the farce, of continuing up the street, taking Oliver for a walk. I didn't feel like passing Paul's house. Clearly, he had gotten to her. It was Erin who had grabbed me, yet she thought I was a killer.

Mrs. Jensen had been my only hope, for the time being, for gaining a better understanding of what was going on. For gathering more informa-tion.

I brushed tears from my face as I returned home. I didn't know what to do, where to go, from here. A car rolled past me, and I kept my head down, ashamed to be crying.

I'd assumed it was the cop, turning around, perhaps following me. But the car was expensive and white, not darkly generic, and it pulled into the driveway beside my own. A woman climbed out. She wore sleek, black ankle pants and a tweed blazer shot with red and gold, an outfit I might have coveted and copied in my former life. It was Linda, my next-door neighbor, returning home from work much earlier than usual. As far as I could tell, she worked long hours outside the home, and she always parked in her garage. I had barely seen her since we had moved in. I could never tell when she was home and when she wasn't, except when I hap-pened to catch her car coming or going or saw her retrieving her mail.

I just wanted to get back inside—now was not the time to get to know each other, for formal introductions and pleasantries—but it was clear that she was approaching me.

"Everything alright?" she asked.

I almost laughed. "I'm fine," I said. I tried to smile at her. She'd never taken the time to chat before. Why now?

She nodded, but she didn't turn away. She fingered the handles of her handbag, glossy and chestnut brown. "Would you like to come inside for a minute? I could make you a cup of coffee. I'm about to make one for myself."

I didn't want to, and I couldn't have any more coffee. But declining felt more difficult than simply agreeing with her and letting her lead me inside, so that was what I did.

I followed her into her kitchen and stood here, rocking and bouncing Oliver so that he would remain quiet, would not awaken due to a sudden lack of movement. Linda popped a pod into a Keurig machine and it hissed to life.

"Awful what happened to Erin, isn't it?" she asked, over the burbling coffee behind her.

I nodded weakly. I didn't want to talk about Erin.

"It's hitting me harder than I thought. We weren't even close, really, just friendly. Mostly we just referred clients to each other. But I can't stop thinking about what happened, so near to where we all live. I canceled my appointments for the rest of the day. I'm having a hard time working right now, to be honest."

It was a personal admission for a stranger, and I shifted from foot to foot, feeling uncomfortable. Linda was just lonely, I thought. Looking for a listening ear, someone she could burden with her feelings.

"I'm mostly just sad for Petra, you know?" Linda continued. "My own kids grew up in a single parent home—but two of them. Their father and I divorced when they were around Petra's age, and they went from house to house, and that was hard on them. I can't imagine how hard it must be to lose a parent entirely at that age."

Linda was blinking at me, and I realized I'd not said a word since entering the house. "I can't imagine, either," I said. I could have added an anecdote about losing my own mother in my twenties. How that had been impossible. How losing her at age ten must be even more so. I didn't.

"Cream or sugar?" Linda asked. "I take both."

"Both. Please." I wasn't planning to drink the coffee, but when she pushed it toward me, it smelled rich and faintly vanilla, so I wrapped my hands around the mug and took a long sip over the top of Oliver's head. It seemed to fill me with life.

"Have you spoken to Paul or Petra at all, since Erin's death?" I asked. Linda wasn't Mrs. Jensen, but she'd been friendly with Erin. She might know something.

"Well, Paul was going door-to-door, I guess. I missed him while I was at work, but I caught up with him later, and he asked me if I'd seen Erin. That was before the body was found, of course. I hadn't seen anything. I was at work when Erin went missing. I didn't get home until late that evening. There was that thunderstorm, it was strange. I stayed at my office until things had cleared."

Linda began brewing a second cup of coffee for herself while she spoke.

"And yesterday evening, I stopped by. I brought a lasagna. I brought it for Petra, really. I just wanted to see her, to see how she was doing. But she wasn't home. Paul took the lasagna from me and said he'd put it in the freezer because they had plenty of food, and Petra was staying with Erin's sister at the beach for a couple of nights. He would be headed there, too, to pick her up."

"The beach?" I asked, my mug frozen inches from my face. "Like, a vacation?"

"That's what I said. No, he told me. Not like a vacation. Just a change of scenery for Petra. He said that Erin's sister had wanted to see her, so she picked her up earlier in the day. She wanted to grieve with her, and vice versa." She shrugged. "I guess that makes sense."

"Yes," I said. "I guess it does."

I finished the rest of my coffee. I could already feel the caffeine coursing through my veins, my nerves pricking, my mind firing. I'd had too much today, but I didn't care.

"A couple days, you said?" I asked. "Did he say when he was leaving, to pick her up?"

Linda fanned out a hand, inspecting her manicure. "Sometime tomorrow, I suppose. I think he said he's heading down there tomorrow, then he'll spend the night and bring Petra back in the morning. Then, he took the lasagna inside, and I left. That was that." She shrugged. "He was rather rude, actually, rather cold, now that I think about it. But I guess I never was his biggest fan, and I guess he knew that."

"No?" I asked. I placed my empty mug on the counter. When I looked up, it was to find Linda watching me.

"How well did you know them?" she asked. "Paul and Erin?"

"Not well," I said, my eyes dropping to a chip in the granite countertops. I didn't know how much she had seen.

"Well, I didn't know them well, either." Linda scooped an extra spoonful of sugar into her mug and stirred it gently. "Erin was very private. She never said anything to me, but it seemed that things weren't as rosy as they seemed in that household."

"What do you mean?" I asked, even though I'd seen it, felt it, too. There'd been a divide in the home, Paul and Petra on one side, Erin on the other.

"Erin worked so hard. It was so much pressure on her, paying for that big house, paying for private school for Petra. I think Paul could have done more. He always seemed rather lazy to me. What exactly was he doing all day, while Petra was at school?" Linda crossed her arms. "Well, I had an idea. I never said anything to anyone. It wasn't my place, and perhaps it's still not. But Erin's gone, and I can't stop thinking about it."

"What do you think he was doing?" I asked. I was astonished by her perception of Paul, of the family's dynamics, how it so differed from my own.

"When I saw you at the block party with Paul, when Erin told you not to touch him, I thought, *Oh no, it's just like it was with that other woman.*"

A blush tingled on my cheeks. I'd forgotten that Linda had been there, chatting with Erin. She'd seen and heard everything. *Don't touch him!*

"What other woman?"

"The woman who lived in your house before you. I'd seen Paul going into her house on occasion, when Erin and the husband were at work. That was all I saw. But it gave me a bad feeling. What else could they have been doing?"

"You mean you think they were having an affair?"

Linda pressed her lips together, as if embarrassed.

"Have you told the police this?" I asked. It suddenly felt urgent. This seemed important.

"I never said a thing to anyone. This is just pure speculation. But Lara wasn't working, her husband wasn't home, her kids were at school. Call me old-fashioned, but I wouldn't have liked that, if I were Erin. But I never said anything to her. It wasn't my place."

Oliver was beginning to writhe against my chest, to strain against the straps of the carrier.

"He'll need to eat," I said to Linda. "I'd better go."

"Of course," she said. She put her cup down and took a step toward the door, then stopped. "You went back to work, didn't you? But you've been home again?"

"I'm taking a sabbatical," I explained. "I went back, but it didn't work out. I only took eight weeks of leave. It wasn't enough." I felt defensive, and I must have sounded it, because Linda held up her hands.

"We all have to do what's best for our families," she said. "No judgment here."

"What did you do?" I asked, suddenly curious. She had mentioned two kids, a divorce. Now, the house was tidy and sterile, revealing no evidence of messy family life.

"I took ten weeks after each of my sons were born. I didn't want to leave my job."

"Me, either," I admitted. "But it was too hard." It felt so shameful to admit. I'd never been a person who quit, who'd failed.

"I know it is," Linda said. "I never considered staying at home with my kids. 'Don't you want to spend more time with them?' My mother and my in-laws used to ask me that. They thought there was something wrong with me. Things were different back then, you know. My boys are in college now, and most of my friends left their jobs when their kids were born, at least for a few years, if not permanently. Not me. Their father's not staying home with them, is he? I'd point out. I worked a lot, but I spent time with them, too. And when I was home, I made sure I was present. I was a better mom to them, because I was getting what I needed during the day. And being a parent isn't just about being present with them. Being a parent also means supporting your children. That means supporting them financially, too. My boys saw me working, earning money, and that was important. I wire money to pay for their college tuition two times a year. I earned that money, and I'm proud of that."

She sounded defensive, too, and it made me feel desperately sad, that we were made to feel this way, to struggle with these choices, to strike impossible balances. That it wasn't like that for our husbands. Perhaps it was for some. But not mine.

"I want that, too," I admitted. "That's what I want."

"And you'll get there." She made it sound so simple, so matter-of-fact, and I'd needed to hear it, although I was conscious of how much stock to give her opinion. She was a stranger, after all. She didn't know me. She didn't know my baby.

"Thank you so much," I said. "For the coffee."

Linda nodded, walked me to the door. "Anytime," she said.

I paused on her welcome mat. "Do you think you should tell the police what you told me?" I asked. "About Paul and Erin's relationship, that you thought he was having an affair?"

Linda bit her lip. I could tell she didn't want to.

"It might help," I suggested. "It might help Erin, and it might help you feel better." I shrugged, as if it didn't matter. "Just a thought."

"You're probably right," she said. She smiled at me, tightly. "Take care." She closed the door.

I glanced toward the Riley house as I hurried down her driveway, back to my own house. Oliver was crying in earnest now, punching the air. He wanted out.

I'd known, of course, that things had not been good between Erin and Paul, but I'd assumed that was Erin's fault, that she was ungrateful, not understanding. I'd not considered that Paul was at fault. I'd never considered that he might have had an affair.

For so many weeks, Paul had seemed like a hero, like a saint. He'd made me feel hopeful and safe. And I'd hated Erin for taking that away from me.

Now I could see that I'd only been looking at the mask he'd been painting, the costume he'd created.

Beneath it had lain a monster.

It had become quite clear to me that beneath that mask was a cat, claws ready, teeth bared. And I was his mouse.

But everything had changed. Because I wasn't going to be his mouse anymore. I was going to have to make him mine.

FIFTY-ONE

I pulled the sleeves of my coat over my hands as I gripped the handlebars of the stroller. It was early, yet the sun was low in the sky. It was the most depressing time of the year, I always thought. In my old life, in early November, it would be dark when I left for work in the morning and dark when I left work in the evening. The only daylight I saw was through my office window, streaked with smears, speckled with dust mites, not cleaned nearly often enough.

I glanced around me as I walked, looking for signs of movement. Specifically, looking for a navy sedan. I didn't want Detective West to see me visiting Paul, nor any of the other cops, the ones who had been taking turns watching our street, watching me.

Yet, I had to go. It was a risk, and I was terrified. I was equally terrified not to go, to do nothing, to allow the baby wrap to remain in my house.

As I approached the front door, I slipped my cell phone from my coat pocket and initiated the recording app, tapping the little red button before zipping it away again.

I left my stroller parked on Paul's front walkway and knocked on the door. The neighbors might see it; Mrs. Jensen most definitely would, but I wasn't sure that mattered anymore.

"Natalie," said Paul when he opened the door. He didn't step aside to invite me in. I knew why. He seemed surprised, but not displeased to see me. I wondered if he thought I was still clueless to what he'd done, what he was trying to do.

"Sorry to drop in on you with no warning," I said. I thought of the text messages the detective had shown me. Messages purportedly sent by me, painting a picture of unwanted obsession, unwelcome advances.

He shrugged. "No problem."

"How is Petra doing?" I asked.

He sighed. "Petra is with her aunt. I think it was good for her to get out of the house. Her aunt's having a hard time, too. It's good for them to be together. Breaks my heart, though."

"I'm sorry." My heart was thundering. There was a rushing in my ears. It nearly drowned out my words. Was I speaking too quietly? Would the recorder pick up our voices?

"Could I come in for a few minutes?" I asked. "It's a little cold for him." I nodded toward Oliver.

Paul glanced around then stepped aside with thinly concealed reluctance.

I extracted Oliver from the stroller, then trailed into his kitchen, then the family room, at the back of the house, as though this was perfectly natural. The floor plan was just like my own. I thought of the day I had gone upstairs to use the master bathroom, had availed myself of Erin's tweezers, organic hand soap, and face cream. I'd been so foolish. I'd thought I knew what I wanted then. I'd thought I needed an escape, that I needed Paul. Or else, I just needed help, breaks, so that I wouldn't *have* to escape. Look at where I'd ended up. Now, it was time to fix the mess I'd made.

Paul met me in the family room and perched on the arm of a sofa. "Is something bothering you?"

"I just know that I shouldn't be here," I said. "That's all."

"I'm glad that you're here," he said. It was like he'd suddenly stepped into a different role. He seemed welcoming now, his eyes soft. "You've stood by me," Paul continued. "Not everyone has."

"What do you mean?" I asked. "You lost your wife. I'd think you'd have quite a lot of sympathy and support."

"Well, I'm the husband," he replied. "You know what that means."

Heart fluttering in my throat, like a high schooler proximate to her crush, I swallowed, as though trying to force it downward.

"I suppose I'm a suspect. They have searched my house. They've interviewed me multiple times." He shrugged, crossed his arms. "But I have nothing to hide."

"I assume there would be physical evidence," I said. "You know, DNA, footprints."

"Nothing helpful," he said. "The fingerprint and DNA results came in late last night, actually." He arched, stretched his back, the pause, the anticipation crackling like his vertebrae. "The detective called to let me know. No prints obviously. Nothing to leave prints on out there, in the woods. And she was drenched in the thunderstorm that night; her body wasn't found for days after, you know. Nothing useful was preserved, I guess."

Said matter of factly. *It is what it is.* And it was. Nothing to be done about it now. Still, his coldness startled me, and I was scared. But I told myself that he wouldn't hurt me. He needed me. I was part of his plan.

"That's unfortunate," I said.

Paul sighed, a heavy gush of air, and raked his hands over his face. "I just don't know what to do. Erin is gone. Petra is gone. I'm lost."

I looked away, checked on Oliver. He was quiet in my arms, taking in his surroundings. It was only an excuse to turn from Paul, to decide where to steer things next.

"Will you need to go back to work, or something?" I asked.

"I don't think so," Paul replied. "We have savings, then the life insurance money will come through." He rubbed his chin, squinted his amber eyes. "You know, business hadn't been good for Erin lately," he said. "She made a mistake for a new client. A bad investment. She was mortified about what happened, then to make it worse, he posted a negative review about her. She had lost some clients and wasn't getting new ones as quickly as she used to."

"I had no idea," I murmured. Oliver was beginning to stir, his brows pinched low. I knew my baby. Screams were imminent. I swayed and bounced him.

"Should I take him?" Paul asked, looking down at Oliver's scrunched features.

"It's okay," I said, ashamed and appalled that I had ever let him hold my baby. "Anyway, when will Petra be home?"

"I'll drive up there later this evening, to pick her up. Stay the night there with Erin's sister. I think it's been good for her, having time to process with her aunt. But it's time to come home. When she gets here, her mom will still be gone. I'm worried."

"Of course," I said. "This will be very difficult for a long time. For both of you."

"I'll arrange some extra sessions with her therapist," Paul continued. "That will help her."

I nodded, smiled faintly. I'd not removed my coat, and I felt too warm, almost dizzy. Still, I didn't take it off. I needed to be able to make a quick escape.

"Well, Oliver's been sleeping better," I said, although he hadn't asked. "I think I'm finally getting used to it so I can get a bit more sleep, too."

"That's great. I remember that. It's such an adjustment to not get any sleep. Then, once you get used to it, they start sleeping and it's as though you've forgotten how."

"Exactly. That's exactly how it is."

Paul shifted. He was tiring of the conversation.

"He's getting better at napping, too," I said. "I'm able to put him down more for naps. I don't have to hold him as much."

"What a relief for you," Paul replied, sounding disinterested, somewhat insolent.

"He never did get the hang of that baby wrap," I continued. "I thought I might give it another try, now that he's a bit more solid."

Paul stiffened. Or did I imagine it? I could never be sure lately, couldn't trust my own eyes or mind.

"That day you brought me one a month back," I said, "a baby wrap, I mean—you took it with you, right? I haven't been able to find it."

Paul's brows dropped. He watched me with his amber eyes, the sun working its way through the cloud cover and windows, setting things aglow.

"You took it with you," I said again. "I couldn't find it."

"Natalie," he said quietly. "No, I didn't."

"I couldn't find it," I repeated. I needed him to admit something. To give me something I could work with.

"I didn't need to return it," he said. "It was only thirty dollars. I left it for you. We both know that."

"I think you took it with you," I said, but my voice was wavering and high, precarious, so contrary to his smooth and quiet certainty.

"Natalie, we both know what happened. The police found the tag at the scene. I identified it for them. They know how Erin was killed. And you know, too. Let's not do this."

I took a step away from him, putting more distance between us. "Do what?" My heart was thunderingly loud.

"Let's not pretend," he said. So patient. I could tell he was an educator, a father. "We both know what happened."

"What happened?" I wanted him to lay it out.

"We had become quite close, Natalie," he said, still so soft, even, and calm. "We enjoy spending time together, and I have helped you with the burdens of caring for an infant. Erin was an obstacle to that. You wanted to be with me, to have a family like mine. That day at the block party, and the day Erin came home early, it was clear she wasn't going to let that happen."

His words sounded practiced.

"You followed her into the woods. You killed her. You used the baby wrap I gave you."

I shook my head.

"You've been doing everything alone. It's far too much, to follow all the rules, to care for your baby perfectly, especially when he has such a challenging temperament. He's not an easy baby. You gave up your career. You've given up everything, really. You did it because you wanted me to help you. You needed support, so that you could have it all."

Although I'd wanted him to spell out his plan, I hated that the words were hanging there between us, glimmering and obvious, like a neon sign. They sounded more plausible than I'd like to admit.

"That isn't true," I told him. "That's not what happened."

"It is," he told me. "We both know that it *is*. You can tell me. I haven't told anyone yet, Natalie. I don't need to. There was no DNA found on her body. No evidence. They never found the baby wrap. They can't prove who killed her." His eyes were holding mine. They were soft and glittering with kindness and sympathy, as they always had been. Had it always been fake?

"I won't tell you," I said. "Because that didn't happen." I looked away, then forced myself to meet his eyes again. "Why are you doing this? Why me?"

Paul's brows dipped low. He was angry, frustrated. He wasn't going to admit to anything. I'd never really expected that he would.

"I have to go," I whispered.

I held Oliver close, and I hurried from the room, down the hall, to the front door.

I'd spoken with Paul in the family room on purpose.

Even though the meeting had not gone as well I'd hoped, even though he had not admitted what he'd done, I had come here for another reason.

He couldn't see me as I left. He couldn't tell that I paused at the white console table in the foyer, on which several decorative trays, tiled with turquoise and ivory glass, were resting. I'd examined them before, was familiar with their contents. They were for depositing odds and ends as the Riley family entered and exited the house. Wallets. Sunglasses. Half-spent tubes of lip balm. Oozing, pocket-sized bottles of hand sanitizer. But, mostly, keys. And that was exactly what I took on my way out the door.

FIFTY-TWO

As soon as Natalie disappeared from view, Paul slipped his phone from his pocket. She'd stopped herself from admitting anything, and he was surprised. He'd thought that his renewed kindness, his sympathy, might push her into confessing that she didn't know what she'd done, that she was confused and scared.

Just in case he had missed something, he played the recording back.

He'd wanted to create something he could turn over to Detective West, to help her get that warrant, but he didn't like it—it wasn't helpful. In fact, it sounded as if Natalie had been trying to get *him* to say something incriminating. To admit he had taken the baby wrap with him, instead of leaving it at her house. Which, of course, he had.

Why are you doing this? she'd asked. *Why me?*

She was catching on. It wasn't good.

He tapped the trash can icon, permanently deleting the recording from his phone.

He was growing impatient waiting for the police to search her house. He needed that baby wrap found. He'd been hoping that she would come, and she had. Although she'd confessed to nothing, he could still use her impromptu visit to his advantage.

He ascended the stairs, his phone pressed between his shoulder and ear.

"She came here again," he said once Detective West answered.

"Really."

"Yes, really," he continued. He moved into the guest room—his room—and tugged a dresser drawer open. It had been a long time since he and Erin had shared a bedroom. With every year that went by, with every day that he hoped her blatant resentment toward him, toward motherhood, would fade, with every day that it had only seemed to grow, to spin, to cause damage in its path, Paul had grown to accept that his family simply wasn't a happy one. It would never be. Not when Erin didn't seem to care to do what it took to make that happen.

She only cared that they *looked* like a happy family. She couldn't have cared any less about what went on outside of the public eye. He had moved his things into the guest room one day while she was at work, tired of her jerking away from his touch—even that which was accidental—in their shared bed at night. He'd hoped that when she arrived home to find his things missing from their closet and his nightstand, it would be a wake-up call.

It had only been a wake-up call for him. Further evidence of how strong her apathy, her resentment, had become. He had been sleeping in the guest room ever since.

"She rang my doorbell, invited herself in. She thinks we can still be friends. It's outrageous. Remind me again, why she hasn't been arrested yet?" he demanded. "What more do you need?"

He shoved a pair of jeans and a long-sleeved T-shirt into a backpack, collecting what he would need to spend the night at Brenna's beach house. It was the last thing he wanted to do. But Brenna had suggested that it would be good for him to get away for a night as well. She was sick with grief herself, and he'd felt like he couldn't refuse. The police certainly hadn't told him he couldn't go away for a night. Besides, it wasn't a pleasant drive to do twice in one day, even though Brenna herself had done it when she'd retrieved Petra. She'd arrived at the house tear-streaked and red-faced. It was clear she had cried the whole trip.

"We are getting close," Detective West replied. "We're trying to get a warrant, to search her house. Like I told you yesterday, if we could find the baby wrap she used, any other evidence that puts her in the woods that day, we'll have enough to arrest her."

"Don't you have enough now?" he asked. "At least to search her home? I don't understand. She fought with my wife the afternoon she was killed. Erin was seen walking down toward her house. There are the text messages she sent me. All the times she came to my house. She was obsessive. She still is. She's still coming. There's something wrong with that woman." He slammed his dresser drawer closed.

There was a pause. "Not yet," the detective admitted. "We need something more. Do you want a tight case? Do you want a conviction?"

Paul moved to his toiletries bag, the one perched on the chest across the room. He brought it into the bathroom with him when he needed it, then back to the room, as if he were a college student using a communal bathroom. He didn't want to leave his things in Petra's bathroom, didn't want to remind her that she shared it with her father at times.

"The baby wrap must be in that house. It won't help you get a warrant. Not if you won't find it without one," he told the detective.

She didn't reply.

"I don't feel safe here," he continued. "Not with her feeling free to keep coming by whenever she wants. I even had to let her come inside. She asked me, and I was too scared to tell her no. Thank God Petra wasn't home. If she was, I wouldn't have allowed it." He felt he needed to cover his tracks, in case anyone had seen Natalie enter his house.

"And what did she want to discuss with you?" the detective inquired.

"It was just more of the same." He sighed audibly. "She misses me. When can we spend more time together again? When will I be ready?"

Detective West was quiet.

"I will never be ready," he told her. He zipped up the backpack and swung it over his shoulder. "Look, I'm worried about myself, and I'm worried about my daughter."

"Your daughter's not there, you said? Still visiting her aunt?"

"For now, but I'm headed out to pick her up today. She needs to come home. She needs to get used to life without her mom, but she needs to be safe."

Again, the detective didn't reply. He could picture her stony face, blinking dully at nothing. He wondered whether he'd misread her stoicism. Perhaps she was just very, very stupid.

"Look," she said at last. "We're planning to search the area for evidence again, anything that might have been missed. We're hopeful that might yield something."

As if that news would pacify him. It didn't. It wasn't what he wanted to hear at all.

"We need something else to break before we can apply for a warrant. We're doing what we can," she continued.

He ignored her.

"I'll be back tomorrow with my daughter," he said. "And I sincerely hope that Natalie will be arrested by the time we get home. Petra deserves justice. We both do."

He hung up the phone before his words could be met with more silence, with more platitudes. He silenced her himself.

FIFTY-THREE

For once, I was grateful for my coursing thoughts, for my inability to fall asleep, for how deeply my husband slept beside me, while I could not.

I hovered in the doorway of our bedroom, Oliver strapped to my chest. Tyler was whistling faintly, his body still. I was confident that if he awakened and noticed my and Oliver's absence from the room, he'd think nothing of it. He'd assume we were in the nursery, or perhaps pacing through the house, as we'd done countless nights. Tyler rarely came to check on us anymore.

Erin's keys were tucked into the side pocket of my leggings. It had been easy to pick them out. There'd been two sets resting on the tray closest to the Rileys' front door. I'd only had a second to make a choice. But one set had a silvery key chain, shooting my reflection back at me as I'd hovered over it. It was decidedly feminine, but not childish, so I'd quickly assumed that the keys didn't belong to Petra or Paul.

I descended the stairs silently, moving as evenly as I could, lest I wake Oliver. If he began to cry, it would be devastating. Everything would be ruined. I stepped expertly over the floorboards in the foyer that always creaked, and I slipped from the house.

I climbed the hill slowly, my gloved hands resting gently on Oliver's back. It was just past two in the morning, and there was no movement. No curtains being tugged to the side. No cars backing out of garages. No lights flickering to life. No police car waiting at the curb, watching me. Perhaps they hadn't the resources to do so twenty-four hours a day. That felt like a single stroke of good luck, unfamiliar but welcome.

I ducked around the side of the Riley house, through the grass, to the back. There was a walkout basement, and I tried each key in its door—

Erin had five on her key ring, in addition to what were obviously car keys—before the lock tumbled, and I was able to push my way inside.

I held my breath, waiting for the blare of an alarm system, even though I didn't think that they had one. I was met with only silence, and a trickle of relief worked its way down my spine, although it shouldn't have. There was so much left to do.

The house was dark, but I knew my way around the floor plan in the darkness; it matched my own. On the first floor, I returned Erin's keys to the tray, after wiping them clean with the hem of my sweatshirt. I buried them beneath a bottle of hand sanitizer and a business card for a power washer. I hoped that Paul hadn't noticed their absence.

I moved upstairs, into the master bedroom, where Erin's things remained. Upon closer inspection, the room held only Erin's things—on the nightstand, in the bathroom, in the closet. They didn't share a room.

I suspected Paul would move back in here soon, reclaiming what he viewed as his.

With much difficulty, I removed the baby wrap, concealed in a plastic bag and tucked into the waistband of my leggings, between my T-shirt and hoodie, trying not to disturb Oliver. I slid it between the mattress and the box spring, as deeply as I could.

I didn't know if the police would find it, and I wasn't sure that I cared. I just didn't want Paul to. I just wanted it out of my house.

I had washed it, concerned about what evidence it might hold. Had he used the same wrap I'd looped around myself, into which I had tucked Oliver? Was it rife with my DNA, as well as Erin's? I'd tossed it into the laundry machine earlier in the day, while Tyler was still at work and Oliver was snoozing in his swing, using hot water, but no soap, hoping that would be enough to remove my traces from its fibers. I'd watched it spin and tangle in the dryer, wondering when exactly Paul had been able to plant it in my house. I'd been so careless, so oblivious.

I returned to the basement, then pushed out of the house, locking the basement door behind me and pulling it closed. There was nothing I could do about the dead bolt. I could only hope that Paul would think he'd left that unlocked by accident.

My strides were wide but smooth as I descended the hill, my arms around Oliver, holding him steady and close. I hoped we were only a streak of black in the dark of night. My hair was concealed beneath the hood of my sweatshirt, nearly all of my skin covered in fabric.

I closed my own front door behind me and flipped the lock, then leaned against it, waiting for my breath and heartbeat to slow. I tipped my head forward to press my lips to Oliver's head. "Thank you," I whispered. Because he was still quiet, still asleep. It felt like my son had given me a gift.

I was suddenly struck by a wave of exhaustion, so crushing that I could barely drag myself up the stairs. In the nursery, I pulled the gloves from my hands, then extracted Oliver from the baby carrier. He stirred, then fussed. I'd known that he would awaken, but I couldn't very well let him sleep in the carrier for the rest of the night.

I changed him, then nursed him back to sleep. When I put him back in the bassinet, his eyes remained closed. This time, he wasn't startled awake. Although he did this sometimes, I was still riddled with anxiety every time I put him down. There was no predictability, no pattern, to when he awakened, and when he did not.

I stripped off my sweatshirt and leggings and changed back into my pajamas, then slid into bed beside Tyler. He was still fast asleep, still breathing his whistling breaths.

Had anyone seen me leaving my house? Had they seen what I'd done?

I was so desperate to know. I was desperate for it to all be over. But for now, there was nothing more I could do. I closed my eyes, and I slept.

FIFTY-FOUR

Perhaps it was relief, because of the fact that the baby wrap was finally gone from my house. Perhaps it was that I'd come to understand what had really happened. What Paul had done. Perhaps it was that I'd finally started to get used to Oliver getting a longer stretch of sleep each night, and something had clicked in my brain.

Regardless, I'd slept, for four straight hours—the most consecutive sleep I'd had since the penultimate night of my pregnancy. I'd awakened to Oliver's screams four hours after I'd managed to fall asleep, still with a foggy mind and an aching head, but after I changed him and nursed him and put him back down, I realized that much of the fog had cleared, as though burned off by the rising sun.

"How was your night?" Tyler asked as we moved around the kitchen, dancing around each other.

"I got some sleep," I replied as I poured half a cupful of coffee. I allowed myself a little more than usual.

"That's good." He hesitated, then reached into the fridge, removing bread and lunch meat and sliced cheese, hastily packing his lunch. I wondered cruelly how many other partners packed themselves a meal fit for a third grader.

He didn't ask me where I'd gone the previous night, didn't mention hearing the front door open or close. The secret of it all seemed to flicker silently between us, a ghost only I could see.

When he was finished, he kissed me briefly on the forehead. "See you later."

"Bye."

I moved into the dining room, listened to the front door squeaking closed, the lock flipping, his car door slamming outside. We'd stopped saying "love you" completely, it seemed. Not before bed. Not when he left for work. I wasn't sure if that meant that he no longer loved me. Did he see me for what I was? What I'd become? Did I care? Did I feel the same? Or were we just too tired to bother? There was too much else burdening my thoughts to figure it out. I couldn't explain it, couldn't fix it. I sensed that we needed a babysitter who could watch Oliver while we sat awkwardly on a too-firm sofa, a box of tissues on the coffee table before us, and spilled our mutual resentment to a professional counselor. Maybe it wasn't a bad idea. But that would have to wait. There was too much else to get through first.

I stood before the dining room windows again, letting the early morning silence fall over the house, sipping my coffee.

Tyler's car had disappeared. All was still.

Until it wasn't. Several vehicles rolled into view. Two police vans. One marked police car. They parked along the street. I froze, my hand on the curtain. Should I drop it, let it close, walk away? I couldn't move.

One more car was driving down the street now, toward my house. It was an unmarked sedan. Navy blue. Familiar, and not just because it was a generic-looking car. A woman climbed out, her tiny red ponytail bobbing. She looked around her. Her eyes landed on me.

Detective West was back, and she had company.

Perhaps this was how it would end.

She stood in the cul-de-sac with her colleagues—uniformed officers, crime scene technicians. She was speaking to them urgently, seriously. They were all watching her, receiving their instructions.

But instead of knocking on my door, a warrant in her hand, the detective climbed back into her car. I watched the other police officers and crime scene technicians spill into the woods.

They weren't back to search my house. Not yet. Instead, they were returning to the site where Erin's body was found, I assumed. Where she'd been killed.

Where Paul had killed her.

There still wasn't enough for a warrant. They needed more.

Baby monitor in my hand, I looked outside, and I paced.

FIFTY-FIVE

Detective West climbed out of her car, all the while staring at the Fanning house. She could see Natalie Fanning standing at her window, watching. She thought of Paul Riley's insistence that they had enough to arrest her— she was quite used to it, to people in his position, people who were grieving and shocked and angry, thinking that they knew better than she did.

But they didn't know. There wasn't enough for an arrest. There wasn't enough for a warrant. Not yet.

That's why they were here. Juries loved physical evidence. They didn't like it when there was no murder weapon. She needed to find that baby wrap. But without something more, she couldn't properly search for it. She felt like her case was trapped in a hamster wheel, spinning, running to nowhere.

She met the techs and her backup outside the crime scene vans, where they'd parked a few houses up from the Fannings'. She went over their instructions, even though she had already done so, back at the station. She watched them trail down the path between the Fanning house and the one next door, into the woods. Officer Price was leading the way. Once they'd disappeared, she turned away and climbed back into her car.

She had paperwork to do, notes to review, but she would do it here. She wanted to be close by if they found something.

She unlocked her phone and placed another call to Lara Tucker. The call rang through to voicemail, so she left one, identifying herself as a detective with the Patuxent County Police Department and requesting a callback immediately. "It's important," she said.

She'd been surprised to receive a phone call from Natalie Fanning's neighbor, Linda Molloy, the previous evening. Linda had nothing of interest to share with her the first time they'd spoken—Linda was at work when Erin disappeared, and when she was killed. Detective West had been even more surprised when Linda had said that she wanted to share something about Paul Riley, not Natalie.

She did not want to be a gossip, Linda was clear about that, but there was something niggling at her. She'd not said anything before, because it was all speculation, but a conversation with Natalie had caused her to reconsider.

Apparently, Linda had a theory that Paul Riley had been having an affair with the woman who had previously lived in the Fannings' home. She had no evidence of this, aside from witnessing Paul dropping by to visit Lara Tucker while their respective spouses were at work.

Detective West had thanked her. She'd quickly tracked down Lara Tucker's new address and contact information and left her a message. But she was skeptical. What Linda had witnessed seemed to be nothing more than speculation from a nosy neighbor—notwithstanding one who insisted she was anything but. It was not evidence of an affair. And most interestingly, Linda had come forward only after she'd spoken with Natalie. Detective West had to wonder whether the call was born out of influence by Natalie, who seemed to be finally catching on to the fact that she was, at least, a person of interest in the homicide of Erin Riley.

Still, she'd track down the lead, such as it were. She'd keep calling Lara, would send someone out to her home in Pennsylvania if she needed to.

She tucked her phone back into her cupholder and reached for her laptop. She navigated to the case file and started reviewing her notes. She looked over every piece of physical evidence logged, every interview she'd done.

She looked up at the Fanning house. She could no longer see Natalie standing in the window. *There's something wrong with that woman.* That was what Paul Riley had said on the phone the day before.

She'd thought it, too. Something was wrong. Something was off.

Well. Jill West had felt off herself for months after she'd had a baby. Her identity as she'd known it, as an investigator, as a cop, had shifted into something else. Something hard and intense had been tugged away, and something soft and warm and fragile had been shoved into her hands. Days had blurred together. Her son, Jacob, hadn't slept at all, except for when he was in her arms, or if he was riding in the car. What she'd told Natalie that day on her driveway had been true. West had bundled her baby into the car and gone driving for hours a day, for hours during the night, while her husband was working shifts at the hospital. He'd noticed the increased charges for gas on their credit card statements. He'd said nothing.

Jacob was sixteen now, and they were facing a whole new set of challenges. He was taking his driving test in three weeks. The thought gripped her with fear.

But it was more than just sleeplessness, confusion, and change, with Natalie. It seemed to be something more. Those text messages had reeked of desperation, as had her actions at the neighborhood block party, all her visits to the Riley house, long after she was no longer welcome. Carol Jensen had attested to that. *She just couldn't help herself,* Detective West had quoted from her interview with Mrs. Jensen. *She just kept walking over there.*

And there was the murder weapon. If that didn't point straight to Natalie, what did?

Everything was there. It seemed to fit. If only she could find that wrap.

There was a tap on the driver's side window. Detective West glanced up from her laptop, then snapped it closed. She climbed out of the car.

Kris Watts, one of the more inexperienced techs she'd brought with her today, was holding a plastic bag with something small and white inside. The November wind had swept his always unruly black hair into a tangle of waves. He looked quite young and seemed threatening to brim over with excitement.

"You find something?" she asked.

She looked over his shoulder to see the other officers and techs on the path, approaching her car as well.

It had been hours, but finally, they were back. With something. Kris passed her the bag and she held it up, peered inside.

"That's all we've found so far. A button," Kris said, redundantly, for Detective West could see that it was a button. A small, white button, with a brand name printed along its rim. One she recognized. An expensive brand. The button could be from a male or female garment. It was impossible to tell. It had several burgundy threads still wrapped around the tiny holes, where it had been sewn onto a shirt. Clearly, it had been torn away.

"Could be related," she said. "But maybe not. Where did you find it?"

"It was close to the scene, but not right there. Maybe the rain or an animal carried it a bit farther away."

She nodded. Kris was looking at her, as were the other techs and officers who had joined them. Price was practically levitating with excitement. She glanced at the Fannings' house, then to the Rileys'. A compact SUV was driving down the street. It swung into the Rileys' driveway, then disappeared into the garage. He was home, with his daughter.

She made a decision.

"Let's go to the Riley house," she said. "We'll start there. Ask to have a look around for a shirt this button could have come from. We'll need to rule him out first. But to do that, we'll have to search thoroughly. Look in dressers and closets, of course, but look everywhere. In the basement. In the back of the toilets. Under beds, beneath mattresses. We can't rule him out unless we search everywhere."

"Got it," said Kris. The others nodded their understanding, too.

Detective West slipped the plastic evidence bag into her pocket and led the way up the hill.

FIFTY-SIX

Petra had been silent the entire three-and-a-half-hour drive back to their house. He had peeked at her in his rearview mirror as he drove. Her hair was unbrushed, her part uneven. She had refused his offer for French braids.

Time, he told himself. She only needed time.

There was activity, farther down the street. Police vans and cars. The detective was standing beside her car with several other personnel. They'd been searching the area again, he suspected, just as she had told him.

He pulled the car into the garage, beside Erin's Volvo. She had bought it with cash several years ago, back when business had still been very good. He would sell it, he decided. He could probably use the proceeds to pay an entire year of Petra's tuition, maybe more.

Petra trailed quietly into the house. He collected their bags from the trunk, then followed her.

"Do you want some lunch?" he asked. He dropped their bags onto the floor in the kitchen. "Grilled cheeses?" She loved his grilled cheeses.

"I'm not hungry." She turned and made her way slowly, heavily toward the stairs. She looked about a hundred years old, not ten. He heard her bedroom door close.

He moved to the fridge and inspected his options. They had Irish butter, buffalo mozzarella, and a block of sharp cheddar. He would make the sandwiches anyway.

He was pulling out the supplies he needed when the doorbell rang. Puzzled, he left the cheese on the counter.

There was Detective West, waiting on his front porch, several other officers and technicians behind her. He smiled, hoping she was here with good news.

He opened the door, remained standing in the doorway. "Can I help you?" he asked.

Detective West slipped a plastic bag from her pocket and extended it toward him, close enough that he could see inside.

Immediately, he recognized what was inside the bag, and his heart dropped. But only for a second. Because it was a button from the shirt he'd been wearing the day he'd killed Erin. The long-sleeved, burgundy polo. He'd worn a sweatshirt on top of the shirt, pulled the hood tightly over the top of his head. Erin must have managed to tear the button loose, perhaps from his cuff that had peeked out from the sweatshirt's sleeve. But it was fine. Because he'd burned that shirt in the fireplace before Erin's body had been discovered. He'd burned everything he had been wearing. He'd swept the ashes into a trash bag and thrown them away. They were long gone. This button would not lead back to him.

"We've been searching the area again," the detective said. "We found this in the woods. Do you recognize it?"

He squinted at the button, shrugged. "No," he said. "I don't think so."

"Mind if we come in and take a look around?" asked Detective West. "Either we find the shirt to which this button belongs, or we don't. I'm sure you understand. We'll need to rule you out."

"Have you searched Natalie's house?" he asked. He couldn't help himself. "You might want to start there."

"Not yet," she replied. "We need to rule you out first. I'm sure you understand," she said again.

A beat passed, then he nodded. "Of course," he said. This was just a formality, he knew. He had nothing to hide. Nothing in the house. Not anymore.

"Of course, I understand," he said. "Please, come in. Take your time. Look everywhere."

EPILOGUE

I hesitated, the candy-looking pill between my thumb and index finger, then tossed it back with a swallow of water.

I hated to take medication, hated putting the chemicals into my body. Hated that they traveled through my blood, through my breast milk. Hated that Oliver received the chemicals, too, even though my doctor had assured me repeatedly that they were perfectly safe. She had been sure to select a prescription that was acceptable for ingestion by nursing mothers.

But the saddest thing about the pills was that the only reason I was taking them at all was because of Detective Jill West, a veritable stranger. It was she, and she alone, who had shown me that something was very, very wrong. Not my husband, nor my best friend. Not my dad or my in-laws. Not Oliver's pediatrician, despite that she'd had me complete a questionnaire about postpartum depression at least twice since his birth. I didn't blame her. It wasn't her job.

"It's not my place," Detective West had said when she had stopped by my house to let me know that Paul Riley had been arrested for the murder of his wife, that the baby wrap that had been used to strangle Erin had been found in the house, "but it seems like you could use some rest."

I'd laughed, sharply and suddenly, tried too late to swallow it down. "Sorry. It's just, that's quite an understatement."

"Again, it really isn't my place," Detective West had said, looking embarrassed. "But have you seen a doctor?"

I'd squinted at her. "Yes," I said. "He goes rather often. For his weight checks, and for monthly appointments."

"Not him," she'd replied, tipping her head toward Oliver. "I meant a doctor for you."

"A doctor? For what? 'Doctor, help! There's something wrong with me. I have a baby. I don't sleep. I feel like I'm going insane.'"

I'd laughed again. She hadn't.

Detective West had cleared her throat. "Ms. Fanning," she'd said. "It seems to me that you have been struggling. Paul Riley had concocted an entire trap for you. He nearly framed you for killing his wife. Having a newborn baby is a vulnerable time for everyone, and he was manipulating you. I know that. But it went quite far. I don't see that happening to someone who is well."

She'd been right, of course. After they'd found the baby wrap in Paul's house, exactly where I'd left it, she'd come to understand my role in the murder, which had been mouse to Paul's cat, trapped beneath his paws.

I'd told her as much, and I'd shared the recording with her, the one I'd made in secret the day I'd taken Erin's keys from the tray in the foyer. It was inadmissible in court, of course—I'd taken it without his consent—but it flew in the face of everything Paul had told the police. It was reinforcement that they had it right. Paul might have insisted to the police that I had planted the baby wrap in his house, or maybe he'd said nothing at all. I don't know. Detective West hadn't told me, only asked me to send her a copy of the recording. Even though it wasn't usable, she'd wanted to have it.

I'd done so. Then, after she was gone, I'd called my doctor.

Postpartum depression was the diagnosis, as well as the rarer postpartum psychosis. I'd never heard of the latter, and that was sad, too. I should have been aware of it. I should have known the signs, known what to look for. If I had, perhaps that would have prevented so much.

"Take care of yourself," Detective West had said over her shoulder, before she left my house. "If for no other reason than you need to, to take care of him."

I enjoyed the silence flowing through the house as I brushed my hair back into a ponytail. Downstairs, I slung the diaper bag over my shoulder and found Tyler and Oliver on the family room floor. Oliver was on his play mat. He was five months old now, but he still loved the spinning butterflies.

I bent down to lift him up.

"Ready to visit your aunt Elaine?" I asked, even though she wasn't really his aunt. Not by blood. And in a way, I felt betrayed that she, as my best friend, with her medical training, hadn't recognized what was wrong with me.

But perhaps I hadn't given her a chance. I had barely seen her, had barely spoken with her. I'd been isolating myself in my spiral of confusion and sleeplessness, of swinging moods and irrational thoughts, of missing hours and panic attacks.

"We'll be back in an hour or so," I told Tyler.

"Sounds good," he replied, pushing himself up from the floor. "Love you." He leaned forward to kiss my cheek.

I said it back.

I was able to slip Oliver into his car seat without worrying about his fragility and comfort. I'd come a long way.

There was the one thing on which I could rely: just like Detective Jill West's unnamed, potentially fabricated, baby, my son always fell asleep in the car.

I stopped at a restaurant by Elaine's house to pick up the curbside delivery I had ordered ahead on my phone. A waiter ran out and placed it in the backseat of my car, next to my sleeping child. She marveled quietly at his cuteness before closing my car door with conscientious care.

Oliver was still zonked when I heaved the car seat out and lugged it up to Elaine's front door.

She wasn't beaming when she answered the door. Wasn't glowing with natural, maternal beauty. She looked drooped and exhausted. She moved delicately, as though she was in immense pain. She looked like a mother.

Brynn was curled against her chest, wrapped in a swaddle blanket.

"She's perfect," I whispered, then moved past them, into the house.

I wouldn't stay long. She wouldn't want me to. That was the key with visitors. Bring food and don't stay long.

I placed Oliver's car seat and the bag of food on the floor, then hugged my friend gingerly, wrapped my arms around both her and her daughter. They were warm and soft, smelling of lavender and milk. Elaine's body went slightly slack. My presence was a relief to her, a comfort. In some ways, I was a walking exhibition of what rock bottom might look like.

Because it had happened to me, statistically speaking, it probably wouldn't happen to her, too. Because I had lived it, I would know the signs.

Seeing things that weren't there. Hearing things that I couldn't have heard. Remembering things that hadn't happened. Feeling disoriented and lost. The mood swings. The violent thoughts. The frantic insomnia when my baby was sleeping. The despondency. The loss of self. Even with all the love—too much love, perhaps—there'd been room for these other feelings to creep in, to sneak up on me, to break me down.

I'd thought it was self-inflicted, that my type-A, singular focus to follow all the rules, to be a perfect mother, to exclusively, compulsively nurse my child at all costs—at so much cost—had led to my downward spiral, my flirtation, perhaps affair, with insanity. Maybe it had. Maybe it had contributed. But there had been more than that. Something chemical, too. The medication was helping. That, and the sleep. With Oliver growing older, his colic, his food sensitivities, had seemed to work themselves out. I wouldn't call him an easy baby. He was still quite temperamental. We still had our challenges. But we were getting better.

And I'd taken Detective Jill West's advice. A mother was selfless. A mother always put her child first, I thought. But if it was at her own expense, to the point that she was prevented, actually, from being a mother, then her baby was suffering as much as her. It was this line of thought that had forced me to consider what I needed myself, to reclaim some semblance of who I was.

Some semblance of who I was meant work. Just as I'd known that it would, the sabbatical had become permanent. But in a surprising turn of events, that had been my choice. In two weeks, I was starting a new job.

It would be the same type of work, the work I enjoyed, but with a completely new firm with a suburban office, only fifteen minutes from the house on Ashby Drive that had finally started to feel a little bit like home. It was a smaller law firm, too, one that prided itself on being family friendly. I hadn't known that such a thing existed—it seemed oxymoronic: a family-friendly law firm, a workplace that permitted, even encouraged, some modicum of balance. My billable-hour requirement would be a third less than it had been at my previous firm, and I'd be working from home up to three days a week. All employees were offered that perk. I wasn't sure I'd be taking advantage of it. At least for a while. I might enjoy sucking in my stomach while I buttoned my sleek ankle pants and rubbing my high-heel-sore feet at the end of a long day. I might like the separation between work and home, shutting down my computer, leaving it behind, compartmentalizing each aspect of my life. I would miss Oliver while I was gone. That would bring me comfort.

Time apart from my baby, time that also allowed him and Tyler to bond, along with work, sleep, exercise, therapy sessions every few weeks— and, I hated to admit it, the medicine—would help. It already had.

I was dreading my return to work. I longed for it, but I dreaded it, too. This seemed like the right way to feel.

I settled onto Elaine's sofa, pushing aside a bit of clutter, and rocked Oliver's car seat gently with my foot.

"Do you want to hold her?" Elaine asked, peeking down at her daughter, impossibly small and pink, still cradled against her breasts.

"That's okay," I said. "I don't want to wake her."

"She sleeps all the time," Elaine said, grimacing in pain as she settled onto the sofa beside me.

"That's how it is at first," I replied knowingly. It wouldn't last. "How are you feeling?"

She launched into the gruesome details of her birth experience, then, even though we'd already exchanged rapid-fire text messages about the whole ordeal. I understood, though. She needed to share it again. She needed to speak of her unending bed rest, her scheduled C-section, the feeling when they'd pulled Brynn out of her body.

I listened and murmured sympathetically.

I got her lunch set up at her dining room table, then, and she ate one-handed, standing up, as she swayed back and forth. She was already well practiced at the sway.

Before I left, I hugged them again and told her to text me if she needed anything.

I would be here, to look out for her. To make sure that what had happened to me didn't happen to her. As if that was likely.

But perhaps it was more likely, more common, than any of us imagined.

I carried Oliver, miraculously still asleep, back to my car and clicked the seat into place.

I glanced around at the houses in Elaine's neighborhood as I drove, so similar to mine, spacious colonials with trim, green yards. The streets were lined with trees, their branches bare in the January cold. I wondered if Elaine would bundle Brynn up and walk for hours a week, like I had, talking to her baby. I hoped she didn't have a neighbor like Paul.

Paul, who, in my fragile state, had acted like my friend. Perhaps he'd been the first to understand what was wrong with me. After all, he'd known the most. I'd confided in him. He'd been there to witness it. Being so exhausted that I'd had to leave my job. Forgetting Oliver's doctor's appointments. Breaking into my own house. Hearing my baby screaming when he wasn't. Getting lost in my neighborhood while walking a loop I'd walked dozens of times before. Subtly and methodically, he'd pulled me closer. He'd behaved as though he was my savior. He'd been trying to trap me, had manipulated me handily.

More details had emerged, in the news, but mostly from Detective West. Linda Molloy had been right. The detective had made contact with Lara Tucker, the woman who lived in my house before me. She and Paul had been having an affair while their spouses were at work. It made sense now, Erin's displeasure with me spending so much time alone with her husband. If Erin had known about Lara, she would have been livid with Paul, with me, for having a relationship, even one that was platonic. There'd been Lara, and the allegations the student had made against Paul, back when he'd been working. I could only imagine what more there might have been, to make Erin so suspicious.

Meanwhile, Erin's business had been struggling, just as Paul had told me. Apparently, their marriage had been especially unhappy of late. They'd been disagreeing about Paul returning to work. Petra was ten and there wasn't a need for him to stay home full-time anymore. He'd still not managed to finish his novel. He had wanted to escape Erin, to maintain his lifestyle. A divorce wouldn't have worked. She needed to die. That would give him money—several million dollars of life insurance proceeds—and freedom.

But not if he was implicated in her death. So, he'd used me. He'd assured me I was just tired, I just needed some rest, when it was something more nefarious and dangerous than that. He'd lied to me, tried to make me believe I had done something that I hadn't. Tried to make others believe it, too. He had almost succeeded.

Almost.

I was ashamed. But I tried to be kinder to myself. Detective West had demanded that. I'd been sick.

Meanwhile, the Riley house sat vacant, not as pristine as it once had been. I averted my eyes as I drove past, as I always did.

When would they sell it, I wondered? Would it fall more deeply into disarray as Paul sat in a jail cell, awaiting trial?

I still thought sadly of Petra sometimes. I'd heard that she had gone to live with Erin's sister, in her house at the beach. I hoped that she was okay.

Oliver awakened as I removed his seat from the car. I hurried into the house and lifted him out. Tyler met us in the living room. He had probably been working while we were gone, even though it was Saturday. He had been, I thought, appropriately mortified by my diagnoses, by what had occurred while he obliviously toiled away at his office and his life marched on as though we'd never had a baby.

The week after Detective West had left our house, had told me to see a doctor, Tyler hadn't worked at all. He'd taken a week off to spend time at home with Oliver and me. He'd watched Oliver while I went to my appointments, so many of them that first week. He picked up my prescriptions. When he returned to work, he didn't stay as late. His billable hours, his profits, were suffering. I was relieved to see that he didn't care as much as he used to. He'd received the wake-up call he needed, I thought. I could only hope that he wouldn't need another.

"How was it?" he asked, as I settled onto the sofa. It was time for Oliver to eat.

"Fine," I said. "Elaine seems tired, of course. Brynn is so adorable. I can't believe how tiny she is. Much smaller than Oliver ever was."

I gazed down into my son's face, smoothed his faint brows, grazed his impossibly silky skin with the pad of my thumb. His eyes were still a brilliant cobalt. I wondered whether they would change. I hoped they never would.

"Was she giving you a bit of baby fever? Time for another one, you think?"

My head jerked up. Tyler was grinning at me.

My pulse quickened. My breath caught. I'd thought it was gone for good, but there it was. The rage. Trickling in.

Eyes closed, I took a slow and steadying breath. I held on to Oliver more tightly, as though he were my life raft. Then, I shifted and used the palms of my hands to cover his minuscule, kitten-soft ears. He peered up at me in confusion.

I looked at my husband.

"If you ever say that again, I will kill you."

ACKNOWLEDGMENTS

I think that of everything I have written, I am the proudest of *The New Mother*. Of course, my pride and love for this book are a privilege given to me by the thoughtful and tireless work of many people. That you, reader, chose this book is also a gift for which I am truly and eternally grateful.

Thank you, as always, to my brilliant agent, Helen Heller, for reading every word I wrote and steering me in the right direction. Your insights have transformed not only my words, but my life. Thank you to my wonderful editors, Catherine Richards and Trisha Jackson, and their respective teams at Minotaur Books at St. Martin's Publishing Group and Pan Macmillan, for your incredibly astute notes, and for every amazing thing you have done to shepherd this book along. Thank you to Nettie Finn, Steve Erickson, Kayla Janas, and Becca Bryant for your support and hard work. I'm so lucky to have all of you on my team. Thank you to Kelley Ragland for helping brainstorm titles and to Jennifer Enderlin for coming up with the winner.

Thank you to all of the early readers, reviewers, and bookstagrammers. Your support for my books means so much. Thank you to my parents, for sharing with me a love of words, and for everything else.

Thank you to Ms. Bri and Ms. Missy, my first son's first caregivers, who were with him from the time he was twelve weeks old until he turned two. I am incredibly grateful for the love, patience, and care you provided to our son. I have seen your kindness and compassion reflected in him as he grew from an infant to a toddler. You made it possible, and even—eventually—comfortable for me to be away from my son so that I could work. What you do is amazing. Thank you.

Finally, to my husband, for your endless support and encouragement, for helping me reach for my dreams. And to our boys. I really love to write, but there is *nothing* like being your mom.

AUTHOR'S NOTE

The New Mother is not my autobiography, but in some ways, Natalie's story is like my own, and like that of so many new mothers.

In the summer of 2019, I had a baby. I didn't sleep at all for the next six months. At least, that was how it felt. My son was colicky. He would sleep only when he was being held, including during the night. I spent hours nursing him, then putting him down, hoping each time that it would stick, that he would stay asleep in his bassinet so that I could sleep, too. Sometimes, I would blearily and persistently continue trying to nurse him to sleep and put him down until four or five in the morning, refusing help, until he would finally stay down for a couple hours.

In the middle of the night, I devoured baby care books and treated them like gospel, latching on to the advice they propounded, no matter the cost. I behaved as though my son would die if I didn't exclusively breastfeed him, never mind that there were some days I felt like I was dying myself. I spent the vast majority of my maternity leave sitting in our rocking chair, nursing my baby, even during his sleep, because I couldn't stand to hear him cry, and nursing was the only thing that worked. I wouldn't let him drink from bottles in case it interfered with breastfeeding. I took only eight weeks off from a demanding, emotionally exhausting job I was struggling to admit was not right or healthy for me. I became resentful, often rejecting help, terrified that passing my baby off to others would lead to me failing at breastfeeding, would lead to him consuming formula, would lead to failure (mine) in general. I wanted to persevere, to do everything, to be tough, a perfect mother. Nothing about this was rational, but I was far too tired and overwhelmed for rationality.

When my baby was not even two months old, I returned to work. I drove to my office, while my son stayed home with my husband. I started to cry promptly upon encountering a coworker's friendly face. I wanted to work, yet being away from him felt impossible. My husband stayed home with our son for the next four weeks, and when he was twelve weeks old, we dropped him off at daycare for the first time. Despite all the impossibility I'd already experienced, his first few days of daycare, where he refused bottles and was placed in a crib to nap, where he simply *couldn't* be held or nursed for hours at a time, were the most difficult days yet. We were lucky that his teachers were the most wonderful, loving, patient caregivers we could have asked for, and I am eternally grateful to them.

While I felt like I was drowning, there were also times that I was buoyed by immense happiness, because I was so lucky and so grateful to be a mother to our baby. Seeing him after work each day gave me something bright and sparkling to which I could look forward. My love for him was crushing and consuming, and my life, the way I felt, was so unfamiliar, bearing so little resemblance to its pre-motherhood state. Everything seemed so confusing and exhausting.

I dutifully told healthcare providers that I was *fine*. I responded to the seemingly extreme postpartum depression questionnaires when directed to do so, and I passed, which always left me feeling both unsettled and relieved, because while I was trying to be *fine,* while I was in denial about not being *fine,* I was, in fact, *not fine.* It was not until years later that it occurred to me that I could have used some help. That I could have sought it. That I should have. And by "help," I mean for my mental health, not another pair of arms to hold my baby (or perhaps set of breasts to feed him). Because I spent those early weeks riddled with guilt and coursing with anxiety. I never knew that caring for your baby *too much* could be a sign of postpartum depression.

I was so consumed with caring for my baby that I stopped caring about myself, as a mother should, I'd thought (wrongly). I should have cared more. Not just for his sake, but for my own. Because there is no reward for being the most selfless, the most tired, the most overwhelmed. Because when we behave that way, despite our best intentions, our kids may actually suffer, but also, importantly, we suffer, and *that matters, too.*

I hope that you enjoyed *The New Mother.* I hope that if you don't have a child, it doesn't scare you off from doing so (if that is your choice). I hope that if you have had a child, it makes you laugh and cry and feel seen. I hope that if you ever find yourself feeling like Natalie felt, or feeling like I did, you really think about whether you need help. I hope that you let your mind go there, let yourself truly consider whether you are okay, because doing so is brave, and it's a kindness that you deserve. And if you're not okay, I hope you get the help you need. Getting help doesn't mean that you are weak. It means that you are strong.

Anyway, there is hope. After my son was six months old, we tried sleep training, and he started to sleep for five or so hours at a time. He's three now, and there have been sleep regressions, tantrums and tears over everything and over nothing, bursts of frustration (his and mine). It really doesn't get easier, but it gets different, and he is amazing. He is the brightest light. He makes me laugh every day.

I am writing this note while I am on maternity leave with my second son, as he sleeps peacefully in his swing. There is dried spit-up on my shirt, but there's no point in changing. I've learned so much, and every baby is different. At night, my baby sleeps two to four hours at a time, and I sleep too. I don't spring from bed if he so much as coughs. Sometimes, when he starts to cry, I'm not able to get to him immediately because I'm doing something for my firstborn or for myself, and my baby completely shocks me by putting himself back to sleep. I hardly ever stand over his bassinet and squint into the dark, making sure he's breathing. My days of maternity leave have been largely peaceful, almost always relaxed. This time, I really am fine.

But now I know that if I wasn't, that would be okay, too. It's okay to not be okay, it's not your fault, and there are resources to help.

POSTPARTUM SUPPORT INTERNATIONAL
1-800-944-4773

Postpartum Progress: a nonprofit organization with a website that provides a list of providers by state who specialize in PPD treatment

NATIONAL SUICIDE PREVENTION LIFELINE
988 in the U.S.